WISH
UPON THE
STARS

MALCOLM TENT

WISH UPON THE STARS

A Superhero Cultivation LitRPG

Book 3

MALCOLM TENT

Timeless
Wind

Line editing by Stefanie B. (Red Adept Editing). Proofreading by Lorne Ryburn.

Beta read by Morcant.

Cover art and typography by Richard Sashigane.

Recap of Book 2

Shane, Callie, Jessie, and Benny travel to the Ascendant Academy in the planet's capital, Rajak. Shane reveals his Wishmaster powers to his friends and grants them numerous wishes to gain and reallocate stat points. After enrolling, the group participates in monster culling missions to give Jessie and Benny more practical combat experience, gain renown, and acquire crafting materials. During one mission, the group meets Grimmengap, a team with ties to Faerieland. Its elven leader, Celine, shares information about the job system in Faerieland, which works differently than the heroic system in Unity.

Meanwhile, Shane receives threats from a mysterious organization called the Heartrippers with ties to the far-reaching Black Sorrow Cult. One of Grimmengap's members, Sarah, is a cleric of the Red Revenant Church, the enemy of the Black Sorrow Cult. She arranges a meeting between Shane and the local Church's leader, Aiden, in the Wish Curse Palace (WCP).

Shane ventures into the WCP with his friends by his side. While investigating the Heartrippers, he encounters Tony Cark, a local bounty hunter searching for his kidnapped sister.

Eventually, Shane learns that the Heartrippers steal children, converting them into sleeper agents before returning them to their families. Recognizing that Cark's sister Cassidy is likely one of their victims, Shane invites Cark to help eliminate the shadowy assassin organization for good.

Shane and his friends hatch a scheme to draw out the Heartrippers and put an end to their activities around the Academy, one that revolves around the Academy's annual scavenger hunt: a days-long event where teams of heroes track down strange objects in a variety of bizarre locations. Allied with Grimmengap and Cark, the team establishes their base, prepares for the hunt, and sets their trap for the Heartripper sleepers who double as Academy students.

The plan is successful and the ringleader of the Heartrippers, Aiden, is unveiled. Before he dies, Aiden reveals a bombshell: Shane's mom is the youngest Saintess in the history of the Church of the Red Revenant, a powerful faction to rival the Wish Curse Palace.

Reeling from the discovery, Shane calls for Uncle Zeke to officially apprehend the remaining Heartrippers and rescue the kidnapped children. Cark's sister is safely rescued and the Heartripper threat is finally over.

Now, Shane and his friends can focus on completing the scavenger hunt.

Chapter One

THE NEXT DAY found my entire team on the top floor of the hatchery, meeting with Jessie. She'd taken the rest of the night off to spend time with Cassidy, to eat, and to generally just relax a bit. The siege had been hard on everyone, and it seemed like the right call to take a break. I'd spent the evening with Callie, just talking and telling her how I was feeling about everything. Once I was fed up with babbling, we just sat together, watching the stars, which were infinitely more visible out here than in the city.

Most of today had been spent relaxing, too, at least for us, but Jessie was working with the ravens and had all three of them out combing the forest to identify every nearby faction. As expected, Callie wanted to see what was going on nearby before any of us moved out, and Jessie was more than happy to check out the surroundings. I think she felt like she hadn't done enough during the siege. Personally, though, my ribs and I were well aware of how vital she'd been to that whole battle. No one is more important to a team than the healer.

Regardless, she seemed thrilled when we all arrived. Cark had tagged along with Callie, Grimmengap, and me.

"You're here!" She nearly bounced with excitement. "I've been watching the woods nearby, and even close to us, I found out so much! I don't know who everyone is, but I think with Celine's sources and the research she's already done, we can put some names to faces." She held out her fist for the elf girl to bump, which she did, though she seemed almost confused by the action.

Celine and Jessie had bonded over their mutual love of trees, and it was amusing to see my outgoing teammate engage with the taciturn elf. Admittedly, Celine had put a ton of work into this hunt, and she seemed energized now that we were ready to start putting in the work.

She was still as stoic as ever, but her eyes burned as she addressed us all. "While Agria may not be able to identify everyone involved, my files on the notable participants this year are extensive. One of the first things a noble learns is cultivation of sources." She nodded to Jessie. "If you can describe the nearby participants, I can do my best to fill everyone in."

Jessie gave a serious nod. Her face smoothed out, her eyes glowing green as she slipped back into the driver's seat of one of the ravens. "Can do. Okay. First up, the closest group is a set of three. All dressed in yellow and blue. A short, bearded guy with green hair, a tall dark-skinned guy with really heavy bracelets on, and a smaller girl with short red hair. I haven't seen most of their abilities, though the girl looks like she might have some kind of teleportation power. She's been spending most of her time in the branches of the trees nearby, scoping out the area."

Celine blew out a breath. "One of the notable teams. The Wavestriders. The shorter man with the beard is Boreas, a wind ability user with a noted Might focus. He does powerful bursts and is a bruiser in head-to-head combat. The taller man is Raleigh. He can change the weight of things he touches. He uses those bracelets as blunt weapons, mostly by dropping them on people's heads. He also carries a hammer most of the time. The two of them are fairly high up the Might rankings, and are usually together."

She bit her lip, looking out into the tree line. "Astara is the last one. Teleportation with a notable lean toward Fantasy. She's extremely skilled at tracking and is one of the bigger threats in the hunt. If they're nearby we need to find out what's on their list. Agria, did they notice your raven? Can you keep them under surveillance and try to get a peek at what objects they're looking for? Will they notice?"

As expected, they hadn't. Jessie was as cool as a cucumber during actual jobs, and she hadn't given away a thing. A fact she confirmed immediately. "Not at all. No one ever looks at normal-sized birds, and the ravens have such good eyes, I can stay well away from them. I'll have that one lurk around to see if they take the list out. In the meantime, I can move onto the other two if you're okay to keep going?" Celine indicated that she was, and the glow faded from Jessie's eyes before reigniting.

She had switched birds, and her brows furrowed at whatever she was seeing. "The next closest guy is alone. He's really big and not wearing a mask. His hair is long and red, and he's pale and covered in dark tattoos. Lot of chains on him. He's riding a motorcycle somehow. No clue how he got it out here... and he just drove it through a tree. Like literally *through* one. Like a ghost or something. Guessing that's his ability."

Celine winced. "That's Fisher. Real name as far as I can tell. He doesn't bother with costumes or codenames. His style is closer to Mr. Cark's. He's... very dangerous. His ability is intangibility as far as I can tell, also Fantasy-geared. He's got a fearsome reputation on campus already, and is one of the highest ranked on the Fantasy leaderboards among the freshmen. He's another one we want to avoid if at all possible."

Callie nodded. "I've heard of him actually. You're going to want to hang back a bit, Jessie. He's on the Perception rankings too. I saw him when I was doing my test. You still have one more raven out, right? Hopefully, the last one won't be aimed at anyone who will give us trouble. They can't all be terrifying competition." She sounded like she was joking, but I could tell from the stress in her tone that she was really hoping the final raven was a dud.

Jessie shrugged. "I couldn't tell you. I don't know who is who. But the last raven I have out is following a pair of small guys in cloaks. They're quiet and careful, and I keep losing them, but they don't seem overly threatening in any direct way." She looked at Celine. "No real identifying features. Are there any people you can think of that fit that description? I realize that you don't have much to go on."

It was honestly a relief when Celine responded. "No. Nothing just based on that. Keep an eye on them if possible. The fact that you've lost them at least once isn't reassuring. I would suggest rerouting the raven following Fisher to search for other targets. He's likely to notice it, and I doubt he's going to expose his list anytime soon." She looked to Callie. "Assuming that works for you, I realize you're the one in charge of this operation. I don't mean to step on any toes."

My girlfriend was pretty much the opposite of petty, however. "Not at all. I agree. I know how scary his Perception is, and that raven could be looking for other possible threats. You heard her, Agria. Peel off and do a sweep for any more incoming hunters." Jessie gave a salute and cycled back to the specified bird. Callie turned to the rest of us. "So, with all that in mind, we need to figure out what our next move is. I have a decent idea of where we should go from here, but I'm open to suggestions."

Cark looked out over the clearing from the opening in the hatchery. "Hard call. Depends on the overlap from the lists. If it's a common thing, we need to leave people here to play guard for the stuff we've already gathered. We have two items down, and if those are things others will need we can't leave them unattended. If it's uncommon, then the two we have are unlikely to be on anyone else's list, much less the people nearby, and we can play offense. Celine, do you know how much the lists coincide?"

The elf girl sighed. "No. They purposefully kept the lists from everyone. It's one of the aspects of the hunt that they conceal to make it more diffi-cult, a second layer of security in case anyone finds out the location ahead of time. Your point is well-made, though. I know there is at least some overlap, because they mention that as a warning, but I'm not sure exactly how much of our list will appear on the others. Thinking about it, though, given the sheer number of participants and the scarcity of Ascendant materials, I would guess even if the overlap is small, we'll have quite a few people after us."

That was less than ideal. Clearly, Callie thought so too. "I hadn't consid-ered that. But it fits with what I was thinking. We need a small team that can track and hunt out there. G-rankers with combat potential who have mobility and the skills needed to find and identify materials. Some of them will need more, and we can call in backup, but initially, I think Solomon and I should head out as a scouting party. That work for you?" She raised an eyebrow at me.

It did work. It sounded like a great way to spend my time, actually. But it wasn't something I could do just yet. It was a new day, which meant I had new wishes. "I'm in, but I have something to do first. Tony, you free for a quick chat, buddy? Wanted to go over that thing we talked about yester-day." I tried to be as vague about it as possible, but I saw Cark's face light up as he got what I was talking about. Just a short while ago, I'd revealed my ability to grant wishes to Cark, informing him that it might be possible to fully deprogram his sister Cassidy using a wish.

Callie obviously understood too.

4

She gave me an encouraging smile. "Sounds good. I'll wait outside, and we can get going as soon as you guys finish your talk." She winked at me before heading downstairs, and I gestured to Cark, who followed me outside.

In the meantime, Jessie went back to filling in Celine about all the details of what was nearby, presumably to make sure we had a decent idea of where everything was for her next report. It distracted the elf and her team enough that I knew they wouldn't overhear my talk with Cark. I still took him downstairs and then outside, though, just in case.

We made it outside, and he turned to me. "Okay. Is it time? You said it was going to be soon, but I didn't think it would be this soon. You can really fix my sister? I just need to wish for it?" He looked so excited, I was surprised he could stand still. I just chuckled.

He noticed and took a few calming breaths. "Sorry. This is just a big deal. So all I have to do is say the words? I wish my sister was free of any Heartripper influence? Does that work?"

Wish detected. Grant wish?

I confirmed, as usual.

Stat points sufficient. Requirements: 10 Focus, 10 Impact, 10 Fantasy, 10 Might. Compensation required.

I was surprised by how many points the wish required. Wishes on mortals were usually pretty cheap, and it was shocking they'd done enough to her for the repair wish to warrant ten Impact. That said, it was definitely affordable and well within my reach. That was a load off my mind. I'd been worried I wasn't strong enough yet. "All right. Looks like we're a go. All we need to do is sort out payment. I'd like to waive it, but these premade wishes are pretty strict. So. Let's get to haggling."

I was determined to get him the best deal I was capable of.

Chapter Two

I TRIED to trade him for his service for the rest of the hunt, but unfortunately, that wasn't enough. In the end, he traded me another two points of Might. I was happy enough with it. I hadn't actually gotten any Might from taking down Aiden, but I suspected Tony had. Might was a key stat in so many skills and abilities, and that made it an important part of my Wish power, not to mention my DS Mastery. Once it was done, Cark ran off to find Cassidy, and I headed out to meet my girlfriend, checking my stats as I went.

Wishmaster Candidate Status: G-rank.

Ability: Beginner Wish—Five times a day, grant a Beginner wish in return for proper compensation. Wish must be feasibly achievable by the candidate's own efforts within a three-day period with current statistics.

Might: 58
Impact: 12
Fantasy: 21
Vitality: 25
Focus: 38
Perception: 40

Creation: 32

Skills: Beginner Doom Sovereign Mastery, Lesser Enchanting Mastery, Lesser Cooking Mastery, Lesser Inventing Mastery, Minor Piano Mastery, Minor Gymnastics Mastery, Minor Swimming Mastery, Minor Guitar Mastery, Minor Singing Mastery, Minor Poker Mastery, Minor Archery Mastery, Minor Boxing Mastery

I was in fucking shock. Aside from the two points of Might from the wish, I'd gotten a full ten points of Focus, seven of Vitality, and *fifteen* of Perception. No Might, sadly, though I wondered if that had to do with the fact that everyone who would hear about this was high up in the WCP, and they would consider beating G-rankers nothing. Still, I wasn't complaining about the huge bump in my stats. Big crazy capers like defeating an organization of assassins paid off big time. It was a shame they were so annoying and time-consuming.

Still, this would pay dividends during the hunt, and I was looking forward to showing off the extra power in front of Callie, as well as seeing what the results had been for her.

She was waiting for me out front, and she gave me a big smile when she saw me. "Hey, that didn't take too long. Things with Cass all sorted out? That girl is a real spitfire—no pun intended. I'm glad you decided to help make sure her brain was cleared out."

I fell into step next to her as we walked out into the forest.

I put an arm around her shoulders, and she smiled, taking a deep breath of the forest air as we picked a direction. I activated my Seek Hidden skill, though I didn't stretch it to include multiple items. I just picked a random object off the list, Hummingbird Blossoms, that I knew grew on trees and kept a casual eye out.

Finally, I had a chance to bring up the boost. "So, did you get any points from taking down the Heartrippers? Because I got a decent chunk."

Despite my casual tone, she burst out laughing. "How long have you been waiting to ask? Yes, I did, and you could have just said you wanted to know earlier. You didn't have to wait until we were alone. Ten Focus, eight Vitality, and six Perception. Not a bad haul for something we were going to do anyway. How about you? What did you end up getting?" She had a wry tone, implying that she'd already expected me to get more points than she did.

I muttered my numbers under my breath.

She barked out another laugh. "Of course you did. You're going to hit F before me—I just know it."

She didn't sound upset, just amused.

I just shrugged. "Maybe, but I'll make sure you get there not long after. Further than that too. Our whole team is headed way higher than just F-rank. Besides, it's not just me. I wouldn't have gotten half this far without you guys. We're a team. Sure, my ability helps, but yours is pretty damn impressive, and your experience is why we've gotten half as far as we have. I'm under no illusions that I'm doing as well as I am on my own. Don't worry."

That got an actual giggle from her (a sound she didn't make too often) and it surprised me. "I wasn't worried about you leaving us behind. I was just frustrated at how long it took me in comparison, but honestly, I can't even stay frustrated, because you're so cute when you worry."

I was glad to be wearing a mask, because I was definitely blushing.

"I'm glad to know you think of us all as a team, though, despite your... clearly impressive qualities. We're with you all the way. Through the hunt and past it." She paused, looking around. "Speaking of the hunt, what are you looking for out here?"

I scanned the tree line for any hint of red glow, not finding anything yet. "Hummingbird Blossoms. I remembered them from the list. They grow on trees, so they seemed like a safe bet for a first target. That work for you?"

The list had plenty more on it than that, so if she wanted me to switch it up, I was game. I had twenty-three more charges today, so it wasn't like I couldn't afford another few tries. I just wanted to make sure not to use them all up in case we ran into other hunters out here.

Luckily, she seemed to agree. "Yeah, that works as well as anything. Until we get a better lay of the land, it makes sense to look for anything tree related first. I'm sure there are some other biomes hidden around here, given the list we have, but we have to actually find them first. Keep an eye out for a volcano, by the way. There's at least two items on the list that are native to that habitat. Luckily, they let us keep our scan rings. I've been searching for stories about any of the things we have on our list. Anyone who isn't an expert on Ascendant flora and fauna is going to be combing the internet for clues."

That brought me up short. "Wait. So, there are a ton of people out here searching the internet for obscure Ascendant materials they need to look out for? Any chance someone is going to use that to track down some of the mats? Like, can they hack your scan ring?"

I knew they couldn't hack mine. It had been a gift from Zeke ages ago, and it was secure as hell. Still, gathering information to crack into the networks the hunters were using would be a viable strategy.

I was glad to see she'd already thought of that. "No. I mean, I'm sure it's happening, but the searches are for information on things they haven't found yet. Identifying who had what list is useful, but in the end, it won't mean much when most of them won't end up finding their stuff. Besides, I'm using the ring Batty left behind. After they cracked it, the guild master gave it to me as a keepsake. The info sec on this thing is top-notch. Since I'm the only one doing the searches, it won't be a problem."

Distracted by a flash of red in the corner of my vision, I stopped. "Hold up." I pulled her to a halt with me as I stared up into the branches. "I see something. Hummingbird Blossoms. Don't suppose there's any tips you can give me on collecting them? Wasn't sure if you got to them in your research yet, and if we're going to be grabbing them, we should be sure to handle them properly."

She waved a hand, and a layer of shadows gathered around us. It wasn't the same as our cloud trick, but it would keep us obscured at least a bit. Anyone looking for us specifically wouldn't be fooled, though, so we both lapsed into stealth and started making our way toward the tree the blossoms were situated on.

I leaned down to whisper to Callie. "Keep an eye out for any animals watching it or anything. My perception isn't nearly as high as yours, so I'll be relying on you to detect any defenses."

She nodded sharply, keeping her eyes peeled for anyone or anything lying in wait. When we finally reached the foot of the tree, I had to fight down a whistle. The thing was *huge*. Granted most of the trees here were on the large side, but this one was as wide around as a small house. The branches were about as wide across as a sidewalk too. I put my hand on Callie's shoulder to let her know we were stopping then waited for her to tell me what was going on.

Callie was going hard on her Perception, and after only a few minutes, she seemed to discover something, turning to me as quietly as possible. We weren't exactly in the open, and given our stealth skills and the shadows gathered around us, we were tough to spot. Despite that, she didn't bother to keep her voice down. "We have company Solomon. Two of them, though I can't pin them down exactly. They've been watching the blossoms, I think, not us, but they're definitely keeping an eye out for hunters." She raised her voice. "Isn't that right?"

A pair of shapes blurred into existence on the branch of the tree across from us, and I cursed. Two men, not particularly large or intimidating, were wearing shapeless black cloaks. Either these were the same two guys Jessie had seen and they'd actually slipped her watch, or they were part of a team of at least four.

The closest, a fair-haired man of young but indeterminate age spoke calmly. "An impressive show of Perception, to be sure. Yes, we have been keeping watch on these flowers. We seek to lie in wait for our competition."

Callie raised her brow. "Did you have these on your list and just assumed someone else would come looking, or did you just find an Ascendant material and assume *someone* would be searching for that? Either way, not a bad plan. But if I were you, I would go and watch another target. The two of you aren't enough to deal with us."

The man just smiled placidly down at us, saying nothing at all, and his friend, whom I realized was actually a girl about my age, started laughing loudly.

I rolled my eyes. "I've heard this one before. This is where you tell us how tough you are, right? You tell us we don't want any part of messing with you and try to scare us off with your reputation or ability, right?" After dealing with the Heartrippers, these guys and their ridiculous cloak vibe weren't nearly as unnerving as I suspected they were hoping. I had no issue picking a fight with a couple G-rankers over some flowers. It would be nice to fight for some lower stakes, honestly. I did love a nice dustup.

To my surprise, though, the smiling man just shook his head slowly. I didn't like the look on his face at all. He was way too self-assured and smug for a guy who was dealing with even odds. I could understand him being confident since he didn't know us, but there was something about his demeanor I didn't like.

"Not at all. I was mostly going to ask what exactly gave you the impression there were only two of us." That, of course, was when the other six-cloaked figures blurred into existence up on the branches of the nearby trees. I cursed internally. Okay, I'd kind of walked right into that.

Chapter Three

THIS WAS STARTING to feel depressingly familiar. Still, eight wasn't too bad. That was two less than the group standard of ten. Presumably the two Jessie was following were scouts. What an annoying bunch. Still, it was surprising they'd stayed hidden from Callie. They were far enough away to make hiding easier, but still, the idea that all of these people had higher Perception than my girlfriend's one hundred fifty was intimidating.

I didn't want to jump to conclusions, though. I didn't know the particulars of higher level stealth or if them outnumbering us affected things, so I just decided to move on. I stared at the calm man, not letting my eyes wander to the new figures. "So, eight to two, less favorable odds, sure, but then again, based on your vibe, I'd say you're all stealth-geared. We're not a great match up for you, and you gain nothing from fighting us."

He gave me that same humorless smile. "There are a limited number of G-rank Ascendants in this little hunt. Two less is nothing to sneeze at. We can just disable you and trigger your beacons."

I didn't actually know that was an option, but I would keep it in mind for later. It seemed like a great way to get rid of enemies.

"But we aren't exactly eager for a head-on confrontation. The lady noticed us early, meaning she's got an impressive Perception stat. That will make this fight... messy."

Callie sighed. "Which means this is a stalemate. You don't want a losing fight any more than we do, but if you let us go, we might hold a grudge and come after you. Not to mention neither of us wants to give up the blossoms, assuming they're on your list too. So, what do you want to do?" She was looking around subtly, and I was betting she expected the other two members back soon and that Jessie would find us. In the worst case, we would fight them head-on, but that might not be necessary.

The fact remained, however, that we needed to do *something*. That meant this would probably break into a fight. Hell, they were probably planning something as we spoke. I reached out for Callie's hand, wrapping my fingers in hers. Our little smoke trick would work well here. Combined with Seek Hidden, it would let me identify where they were, but it was Callie's call. I would at least wait for her go-ahead. She might have a better idea for getting us out of here than just vanishing into black smoke and attacking them all. That tended to be my go-to response to stress.

Callie was as cool as a cucumber. "How about we do this? There are a few blossoms. Maybe enough for us to split them and hit the quota. Why don't we just do that and go our separate ways?" She sounded calm and reasonable, but the hunters got to keep their findings. This wasn't just about the quota. Giving us any of the flowers meant money they would be giving up.

That was the trap in this whole thing—letting us keep the treasure meant this wasn't just some school scavenger hunt. This was building a fortune, and they'd put us in a position where giving up even a single thing would impact us personally. Any sort of alliance outside of a team was pretty unlikely. The damn academy had effectively put us on opposite sides of a war for resources, and there was no real reason to expect anyone outside your team (whose performance impacted yours) to honor a deal.

That was obviously apparent to Callie, too, because she clearly noticed them starting to move off to one side when I did. She squeezed my hand, a signal to get ready to use mistwalking. "If not that isn't a problem, we can always just leave. There will be other Hummingbird Blossoms. No need to get mixed up in anything so early—shit *now!*" Her head snapped to one side.

Callie was clearly picking up on some kind of imminent attack, and I pulled up my mistwalking as she spread the shadows around us, merging the two together.

As we did that, though, it gave me another idea. I'd practiced flexing my skills, and I'd accidentally managed to merge skills with Callie then repeated it plenty of times. I wasn't sure if the way we were doing it was really the same as synergizing skills myself, but if I could interact with her skills at all, then maybe she could do the same. I dropped then called up Seek Hidden again, aiming at the hooded assholes around us.

Instead of letting it settle as normal, I reached down and strained it. Rather than layering another version of the skill on top, I did something more like what I'd done in the siege with the poison. I stretched out Seek Hidden, pushing it through my hand and into Callie, trying my best to give her access to the same vision I had. She stiffened when the energy slipped between us, but then, slowly, she relaxed as the skill took hold and suddenly, she could see.

Just like me, she had the red outlines of the hooded figures in her view. If anything, she could see them more easily because of her Perception. Luckily, the cloud skill actually fucked with their stealth. Since the stealth Skill worked by erasing the traces a person left, making them unable to see where they were going degraded its effectiveness. They still had Perception and other senses, but still, it definitely helped us and hurt them.

We crept out of the way of the attack, stopping a bit away to look over the battlefield for their locations to plan out our next move. The cloaked figures were all on the ground now. Even the original two had dropped down to avoid presenting obvious targets on the branches. I turned to Callie. The slight muffling of the mist made whispers viable so I pulled Callie close. "You see them, right?"

She nodded silently.

"Good. Then we need a plan. What's our method of attack?" I kept my voice as low as possible, basically exhaling the words.

She scanned the battlefield, clearly not sure she could get away with the same trick without a mask to muffle the sound. She pointed out one specific hooded figure, and I nodded. Before she could move, I swept her up into my arms and triggered Leaf in the Wind, covering us both. Pushing both skills at once was a strain, but covering a second person I was touching wasn't nearly the imposition trying to force a skill to work double-time had been. I pushed off in a leap, carrying us both across the clearing through the smoke.

Given the Perception-based skill set at work, coming in from the air gave us a better chance of getting close without being noticed. I caught a branch as we sailed up and pulled us both onto it. While within the smoke, we could still see because of Seek Hidden, and I figured the high ground would give us an advantage against our opponents. I'd seen that on a movie somewhere, and the guy who'd said it seemed really sure it was a game changer.

At the very least, though, it was useful for battlefield control. Callie was looking down at the enemy, who were all surrounded by her shadows, and she was grinning. When she closed her eyes, I knew to look down and watch the show. Watching it from up in the branches was actually really weird. My Seek Hidden let me see through the shadows, literally, but I didn't see the shadows themselves. So despite them theoretically moving, I got no hint as to what was coming.

To me, it just looked like the enemies started tripping and slamming into things. Callie was playing this smart—ankle grabs and rope trips. Based on the pinwheeling I saw from at least one of them, I was pretty sure she'd managed to create a slick of frictionless shadow under the feet of some of them. It wasn't just making them fall, though. She manipulated the battlefield perfectly, tripping them into each other's range of perception so they would hear their companions and think they were being attacked.

Unlike the last batch of enemies we'd fought, despite being fairly well practiced at working together, these guys weren't all being puppeted by a seamless puppet master. They had no innate sense of what was what, and apparently, Callie's frustration at dealing with the Heartrippers had made even handling a group of well-trained opponents seem like a cakewalk. The spots where their cooperation wore thin were easily visible when you compared them to the kind of perfect synchronization our last group of enemies were capable of.

Leaving Callie to her controlling, I slipped off the branch and drifted down to the ground using Leaf on the Wind. Once I hit the ground, I homed in on the closest cloaked figure. It was the blandly smiling man. He was nursing a head wound, presumably from one of the others attacking him when Callie tripped them up. I leapt forward, sailing through the air and bringing my tonfa down on his head.

His Perception let him pick up the sound before I managed to hit him, but his dodge was slow and jerky because he couldn't actually see me coming. My blow landed on his shoulder, and the force flooded from my tonfa.

Surprisingly his cloak absorbed most of the force. It didn't take all of it, though, because he staggered. I was on him in seconds, beating him heavily about the head and body. I didn't use the poison fire because they were classmates, not evil cultists, but I also didn't hold back. This one was G-rank, so he could take the hits.

It took about two minutes to put him down, and I ended up stripping off his own cloak and tying him up with it before leaving him there to move on to my next opponent. Ten minutes later, we'd taken down all of them, and we banished the smoke.

Callie dropped from the tree on a rope of shadows, raced over, and tackled me. "That was amazing! That trick is so much more fun when we can both see! We kicked their asses!" She was grinning like a maniac as I held her up, and I couldn't help but laugh at her enthusiasm. I leaned up for a quick kiss, and as I put her down, her grin turned sly.

"I also grabbed this while I was up there." She held up a multicolored Hummingbird Blossom. "Three down, twenty two to go. Now, what say we search these guys and find out if they have any of the rest of the stuff we need? Or any other materials we can sell before we trigger their beacons." She turned and happily raced off to pat down the cloaked figures.

As I watched my excited girlfriend search our most recent defeats, a grin spread over my face. I felt amazing. This was what I was out here for. None of the hard moral choices or the evil assassin cults. I just wanted to fight, to get stronger, to help my friends, and to spend time with my loved ones.

Cracking my neck, I headed for the nearest limp figure. I was pretty sure Callie could use some help.

Chapter Four

We didn't find anything on our list when we searched the cloaked guys, and when we set off their beacons, they all got picked up quick as possible. Then we headed back to the hatchery with our spoils, which included the Hummingbird Blossoms and a fairly rare golden pear called a Calamity Fruit. The fruit was at the very least worth money, given how rare it was. The thing looked delicious too, but my girlfriend warned against eating it.

When I'd found it, she plucked it out of my hand before I even got a good look. "Careful. That's a Calamity Fruit. Staring into them too long can cause hysteria, and eating them causes delirium. Still, bet it's worth a pretty penny. Plus, if we run across someone else with a stockpile who has it on their list, we might be able to trade for it."

I hadn't considered that, so I'd stashed it for later. Once we got back, we checked in with Jessie about the missing two members of the cloak brigade.

Our enthusiastic overwatch was excited to see us, as always. "Hey, guys! You're back pretty quick. It's only been an hour or two. I don't really have any new info for you. That last raven hasn't found anything yet. Well, no other people anyway. There was a weird building I was going to report." She was sitting on the floor, playing cards with Cassidy.

Based on the large pile of acorns in front of her, Cassidy was cleaning up in their friendly game, not that Jessie seemed to care.

Callie was fighting down a smile as Cass slammed down a full house with a cheer and scooped up another pile of acorns, but she shook off her amusement to focus. "Not a problem. We wanted to check in on the cloaked pair you were watching. We ran into some of their friends. Also what do you mean a weird building? What kind of building? We're in the middle of the forest. There shouldn't be any buildings around here." She paused, looking around. "Well, current location excepted anyway."

As Jessie turned to us cheerfully, she looked up from her most recent hand, accidentally showing her cards to the nine-year-old in a way I somehow doubted was a surprise to the smirking kid. "Oh! Those guys freaked out about thirty minutes ago. They've been running nonstop toward some random spot, but they haven't gotten there yet. I followed them and figured I'd tell you where they ended up. As for the building, it's pretty weird. It's like an old crypt or something. It's in the middle of this huge empty field of black grass full of graves. Seemed weird and out of place."

My eyes widened, and I turned to Callie. She'd hurriedly pulled our list out and was searching through it. She finally shouted with excitement when she reached a specific entry. "Hundred-year-old corpse-eating grass! Plus a Bone Goblet that might be in the mausoleum! That biome is probably crawling with valuable materials we can stock up on too, either to sell or trade! Agria, where did you see this place? Also, were there any bodies around it? Skeletons? Really pale people with fangs?"

That brought me up short. "Wait. Are you asking about vampires? Those are a thing? Like, Skeletons, I get. That's power shit. But how the hell does someone become a vampire?" I knew about fae and devils, but the revelation that vampires existed was just… weird. I guessed it made sense, but at the same time, it just didn't fit with my worldview. What was next? Werewolves?

"There are no vampires here." Zeke's voice cut in from behind me. I hadn't even noticed him there, though given he was guarding Cass, I should have expected him. He was lying on a couch I knew hadn't been there before, eyes closed. "They do exist, but they're stupidly rare. They're all descended from an absolutely terrifying S-ranker named Morgan Lark. The Vampire is considered the most likely candidate to ascend to godhood next, and his clan is usually treated as the next best thing to their own faction. No vampire would be caught dead on this hellhole."

That news was disturbing and relieving all at the same time, but I didn't necessarily share his confidence. "And you're sure there isn't one here? The Black Sorrow Cult aren't exactly all over the place, but we've met a few of them. What's to say there isn't some distant vampire cousin around here snacking on people? If Nightstrike is bringing them up, they have to exist here in some form."

Zeke snorted, opening one eye. "No. The Vampire and Unity aren't fans of each other. They've fought several times. The Vampire has managed to get away every time and usually gives the youngest god a run for his money. His spawn steer clear of the conglomerate for that reason, though. Regardless, she wasn't talking about vampires. She was talking about ghouls. *Those* are fairly common, actually. The fangs aren't for sucking. They're for chewing. Think shark. It's a racial trait, though, with more in common with devils than fae."

Callie nodded. "Yeah, I've heard about ghouls in cemeteries a few times. They're known to be kind of a menace. They're pretty Might heavy. But the place Agria saw sounds like a Necropolis. They extend a ways underground. Usually pop up in graveyards, but if there's one in the area, the Academy must have taken it into account." She turned to Zeke. "Don't suppose you can tell us anything useful about the materials there?"

He just shrugged. "The Vampire and his clan fall in the category of 'so far above your paygrade, it's not covered under my geas.' Random graveyard monsters very much do not for the most part. If you want info, then do your research. I'll stick with the kid like I said, so it's not like I'd be along for the ride to ask anyway. Freebie, though—take the firebug. His kind are usually useful in death traps. Same with the churchie." Then he rolled over and faced the couch, clearly no longer willing or maybe even able to talk.

With that information, Callie decided it would be easier to involve everyone. "Okay, Cass, Agria, go get the others, please? I think we know our next move, but I want to get everyone's input here." She wanted feedback before sending out a bigger party, which made sense, so I settled in to wait.

Cassidy and Jessie bounded off to collect everyone from who knew where.

As I waited, I took in the changes to the hatchery. I didn't know if Benny had been inventing stuff or if one of the others was a crafter. Or maybe Zeke just traveled with a whole furnished house on his person. Whatever had happened, furniture was scattered all over this place. The raven baskets, which were mostly still full of eggs, sat in the back half of the building farther from the open side exposed to the clearing. They'd just moved some of the egg baskets closer together to make space.

The rest of the area was empty wooden floors and rock walls just like the rest of the building, set back into the cliff to provide some room. Aside from Zeke's couch, there were two big ass chairs and a love seat scattered around to create a nice homey atmosphere. I slumped into one of the chairs facing the open side of the building to wait as I watched the tree line. Even at this angle, the view was beautiful, and once again, I basked in being in the outdoors. Letting off some steam during that fight and talking to Callie last night had helped me a ton.

I wasn't magically feeling fine, but taking off some of that pressure let me focus on the good a little more. I could unpack the other stuff a little at a time instead of wallowing in it for ages. I'd always been the kind to repress then let off steam in small bursts instead of blowing my lid when I had a problem, and it had been working out for me so far.

After a few minutes of staring out into the wide-open wilderness I heard sounds, and everyone came filing up the steps. Benny looked noticeably annoyed even with his mask in the way, and I guessed he'd been talking to Celine, who was as blank faced as ever. I genuinely couldn't read that girl, Perception or not, and it made me wonder if she had a noble skill for keeping a straight face. Still, whatever the case was, I hoped Jessie and Cass didn't invite her to their card game unless they were okay with losing some serious acorn.

My best friend scowled over at my girlfriend. "Weren't you guys supposed to be out... doing something?" He sounded frustrated, but more grumpy than actually mad.

I detected a slight twitch at the corner of Celine's mouth. Apparently, he was making her smile, or her version of it, which seemed like a good sign to me. Callie just rolled her eyes and ignored him as Martin the Knight and Sarah the Cleric made their way up behind them.

Callie gestured to Jessie. "Now, Agria has informed me there's a necropolis nearby, and we have some death-related materials on our list. I was planning a trip down there, both for the things we need and for whatever else we find and can sell. Given the area, I think this should be safe to bring Grimmengap along for this trip, which is good because Sarah's Holy Hand skill will probably come in handy. Tony, we were hoping you would come along, as well, if you're willing to be backup on this."

She directed that at Cark, who had followed the others up when Cass and Jessie called them.

He just shrugged. "Yeah, I stayed so I could help. Zombies or heroes, doesn't matter much to me. Hell, if anything, this works better. I don't have to hold back and worry about burning some school kid. I can just burn the bastards to ash." He paused. "I… can just burn zombies to ash, right? They're not like… sentient or something? Because I don't know how that would even work, but it seems awful any way I can picture it."

Sarah, surprisingly, was the one to answer that. "Not at all. Zombies are animated remains brought to a semblance of life by necromancy. They have no consciousness aside from the crafted spirits the necromancers can imbue them with at higher levels. Unlike some other variations of undead like Ghouls or Liches, which are transformed from former living people, there is no moral questionability to destroying a zombie. Same with skeletons." We all turned to stare at her, and she blushed. "The church is often called to deal with the undead, so learning the particulars of their existence is one of the first tasks for Initiate clergy."

Callie just nodded dumbly. "Okay, well, it seems like we found our resident expert, discounting Zeke, who can't come with us because he's going to be staying with Cass."

I felt a surge or gratitude to her for heading off any complaints by reminding everyone he was on guard duty. Zeke was unable to help, but I knew that wasn't by choice. It meant a lot to me that she'd taken his feelings into account.

"With that out of the way, I guess it's time for us to head out. Who's ready to go destroy some undead?"

Chapter Five

AT THE VERY LEAST, the trip to the necropolis wasn't too long, not even moving as slow as the H-rankers. Jessie hadn't been ranging out that far, so it only ended up being about twenty miles. It was actually really nice to bolt through the woods, dodging trees and swinging off branches. The kind of speed we were reaching even without going all out was absurd.

The fastest mortal in the world could sprint just below thirty miles per hour. That could be considered a single point of Might, much like a thousand pounds of lifting force could be considered the same. At more than fifty Might, my top running speed was over fifteen hundred miles per hour. Now, allowances needed to be made for my much lower Vitality. I couldn't keep up that level of sprinting for particularly long, but that was irrelevant since the others were with us.

We kept it to a brisk jog requiring ten points or so, and three hundred miles per hour was more than fast enough to make that trip in a few minutes, even with time shaved off for tree dodging. It felt amazing to really let loose with my power in a controlled activity, even a non-combat one. I decided I would run more often. That wasn't practical in the city, but while we were out here, it was a fun and easy way to get around. We made it out of the forest without much trouble and slowed down as we approached the city of the dead.

The relatively small crypt stood in the center of a giant ass field of black grass. The entire landscape looked like something out of a nightmare. Black twisted trees clawed their way up from jagged hills that jutted up between the tufts of ebony grass. It was hard to spot them in the dark, but I could make out shambling, creeping forms in the shadows between the hillocks.

Benny, who was staring hard out at the dark landscape, tilted his head back and whistled. "Anyone else notice that? Because I'll be honest, I didn't even think to question why it got dark so suddenly at first. Now I kind of wish I hadn't looked."

We all looked up and winced as we saw the swirling vortex of black clouds shot through with icy-blue light. It diffused out over the area just enough to make things vaguely visible.

He turned to Sarah. "Don't suppose they covered this in your church classes?"

She sighed and nodded. "It's called an Omen Star. It's a meteorological manifestation of a massive concentration of necromantic energy. It's not an actual star, obviously. It's just named based on the placement, but if there's one here... we might have to fight a Lich. I imagine if there's one here, it's only going to be a Beginner Lich at worst. The Academy wouldn't have left it here if it was any stronger. Still, they are... problematic to deal with. I'm not even sure how one would have ended up on a planet like this, much less have established a presence strong enough to form an Omen Star."

That sounded unpleasant to say the least. "So Liches are like undead magic users? You mentioned they were one of the races of undead you can transform into, which makes them part of the devil faction, I take it?" I knew the devils were a faction of monstrous cultivators with a racial trait, similar to the fae, but I didn't know too much about them in general. "What's the difference between devils and the fae exactly? Sorry if the question offends, Celine." I gave the elf girl a nod of acknowledgement.

Luckily for me, she didn't seem upset and just shook her head. "It's... somewhat arbitrary in all honesty. The devil factions split from the Faerieland for one reason or another. They're basically a mishmash of cultivators that aren't technically fae. They gathered under the actual devils, which *are* a race of their own, and declared their independence. For simplicity, most people call the devil factions as a whole 'fiends,' because devils are a specific subset of the fiends as well as the leaders of the faction. Regardless, yes, Liches are fiends, and dangerous ones, at that."

Sarah's worried frown testified to that. "They're magic users, which isn't something you see often in the Conglomerate. It's part of the Job system and not ability-based cultivation. Liches are unpredictable and difficult to defeat because they rarely have the same Skills. The only real consistent skill set is necromancy. Regardless, if we're lucky, we can avoid the Lich altogether. They're best given a wide berth." She turned to Callie. "So, what's our plan of attack, Nightstrike? I assume you have a specific method of approach in mind?"

Callie nodded. "I was thinking I could cloak us in shadow. I wasn't sure if the undead have a way to pierce that kind of concealment. This seems like a good environment to use my ability, though." She gestured out at the faintly lit ebony landscape, and I could see her point. Her shadow embodiment should get us to the crypt itself easily enough if they couldn't see. "Based on stories I've read about necropoli, chances are pretty good there's a series of catacombs under that crypt, so the closer we get before being discovered, the better our chance to get in without a fight."

Sarah pursed her lips, staring out into the dark, as if trying to identify exactly what we would be facing. "I can't say for sure, honestly. It depends on which undead we come across. Some of them see with senses beyond those of mortal eyes." That was actually an interesting thing to know. I wondered how Perception interacted with that difference in sight. Regardless, that meant we really had nothing to go on.

Callie knew it too, so we could only go with the obvious plan. "Then I guess we just have to check and see. We'll try to breach the borders and check if they notice us. If they do, we run, and hopefully, only the closest undead will come after us. We can mop up the few that follow and then try another plan of entry, or barring that, just run back to the hatchery and use it as a fortified position. Either way, our best move here is to test the waters." She glanced around inquisitively. "Unless someone else has a better plan? I'm always open to suggestions."

I had to give it to Callie. Aside from being open to new ideas from teammates, her timing was always good too. She made sure to give us all input at times when it wouldn't affect the flow of battle. Whether we took her up on it or not, we all felt heard, and it didn't screw with our operational efficiency. Besides, her plans were usually pretty solid, which was why we'd picked her as leader to start with. As usual, no one had any big problems with her strategy, so we all just indicated that we were ready to go.

Callie raised her hands, closing her eyes in concentration, and the shadows surged beneath our feet. They wrapped around us, and I felt them shift slightly as Callie synergized her stealth skill with her ability in a monumental feat of power I was pretty sure I couldn't have managed. Even if I had the tools like she did, the amount of shadow she was perceiving and the traces she had to suppress were mind-blowing. It took her a few minutes to even get the whole thing in place, and we all just waited and watched.

I'd done plenty of tricky operations with my Skills, but I hadn't used my ability much. It wasn't really functional in a combat situation. Still, I knew very well how much it could wear on a person to make changes to the world around them like she was doing now. I had enough trouble effecting my own individual skills or even pushing them to one person. Cloaking an entire group in stealth was enough to reinforce my already-heavy respect for my girlfriend and her capabilities.

When her eyes opened, she began to walk, slow and steady, trusting us to follow. The second she stepped out onto the black grass, she froze. We all stood stock-still behind her, waiting for the other shoe to drop. Despite the tension, she just stood there in silence for a beat and then started walking forward again slowly. We followed, and again, she stopped. It finally occurred to me what she was actually doing. She was trying to process the sounds and traces the rest of us were making then erase them, and it was taking a bit to manage.

I held a finger to my lips to show them they should try to be quieter. Then I slowly started to step after her, doing my best to creep across the grass without disturbing it too much. The others clearly understood my intent because they began to do the same, trying to make Callie's job of hiding our presence easier. The effort brought our speed down dramatically, but it was worth it. We slowly crossed the field of death, avoiding trees, sharp hills, and any undead we noticed.

Of which there were *a lot*. Skeletons were pretty common, but wights, a sort of creeping undead that scurried across the ground on four legs, were more prevalent. Once the first one we saw was out of earshot, Sarah gave us a hushed explanation of the things, and we saw plenty more of them over the next hour or so of careful creeping.

We also learned something new. The crypt was *much* bigger than it looked. The whole tiny mausoleum thing was a trick of perspective; the massive marble edifice was actually the size of a pretty decent house. Even the raven hadn't been able to spot that because it was so fucking *far* into the field. Jessie had stayed on the outskirts of the black field to avoid drawing attention from the undead, and because of that, she hadn't had the perspective to notice the size difference.

We took things one step at a time, and the actual distance was pretty much irrelevant to the journey beyond making things harder on Callie. We had to stop multiple times on the way to lighten the burden, but eventually, we got within sight of the huge marble crypt. Once we could see it, we realized the place was guarded by more than just skeletons. A quartet of massive black skeletal knights in plate armor flanked the front of the crypt, attended on either side by smaller bone constructs.

Unlike the others, these skeletal knights didn't seem to have any trouble with Callie's stealth. They turned to glare right at us as we approached. I wasn't sure if Callie was tired, if they could see better, or if their G-rank made up the difference, but in the end, it hardly mattered. Callie dropped the stealth field and slumped against me. I held her up before passing her to Jessie for a pick-me-up and turning to Cark and Benny. "Well, looks like we're fighting our way in after all. So, who gets to fight two of them?"

Chapter Six

CARK GOT to fight two of the knights. His stats were the strongest, though I didn't know exactly how many points he had, so he decided to take the initiative and hit one of the two duos himself. I personally was annoyed by the fact, but it made sense, so I backed down. Benny and I each took one of the other death knights, as Sarah informed us they were called, while the H-rankers mopped up the basic skeletons.

Callie was sadly unable to fight with us, being exhausted from keeping up the shroud around us for literal hours. Jessie was pumping life energy into my girlfriend with her ability, so she was out of this too. That left us with just the three G-rankers on our side. Still, Cark, Benny, and I were more than up to the task of taking on some undead knights, so I wasn't worried and could focus on just having fun.

Obviously, the first thing I did was light up my tonfas with poison fire, and the second was activate Leaf in the Wind to allow me to jump around a bit more and compensate for the fucking horse the skeletal knight was sitting astride. I wasn't too familiar with fighting someone on horseback, but I figured not being ground bound would be a benefit. Not to mention that horse was probably G-ranked, as well, so I wanted to be free to dodge it. Getting trampled by a nightmarish bone horse was pretty low on my list of preferred ways to die, not that there were any ways to die that I would like better.

With the strength in my legs, jumping around was easy enough to manage, and with Leaf on the Wind and Cloud Step, I could change directions pretty easily. I wasted no time sending myself streaking toward the skeleton knight in a shallow arc, my tonfas flashing out to slam into the thing. As I came in at it, the ghostly blue flame in its eyes, a twin in color to the Omen Star, flickered steadily. It lashed out at me with black metal sword on its back, a weapon that matched its spiked and jagged armor.

One thing I appreciated about the skeletons was that they didn't talk. There was no monologue or boasting. Much like the sleepers, they got straight to the fight without saying a word. Unlike the sleepers, though, the skeletons weren't actual living, thinking beings. They were piles of bone animated by dark magic, so I didn't feel bad about crushing the damn things without mercy.

My tonfas seemed to be pretty well suited to normal skeletons actually, as I ended up smashing two of the H-ranked bone constructs when they got in the way of my attack. They didn't even slow me down. The knights were wearing armor, however, making them much less susceptible to blunt force. Still, I quickly got in close and start lashing out at joints with my weapons, doing my best to take the things apart, even through the armor.

The downside to fighting bone constructs in armor became apparent. While the poison fire spread through the bones, burning away at them, the skeletons weren't even fazed. No flesh meant no muscles to wear down or burn away. Whatever the hell moved this thing, presumably stat points and a skill, even the slow destruction of the materials didn't seem to do much to stop it.

Still, aside from the bones, I landed several blows on the armor, and the force enchantments dented and cracked the black plate as the poison fire seared it away. My attack unfortunately had to end early as I dodged that big-ass sword, using Cloud Step to bounce myself over it and activating my gymnastics skill to maneuver more freely in the air and reposition myself for my next attack. A smashing blow to the helmet didn't do much since the skeletons didn't use their eyes.

As the second one's sword came in at what it probably thought was my blind spot, I juked hard to the side and turned to glare at Benny, who was looking somewhat irritated that his tranquilizer punch wasn't working. He shrugged apologetically, and I stepped forward hard, skating through the air in an incredibly short forward arc that let me travel just above the surface of the ground to land next to him.

He grinned at me as I landed. "Hey, sorry about that. These bastards are fast. How about we tag team the two of them?"

I blew out a breath. "Probably not a bad idea. You have any ideas for dealing with them? We can just crush them through brute force, but I feel like that might take too long. You notice any special weaknesses?"

It would have been useful to ask Sarah, but the Cleric was among the H-rank skeletons with Martin and Celine, so we would have to rely on our own observations here, as unhelpful as they might be. All I'd been able to grasp was the obvious "break bones so they can't move" strategy, so hopefully Benny had more.

Sadly, I had no such luck. "Nope. They're skeletons. Blunt force breaks bones, so that's probably our best bet. My punch and probably my density shifting are my most effective weapons, from what I can tell. You seem to be doing okay, though."

He pointed over at the second skeleton I'd just been fighting. "That poison fire will probably melt them if we leave it to work long enough. Looks like it's having an effect already." He pointed out a specific spot where the skeleton's leg seemed to be barely attached. It had little effect, given it was sitting on a horse. Still, he wasn't wrong.

Though that did give me an idea. Unlike Benny's punch, my Mercy Kill ability let me apply a flat increase to any attacks I used. It didn't matter what weapon or skill was involved; as long as I was making an attack, Mercy Kill would work on it. I put my hands together and turned to Benny. "Here, I have an idea. I'm going to launch you up, then you use the density shifting in your leg to come down hard and slam your fist into the one that's already damaged. Just concentrate on the triple punch."

He seemed unsure about the instruction, but he was the one who'd wanted to team up in the first place, so he did what I'd told him to do. As I launched him up into the air, I triggered Mercy Kill, designating Benny himself as my attack in this case. My friend went sailing up into the air, his arc actually improved by the skill, and as he came back down, he slammed his fist into the chest of the skeleton knight. The triple punching force amplified by the hundred fifty percent boost of Mercy Kill and his increased speed and momentum crashed down on the death knight with a deafening roar of shattering metal, driving the skeletal being right off its bony mount.

I was already in motion before it hit the ground, sailing in with Leaf on the Wind to rain down as many blows as I could. Given its missing leg and position on the ground, my blows had the added effect of not just slowly corroding it with acidic poison flame, but also driving the thing into the ground. Despite not having seen any actual rain lately, the earth here was loose and easily disturbed. I smashed the bastard into the dirt as hard as I could, letting the ground restrain him as I tried to deal maximum damage.

Bone cracked and plate fractured as the increased force of the blows and the poison flame effects compounded to degrade the death knight. Of course, we were fighting more than just this one knight, but Benny was up to blocking the second skeletal charge with his hyper-dense leg, kicking out hard at the head of the horse to turn the knight off course and prevent me from being trampled.

I still had to dodge the horse of the knight I had downed, but without a rider, it seemed jerky and easily frightened. It shied away from the loud noises and bright lights of the smashing attacks as I pummeled its former rider. After a minute of constant wailing, I managed to get the monster broken up enough that I was pretty sure it couldn't move. I turned to help Benny with the other one.

Benny was using his legs' weightless mode to make himself more mobile, and combined with his Might stat, he was managing to stay ahead of the skeleton. I suspected his high-speed perception was coming into play, because he was barely dodging, clearly trying to stay in close to prevent it from building up too much momentum. It was a solid way to deal with the knight, and as it wheeled yet again, I slipped in close to deliver a Mercy Kill empowered blow to the horse's leg.

The big thing that people rarely realize about horses is how absurdly delicate their legs are. The sheer amount of weight focused on such a small area, combined with the delicate artistry of equine legs meant that they were actually one of the animal's most vulnerable parts. My blow fractured the leg, and the poison fire started to degrade the limb pretty soon after.

The horse didn't really seem to notice, given the bone was still holding together, but it did give him an active debuff that would drop him eventually. Despite not being a flesh-and-blood horse, it was still pretty heavy, and the more it used that leg, the worse it got. As the horse spun on me, Benny dipped in with a triple-strength punch aimed at unseating the knight. Though the creature had learned from its companion and wouldn't come off its horse so easily, Benny's attack *did* get the thing's attention.

We played it like that for a while—whittling away at the death knight from either side. The initial skeleton was gone at this point, the poison fire having been stacked enough to completely consume the bone, though there were still some pieces of armor left.

Finally, it was done. The horse collapsed once its leg had dissolved too much to be usable. It toppled over, and we fell on it, pounding it into the dirt like the last one and making sure not to let up until it was no longer functional. It was one of the more satisfying fights I could remember because it was just pure combat. No worry about humanity, motivations, or even sentience, like with animals. It was just raw force against dead bone, and it put me in a great mood.

Once we finished, I turned to check on the others and had to chuckle at my own worrying. They hardly needed my assistance. The skeletons were demolished, bones and weapons littering the ground, and everyone was waiting for us to finish. Cark was just polishing off his second with his blue flames, and I turned to Callie as I finished, grinning behind my mask.

"Now that's what I'm talking about. So, what do we do next, boss?" I couldn't wait to get into the necropolis. I wondered what new monsters would be waiting.

Chapter Seven

CALLIE LOOKED MOSTLY unamused by the question. "We go in, obviously, before the fight attracts even more of these damned undead and we end up ass deep in a skeleton army."

I snickered slightly. There wasn't really any other valid move after all this, but I felt like poking fun at her for checking in with us all the time, even if I did appreciate it. I knew from her smile that she didn't take the ribbing too seriously, though. With her eyes still blazing a now-fading emerald green from Jessie's ability, she was more than up to leading the way.

Everyone gathered up in front of the door to the crypt. The entrance was (despite being ten feet if it was an inch) ludicrously small in comparison to the rest of the massive marble building. The iron double doors were thick and dark, with intricate scrollwork displaying screaming faces and huge skeletal figures. It was literally the most morbid piece of decoration imaginable, and the pair of cold blue torches on either side of the doors were yet another chilling touch that made it clear how absurdly creepy this place was.

Luckily, the doors were just normal iron. With our Might stats, opening them was child's play. We could have ripped them out of the marble if need be, so we were able to open and close them quickly enough to not have to worry about the undead swarming us. Once we were inside, I expected to have to find some light. Sure enough, those same creepy blue torches flickered eerily down the length of a dimly lit marble corridor. The split-off just ahead of us went in three different directions, all headed into the building at a downward angle.

With the door closed, we were able to relax a bit and stare into the depths of the building.

Sarah nodded unhappily. "Like I thought. This is the tip of the iceberg. We're standing at the peak of a massive underground complex." She bit her lip uncertainly. "I was really hoping it was just a few underground tunnels. We're probably looking at a real city of the dead. Maybe even a kingdom." She turned to Callie. "This isn't going to be a short trip. Is this really a good use of our time?"

My girlfriend sighed unhappily. "I think so. There are only a few death-aligned materials on the list, but if this place is that big, the undead may have been collecting materials of their own. Even if we don't find the exact things we need, we might stumble on a treasure trove we could trade or sell. We might lose a few days or even a week down here, but in the long run, this is going to be the best way to get ahead quickly. Solomon, can you find the right way for us to go to get deeper into this place?"

I'd been expecting that, and I triggered Seek Hidden. Finding the "right way" was an amorphous concept. Although there were only three routes, it was a strange experience searching for a path. A waist-high cloud of red mist drifted up off the marble floor down one hallway, demonstrating where we should be heading. It was almost as difficult as straining the skill to show me two things at once to change the input, and I stumbled slightly before Callie caught me.

I gave her a nod of thanks and pointed down the hall that was marked. I relaxed my hold on the skill and managed to keep a faint trace of red active. Letting it fade eased the strain, and after some rest, I was able to continue. "That's the way. Can't see much besides general direction, but that's where we need to head. Keep an eye out for any other undead we might come across. I won't be able to watch for them and pathfind at the same time."

Jessie's hand on my arm was accompanied by a rush of energy as she pushed life force into me, helping me get back into fighting shape. It put a nice pep in my step. We started forward down the tunnel, eyes peeled for wights, skeletons, or even new types of undead we'd never seen. The death knights were probably out because of the horses, though it was hard to say if they could walk around without them.

"Hey, are those bone horses part of the death knights?" I asked Sarah, our resident expert on all things undead.

She shook her head, clearly happy to have something to focus on other than the creepy marble hallway lined with ghostly torches. "No. They can walk normally, though the ones summoned as cavalry tend to be slightly stronger in exchange for the loss of their ability to dismount. We might run into some down here, though, so we should keep an eye out. Bone archers are common in confined spaces like this, too, and that's going to be a big problem if we come across them. Do you have some way of dealing with projectiles?"

I pointed at Benny, who held up his arm triumphantly.

Callie rolled her eyes. "Yes, we can shield. It's much more effective than using one of our party members' limbs as a long-term pincushion for foot-long shafts of wood." She curled her fingers, and the shadows rose up off the floor, washing up in front of us in a sort of translucent dome. It was like looking through black glass, and I was shocked to see she'd mastered yet another use of her power when I wasn't looking. I was really starting to lag behind. I needed to get with the program.

We walked like that for about two hours before I needed to take a break. We decided to stop in one of the few alcoves off the main hallway, stepping into the side room and slumping down in exhaustion. Well, mostly that was just me. Flexing my skill like that (even minimally) for hours, was exhausting. The others had pretty much just been walking around, so they were fine, but it got pretty banal walking down the same stretch of corridor for that long, so the change of scenery was nice.

Jessie, angel of mercy that she was, came over to charge me up while we rested, and I sighed with relief as my body flooded with life energy. With her this close, even through the mask, I was able to spot some telltale signs I'd missed until now. Given how busy everything had been, I hadn't been as focused on my team as I should have been.

I put a hand on her shoulder. "Hey, you doing okay? You seem tired. If this is wiping you out, you can say so. We don't need you to top us off every five minutes."

She gave me a small smile. "No. It's not that. I just haven't been sleeping well. My lifeforce comes from inside, so I can't really energize myself by putting it back. I've just been having trouble getting rest. Even with Vitality like mine, you need *some* sleep. It'll be fine, though. I'm figuring it out." Despite her confident words, her tone sounded... off. Sad and beaten down.

I reached up to remove her hand from my chest, where she was pumping in the energy. "Hey. Talk to me. I know it hasn't been that long since you lost your brother. No one expects you to pick up everyone's slack. You don't need to work so hard all the time."

She looked surprised.

"Please, like I haven't noticed how much you've been doing. Callie is the leader, but I do pay attention. You've been working your ass off. I guess I just hadn't put it together how tiring that must be for you. I'll talk to the others, ask them to lay off."

She grabbed my hand tightly. "Don't!"

I tilted my head, the universal sign for being confused in a mask.

She let go of me, sighing. "I need to get stronger. I've been trying for a while now. At first, it was to be useful and because it helped take my mind off things. But now I can't stop thinking about an idea I had. My powers... They let me give life to things that aren't alive, they heal and animate, and they're still so weak in the grand scheme of things. If they can do this now, then maybe—"

I swallowed as her question hit me like a speeding train. "Maybe you can use them to bring back your brother someday." It sounded crazy. Dead was dead. Everyone knew that. But was it really? In a world where you could bend and break the fabric of reality, was dead *really* dead? "I... want to try to talk you out of that. To convince you to move on. But I can't. Not really, not in the world we live in. So all I can say to you is that if you do manage it—and I believe you will—he would want you to be happy. To be safe and healthy. He wouldn't want to come back to find you a shell of yourself."

She bit her lip. "I know. You're right. But it's just... It's right there. Every time I close my eyes, I see the next step. The training I could be doing. Relaxing feels wrong, like I don't deserve it. It feels like I'm betraying his memory every time I stop to smell the roses. I have so much to do, so far to go before I can even think about fixing this, but I know if it was him here, he would move mountains to bring me back if he could."

I couldn't argue that, but I did dispute one point. "You still need to live your life. You can't just pour yourself completely into this. Have you even talked to Maria lately? I know how much you look forward to those talks."

It was only now dawning on me how oblivious I'd been to my teammate's suffering while I was worrying about my own problems. Jessie had been hurting all this time, and I hadn't seen a thing. Like her pain had just magically gone away for some reason. I felt like an asshole. "Plus you're acting like this is all on you. Like you're alone here. We're a team—trust us to help, to have your back. If you can't get this done with your powers, we can do it with mine."

Her eyes widened in realization. I had never actually considered a resurrection wish before, but it seemed like it... should be possible. Probably not anytime soon, but if trying helped Jessie realize she wasn't in this alone, then I was all for it. She looked at me with a flicker of hope in her eyes, and seeing it there after not noticing its absence broke my heart a little.

"I wish my brother was alive again." Her voice was rough, as if saying it out loud was almost too difficult for her to bear, but she did it anyway.

Wish detected. Grant wish?

I confirmed.

Insufficient stat points. Requirements: NA. Resurrection beyond the capabilities of Beginner Wish ability.

I'd expected that. But it wasn't actually bad news. I shook my head, but before she pulled away, I gave her a grin. "It's beyond my ability right now, but it *is* possible. If your power can't bring him back, then mine will. We can do this. We can bring your brother back to life."

The sobbing missile of healer that slammed into my chest in a grateful hug was enough to lift my spirits like nothing else had in a while, even spending time with Callie. I'd forgotten something important—things that were broken could be fixed. Even hearts.

Chapter Eight

It took a few minutes for Jessie to cry herself out. I imagined she had been building up quite a bit of pressure and frustration, and having a release for all that tension in the form of hope was bound to take the wind out of her sails. Since she couldn't use her energizing ability on herself, she fell asleep on my shoulder after crying herself out. I considered waking her, but we were as safe as we were going to be for the foreseeable future, and having our healer running on fumes seemed ill advised.

Callie came over to smile at me as I set her down. "She finally decided to talk to someone, huh?"

I cocked my head in confusion.

She chuckled sadly. "She's been running herself into the ground trying to get stronger. I would have brought it up, but it was something she needed to open up about on her own. I honestly have no idea what you said to her, because I couldn't think of a way to help. You can't just shrug off losing a loved one like that." She gave the younger girl a soft smile as we bunched up Jessie's cloak under her head so she could sleep on the hard marble flooring.

Callie turned to look at the others. "We're stopping here for a while. Agria needs some rest, and I think the rest of us could use a bit of time to decompress. Solomon and I will take first watch. The rest of you should have something to eat and relax a bit. Maybe catch a nap yourselves. We'll wake you up well before any undead get close."

Everyone else seemed happy to take the time off and was able to relax a bit, though I saw Benny looking at Jessie with concern. He tapped Celine on the shoulder and pulled her over to stand by our teammate so they could talk and watch her at the same time as Callie and I pulled off to stand at the door to the hallway.

Despite being on watch, I could tell Callie was relaxing a bit herself, and I put an arm around her shoulder, pulling her against me as we watched the hall. She let herself snuggle into my side, and I saw a tension ease from her that I hadn't even noticed was there.

I reached up to remove my mask since my back was to the others and my hood kept me mostly protected from sight. "Wow, you were really worried about her, weren't you? Am I just a giant asshole for not noticing she was hurting so much? I just picked up on it today, and I kind of wish I'd known. I might have been able to... help somehow. I don't know."

She leaned up to press a kiss to my lips. "No. You aren't an asshole. You've been dealing with problems of your own. I was worried, but I'm the leader. That's my job. The emotional health of my team, especially yours, is important to me. I had faith she would confide in one of us soon, and if she really did bottle it up for too much longer, I'd have said something to her. I just... I know how hard it is to lose someone close to you. Not like she did. I know she and her brother were inseparable, but—"

I put a finger to her lips. "Hey, you're allowed to mourn your friend. I know he was there for you in a really dark time in your life. Just because Jessie lost someone doesn't make you less deserving of your own grief. Feel how you feel. If it's your job as leader to take care of us, then it's my job as your boyfriend to take care of you. Someone needs to if you're going to worry about everyone else." I gave her a lopsided smile.

She chuckled wetly, giving me a grateful nod without saying anything out loud.

Callie hadn't really had time to mourn Batty (an old friend of hers and another of Stricture's victims), hell, most of us hadn't had time to process any of this. She'd gone out of her way to talk to me about my issues and check how I was doing while keeping an eye out for Jessie, too.

Benny was the only one of us who seemed genuinely unaffected, but I knew how my friend liked to repress everything. I decided to talk to him about everything soon, to take something off Callie's plate, because she'd been stuck with way too much lately.

We sat there like that for a while. I had my Seek Hidden skill active and scanning for skeletons, and I knew Callie had her eyes peeled even if she was taking a beat to just let things go. I felt bad that I couldn't give her that time with no distractions, but that just wasn't where we were at right now.

After she'd had time to gather herself, she finally spoke. "What did she ask you? You don't have to tell me if you think it would violate her confidence, but I'd like to know, if that's okay."

I couldn't see a problem with answering honestly. I'd promised Jessie the team would have her back, and Callie was part of that. Benny too. I was pretty sure she wouldn't mind them knowing what we had planned. "Her brother. She wants to bring him back. Either on her own or with my help. She tried wishing for it to see if it's possible, and while it is, it's beyond the scope of my ability, which means it's probably absurdly expensive. Still, one way or the other, it can be done, so I agreed to help her." I kept my tone even, though I was curious what Callie's reaction would be.

She flinched away, looking almost confused. "That's… sweet Revenant. I didn't even know that was possible, though now that I say that out loud, it seems silly. It's just… death. That's so final. I can't even imagine it not being a constant. I wonder if that's a common option for people who are ranked high enough. It just kind of highlights how different the world gets as you grow stronger. How much the rules change. If you can help her like that, though… to bring him back. Can you do that for me? Can I wish for my friend back?"

I just shrugged. "I don't see why not. I mean keep in mind it might be a while. Judging by the feedback, this might be pretty damn late game, but if you want to wait… yeah, I don't see a reason I couldn't. You don't think it's stupid? Or crazy? You'll help? Because honestly, even thinking about it feels crazy in a way. Living for a thousand plus years because of Impact is one thing, but death just being something you can fix is such an absurd thing to even consider. I half expected you to bust out some obscure cultivation factoid to tell me it wasn't possible."

That got a snicker. "Nope. That kind of thing is well above my paygrade. This isn't exactly a top-tier planet, not that I've been to one. There's plenty about cultivation I don't know." She smiled wetly and poked me in the ribs. "I just seem knowledgeable to you because you have no idea what the hell is going on."

That was probably fair. I had no clue what was happening to me most of the time, as much as I had fun with the process.

Callie glanced over her shoulder. "You might want to put your mask back on, by the way. Looks like our watch is over."

I was surprised it had ended so quickly, but I guessed we had been here longer than I'd thought. Spending time with her had been nice. Callie had this knack for keeping me in the moment. I didn't overthink or analyze everything when I was with her. Whether it was helping with her burdens or just sitting with her and talking, I was always present when we were together. I shot her a grateful smile and gave her another quick kiss before I slipped my mask on, and we stood up to turn and meet the next pair of watchers.

Benny and Celine were waiting for us, Cark having taken over sitting with Jessie, and it was all I could do not to laugh at the image of them switching places with us.

I gave my best friend a sarcastic nod. "You guys have a reservation? Apparently, this is the hot new place for couples to spend time together, so I'm gonna have to check the guest book." After the shit he'd given me about Callie before we got together, I wasn't going to miss a chance to rib my best friend about his new romance.

Celine's incredibly pale cheeks reddened so imperceptibly, I would have missed it without my enhanced Perception stat.

Benny just gave me the finger. "Yeah, table for two under 'go fuck yourself.'"

I cracked up, and we stepped aside to let them through. Benny kicked my ankle as I walked by, and I yelped as it landed right on the bone, getting a snicker from my friend. I didn't begrudge him that back-and-forth. I could tell he was as worried about Jessie as I was. The familiarity of us messing with each other was a comfort with so much changing.

I expected Callie to mention it, but she just shook her head in exasperation at the two of us. We found Cark sitting back against the wall, napping, and the two of us sat down on the other side of him near Jessie to close our eyes too. I spread my cloak out on the floor at the base of the wall as we settled in for a nap.

I didn't know when the next chance to sleep would come, so since we were here, it made sense to at least try to rest. Callie seemed to agree with me, because she snuggled up next to me. Then we both did our best to drift off to sleep.

As we lay together, I thought back to what I'd learned from Jessie, to what I'd seen in Callie's eyes. I spent a lot of time focusing on the good and trying not to get lost in the various terrible things interspersed throughout my time as an Ascendant. My dad disowning me, finding Batty's body, and those eight sleepers Aiden had killed in G District. As much as I tried to avoid thinking about it, there was real darkness there. But I'd been ignoring the most important thing—my own team.

Benny had left home for the first time and basically abandoned his family to follow me. He and his parents hadn't always been that close, but they loved him, and he loved them. He and his sister Maria were as thick as thieves, and he had left all that behind to come with me. Some of that was a desire for adventure, but I knew him well enough to know some of it was looking out for me, even if he would never say it. Callie was dealing with Batty's death and everyone else's problems, and Jessie had been suffering without me even noticing.

I made a promise to myself. To help my friends with their demons even as I tried to work on mine. To take care of my team for real, not just ignore them outside of fights. I planned for us all to be together for a long time, and I wanted us to thrive, emotionally and in terms of power. I fell asleep like that, my girlfriend warm against my side as I nodded off. Despite the dire revelations, I was smiling. Knowing there was a problem was a good first step. Tomorrow would be a better day.

Chapter Nine

We woke up about two hours later, and Jessie was already awake and ready to take on the world. It made me smile to see how much happier and more energetic my friend was—not just because of the rest, but because she had hope. She had been keeping her plans to herself and had probably half convinced herself she was crazy and chasing ghosts, and knowing that I not only believed in her but had another solution if hers failed clearly made a big difference.

Now that her light was back, I was determined to keep it there.

We formed up ranks in the doorway. I did a quick scan with my Seek Hidden for skeletons while Callie used her tracking skill to look for traces of passages or traps. The former was unlikely, given our lookouts, but we could never be too careful. We scanned the hallway in both directions, and once we were sure there were no traps, we started slowly forward again. I felt refreshed after the downtime and the nap, so I was ready and waiting for any danger.

It took quite a while before we hit the next blockage in the path.

We were walking through a shadowed portion of tunnel, the ghost fire torches guttering low on the walls, when we got jumped by wights. They came out of the walls, literally two dozen of them, but the wights were hardly the biggest threats. A pair of massive armored forms stepped from well-hidden alcoves in the path, clearly having been waiting to ambush us.

They barreled toward us at top speed. Each gargantuan shape was covered in black metal and wielding an enormous two-handed axe... and missing its head.

Sarah squeaked in fright. "Dullahans! They're an elite vanguard unit of the undead. They're legendary for their power!"

The rest of her warning was cut off as I leapt forward to meet one. Cark went at the other to stop it Might to Might. The axe smashed down at the bare-handed brawler, and his blazing blue hands caught it between his palms. He wasn't able to stop it cold, but he sure as hell came close. The heat also softened the metal enough that what little force did hit him dented the axe.

I... was less fortunate. My arms buckled under the weight of the axe as I slammed my tonfas into the blade, releasing my force enchantment and... nothing. I was lucky I managed to hit the thing as hard as I had, because I was pretty sure my armor would have split in two without the force my blow had leached off. It still wasn't enough to prevent the battering ram of pure force that impacted my chest. I sailed back to skid across the floor. Callie screamed my name frantically, but it took me a second to clear my head enough to actually process what was going on.

One of the wights was on me, but since it was H-rank, its scratches and bites were more annoying than deadly. I reached up absently and crushed its fucking head with my bare hands before crawling to my feet to look around for my weapons. My chest hurt, my head hurt, my arms hurt, and I was pretty sure that blow had cracked my sternum, but I was recovering from the shock quickly thanks to my Focus and Vitality, which left me dealing with something else.

I... lost. I mean it wasn't over, obviously. I would be getting back into the fight, but I'd gotten used to my tricks and skills being enough to dominate things in my own weight class. I guessed now that I was higher rank, the variation in enemies even at my own level would make those fights much less certain. I finally found my weapons, and I stopped to think about what I should do. I could use my Mistwalking skill, but that would impede my friends and allies. I needed to focus on the one I had committed to. Cark was clearly able to handle his opponent, but the others would need me.

I stood and looked down the hall at the towering form trying to bisect my girlfriend, and blinked. Callie was... pissed. Her face was set in a mask of cold rage, and Jessie was headed my way as Callie basically single-handedly dealt with the Dullahan. I'd expected her to run into the same issue as I had, and she had, but her response was much different.

The Dullahan was raining down blows with its axe, but unlike my dumb ass, Callie wasn't meeting them with strength. She moved like a shadow, whispering between swings, her fists covered in shadow gauntlets that occasionally flicked out to guide the blows a bit to one side. A series of chains with spikes on either end hung from her arms. Each time the Dullahan stopped to retrieve the axe, she darted in, jammed one end into a joint and the other into the marble floor, then darted out.

She was circling the thing, slamming the spikes home quickly and efficiently. It broke several of them—easily, in fact. But Callie kept shoving more of them in, and the creature struggled to free itself. She was slowly weighing it down, stripping its mobility. I was in awe. I'd thought I was doing okay with the fighting (not perfect but pretty well) but seeing Callie actually fight with an opponent who was her equal was an absolute revelation.

I needed to step up my game. Jessie reached my side and smacked her palms on my chest, which fucking hurt. She shoved a bunch of green energy into me, and I almost groaned with relief as the damage started to knit back together. Bones mending, muscles reknitting. My armor was still pretty fucking banged up, but it was also totally full, so I knew exactly what I could do next. Glaring up at the slowly lagging form of the Dullahan as Callie stripped its freedom, I reached for my DS Mastery.

Touch of Tears, Consecration of Flame, Leaf in the Wind, Mercy Kill, Flurry of Blows, and Afterburner. I layered my strongest and most effective series of skills on top of each other. Jessie jerked a bit as her power yanked more life force out of her. She was trying to get me to full, and the big drop in my body's energy had forced her to compensate with a new burst of life force. I was grateful for it, too, since I'd forgotten how much strain fast-triggering skills could put on me. Luckily, the extra power from Afterburner and the life force were more than enough to keep me upright. I caught her, offering her a grateful nod before I hurled myself down the hall at the Dullahan.

Callie had pinned its legs, and I timed my lunge for right after a swing of that massive axe. I felt like a fucking flaming meteor as I sailed down the hallway at the undead powerhouse, raising my tonfas in preparation. When I finally came within range... I struck. A hail of flaming green attacks thundered across the shoulders and chest of the armored abomination, leaving blazing green cracks and dark-green smoke behind as the plate splintered under the force.

Sadly, the damn thing didn't go down, but I was able to push off and drift lightly to the ground to land next to Callie, who looked relieved.

She smiled happily at me. "You're okay. I saw that thing hit you, and you just… went flying." Her voice was shaking a little.

I winced since I hadn't actually considered how complicated the team dynamic could get in combat with us dating, but then again, it wasn't like she wouldn't have cared before we got together. Any of us getting hurt would shake the others, but we were both fine, so now was the time to focus on dealing with the Dullahan.

I holstered one of my tonfas and grabbed her hand, squeezing it gently so she knew I appreciated the concern, even if she couldn't see my face. We turned to the Dullahan, which had finished tearing free of the bindings while we talked. Despite that, the effort seemed to have worsened the damage to its upper body.

I turned to Callie. "I think my big mistake before was trying to meet it head-on. I got so used to being able to muscle everything because of my Might stat, I forgot I've been dealing with freshman and rookies… and cultists, I guess, but they're on the low end of the spectrum too."

She nodded. "It's not an uncommon mindset. It's honestly better you're dealing with it now. I've heard it can be really dangerous at higher ranks, where there's a much wider variance. Anyway, can you keep the legs busy while I handle the shoulders and torso? With all your damage, I should be able to finish it quick."

That wasn't even a question. I was still in Afterburner, and I felt like I could punch out an F-ranked bear. Without needing to say anything, I bolted at the Dullahan.

I activated Sucking Mud as I leapt, confident that between the walls and Cloud Step, I could maneuver pretty easily. I came in at the legs and used my second-tier rogue ability. Kidney Blow bypassed armor, and since this entire thing was armor, the blow, stacked with all my other skills, would basically be a hole punch. There was a shattering crash as I hit the knee, Kidney Blow increasing the size of the cracks created by my poison fire ability.

I had to dip back out fast to avoid the axe blow, but I succeeded in distracting the thing long enough for the Dullahan to start sinking. Luckily, marble counted as earth for Sucking Mud, and this big bastard was heavy. I continued to harass the thing for another minute or two, managing to batter the knees so bad, it was about to literally fall off its own calves. Callie had already finished up the fight by that point, and I was glad because I felt Afterburner ticking down.

Callie had made more spiked lengths of chain. She had been driving them into the cracks in the shoulders while the Dullahan was completely distracted by me cutting it off at the knees. I was wondering why she targeted the shoulders until I saw her merge all the chains at one end into a giant lasso and toss them across the room to wrap around the other Dullahan, the one that was on its last legs fighting Cark.

When it felt the restraints, the Dullahan roared in defiance (which was weird since it had no head or mouth) and hurled itself against the chains to escape. Given how fucked up the first Dullahan's shoulders and upper arms were, not to mention the sheer mass of the chain lasso, the second Dullahan's escape attempt managed to rip the arms and legs clear off the one we were fighting.

The limbless armor collapsed into the pool of Sucking Mud. I touched down outside of it and slumped against the wall, exhausted. That fight had been tiring as hell. Luckily, Cark didn't seem to be having any problems. One down, one to go. But I needed a breather.

Chapter Ten

CARK TOOK the other Dullahan apart. We literally just sat there and watched him slowly demolish it. The wights were downed fast enough, and the others came over to sit with us as we spectated. We offered to help, but Cark seemed pretty into it, so we mostly just enjoyed the show. Zeke hadn't been kidding about undead having a weakness to fire, and given his high Might, Cark was already the optimal choice to take one of these things down.

I was staggered by how different his fighting style was from mine. I had a bit of boxing knowledge from one of my minor skills, but mostly, my combat abilities came from tons of DS and massively overpowered stats. I knew absolutely jack shit about fighting, and it was never more apparent than when I watched Cark solo that Dullahan bare-handed.

When he finally finished prying the warped pieces of armor apart with his bare hands we all made our way over to congratulate him.

"Damn, man, you crushed that thing. If it was as strong as the other one, you are *way* more powerful than we are." I hadn't actually asked what Cark's stats were, but judging from that showing, I was guessing he really was *highly* specialized toward Might.

He just shrugged. "It was weird. I felt like the things were made of like… concentrated darkness somehow. My flames seemed to weaken them. But even so, yeah, I'm positive your Might is way lower than mine. Still, those things were no joke. Glad you took yours down." He clapped me on the shoulder. "Scared me a bit there after you took that hit. Glad to see you're alright."

The others arrived to congratulate him on the solo fight, and that was fine with me because I still needed to check in with my girlfriend. She'd been pretty freaked out there.

I jogged over to where she was standing off to the side, and she fixed a smile on her face. I just pulled her into a hug. I could see the adrenaline draining away as she stood there, and I wanted her to know I was there for her.

She clung to me for a minute before letting go with a rueful chuckle. "Sorry, I know it's over, but that was just… I've never worked with a team before, really, except people stronger than me. Ever since we started working together, we've been punching down. It's just kind of a shock to see you take a hit like that."

I shook my head. "No, I get it. Hell, it kind of knocked me for a loop too. I think I've been so focused on raw power, I haven't been doing enough actual training. When we spar, it's always with powers, and between stats and skills, I kind of just brute force it. Can you teach me how to actually fight? Like no skills or tricks, just real combat lessons?"

I could have traded her for the memories, but then she wouldn't have them. I didn't want to make her less able to defend herself.

With skills, losing progress didn't rank them down, so a small hit here or there was fine. Losing combat ability, though, would make her less able to fight, and while the skill portion would still synergize with other skills, that didn't fix my problem at all.

She nodded, seeming a bit pensive. "Yes, but my actual combat abilities aren't really that impressive. Like most Ascendants, I tend to lean on my power way too much. I have an idea, though. I wish for the most in-depth mastery of the most suitable martial art for the two of us to learn."

I blinked. That was… really vague. But to my surprise, I saw the usual prompt.

Wish Detected. Grant wish?

I confirmed, and was treated to the sight of:

Stat points sufficient. Requirements: 150 Might, 36 Impact, 104 Focus, 96 Creation, 75 Vitality. Skill name Lesser Balam Mastery. Compensation required.

I was just kind of speechless. That was… so fucking many points. That was more than five hundred points for a *lesser* skill. "Okay. That actually worked… kind of. It's insanely expensive, but have you ever heard of a martial art called Balam?"

Some part of me was expecting her to gasp, put a hand to her chest, and tell me about the forbidden martial art she'd heard whispers of in the underground when she'd been on the run.

Sadly, she just shrugged. "No, sounds weird, but if your power says it's the best style for us to learn, then I guess that works. I assume I still require payment?"

I nodded.

She blew out a breath. "Fine. I'm honestly shocked I was even able to wish for that considering you were involved. I guess since it was my idea, it works. In exchange for the skill, I'm willing to do everything in my power to keep you safe and dedicate my time to training you in both this martial art and any other combat style I know of until you surpass me in skill. Does that work?"

I felt the electricity build on my skin, signalling the beginning of a wish. I guessed that it did, which was a relief, because I wasn't sure the skill would have value if I gave it to her. Luckily, as Benny and I had established, training could work. I supposed the actual time expenditure counted as a payment if nothing else, or maybe her other combat skills made a difference. It clearly meant a lot to her that I was safe, so that probably played into things. I reached up and pulled my mask off, and she looked confusedly at me.

With a wince, I leaned down and whispered, "Wishes like this are incredibly painful and obvious. Most of the team doesn't know about my power. I figure if I kiss you to trigger it, my mouth might muffle some of the noise so the others don't notice."

She looked wary but didn't stop me as I leaned in and pressed my lips to hers. The static flowed into her through my mouth, and I felt the energy rampaging through my own body—literally the most powerful wish I'd ever granted. Callie bit off a strangled scream and bit into my tongue by accident, so I wasn't exactly quiet myself. Luckily, we were a bit of a distance away, so no one noticed us seizing up in agony.

I pulled away, wincing. I didn't know why I'd decided that would be a good idea instead of, like… covering her mouth or something. It was probably some attempt to be romantic, but it had been a terrible decision that I definitely wouldn't make again. I would need Jessie to heal the big hole in my tongue now. While tongue injuries tended to heal pretty fast, they were also absolutely awful to sit through, and I refused to go through that if I had a choice. I left Callie to get accustomed to her new skill while I slipped over to have Jessie heal me up. Thankfully, the process was fast and quiet, and it took relatively little energy on her part.

Then I made my way back over to Callie. I felt the geas on her slip into place, a self-imposed binding that locked her into her promise to train me for as long as necessary and to keep me safe. The latter was less of an issue since I believed she would have tried her best to do that even without the binding, but still, I could see how this would count as payment for that huge wish. She was basically my trainer and bodyguard for as long as it took for me to get better than her at combat, potentially years given that she was incredibly skilled in Balam now and would be learning more even as I did.

Luckily, my girlfriend seemed more upset than regretful. I assumed she wouldn't have made the offer if it was something she couldn't live with. I pulled her against me, letting her relax without needing to worry about standing up.

It took her a few minutes to speak. "Ow."

I winced; I'd seen how much that had hurt Benny. If anything, she'd gotten off easy because she was G-rank, but still, I couldn't imagine having all that information shoved into her head was comfortable. I just held her until she was feeling better.

Callie pulled away gently. "Okay, now I get why you decided to make sure they couldn't hear me."

I massaged the roof of my mouth with my tongue. Remembering the pain made me wince again. "Yeah, but I picked the dumbest possible way to do it. Still, glad you're feeling better. So, what exactly is Balam? Is it anything good? I've never heard of it, but then again, this is a pretty small planet. I imagine I haven't heard of most martial arts. Can't tell much about it from the name, though. How does it work?"

I was pretty excited about the fact that this skill came essentially out of nowhere. We'd just asked for something that would work best and gotten it. We'd overpaid a *lot* for a Lesser skill, probably for that reason, but still, this was fascinating.

She chuckled. "I actually have a bit of background info. It's a relatively prevalent style among the dark elves. Mixes well with stealth. Mostly striking and holds best used from surprise, though there's a dueling component aimed at dual blades—sword and dagger specifically. Still, it's definitely something we can get some serious use from. There are even actual Masters and Grandmasters of Balam among the dark elves, so the route to advancing it is established if we can get some instruction later."

That was a big deal. Skills in general were a pain in the ass to rank up. Knowing this combat style had a carefully laid out progression was extremely useful to us. We would need to actually go and *find* one of those Masters, but still, it meant one more skill we could definitely rank up. The whole thing was incredibly interesting. I couldn't wait to actually do some training with Callie and start learning it. After a few minutes for her head to clear completely, she stood up, stretching and right as rain.

The others had been talking to Cark the whole time. I was pretty sure at least one of them had noticed us and figured they would leave us alone for some private time. That was... slightly embarrassing given how everything had just gone down, but better than anyone new figuring out about my ability. Callie was blushing slightly, having obviously picked up on the same thing. When we rejoined everyone else, we all just kind of acted like nothing had happened, and I was grateful for it.

We kept walking along the marble corridor the same way we had before. Callie and I searched for traps and enemies. We hit another few patches of wights but nothing like the Dullahans again. H-rank monsters were easy enough to clear out without any G-rankers to hold our heavy hitters back. That went on for about two more hours before we finally emerged from the corridor. We stepped out into a massive underground chamber the size of the WCP back in Velan, and all of us stopped at the entrance to look around for any undead who might be waiting.

We didn't see anything nearby, but off in the distance were the unmistakable forms of lumbering undead. They moved in huge packs along the floor of the cavern, with tombstones and much smaller crypts scattered among them. In the middle of all of it, a black stone fortress towered above the entire area, barely illuminated by the ghostly flickers of blue coming from some of the flowers among the fields.

I stared for a second before whispering. "Who wants to bet the Lich is in that fortress?"

Oddly, no one took me up on the offer.

Chapter Eleven

THE CHAMBER WASN'T the biggest underground space I'd seen. The WCP in Rajak was bigger, but something about this one just made me feel... small. Not its size so much as the untamed wildness of it gave the impression that this was a place beyond the world of men. It was just so other. All my encounters with Ascendant stuff had been in the context of cities, heroes, and things I was familiar with. Sure, I'd seen some odd things, but they had all been part of that same structure I'd grown up with.

This, though... this was new. It was like something out of a storybook, and it just drove home the fact that it was a big weird universe, and I had plenty left to see in it. I wanted to explore with my friends and get stronger, and that meant coming into contact with a lot more crazy stuff, so I needed to adjust sooner rather than later.

In the spirit of that, I turned to Sarah, our resident expert on all things that were formerly alive. "Okay, I take it you can see some of those things down there? Any idea what they are?"

She worried at her lip as she stared down into the cavern. "Several, but I have to give you a bit of context. To understand what we're dealing with, you need to know a few things about how the undead are categorized. To sum it up, there are three basic categories of non-sapient undead: bone, flesh, and spirit. We've come across bone and flesh so far, but I see at least a few spiritual undead down there. Luckily, they're all H-rank, from what I can see, but we might run into some higher-level ghosts later on, so you need to know how to deal with them."

A quick finger point down and off to one side brought our attention to a glowing blue figure in a cloak. "That, for instance, is a phantom traveler," the priestess continued. "Their main form of offense is stealth, and they're known for falling upon the unwary and smothering them with their cloaks. My Holy Hand skill can deal with them fairly easily." She motioned to a different spot. "That, on the other hand, is a Banesidhe. Their bodies are made of ectoplasm so dense, it might as well be physical. Fire is a better counter to them than holy energy, because it can take a while to erode them with light-based skills."

This was much more complex than I'd expected, but Sarah was on a roll and just moved on to the next shape in the darkness. "That one is a jumping corpse, a type of high-level zombie. They aren't particularly dangerous alone, but they tend to travel in packs. If you see one, there's probably another dozen nearby. They're almost always followed by a type of ghostly fish called a silvermist minnow. They swim through the living and tap their strength by draining their Vitality temporarily. I can help with those, as well, but there's usually a massive number of them, so Mr. Cark may need to help."

She continued on in the same vein for a while, explaining the various undead and their functions before finally coming to a rest, staring at the keep. "Now, the Lich is going to be up there—that much is clear. They prefer height and range for their magic, and they tend to gravitate to forti-fied strongholds because they lack defense. Most likely, there will be a regi-ment of Death Knights in there too. That's going to be a problem, but it's the best-case scenario, because if there isn't, the Lich will most likely be attending a spectral court."

That didn't sound particularly pleasant, and I had to cut in. "Wait, Death Knights are G-rank—a regiment of them would be all but impassable. Why is a spectral court worse than that? Wouldn't the ghosts be easier to deal with? You said light and fire work on them pretty well, right?" In all honesty, I didn't relish the idea of fighting a regiment of Death Knights. I'd had a bitch of a time taking down the two Benny and I had fought.

She shook her head seriously. "Not in this case. Spectral courts are usually attended by an undead noble. At this rank, it'll be either an Ectoplasmic Earl or a Grave Lord. Most likely the latter, given the presence of Dullahans. Grave Lords are powerful support-type undead that empower others of their kind in the vicinity. The issue there is that it would be not only another sapient undead, but another source of power for the Lich. The Grave Lord would strengthen the magic user even more."

I winced. "And the Lich summons the other undead, which are also strengthened by the Grave Lord. The synergy there is not fantastic. So… what do we do? I sincerely doubt you would have bothered explaining all this if we had to turn around." As neat as the information was, I assumed Sarah had at least an idea of how to bypass the monsters down there. I admit, I hoped it would be something good, because I didn't really feel like fighting a ghost army.

She smiled brightly, her blue eyes shining with a sense of excitement and enthusiasm that told me she liked being involved in the higher-level planning. "I do. See, Grave Lords are powerful, but their main weakness is that they can't interact with the living directly. They're proxy fighters, and they're so specialized that they can't even *see* excessive sources of life force. Our normal Vitality isn't enough for that to be a factor, sadly—a Grave Lord will be able to sense us—but we just so happen to have someone with us who can supercharge the life force of a being, thus rendering them invisible to the Grave Lord, and possibly some of the sentries they've enhanced." She shot Jessie a wide grin, clearly thrilled with her own plan.

I had to admit, as plans went, it sounded pretty good. I wasn't entirely sure how well it would work, but she was the expert. Being able to sneak past the defenses and rob the castle sounded awesome, but there was a small hole in that idea. "Okay, but will that be enough to get us past the *rest* of the undead? Because if we could have been invisible to them this whole time and weren't, I'm honestly going to be pretty pissed." My ribs creaked with phantom pain and my arms ached with remembered agony. I would've preferred to skip that.

She just waved me off. "No, the whole life force thing is only really relevant against Grave Lords. Their connection to death means they're much less solidly anchored to this world than even other spirit-type undead. Regardless, it won't do much against anything else down there, so we're going to have a long way to go to put the plan into action." She looked embarrassed. "Plus, if I'm wrong and it *is* Death Knights we might have a bit of trouble. Still, this concentration of spirits makes that unlikely. I'm almost positive it's a Grave Lord."

Her confidence kind of tanked at the end there, but I was impressed she'd managed to get up her courage to make a suggestion like that. Callie had stated multiple times she was open to people's ideas, and Sarah, aside from her regular updates about the undead when asked, tended to be extremely quiet and shy. The little Cleric clearly felt more at home with her own team than the rest of us, but she was actively making an effort, and that was more than most people could say.

Callie clearly thought so too, because my girlfriend gave her an encouraging smile. "I think it's a great plan. We need to do some recon to double-check the enemy ahead to make sure it's viable, but if it really is a spectral court, I'm all for it." She fished in the pocket of her coat and pulled out a small white shape, which she held out to Jessie. "Luckily, I considered the possibility of needing to do recon here, so I decided to try something. It seems like it worked, at least if you can still hatch this outside the base?"

I blinked. I hadn't even considered grabbing one of the raven eggs, and neither had anyone else apparently.

Jessie looked pretty much poleaxed, then she got really excited. "I bet I can! I'd have to try, but I bet the raven egg works just as well out here. Give me a few minutes to sort this out, and I'll get us a bird's-eye view!" Without any further conversation, she closed her eyes and started pouring green energy into the egg.

We waited for her to finish, but a minute turned into ten, and she showed no signs of being done. Apparently, without the building to help boost efficiency, hatching the eggs was *much* more energy intensive, so we all settled in to wait.

I saw Callie talking to Sarah, obviously trying to bolster the Cleric's confidence, and I made my way over to talk to Benny. "Hey, man, you psyched about this? We're going to be breaking into an evil ghost castle. How cool is that?"

He snickered a little. "It does sound like something out of a bad movie. Easily the coolest thing we've done since we left home. Of course, I'm obviously going to kill way more undead than you on the way there, so I guess you can do the break-in if you want. Assuming Nightstrike doesn't do it, since she's so much sneakier than you."

I cursed. He was right—she was definitely going to be the one to sneak in and raid the treasury or whatever.

Still, the first half of that little boast had been nonsense. "She's the best person for the job, so she should definitely do it. That aside, you have a better chance of spontaneously growing wings than killing more undead than me. Unless you were expecting me to fight them barehanded, and even then, I would still probably outscore you by a bit." I made sure to use just the right amount of smugness, which got an eye roll and a middle finger from my friend.

It was all nonsense, of course. Neither of us cared who beat up more zombies or skeletons, but the familiar routine of shit-talking helped calm our nerves. I was excited to go out there and wreak havoc, but a part of me was worried about my friends too, just like every time we went out to fight. In a weird way, knowing that Benny felt confident enough to trash-talk me about this helped me calm down.

We lapsed into silence, looking out over the cavern. Despite the palpable anticipation in the air around us, it was still chilling to see all the shadowy forms moving in the dim light. Some huge and lumbering, some small and fast, and some barely even visible. We stared out into the dark, psyching ourselves up about the adventure to come, until we finally heard a cheer from behind us.

I turned to find Jessie cradling a small bird that was still growing even before my eyes as she pumped energy into it. Seemed like our scout was up and running. We joined the group as Jessie finished pumping in enough life force and then sent the bird soaring off toward the castle. It took a few hours to cross the cavern while having to constantly avoid enemies, but Jessie kept us updated on its progress and gave us details about the terrain until finally we got the go-ahead from our healer. With the presence of the spectral court confirmed, our mission was a go. Time to head for the castle.

Chapter Twelve

ALTHOUGH THE CAVERN wasn't bigger than I'd expected, it was a *much* longer trip than I'd thought, because we had to work our way slowly down from the entrance. We might have been able to jump (some of us anyway) but the undead would have noticed and swarmed us. So we ended up having to take a series of winding tunnels to get to the base of the wall we'd been standing on. Luckily, I had access to Seek Hidden, so we didn't have to wander around down there for hours.

Since we'd learned our lesson about me not being a frontline fighter after the Dullahan fight, Callie and I did *not* go first. We let Cark lead the way so he could tank any big hits from stuff that noticed us early. He wasn't actually any tougher than we were, but he could cloak himself in roiling flames, which tended to be a good deterrent for undead. Still, we did our best to avoid fights. Because we were so careful, we noticed the first patrol well before we ran across them and had plenty of time to prepare.

We ran into the first bunch of enemies in a large subchamber, but there were no G-rankers among them. Despite that, there was about a hundred of the damn things. We made our way into the chamber slowly, grouping up to make sure we were all in the best positions to take advantage of the fights. Each of the H-rankers was paired up with a G-ranker just in case. Not to interfere but just to keep an eye on them. Benny was with Celine, Cark was with Martin, and Jessie was with Sarah.

Callie and I were free to go into stealth and sneak around the edges of the cavern to attack from the opposite side in an effort to draw attention. Then we both waded in from opposite edges. The entire place was wall-to-wall skeletons, and when I slipped out from cover, they immediately spotted me and rushed my way. I didn't use my weapons or my DS Mastery this time. I reached into my bag of tricks and pulled out my Minor Boxing Mastery. I had the Balam style to learn from Callie when we had some free time, but until then, I figured this was a solid place to practice my combat skills without much danger.

I pulled up my guard as they all came in at me and tried my best to focus on what was in front of me. I threw a punch, and the skeleton I hit basically exploded. I jerked the fist back in to guard myself and rethought my strategy. I felt the pretty much pointless attacks from all the skeletons landing on my armor. My damage absorb combined with my Impact made it pretty much impossible for them to hurt me. This wasn't training. A single punch would kill any of these, and while I could train one punch at a time, it wouldn't do much good.

I considered my options and decided to make use of my stats to do some actual training. My Boxing Skill wasn't the be all end all, but it came with the basics. The person I'd traded it from had decent fundamentals, so I knew the most important part of boxing was footwork. I closed my eyes and took a deep breath, and when I opened them, I changed my perspective. My enemies weren't one skeleton and then another. This entire army was a single foe. One enemy swinging at me a thousand times a second.

I waited for a single swing to come in, and I ducked out of the way. Then another. I shuffled my feet, drifting between blows. I didn't dodge them all. There wasn't enough space. For every ten swings, one or so connected. I started to get into it, learning the rhythm until I could finally create an opening to actually move safely. I knew when they would attack, and by throwing punches and breaking a specific skeleton, I could open up a space to move into where there would be no attack. Once I got the hang of that, my goal became making sure I didn't get touched at all.

I weaved around the blows, opening up safe spots with my fists. While my stats were much higher than the skeletons', they were much more numerous, and even with my Might and Vitality, dodging a whole army was tough. Despite that, I loved it. I felt like I was a machine, constantly moving, constantly shifting. My blows became more precise. I learned to use my weight better, leverage my power and reach, and I started taking out two or three of them in a single hit.

With my stats as they were, I was more than able to understand positioning and leverage for a normal mortal martial art, and the massive amount of trial and error was a godsend for my skill. I didn't master it instantly or anything, but I could feel myself getting better at it, and it was fun. My footwork became more and more fluid, my weaving more seamless, and between my Perception and my improving skills, I moved among the enemy like a ghost, laying two or three of them out with every blow.

I could have gone faster and done more, but this wasn't an exercise in skeleton smashing—it was training. I only broke what I needed to give me room to move in. I didn't want the action to end too soon. I threw a punch every minute or two, the majority of my time and effort going into foot-work and dodges. I slowly improved my Boxing Skill, basically brute forcing my progress with stats that were way too high for my Minor Skill's complexity. Once I hit Lesser, this would become a whole new beast since I was creating my style from scratch, but for now, I enjoyed the progress.

On the upside, I was pulling plenty of attention from the skeletal army. The waves of enemies crashed over me like surf breaking against rocks as they recognized a clear threat. I didn't know how long I was there, moving between blows and smashing bone constructs. The longer the fight dragged on, the more I started to see the patterns. Timing and force became easier to gauge as I saw the same basic form from a hundred different enemies. I started working my understanding of the skeletal attackers into my form and just lost myself in the press of battle.

Finally, I threw a punch, and there was nothing on the other side. I looked around, shocked to see all the skeletons had been dealt with. Not just by me mind you, everyone had done their part taking apart the army, but my sparring partners were gone, nonetheless. I felt energized. My heart was pounding, and while I wasn't tired, I was definitely breathing heavier after the exertion.

I turned to check on my friends. "Everyone okay? That was pretty crazy, right? Honestly, I've never been in a fight that nuts." I knew my grin was obvious from my voice despite my face being covered.

I got an eye roll from Benny and a fond smile from Callie as everyone sounded off that they were okay.

"Man, I really hope there's some kind of recording of that I can study. They stream this, right?" I'd actually been wondering about that during the Heartripper siege.

Celine shook her head. "No. While the scavenger hunt is televised, they mostly focus on the parts that will gather the most interest. The first few days, there's no way to tell how well someone will do or who is impressive. Once the teams start getting further into their lists, they can see who is the most impressive and focus on them. Besides, they air it all at the end of the hunt so they can cut out the useless parts. The preliminary recordings should be starting within a day or two, however."

That made sense actually. I imagined it took power to send out recording devices. Waiting until people had a chance to settle in was reasonable. Most teams would probably still be building their bases. That also explained why Aiden had rushed his assault. He'd clearly been trying to avoid the notice of local leadership. It was a smart call, given how out of his depth he would be against an E- or even F-ranker, not that it had mattered.

Still, it was a shame I couldn't see my training directly. I would've loved to study how I was moving to try to improve. I thanked Celine and headed over to Callie.

She seemed excited by my fight. "That looked like a blast. I could tell you were really improving. Maybe next time we can make sure there are no G-rankers and then take them on together, use it as a chance for me to teach you some of the Balam Mastery skill. Still, that was an amazing amount of progress. What skill was it? Boxing?"

I wasn't surprised she'd noticed that—boxing was a pretty distinctive style of fighting. "Yeah, I picked it up ages ago but haven't put much time into it. It's still at Minor even after all that, but I bet a few more fights at that level would let me rank it up. Even if I don't usually do fist fighting, the footwork is going to help in my normal combat, and hey, I punch some-times, so getting some practice in won't hurt. I hadn't considered tag teaming a mob of weaker enemies for training, though. You think we can find another army like this?"

She giggled. "Obviously, this is a necropolis. I bet there's at least ten of those hordes down here, mixed in with a hundred different parties of other monsters for us to get through. Necropoli are infamous for being more quantity than quality, which is part of the reason we were even able to bring the H-rankers. We'll hit another grouping like this soon enough, and we can get started on those lessons. I used some of that Skill training during the fight, and it was… amazing. I can't wait to show you."

Having a girlfriend who was as into combat and cultivation as I was definitely made this more fun, and once again, I felt the adrenaline and excitement shove aside my worry and regret. In the moment, it was much easier not to focus on all the bad stuff, especially when I was with Callie. I pulled up my mask and stepped forward to pull her into a kiss, one she happily responded to, but unfortunately we were cut off almost immediately by someone clearing their throat.

I pulled away, and we both turned as I replaced my mask to glare at Benny, who ignored the unhappy looks. "As cute as you two are together (and by cute, I mean sickening), we're in the middle of a giant chamber full of crushed-up skeletons, so now might not really be the time. We need to search this room for anything valuable. Some of them were carrying gear and pouches."

I huffed, but he wasn't wrong. Callie nodded grudgingly, showing that she agreed even if she wasn't happy about it. I squeezed her hand once, and her soft smile promised we would spend more time together later. Then we got to work. We had loot to find.

Chapter Thirteen

THE TUNNELS WERE PRETTY CRAMPED with the exception of the occasional big side cavern, and we'd expected to trip over undead every ten steps. We ran into a few groups of wights on the way down the tunnel, but it was less of a problem than I'd expected. The wights were few enough that they wouldn't have made decent targets for training, so we let the H-rankers handle them.

We were forced to go slowly because of Seek Hidden and trying to keep an ear out for ambushes.

Aside from the wights, we ran into a single pair of Dullahans patrolling alongside a few ghosts. Turned out poison fire worked as well on ghosts as normal flames, and I was able to help wipe them out easily enough while Cark, Callie, and Benny worked together to take down the big guys. I jumped in to help Benny and Callie with the Dullahans after I finished clearing out the ghosts. Callie had been giving them a ton of thought since our first fight, and she had a detailed plan of attack to use on the armored brutes.

Finally, we made it to a cavern like the one we'd been in before, packed wall-to-wall with zombies. It was my first time seeing normal zombies, and the H-rank animated corpses were surprisingly spry for the walking dead. We waited outside, staring in at the rabid corpses, who seemed to be switching consistently from standing eerily still to lunging at each other like animals. Sarah, of course, was well aware of what the deal was. It was nice to know we had an expert on hand for all this nonsense.

She actually seemed fascinated. "H-rank flesh-based undead, revenants. Zombies are the I-ranked version, though most people use it as a descriptor for the whole category, since it covers quite a few varieties. Revenants are vicious, hair-trigger attackers who are often used for guards. They're extremely Might heavy, though only for H-rankers, so the two of you should be fine. Are you absolutely sure you want to go in there just the two of you? I know they aren't a threat, but this is going to take quite a while. There's easily two hundred of them."

It was a valid concern. Given the location, there was a non-zero chance we might get jumped from behind by a higher-level enemy. Still, we couldn't pass up this chance. Callie had seen an opportunity, so her geas was pushing her into this. I also wanted to learn that Balam fighting style because I was pretty sure it would apply well to my DS skills and would really push my combat abilities to a higher level. We nodded solemnly, and Sarah, knowing Callie was the boss and it was ultimately her call, didn't say another word.

Instead of stealthing around, we left the others in the hall and walked in through one door, making sure it was obvious where we were coming from.

Callie gave me a confident smile. "All right, to start out, I'm going to demonstrate a few forms for you. Just watch how I move."

Her confidence was intoxicating, and my eyes were glued to her as she stepped forward to engage the revenants alone, easily the most captivating thing in the room, angry horde of rabid zombies included.

We didn't have time to continue the conversation because we'd come in range of the revenants, and those bastards did *not* waste time. The instant they sensed us (low Perception to offset the high Might presumably) they swarmed us both, and I took a step back just to make sure I was out of range of her fight. It was pretty overwhelming to watch the tide of rabid corpses fall on her like that, and I had to remind myself they couldn't hurt her... for about five seconds. Then she started moving, and I didn't need any other reminder.

The forms of Balam were intricate and circular, lots of rotation and momentum. The almost-dancelike quality made the style seem like it was made for this situation. I knew some of that was stats and the experience she'd gotten from the Skill, but some of it was just the constant movement and extremely precise steps. Callie spun through the forms, and rather than use them in a sequence, she demonstrated them as they were meant to be used, showing me exactly which situation each form was made for.

She made a few moves between her spinning, pushing the revenants into position to set up the next attack. Those linking moves were obviously part of the style, and as I watched, I started to understand how it worked. Much like in boxing, the key to Balam was footwork. Placement of the feet decided how far, how fast, and even which direction she could spin, and she had to read the steps of the revenants themselves to decide where best to place her own feet even before their next attack.

It really was like a dance, except Callie didn't get to know the steps ahead of time. She had to read the room and understand the directions and movements of the enemies. That was where the forms came in. Certain stances or patterns evoked certain responses, the original creators of the style having identified certain keystones of movements and created reactions to those. The rotations and footwork were precise, but Callie was able to work her own movements and attacks into the patterns, creating her own flavor of style even as she used the move set she was trying to teach me to mimic.

She was using the sword and dagger forms, and seeing them in action was amazing. Blades whirled through the air as she spun, taking heads and limbs. No matter how many of them attacked her, she managed to spin between the rampaging corpses without letting them touch a hair on her head. She spoke as she moved, talking steadily and describing the basic principles of her movements and how they chained together into an effective fighting style.

After a few minutes of demonstrating, she flicked her fingers. A wall of shadow rose up, cutting them all off from her as she stepped back to look over at me. "All right, those are the basics. You won't get the skill until you actually try the style out and make it work. You ready to give it a shot?"

I could hear the revenants clawing at the shadow wall, but they weren't making any progress, so there was no rush. Callie looked excited to see me try though, so I stepped up to fight.

Before she dropped the wall, I decided to get ready for the fight by setting up my weapons. I didn't have a sword and dagger, and I didn't want to use my tonfas because I was already overpowered for this fight. So I knelt down and used stone limb on each of my arms. I straightened my hands out like they were blades and then decided to stack Consecration of Flame on my hands just to be safe. The earth on my limbs lit up like magma, and I nodded to Callie that she could drop the wall.

Just like she'd told me at the beginning of her demonstration, I took the first stance. Like I'd noticed early on, footwork was important in Balam. By placing my feet at a certain angle and then using the rotation of my ankles to align myself with them, I could build up twisting momentum and lend that force to my blows. I lashed out with a pair of magma-infused chops at two revenants coming in to attack. With my Might and the fire-imbued coating on my arms, my arms tore right through them.

I cut down both of the zombies... then tripped. Callie muffled a slight giggle as I clawed my way back to my feet, very deliberately not looking at her after the embarrassing move. I wasn't hurt—with so little Impact, they couldn't have actually damaged me. I just focused on my training. The movements for Balam felt odd and stilted. I wasn't used to standing in the weird positions required to start the rotations, and with literally no room to move, it was easy to trip over one of the revenants. Still, I got back in position and tried again.

Getting the first form took me two tries. The second took about six. As I moved through the forms, it got harder and harder to perform the unusual actions necessary, but at the same time, I got more comfortable with the strange way of moving and standing. So while each stance took longer, it also made the next one easier. Despite my stats, Balam was a complicated and off-putting series of movements, but I *was* learning.

Over the next twenty minutes, I learned all thirteen primary forms of Balam one after another, and by the time I was finished with them, I knew for a fact I'd gotten Minor Balam Mastery. Granted, Minor was the lowest level possible, and I wasn't really very far into even that. Still, I'd picked it up. Callie spent quite a bit of that training time correcting my form, giving me notes on my movements, and generally helping me adjust until everything was good enough to count toward the skill.

Once that was done, I took my time with all the easy enemies, repeating the forms over and over until we had cleared every single zombie from the cavern.

Callie threw herself on me happily, easily avoiding my magma-clad arms as she tackled me from behind. "Baby, that was so great! You picked it up so quickly! Most people don't learn the skill so fast on their first try."

I personally thought she was being too nice, given that I was also way higher ranked than most people learning it, but I was happy she was trying to be supportive, so I just took the compliment.

I groaned and slumped to the floor in an empty spot. "Okay, ow. My muscles are not used to moving like that at all. You'd figure my Might stat would make that a non-issue, but I'm crazy sore." I was guessing since my muscles were exerting tension on each other, it was a workout regardless of weight or strength, sort of like some of the stretching exercises I'd seen people doing at the park when Benny and I were growing up. "Can you have Jessie come over and fix this up for me?"

Callie smiled sweetly and pressed a quick kiss to my mask. "Nope. You'll have to suck it up. With your Vitality, the soreness should be gone in a few hours. It's best to recover naturally—the pain helps you learn the right way to position yourself and helps you figure out what motions to avoid in the future. Sorry about that." She didn't sound sorry. She sounded kind of smug, but I didn't hold it against her. Knowing how easily stats came to me, she probably enjoyed seeing me have to work for something.

So I just grunted and held out a hand, letting her pull me to my feet. "Fine. Well, at least I got the basics down. I can continue on from there." Still, I did have one other idea. "I could use a bit more Vitality, though. I still have two more wishes available for today. You want a Might top-up in exchange for those points?"

At the very least, that would help me heal faster. Despite her intention to see me work for it, my girlfriend wasn't turning down easy Might, and I grinned triumphantly as she agreed to make the wishes. Once that was done, I put an arm over her shoulder, and we headed back to our friends. All in all, not a bad first training session.

Chapter Fourteen

AFTER GETTING the wishes out of the way (Callie paid four Vitality for four Might, putting her literally one point short of a hundred), we all took a break in that huge room to once again search for any loot. As everyone looked around, I took a short break and checked my stats for the first time in a while.

Wishmaster Candidate Status: G-rank.

Ability: Beginner Wish—Five times a day, grant a Beginner wish in return for proper compensation. Wish must be feasibly achievable by the candidate's own efforts within a three-day period with current statistics.

Might: 58
Impact: 12
Fantasy: 21
Vitality: 29
Focus: 38
Perception: 40
Creation: 32

Skills: Beginner Doom Sovereign Mastery, Lesser

Enchanting Mastery, Lesser Cooking Mastery, Lesser Inventing Mastery, Minor Piano Mastery, Minor Gymnastics Mastery, Minor Swimming Mastery, Minor Guitar Mastery, Minor Singing Mastery, Minor Poker Mastery, Minor Archery Mastery, Minor Boxing Mastery, Minor Balam Mastery

I'd made some serious progress since we'd arrived out here, but it drove home more than anything how much longer I would be spending at each successive rank. The trek to F-rank was a slow grind, and I wasn't even halfway there. Of course, I expected a nice bump when this hunt ended and all the footage got uploaded, but it would still be a while before I got there. It made it even more imperative that I spend as much time as possible on combat training, because those skills would be what kept me safe against other opponents at my own rank.

Callie was having a field day sorting through the revenant corpses, looking for possibly valuable stuff. Looting was one of her favorite parts of fighting monsters, as morbid as it sometimes was, and I had to admit it was cute how excited she got when she picked up a cursed dagger or something. We didn't find many pieces of gear there or in the skeleton chamber, but did find a few—a knife, a cup, a ring, two rubies the size of golf balls that may or may not have been Ascendant materials, and weirdly, a top hat.

We had zero idea what any of the stuff did, but we packed it all up to be identified later. I was hopeful Zeke had an Identification skill we could pay him to use to help us figure out what everything was. At the moment, my girlfriend was ecstatic about digging up an extremely creepy-looking doll, and I couldn't help but wonder how the hell something like that had ended up down here.

Unfortunately, along with her glee came a lack of caution. I had to walk over and physically take the doll away from her because I was worried she might activate some kind of awful curse. "We talked about this. You need to let Sarah use her Holy Hand skill to move any treasure we find down here. She said there's a good chance some of the stuff might be infused with dark energy."

I dropped the doll on the ground. Neither of us touched it.

Callie just huffed. "Fine. I still say it's okay, but since I was outvoted, Sarah can stow it in the pack with the other stuff. Still, the thing is obviously only H-rank. No way some stupid curse on it will be able to do anything to me."

Knowing what my poison could theoretically do if stacked enough, I wasn't willing to risk it. The whole curse thing could get nasty, and everyone else had agreed with me about it.

"Anyway, this chamber was a pretty good haul," Callie continued. "We found a few objects, and even a box of gold coins. Not that the coins are really useful to us since they're just mortal money, but the box is bigger on the inside, which is amazing!"

I blinked. "Holy shit, really? They had a legit spatial artifact down here, and they were using it to hold gold of all things? Seems like kind of a waste, but hey, big win for us. How big is it?"

Spatial gear was rare and tough to come by at our level. It usually ended up being used in buildings or vehicles. A box like that could be carried in a backpack and would be crazy valuable for storage.

She just shrugged. "I don't know, probably about a hundred square feet. Hard to tell without someone to appraise it. We dumped the coins out to get an estimate and then put them back in. Celine says you can sell gold coins for chits to certain types of fae, though the exchange rate sucks apparently."

I imagined it was probably like I-rank chits too, but that was still better than nothing. I'd been convinced we would have to leave the gold strewn across the floor of our rooms or something as a decoration. Mortal stuff just wasn't really a viable trade good.

Callie sighed happily and slumped against me, surprising a laugh from me as I caught her. She nuzzled against my chest. "I *love* finding treasure. This is so much more fun than shady back-alley crime-fighting. We should totally do more stuff like this." Given the pressure she'd been under, it was really nice to see her so happy.

I gave her a squeeze before stepping back to help everyone continue looking.

I used Seek Hidden to confirm there was nothing left to find. Despite not being able to scan for "treasure," I did use the ability on revenant corpses and sifted through for anything *not* glowing red. Ready to move on, we packed up. When we got to the exit, we verified that the cavern was the last of the tunnels before we reached the main cave area we'd been looking down on when we arrived.

Everyone retreated to talk over our next move before we committed to the next leg of the journey.

It wasn't a long talk, though. We already had a plan—we mostly just wanted a second to breathe and get on the same page. After that, we headed out into the main cavern to see what was going on. Once again, the second I stepped inside, I noticed the thick black grass carpeting the stone, interspersed with glowing blue flowers. In the distance, small banks of fog drifted in strange patterns, with dark shapes moving among them.

Callie lowered her voice to talk to us all. "Okay, we need to be careful about noise down here. This is all one big chamber, so if we're too loud taking out the next group, we might pull too many of them."

We all nodded solemnly.

I lowered my voice to an identical murmur. "What if we don't fight them in groups? If we pull one or two at a time it would be way slower, but ultimately safer for all of us. Sucking Mud would be perfect for this actually, given how slow they move. I could snag one of them, and since they're all mindless killing machines and there wouldn't be a target for them to focus on, they wouldn't group up and attack."

There was no way to tell if that would actually work, but it seemed reasonable, and Callie thought so too, so we decided to give it a shot. We all headed into the fog, moving incredibly slowly and trying to avoid any attention.

We'd considered letting just Callie and I go ahead since we had stealth, but there was a better shot at a quick noiseless kill if everyone was there. So we moved as a group and tried our best to not to make a sound. The black grass was surprisingly good at muffling noise, and we did a decent job of moving unnoticed until we finally closed in on one of the shapes.

When we finally got within range, a small pack of wights was stalking through the fog ahead of us. We stopped behind a small hill that I was pretty sure was just a big rock covered with black grass. I had no clue what the stuff was or how it was growing, but it seemed to be everywhere. Regardless, once we got close enough, I focused on a ten-foot radius around the edge of the pack and triggered Sucking Mud.

The ground started to give way, dragging at the wight that was closest before it could get free. It started to struggle a bit, but the others didn't pay any attention to it, and by the time they were out of range, the skill had worn off and the ground solidified, trapping the wight temporarily underground. I knew it would tear free pretty easily if given a second, but Benny zipped forward and grabbed it with his tranq hand. He held on, and the thing slowly stopped struggling and fell still. Cark stepped up and grabbed it around the head, tearing it off easily without making a sound.

The wight obviously had no treasure on it, but it was good proof of concept. Making sure the others were out of range, we all circled up.

"Okay, that worked, but it seems a little greedy to expect it to keep happening that smoothly." Callie was pleased with the results, but obviously saw the flaw in that plan.

I had to admit it had an element of luck to it that repetition could really screw with.

"Sarah, what's the range on that Holy Hand skill? Like, if we wanted you to grab a straggler and drag it back here, could you do it?"

The blonde cleric nodded thoughtfully. "Probably yeah, if I had to. It might alert the others though. The holy energy would start eroding the undead flesh and it would definitely scream. I'm not sure I could pull the thing back in time." Despite her frown, she held up a hand, and with some concentration, a second hand made of glowing white-gold light manifested above it as she flexed her main skill. I had to admit the thing looked pretty cool. I wondered what it would look like when it burned an undead.

Callie was the one frowning at that, but her face lit up as she got an idea. "Well, what if you grabbed it by the throat? It wouldn't be able to scream, and you could just haul it off into the fog. Assuming you have that kind of range or mobility. I don't know how the hand works."

I was curious to see the thing in action too, but I figured if it was strong enough to use directly in melee, she would have mentioned it. An ambush might be possible, but I was betting that depended heavily on her Might stat. The wights were H-rank, so it was possible.

They got down to talking specifics, whispering furtively as they planned out our next attack, and I gave them space, looking out into the fog and keeping watch. I wanted to make sure we didn't get ambushed just in case another patrol came through. Staring out into the murk, I could just barely make out the shape of the dark fortress in the distance, and I was more than ready for our big infiltration mission. I wondered what we would be doing while Callie broke in to raid the place. All I could do was hope it took more than a day to get there—a few wishes would make sure my girl-friend was as safe as possible.

Chapter Fifteen

THE NEXT SIX or seven hours were an exercise in constant grinding. We spent half the time sneaking around, and we were so thorough about it that Benny actually got the stealth Skill just from the effort. Sarah dragged some of them away, killing more than a few in the process. Some we got with Sucking Mud, and a few we literally just crushed as a group because there were no other mobs near enough to hear and we couldn't whittle them down further.

It took ages to get through them all, but finally, after hours of fighting, we made it to the base of the fortress.

I stared up at the sheer black walls, shooting up from the ground like some sort of monument to human suffering, and I felt the need to point out a pretty obvious fact. "So… anyone else notice there isn't a door?"

The massive building was imposing and wicked as hell, sure, but I saw zero ways to actually enter it, which more than anything just struck me as a design flaw. The creator could make all the cracks about "no escape" they wanted, but not actually being able to enter or leave a place was just… dumb. It made me think less of the Lich who'd designed it.

Sarah didn't seem surprised, though. "It was built for a Grave Lord. They don't need doors. The Lich probably has some kind of winged undead to carry him up there, and leaving out an entrance lowers the chance of having to deal with intruders. Not the most conventional of choices, but it kind of fits with the spirits-only mentality the Grave Lord would be trying to foster. The spectral court wouldn't want a bunch of mindless zombies and skeletons lumbering around their castle."

Which made sense, even if it was annoying. It was also kind of scary because it meant we wouldn't be able to reach Callie if something went wrong. Not that I even knew how she would get up there. I turned to my girlfriend. "Are you sure you want to do this whole infiltration thing? I could use my Mistwalking ability instead of relying on stealth. My Leaf on the Wind skill would make getting down from there much easier too. You should really send me. Just give me a list of what I'm looking for. I can use Seek Hidden to track it down."

She looked like she was going to dismiss that and insist on going, until she heard my actual reasoning. Then she scowled. "That's... shit. That's actually a really good point. I figured you were just being all sweet and protective and annoying, but your Seek Hidden skill would really cut down on the time needed to search the place. Your stealth isn't as good as mine, but Leaf on the Wind might be needed to get out of there." She worried her lip. "Damn. I need to go because I can use my shadows to get us up there, but... you can come with me."

I had to fight the urge to pump my fist. I'd really wanted to go in any case, but even if I hadn't, I would have been terrified for her. Stuck in an enemy fortress with zero backup would be a bad position to be in. At least if we were together, we could rely on each other. We were a good team. Plus, I didn't want to sit around bored and terrified for the next few hours while my girlfriend took on an evil ghost castle. That sounded like literally the least amusing use of my time that I could possibly imagine.

Of course, Benny would still have to deal with that, but I didn't care if he sat around annoyed and worried for a few hours as long as I was there to do something. I worried more about Jessie, but she had the rest of our team down here to help keep her out of her own head. Still, we hadn't taken as long getting here as I'd hoped so I wasn't up for a new round of wishes. Hopefully it reset soon and we could use them inside. I turned to Callie. "All right, sounds like a plan. Do you want to rest up a bit or should we head up there now?"

She looked up the sheer stone face of the massive castle. "I think give it a minute. I have to figure out the best way to get us up there without being seen. In the meantime, are you sure you want to come with me? We have no clue what's up there waiting for us. It could be some horrible hoard of monsters or more ghosts than we could possibly fight. Maybe Jessie's life weaving won't even hide us and we'll get buried in undead the minute we set food in the castle. This could be really dangerous."

I gave her a flat look I knew she couldn't see through my mask, so I made sure my tone was deadpan enough to convey how stupid I thought she was being. "You realize you aren't talking me out of this by describing all the ways your supposedly easy infiltration mission could go horribly wrong right? Because in case you didn't figure this out, I am *against* the thought of your gruesome painful death. Telling me how likely it is that you might be horribly murdered isn't going to talk me out of going with you. Pretty much the opposite."

To my surprise that got an actual blush from Callie. "I don't want *you* to die either idiot, that's why I mentioned it. But... I guess we make a pretty good team." She sniffed haughtily and averted her gaze. "Besides, you should be fine with me there watching your back. I'm pretty awesome." Despite the arrogant words her tone was a little embarrassed and the blush was still on her face, which I found adorable. She got shy about the weirdest things.

Which left us staring up at the giant ass sheer walls of a black stone keep populated by ghosts. Her earlier comments, meant to scare me or not, weren't exactly bullshit. This could be risky, but I'd been telling her the truth when I said I would be more worried seeing her go alone. Besides, I trusted Sarah's advice on this. The issue of how to get up there was the main problem now. "So... can we like... throw a rope up or something? I mean zombies aren't likely to spot us climbing and try to kill us, plus how would they reach us up there?"

Sarah, who was listening nearby, was the one to shut that down, pointing up into the darkness at a series of barely-visible shapes. "There are gargoyles up there. They'll be the ones who monitor the airspace. Gargoyles, contrary to popular belief, *are* a form of undead. Stone statues animated by ghosts. Yes, they can fly—don't ask me how. It's some combination of Fantasy and Might, but the point is they actually can tell what's happening, and they'll be watching. Not sure how you'll get up there, but however you manage, try to stick close to the wall."

Callie looked concerned, but not deterred. I knew she would come up with something, and sure enough, she did. "I have an idea. What if I make us a series of steps up the side of the castle out of shadow, and box them in so they have a roof? Looking down, it would just look like darkness, assuming they even look down. When we get to the top, you can use Mistwalking to get us past the Gargoyles. That kind of fog makes plenty of sense outside, so I doubt it'll tip them off, and we can use our stealth skills alongside it so they don't see us slipping in."

That sounded like a perfect way to get up there, but it also sounded exhausting. My Wish power didn't exactly work like a standard ability, so I didn't know exactly how her shadow power worked, but I assumed it was fueled by Vitality. What I was certain of was that it was fueled by *something*, and it was a *long* way up the side of the castle. "Can you make that many constructs in a row? It'll have to be at least two at a time, and those will need to hold our weight."

Despite the challenge, though, my girlfriend seemed confident. "It'll be tough, but I can manage. Once we get up there, we can find a spot to hole up so I can recover a little. Assuming the Gargoyles can see us at all with the life force running through us." She looked to Sarah, who nodded. "Anyway, once we're past them, we can relax a bit since the other specters will have a harder time. Once we're rested up, we can resume sneaking. Agria, what's the longest we can hold a charge if you juice us up as much as possible?"

Jessie had wandered over to stand next to us. "I have no clue. I've never really used my ability like this. I usually pour in life force to repair damage or fill up someone's energy. I've never overcharged a person. I do it to the ravens because that's how I control them, but they're much smaller and have less energy. If it works the same or similar, at least I'd say probably a few hours. You'll need to be careful not to get hurt or exhaust yourself. Actually, getting up there will probably drain a decent chunk of the power I'll be giving Nightstrike."

That wasn't something I'd considered, but it made sense. "Okay, let's just slow down. We aren't in a rush here. We can do some testing to see how Agria's ability works on people and feel things out before we go. The important thing is to make sure we're as safe as possible up there. So rushing is going to be a bad idea long-term. Right?" I could see Callie psyching herself up to charge ahead (probably my influence, honestly), but at my comment, she seemed to come to her senses and slumped a bit.

Her sigh was long and obviously exhausted. "That's... a good point. We'll see any undead coming well before they reach us. We have time to sit down and strategize before going up there. Maybe the raven can even get a bird's-eye view of the top of the castle from far enough out to avoid the Gargoyles. No reason to rush." She flicked her fingers, conjuring herself a chair to sit down in, which made me grin. Her constant power use was a form of training, but it was also really cool.

I walked over to sit with her, and she conjured one for me too. It wasn't actually super comfortable, though I wouldn't tell her that. Then Jessie joined us, and we all sat together, letting our friend try out her ability on us at varying intensities and through various activities. It felt great getting turbo charged like that over and over again, but eventually, we figured out the timing and the exact drain Callie's ability would put on our reserves, and we were ready to go. The raven got us a bit of intel to help with our ingress, though sadly not very much.

Once we made sure everyone was okay and told them all the plan again to make sure they knew where to wait, we started our journey to the top. Callie created a platform off the wall with a roof to cover the view of us from above, and we started to climb. With one construct under us and one ahead, we began the slow trek. I had to admit the castle was pretty cool, but I was also a little worried about what it would be like near the top. I guess I was about to find out.

Chapter Sixteen

THE SHADOW CONSTRUCTS were surprisingly stable to stand on. I'd expected them to be shaky but my footing was rock steady as we mounted the first platform. It was three sided, a section below, one behind, and one to the side, leaving the front and back open so we could advance. Once we stepped up on the first one, Callie conjured a second about a foot higher, and we stepped onto it, leaving the last one behind.

We'd figured out the least draining way for her to manage this was to slide the preceding construct under the one we were on, arranging it ahead of us. It was cheaper than conjuring a fresh one every time we took a step. Unfortunately, it required extreme concentration and a slow, steady hand, so we had to wait a bit after each step up the castle.

Despite how much power we had and Leaf in the Wind's ability to get us safely down, it was... disquieting to look out behind us and see a massive drop as we started to ascend. By the time we hit around a hundred plus feet, I decided to wrap my arm around Callie's waist to keep her close in case the construct faded and I needed to get us down. "How are you doing over there, babe? Pacing yourself? Don't worry about falling, I've got us, so if your energy gets too low, just drop the construct. We can always try again later."

Her snicker was much more distracted than usual. She was obviously straining, but she did her best to reassure me. "I'm fine, Shane. I could use a distraction, though. This isn't exactly a walk in the park, and focusing on it isn't making it any easier. Take my mind off the process, will you?"

I figured she was giving me something to do to keep me busy as well as herself, but I wasn't going to look a gift horse in the mouth.

It took me a second to figure out what to talk about, but I figured since it was just us, we could talk about... well, us. "So I was thinking about trying to find a nice restaurant to take you out to celebrate after the hunt. I have a whole bunch of meals to replace in your memories. I know how much those mean to you, even if the points mean a little more. If you're up for some company." I'd been wanting to take Callie out to eat for a while, but before we got together, it felt suspiciously date-like, and I'd felt weird about asking.

She smiled, straining a bit but still obviously amused. "Yeah, obviously, you dolt. I think dinner together sounds nice. I was also thinking about maybe taking a trip back to Velan when we have some free time. I..." She paused, and I thought there might have been a problem with the ascent until I realized she was blushing. "I want to introduce you to my mom. I might have mentioned you once or twice, and she's been bugging me to meet you. If that's cool. Not that it's a big deal or anything, no pressure—"

I laughed, reaching out to physically cover her mouth to cut off the babbling. It was nice to know I wasn't the only one who got nervous about things. "That sounds nice, Callie. I'd love to meet her. I've been wanting to introduce you to Maria anyway. She's kind of like the little sister I never had and repeatedly considered trading in for a less annoying model. I think you'll like her, though, and she and Jessie have something going on, so I'm sure our healer would be happy to see her again."

Speaking of our teammate, I was still feeling the blaze of life energy flowing through me. Callie's normally blue eyes were blazing green too, and it needed to last. This would protect us from detection once we got past the Gargoyles. According to Sarah, something about being in physical form made them much more sensitive to things like this than the spirits, so we would need to avoid them.

Callie's smile was softer, though still tinged with strain. "That sounds nice. Maybe I can get Mom to invite everyone over for dinner. Her cooking isn't as good as yours, but it's still pretty amazing, and I think you'll really like her. She's pretty much the sweetest person ever." She stared ahead for a moment, seeming unsure of herself. "So... do you remember anything about your mom? I know you've been thinking a lot about her since Aiden told you the truth, but you don't talk about her much."

She was careful to speak softly, clearly willing to drop it if I was bothered, but honestly, she was right. I had been thinking about my mom a lot. "Nothing much, honestly. I remember she was blonde. Like… platinum blonde. Her eyes were hazel, like this really bright gold color, and she was really tall, though that might just be because I was a little kid. She had a warm voice, though, and she was always hugging me. This was so far back, I don't even know how old I was at the time. My first really clear memory was of living on Callus with Zeke, so who can even say?"

She reached out and gave my hand a tight squeeze. "It sounds like she wasn't the kind of person to abandon her son. Maybe she had a good reason for leaving." I couldn't tell her the truth—that I suspected my dad had forced her to leave to make sure I was alone, except for Zeke, whom he could control. I didn't want her to have to deal with thinking about that. I wished I didn't have to deal with thinking about it. Regardless, her tone was firm when she said, "It doesn't matter. We can ask her in person. We're going to find her, and you can talk to her about it yourself, okay?"

She sounded so sure of herself, it was hard not to be comforted, and I leaned down to kiss her. Just a quick peck so I didn't distract her. We mostly just chatted the rest of the way up, something that became infinitely more necessary the higher we went. Finally, we managed to get close enough that we could see the peak of the wall, a feat that took *way* longer than expected, but at the very least, Callie's eyes were still glowing pretty steadily. As we got close enough to see the edge, we both stepped back under the cover of the shadow construct to talk out our next move.

We kept our voices down; I wasn't sure if Gargoyles could hear, but it seemed like a stupid thing to risk for no reason, so whispering was probably the best move. "Okay, so I can get us up over the edge with Mistwalking like I mentioned before, but I think stealth is going to drain you more than we should risk. I'm hands down the more energized. You should let me pick you up and carry you past them in stealth. My skill isn't as high as yours, but it synergizes really well with Mistwalking."

Callie was looking pretty pale. The life energy was keeping her topped off, but not getting tired didn't eliminate the consistent mental strain of work like this, and I was rather worried about her. Mental exhaustion and physical tiredness weren't the same thing, but the former still took a toll.

"All right," she said, a bit unsure. "But we need to find the perfect spot. Use Seek Hidden and get me positions on the closest Gargoyles so we can pick our point of entry."

I didn't bother questioning, just triggered the skill, trying to locate any nearby Gargoyles. I spotted several above us and reported their positions to Callie. It took some maneuvering to get to a spot on the wall where there was a gap we could exploit, and once we were below it I told her to stop. "All right, this is a good place to start. Just hold us still. Once Mistwalking covers us, I'll let you know, and you can dissolve the roof of the construct. Then I'll scoop you up and carry you to safety."

I made sure to say that last part in as pompous a voice as possible so she knew I was kidding.

She just rolled her eyes then gave me a saccharine smile before saying sweetly. "Yes, you get to carry me literally, like I've been carrying you figuratively since we met." Her tone was innocent, but the sparkle in her eye made it clear I wasn't the only one doing some teasing.

I actually choked out a laugh, though I had to muffle it because of the enemy. "Ouch, you get mean when you overuse your powers." I leaned in for another quick kiss, replacing my mask right after as I triggered Mistwalking. I had to flex a bit to make sure it covered a large enough area, but with a small amount of effort, I had it done.

I stepped up to whisper to Callie, "Okay, dissolve the top only."

I reached down and picked her up, and as the shadowy ceiling above us vanished into smoke, I activated Leaf on the Wind and pushed off the construct into a short leap.

I made sure not to put too much into the jump, not wanting to accidentally screw up and leave the mist. Leaf on the Wind made it possible to control my descent a lot more thoroughly than would normally be feasible, so when I touched down, I was able to erase my traces with stealth. None of the Gargoyles seemed to notice me as I landed. The mist covered us both as I began to slowly sneak toward the nearest opening in the castle parapet. We could use it to access the depths of the fortress.

It was easy enough to find a set of stairs down into the main area of the castle from the roof, and I crept slowly down, being careful not to make a sound as I snuck us down a short stone hall to the first door I spotted. I'd been wondering about the inside because of the ghosts and the lack of an entrance, but apparently that was either a gimmick, or ghosts felt more comfortable in places that reminded them of being alive. There were doors, halls, and everything, though they were lit with glowing blue flames, and there were no windows at all.

We stopped at a door that looked unused, and I set Callie down, letting her open the barrier with her much-higher stealth Skill to make sure avoided making any noise. I wasn't sure if life force stopped ghosts from hearing us too, but it seemed better to be safe than sorry. We slowly eased the door closed, and once it was done, we both slumped down on the floor to rest.

We weren't physically tired, but being on edge for literal hours was hardly the most relaxing activity, and some time to just decompress in private was appreciated.

Callie grinned excitedly at me. "Well, looks like we made it through so far. Now we just need to track down where they're keeping any valuables, and I'm guessing they'll all be stored together, or at least most of them. So… you ready to raid the treasury?"

Despite the dire situation, I couldn't help but be happy I'd come along for this. I loved seeing her so excited. Seriously, best date ever. How did I get so lucky?

Chapter Seventeen

OPENING the door back out to the hallway, I finally had a chance to look around. We had hours of time left on the current life-force charge, and stealth luckily didn't burn much energy, so we didn't need to rush and could take our time studying the castle before we set out.

This went on for about five minutes before I finally decided to say something. "The... inside of this place is literally identical in every direction, isn't it?"

We'd tried pretty much every hall out of the intersection next to the door, and every one of them could have been the same exact hallway.

Callie shrugged. "I mean, the whole place was perfectly square from the outside. Kind of makes sense they went with a formulaic layout. But yeah, this is getting us literally nowhere." She gave me a wide smile. "Luckily, my boyfriend has magic direction finding powers so we never have to ask for directions. I'm the luckiest girl in the world." She batted her eyelashes at me innocently.

I knew she was messing with me, but I still felt the need to point out some key limitations. "My supernatural combat and tracking skills are not a compass or an atlas. They do not exist to make it easier for you to raid treasure rooms." She just stared at me flatly for a few seconds before I rolled my eyes and activated Seek Hidden. "Fine. It's that way. At some point, we should probably have a talk about how gleefully you take to theft."

She just squealed with joy before pecking me on cheek through my mask and taking off in the direction I pointed. Despite my comment, I loved seeing how happy Callie got when we were looting things. Raiding a ghost fortress was a small price to pay to see my girlfriend smile like that. She was so excited, I had to actually stop her a few times and turn her around because she passed our turn. My Seek Hidden ability showed me where the object I was looking for was, but only in a certain range, at least for smaller objects. This time, I was using the trail trick again, and we were following a small path of drifting red smoke that only I could see.

Along the way, we kept up stealth, which didn't slow us down too much despite how intricate the process was. Stealth could be performed while walking at almost-normal speeds provided the user was paying attention and had a decent Perception stat, which I did. With Callie's Perception and her higher-level skill, she could have flat-out sprinted at nearly top speed in stealth, but since she needed me to point the way to the treasure, that wasn't really on the table. We just took our time, looking carefully around corners.

We ran into a few patrols of roving spectral guards, but between stealth and the life force making us harder for them to see, they passed us by without any trouble. As we seemed to get closer, I pulled Callie to a stop. "So, the hundred-year-old corpse-eating grass, is that something we're going to find in the treasury, or are we mainly looking for the Bone Goblet? You mentioned those two things specifically, but a corpse-eating grass sounds like something you would find in a field, not in a vault."

She grinned at me. "You're such a good listener. But no, that stuff is crazy valuable for alchemy. Any plant that lasts more than like fifty years, trees excluded, usually has at least some Impact and is an Ascendant material. As you know, attention and reputation raise stats, and the same is true for materials. Plants start becoming more well-known once they've lived that long, and most fifty-plus-year-old herbs are well on their way to H-rank if they aren't already there. At a hundred, the effect is compounded. There's no way the spectral court had one nearby and didn't collect it for safekeeping."

That made sense. I couldn't imagine leaving precious materials lying around my backyard either. "So when you said we might find some more materials around here, that's what you meant. We're basically raiding the magical version of their pantry. That's pretty convenient. Wonder how many other biomes like this are around here, where some faction of monster or other have collected a bunch of useful stuff that the hunters can just steal." It was a fascinating dynamic.

Callie cackled. "At least one. This is a forest, so there are almost definitely goblins in here somewhere. The damn things are like tree-dwelling locusts that carry knives. I did some research on forest monsters for this hunt, and goblins were, like, top of the list of things to look out for. Well, the forest clans. There are rock goblins, too, but they're different. Usually bigger and much more warlike. Forest goblins are just malicious little shits that steal everything that isn't nailed down and stab you when you aren't looking."

They sounded highly unpleasant to me. "That something we need to worry about back at the base? I haven't seen anything I would describe as a goblin, but if something like that is out there, maybe we should warn everybody." The last thing we needed was some tribe of tree bandits snagging any of our materials before the hunt ended and screwing us out of finishing our list.

Luckily, that didn't seem to be an issue, judging from Callie's disdainful snort. "Not likely. Goblins usually don't manage to rank up. Most of them are H, and they won't go near anyone with higher Impact. The things are cowards at heart. Not to mention Zeke is around, and they have kind of a sixth sense about things that are out of their league. No way they get within miles of anyone that strong for literally any reason. The mats are all safe back at the hatchery with Cass and Zeke, even if they don't actively protect the stuff. Most monsters have better instincts than that."

I couldn't deny that Zeke was way too strong for anyone sane to fuck with, but it was curious the monsters would be able to tell even with him suppressing his power. I wondered if he had some flaw in his suppression or if he wasn't using it to the fullest out of laziness. I still didn't fully understand how he managed to press down on his Impact like that in either case. But once I hit F-rank, I was pretty sure it was a skill I would need. It was yet another reminder that cultivation was so much more complicated than it looked. The basics were simple, but it was a discipline with plenty of nuance.

Finally, after spending about an hour slinking through the halls and stealthing past patrols, we came to the end of the trail that was supposed to lead us to the treasury. We'd gone down more than a few flights of stairs on the way, and our final destination was a massive open room lined with columns. At the far end sat what I assumed were the treasure doors, a pair of massive metal slabs with intricate carvings of dancing specters and wailing ghosts carved into them. Based on the coloration, I was pretty sure they were iron, and based on the Impact, they were G-ranked.

Standing in front of the doors, guarding the treasury from all comers, were a pair of Dullahans. We weren't close enough to be visible, hiding behind a pair of columns, but two Dullahans against two of us with zero backup was not a great prospect.

I turned to Callie. "Any ideas here? Because I have zero clue how to get past them. If nothing else, when we engage, they're going to draw attention to us, not to mention burn our life force reserves. Fighting them head-on seems like a bad idea."

This had all occurred to her already, clearly. She was worrying at her bottom lip. "You're right—a fight isn't optimal. We should look around, I think. There must be another way in. Having to open a pair of giant iron doors every time you want to check on your stuff seems pointless. The specters can walk through walls, but they can't carry stuff through them, and the Lich is around here somewhere too. I bet there's a secondary access point hidden somewhere nearby we can use to get past the guards."

I hadn't actually considered that, but it was solid logic. Using Seek Hidden, I searched the walls and doors for any sort of hidden passage or hatch we could use for access. Sadly, the room was *big*, and the Dullahans could probably see us, so we had to use stealth to make sure we weren't spotted. We slowly made our way up and down each side, checking every column thoroughly.

Since the entrance probably wouldn't be big, Seek Hidden wouldn't be able to find it from too far away, so we had to get in close to search every corner of the room. That meant not just the floor, but also the ceiling and walls, which meant *lots* of climbing the columns. Luckily, the rough black stone was actually pretty climbable, something I assume the specters hadn't considered when designing this place, preferring instead to maximize the whole "living dead chic" vibe. Plus, they had no bodies and had no need to climb.

It took about twenty minutes of searching the hall and about fifteen close calls with the Dullahan guards before we finally found the secondary access point in the back corner, basically opposite where we had started. A small and cleverly concealed door in the column led to a spiral staircase. The door was pretty hard to open. While I could see it, I could *not* see where the fucking pressure plate that opened it was, especially in the dim-ass blue flickering light.

Once I found it, we ascended the spiral steps inside the column then stepped out onto a catwalk like a hundred feet off the ground, so high up that the darkness (combined with the pitch-black stone of both the catwalk and ceiling) had completely hidden it from view of anyone on the floor. We followed it out into the middle of the room and then turned onto a second catwalk (also anchored to the ceiling) and followed it to a small unobtrusive wooden door directly above the much bigger iron set.

We slipped in soundlessly, relaxing as we entered the newer space.

I gave Callie a victorious grin. "Perfect. We slipped right past them. This place is pretty nice for a ghoulish black-stone castle. Love the design."

She smirked at me as we stepped out onto a balcony. Another catwalk led to one of the columns with a passage down, and it was just as well hidden. From up here, though, given the placement of the torches it was much easier to see the floor of the chamber than the reverse.

The whole place was packed with stuff. Lots looked pointless and lame. Some of it was just more gold, which honestly just felt like it was there for ambiance. Several smaller columns rose into pedestals set with objects that I could feel were Ascendant artifacts. One of which was a cup made of bleached white bone and black metal. Another was a small black pot of bone-white grass. There were plenty more to take too. I understood now why Callie was so excited. This *was* pretty exciting.

Chapter Eighteen

ONCE WE GOT down to the treasury, it was even more apparent that we had hit the jackpot. The place was filled wall-to-wall with impressive-looking stuff. Based on Impact, though, a not insignificant portion of the treasures were just mortal crap. Still, I pulled the backpack with the spatial box off my back, ready to grab as much as we could carry.

Callie looked just as starstruck by all the loot as I was, to the point where she was almost bouncing with glee. When she saw me pull out the bag, she grinned. "Isn't that thing the coolest?"

It was kind of bulky, but the idea of having a spatial container of our own was amazing. "Definitely. I've been wanting a spatial container since I heard about them. Sucks the small ones are so expensive. Even this thing is worth more money than I've ever even seen in my life, not to mention a ring or necklace. I wonder what rank we'll be before we have enough to be able to afford to outfit everyone with one of those things?"

Callie just shrugged. "Depends on the planet, I think. I hear they're easier to get on larger-scale worlds, like one at D-rank. Given the gravity on one of those, though, we would barely be able to walk around. Only F-ranks and higher on those planets from what I've heard. The damn things are like ten times the size of a normal planetary body, and that massively increases the gravitational pull. Still, great places to shop." She smiled slyly. "Now, go get the Bone Goblet and corpse-eating grass while I try to figure out if the rest of this is useful or worth anything. And for the Revenants' sake—"

I rolled my eyes. "Don't touch anything directly. Yes, dear, I know. Since we got here, we've been looting everything that isn't tied down. Also some things that *were* tied down. And the ties they used to secure them. Man, we might have a kleptomania problem. This would be really concerning if we weren't robbing dead people." I paused. "I'm going to try not to think too hard about that last sentence, actually. Getting the materials for the list." I headed over to the pedestals with the things we needed.

As my girlfriend giggled, I blatantly ignored the red flag that we had essentially become grave robbers,and I headed to the Bone Goblet first. The goblet's pedestal was a column rising from a massive pile of gold coins. The dark stone ended in a flat platform atop the stone, clutched on all sides by fingers from four different carved skeletal hands. The goblet sat unassumingly on the flat surface, just waiting to be grabbed, and I could see why Callie felt the need to warn me. It was pretty tempting to just snatch the thing up and toss it into the bag.

I was pretty sure that was a bad idea (even if there was no security or anything since the whole picture just screamed cursed object). I opened the bag and the box inside and set it down next to the column. I pulled a rock from my pocket and chucked the stone at the goblet, knocking it over and directly into the waiting bag. Then, I moved on to the pot of grass.

It struck me that trying to steal a pot of grass from a ghost castle was something I legitimately had never considered I would ever be doing, and I had to grin. My life really had gotten weird. I slapped the box down over the pot directly without touching it this time since there hadn't been a problem with the goblet, and sure enough, no response. I refastened the backpack and slung it back over my shoulder before heading over to where Callie was standing next to yet another platform, staring down at a small dark object.

As I drew closer, I was able to see it better, and I realized it was a vial of dark liquid. The vial was capped with bronze on both ends and sealed with dark-red wax. Callie was gazing at it seriously, clearly caught up in whatever the substance was.

I stopped next to her. "Is that some kind of magic potion or poison? Maybe the Lich's one weakness or something? Because whatever is in there looks important." My bet was on some kind of super-powerful blood potion that would make the drinker jump up twenty points or something.

Callie stared for a moment before startling as if she hadn't noticed me. "What? Oh, no, that's blood. Just the normal kind you'd take from a person. It's not valuable to us at all. The vial it's in, however… it's called a life puppet flask. You pour the blood of someone G-rank or lower into it, and you can force them to rise when they sleep and follow your orders." She shook her head with a grimace. "Necromancers. Still, might be useful to have around, if only to make sure no one else gets their hands on it. I think the cult has had quite enough mind-control tricks."

I nodded and scooped it into the pack without touching it. "So, anything a little less creepy in here? I know it's a ghost castle, but does everything have to be all morbid and dark? Like ghosts can't own things unless they look like they belong to a disaffected poet in a frilly shirt? Ooooh, skull cane!"

Callie rolled her eyes at me as I bolted over to a new pedestal and stared down in fascination at the awesome-looking darkwood cane with a silver ruby-eyed skull for a head. It had intricate carvings up and down the length. I turned to her as she came over. "What does this one do?"

That got me a glare. "I'm not an encyclopedia, Shane. I can't just tell you what every random artifact does and where it came from. Just because I did some research doesn't mean I'm a convenient source of info for every time we come across something useful. It's a cane covered with weird symbols. Just put it in the box and move on. We don't have time for this."

That was a fair criticism. I just shrugged and stowed the thing away. She was probably right anyway—I needed to start reading up on this stuff myself instead of expecting her to do it every time.

We didn't bother with talking about the rest of the pedestals. We just shoved everything into the box. We still avoided touching anything of course, but Callie was right about not having much time. The pedestals were all covered with some weird stuff. An hourglass, a glass box with a hand in it, a dagger, a red-crystal butterfly, a rose made of black rock, a pair of gaudy emerald earrings, and a small wooden hammer like a judge would use. A bit bummed there were no other herbs to take, we grabbed a couple of H-rank weapons from the gold piles. We stuffed everything inside until the box was full.

I expected it to get heavier, but nothing happened. Probably for the best because I wasn't entirely sure I could have managed to keep the bag from breaking under any more weight. While I had the Might to carry all that stuff, having to hold the box in my arms would have really screwed with our exit plan.

Once we were packed up, we headed to the column and back up to the balcony. "Okay, we're down to twenty-one things on the list, right? Anything else we can score in this place, or are we good to go?"

Callie just shook her head. "No, we can leave. I officially want to get the hell out of here. Now that there's no treasure left to take, this place is starting to get creepy."

I wasn't a huge fan of the décor either. The torches' blue flames flickered eerily across the dark stone, and knowing there were literal ghosts around didn't help. It wasn't scary or anything, but it was consistently unsettling, and honestly it was starting to make me a little queasy. We made it back down to the entry room easily enough, taking the door to the catwalk and then heading back down the column to the secret door in the back corner of the room.

We had to sneak out of the room to avoid the Dullahans standing guard, but we made it to the hallway easily enough from the back corner. Once we were outside, we looked around slowly to confirm our exit and started our trek out. The sneaking was slow and boring, but it saved us from having to engage the enemy.

I drew close to Callie. "Okay, we should try to rush it a bit. Even if they didn't see us go in, there's no way someone won't go in there eventually. It's obvious that things were taken, so I don't want to be around when they notice."

She nodded solemnly, and we picked up the pace, still moving slowly enough to be stealthy but completely unwilling to go at less than the fastest speed possible. Thirty minutes later and three quarters of the way back to where we'd come in, we heard a series of rattling bangs coming down the hall. I was about to use Seek Hidden, but four massive Dullahans came barreling around the corner, followed by a veritable parade of ghosts.

They paused at the entrance to the hallway, and I froze in place. "I'm pretty sure this answers the whole question of whether the Dullahans can see us. Run!"

I grabbed Callie's hand, and we broke stealth, taking off full speed down the hall. Full speed for us was… fast. I expected to lose them quickly, but those Dullahans were pretty stacked in Might. Despite their huge size, they moved pretty fucking quickly. Not to mention, the ghosts who could pass through walls were hot on their tails. I looked at Callie's eyes, relieved to see she still had the green glow of life energy. They couldn't see us, but they could follow the Dullahans that could.

We used the turns to our advantage, and I activated Afterburner, exploding out with power to keep up with my girlfriend so she didn't have to wait up for me. Finally, we made it back up to the roof, where a ghostly wail had tipped off the gargoyles, who were even now turning to stare at us menacingly.

As we approached the wall, I screamed. "Do you trust me? Because this is going to be pretty crazy."

Her eyes widened. "Yes of course, but, Shane, you were supposed to lower us down with the rope before we jumped. Even with the reduced falling speed, the impact of the landing might break our legs!"

I didn't have time to respond as I grabbed her and swept her up into a princess carry, activating Leaf in the Wind as I hurled myself off the edge of the castle and into open air. Callie screamed and clung to me as I activated the skill, pushing it to cover us both. I wasn't worried, though, as we started to plummet. I had a plan.

Chapter Nineteen

DESPITE LEAF on the Wind we were dropping pretty damn fast. I was spreading the skill over both of us so it was kind of dampened, not to mention I didn't want to drop too slow because the Gargoyles were after us. As mentioned, they *could* fly. Somehow. I was still in Afterburner, but I couldn't fly, even with Leaf on the Wind. When they started swooping down I couldn't do much... at least not without a little nudge from another skill. I used Cloud Step, planted my foot firmly on air, then pushed off hard, hurling myself at the nearest gargoyle.

I slammed into it feetfirst, knocking it away. Callie, who was adjusting well to hurtling toward the ground at an admittedly less than terminal velocity, lashed out with a kick. The heel of her black boot shifted into a spinning drill via shadow embodiment. Her leg flashed out a few times, shattering the Gargoyle's head.

I yelled into her ear. "If I switch you to my back, can you make a glider with your coat?" I'd been considering hopping from gargoyle to gargoyle to get down, but the damn things were all higher than us, and if we slowed down too much, it would run out the clock on my skill.

Her eyes lit up at the idea. "Yeah! I can swing that."

It took some awkward shuffling to get her onto my back midair without letting go, but I got her into a piggyback position. Her coat, which was imbued with shadows and could be manipulated just like her other clothes, flared out behind us and stiffened into a glider.

"Okay! Since we don't have to worry so much about steering, let's take out the other ones!" Her obvious glee was infectious, and I whooped my agreement as I pushed off the dead Gargoyle, hurling us at another one.

The force sent her body flying toward the ground, but gave me a chance to get my footing as I stepped on the air. I managed a relatively small bit of push and a shallow arc, with the coat catching the air as we started to dip again. We went sailing forward at a smooth glide toward the gargoyle I'd picked, and without Callie in my arms, I was able to draw my tonfas and actually attack. I activated Flurry of Blows and Consecration of Flame and rained down punishment as we got within range, shattering the stone shell that sheltered the inner ghost.

The fire helped disperse the rock-glad spirit, and I realized that gargoyles were fairly weak, at least when we could actively defy gravity. The whole flying-rock-death-machine thing probably made them a huge pain for most people, but once we got started, we took out the nearest two or three. The rest of them veered away.

Callie cheered and I turned, sending us in slow circles that would let us descend to the ground. Luckily, with Leaf on the Wind, I was able to go at a steeper angle than would have been safe otherwise.

Still, the destruction of those Gargoyles didn't seem to deter the ghosts. They kept swooping in to attack, trying to exploit any openings. Callie and I were forced to stay on guard as we descended. My tonfas scared them off, though, at least for a bit, until they all scattered of their own volition out of nowhere.

"Oh shit!" Callie yelled.

I tightened the angle of descent so I was facing the same direction she was and felt my blood run cold. I had to curse aloud at our luck, not to mention the ridiculous nature of what I was seeing. "Oh, *come on*! That fucking dragon skeleton is made of *bones*. How is it flying? That doesn't even make any fucking sense!"

Well, it looked like a dragon skeleton. I doubted an E-rank world had actual dragons on it, but whatever it was, it was big and reptilian. It was also carrying what I suspected was a really pissed off magic user in a robe and crown. I was guessing from context clues that this was the Lich.

On the upside, the ghosts didn't seem enthused about getting near the pair either. I abandoned the spiral and went into a straight dive. We needed to get away from this thing as fast as possible, and that meant the quickest drop we could make. I would pull up once we got lower, and Leaf on the Wind should help me come out of the dive. If it didn't, I could *make* it. Callie squealed with joy and surprise as we dove, and I tried very hard not to think about the corpse on the dragon behind me. It didn't work.

Instead of eyes, dancing blue flames sat in a desiccated face, surrounded by poorly contained wispy white hair. It was holding a staff of some kind made of glowing blue wood, and it had a saddle affixing it to the back of its bony steed. Despite not having any expression, I could *feel* the malice coming from the eerie blue glare. Not to mention *both* of them were G-rank, and I was seriously worried whether even the whole crew would be able to take them down.

The ground barreled up at us faster than I was really comfortable with, skill or not, but I was able to pull up as I went. I used Seek Hidden as we plummeted, searching for my party, and a flash of red was enough to bring me in the right direction to meet up with my friends. Mostly. As we came in, I pulled up on Callie's legs to get her to yank back and try to come out of our dive. It… didn't entirely work. Between the skill and the glider, I avoided most of the impact, but I still hit the ground going forward and slid about forty feet, tearing up a long strip of black grass.

My friends were running to meet us even as they saw me come down. I'd managed to get close enough to be visible. The skid had taken me well past them, so it took a minute for them to reach us. As they headed over, I groaned, pulling myself out of the dirt. My costume had tanked most of the impact, but even with all the mitigation, it wasn't exactly comfortable. Luckily, Callie had been on my back, so I had cushioned her fall. Luckily for her, at least. I'd taken twice the damage, not that I was stupid enough to mention that. It had been my idea after all.

I brushed the dirt off me as I climbed to my feet. "That was a terrible plan. I should never have ideas. You okay, babe?"

Callie was climbing to her feet next to me, cracking her neck and checking her costume for rips. There was nothing there of course—I'd taken most of the hit.

I turned to see our friends arriving. "Hey, guys, good to see you. If you didn't notice, the Lich is riding a skeleton dragon down here to kill us.

Which seems bad to me. Sarah, any idea what the hell that is and what we should be expecting?"

Sarah stared up at the sky in trepidation, looking for the Lich and the dragon. I suspected we'd lost them for a second during the fall, one of the benefits of being in a dark cavern and crashing into a field of black grass wearing all black. Luckily, the flowers were in patches, and we'd avoided them in our hit. "Well, it isn't a dragon. At least I don't think so. Bone Dragons are powerful undead monsters. It's most likely a Bone Wyvern. They're much smaller and more common. Still terrifying, but they don't breath frostfire."

She spotted the Lich as it finally drew close. "Okay, wow, yes that's a Wyvern. The skull shape is different. Wyvern horns curl like a ram's, while dragon horns curve back gently, and they're branched. Plus, dragons are universally pretty high rank when they're grown. The younger ones can be lower, but you don't often see them out and about. Point is, there should be a core in there you can target. An organ magically bonded to the bones that supports the spell keeping it animated. It makes them more independent, but for undead of that scale, its more efficient because they can continue to grow stronger."

I winced, though. Honestly, the Wyvern was a distant second concern. I was mostly staring at the withered, eyeless, flame-socketed face of the lich as it sneered hatefully down at us. Now that it was getting closer and I wasn't falling, I could finally focus on it properly. I could see its withered hands clutching the blue staff with twisted black nails and a pair of cloth shoes in the stirrups of the saddle. Flaming eyes seemed to follow us everywhere, despite being literal balls of fire and having no indicating features to show orientation or direction.

The Bone Wyvern crashed down onto the grass in front of us. Its massive weight smashed into the earth with a low boom, buckling the loose, hydrated dirt of the field. The soil down there had been dark and loamy, like a graveyard, and I wasn't shocked to see the ground buckle under the weight of the massive skeletal form. The shadow of the towering beast fell over us like an impending tidal wave as it loomed above our group, a specter of grim judgement that was preparing to enact our final punishment.

The Lich stood, sliding free of the saddle, stepping off the draconic form and floating gently to the grass beside it. Despite the lack of determining features on the eye flames, the Lich was clearly focused on Callie and me when it finally spoke. "Thieves." The Lich's voice was terrifying—a rasping, rustling hiss like the wind through dead tree leaves in the depths of a haunted forest. "Return what you have stolen and die swiftly."

I raised an eyebrow under my mask. "Don't you mean *or?*"

He cocked his head.

I rolled my eyes as I repeated. "Don't you mean 'return what we have stolen *or* we die swiftly'? Because saying you're going to kill us if we give the shit back is clearly not an incentive to do it. Who wants to die?"

The response was an even more raspy and terrifying chuckle. The blue flames danced in their sockets.

The withered head shook slowly. "You misunderstand. Death is inevitable. *Your* death is inevitable within the day. Your choice is not life, but quality of death. If you return what was stolen, I will kill you swiftly. If you make me take it from you, your deaths will take hours, and your corpses will serve as foot soldiers for my army, where I will use them for the amusement of my sapient troops. So, I say again, and for the last time. Thieves. Return what you have stolen, and you can die swiftly."

Ah, that wasn't ideal. I kind of wished we'd had time to plan this out. We'd discussed fighting the Lich, but since they tended to vary, we had no actual idea what the hell he could do. His magic could be any one of multiple different things, so we would need to play it by ear. Not to mention the existence of the Bone Wyvern complicated the hell out of this entire situation.

I pretended to think about it for a second, but eventually, I would run out that clock. Then, I turned to Cark and bellowed, "Wall!"

As if on reflex, the pyrokinetic hurled out a hand and tossed a huge wall of blue inferno out between us and the Lich. The Bone Wyvern roared and charged into the flames, its sheer size creating a break in the fire for the Lich to hurl itself through. As it landed in front of us, bringing the staff to bear, we all readied ourselves.

Looks like we wouldn't have time for a planning session after all. Guess we would have to wing it.

Chapter Twenty

THE FIRST THING I did was cast Sucking Mud on the Wyvern's back right foot. Given how soft the ground already was and the weight of the thing, it seemed like a solid plan. As that took effect, Cark rained down blue flames at the Lich. Callie had picked up my vibe and was trying to chain down the Wyvern. Jessie was imbuing vines with life energy to target the Lich, and Sarah was helping as best she could with her Holy Hand. With them keeping him pinned, I decided to engage the Wyvern with Callie. I was just hoping the specters didn't swarm us.

I activated Leaf on the Wind again then Touch of Tears, turning my already-flaming tonfas into poison fire batons as I hurled myself at the Wyvern's horned skull. The thing snapped at me, and I avoided it with Cloud Step. Bouncing off the midair platform, I slammed down on its head. I was running low on charges for the day, and I winced. I'd used a bunch of them on the raid, and I was going to need to minimize them in this fight. When I landed, I started wailing on the Wyvern's skull, not bothering to speed up my hits as it was distracted.

As I was doing that and Callie kept it pinned down, Benny made his move. Laying into the skeletal drake with his tranq punch, he leapt around with his density-shifting leg. I wasn't sure the tranq would even work on the skeleton, but hell, at the very least, it was some damage. As my blows landed on the skull, glowing green cracks smoldering into existence, Callie slipped past the horns to join me up top.

She appeared next to me, not bothering to attack with shadows. My poison fire was a debuff that would penetrate deeply into the bone and spread. Her shadows were blunt damage, and we needed to find that heart.

"Benny will try to get inside and target that core Sarah mentioned, but until then, we need to stall the bastard," Callie said. "Any ideas on what to do other than stand on its head and punch it a bunch?" She seemed almost as lost as I was in this fight.

I scowled. "Not really. Our best bet is the eye socket, maybe? I have no real idea how to fight one of these. This thing is fucking huge. You ever fought an enemy this size? Also, how is this thing not crushing us into paste? It absolutely has to be Might heavy."

I expected it to be much stronger than a Dullahan, given its size and how it was almost a dragon. This thing was fast and powerful, but not nearly as powerful as it should have been. I'd been expecting nine hundred Might or some shit, and this was anything but.

Callie slammed a pair of shadow hooks into the bone to remain upright as the thing thrashed around trying to dislodge us. I grabbed onto her and was close enough to hear her snicker over the roar of the Wyvern. "Because you aren't thinking this through. Its Might is probably close to mine. Fantasy would be a much higher stat because it has to cheat so much with flying and interacting like a physically whole being." She paused. "We need to get inside the skeleton. We have zero reliable ways to coordinate, which means we have no way to establish a search pattern. Benny is in there alone."

I nodded, and we waited for a lull in its movements. Since I was still using Leaf on the Wind, I scooped up my girlfriend and bolted across the surface of the skeleton wyvern. The thing rocked and jolted. The only thing that had been saving us was that the wyvern tended to keep its head steady, probably just out of habit. I didn't think it could feel us on the bone, so it was just thrashing, trying to get rid of something it barely knew the location of. Still, once we started moving, even on the head, it was tough to stay standing, and I wasted another Cloud Step preventing us from being thrown clear.

Finally, after about five seconds of running, we got to the eye socket. I hurled us both into the gap, dropping into the abyss that was the Wyvern's skull. The whole thing was massive. The socket alone was easily about five feet, and the skull itself was even bigger. We landed on the jaw, bolting forward toward the opening at the base of the throat that would let us drop free and get out of the head. Once we were out, we bounced off another Cloud Step and into the massive ribcage, which was *much* less well-lit than I'd been expecting.

Benny was scrambling around, hopping from bone to bone. I understood Callie's point about the Fantasy stat—from inside and at this angle, I could see an almost-tangible dark aura that seemed almost like flesh coating the bones, isolating the light from outside. It made it nearly impossible to see anything in here… for most people anyway. Luckily, I wasn't most people.

"Hold on, guys. I've got this! I can find the heart." I had to yell to make myself heard in the weird, stilted atmosphere in here. Even sound was muffled.

I activated Seek Hidden, targeting the Wyvern's heart. We needed to locate it as soon as possible, and despite the headache building from spamming skills, I was pretty sure I could last the rest of this fight. I scanned the inside of the darkened skeleton, and finally, after looking around more than a few times, I spotted a faint red glow overhead, obscured by a protective cover of bone. I'd never seen that, but I assumed it was some kind of evolutionary device for beings with chest cavities that could hold whole people.

Unfortunately, it was farther than expected. I was betting something about the thing's massive amount of Fantasy had altered its internal structure. This cavern seemed way too big to be the interior of even the massive beast we'd seen outside. It was a bit like the spatial expansions on buildings, though it seemed less… stable. The world around us was a dark shifting abyss of uncertainty. Regardless, I could see the heart, so we could head for it. I was still holding Callie, and I dashed forward heading for the glow.

Benny had locked in on my voice and was heading our way, though the glow of my tonfas probably helped. He caught up to us within a minute or two, and we dashed steadily toward the heart, hopping between ribs, which the Wyvern had a shockingly large number of.

Finally, we arrived at the spot under the heart and were able to jump up and catch the bone plate surrounding it. The plate itself ended up being the size of a small room. At its center was a pulsing black mass of concentrated darkness with an eerie blue glow lighting up veins across its exterior.

That brought me up short. "Huh. That's… weird. We should take care of this fast—without anyone out there to distract the Wyvern, it might go after the others. Anyone have any clue how to break this? Because I kind of want to just smash it with my tonfas, but that feels like it might backfire." I set Callie down and shrugged. "This one is on you, boss. You're the one who makes the calls."

She stood up easily, the inside of this thing somehow not being jostled by what I'm sure was a madly thrashing Wyver. She looked mildly annoyed, which made sense since we had zero guarantee that destroying the ominous heart would be as simple as hitting it or that there wouldn't be side effects. Sadly, we didn't have time to be cautious, and after a second or two of thinking, she groaned. "Sure, put the completely random decision on me in case it goes wrong. Fine. Do it. We need to get out of here, this thing isn't our main threat and the others are fighting the Lich without us." She gave a resolved nod for me to proceed.

I chuckled. "That's what you get for being the boss. You get credit for the successes and blamed for all the fuckups too." I stepped forward and slammed down one of my tonfas on the heart, and it bounced right off. I frowned. "Okay. That's not… ideal." I tried again, setting my feet and swinging hard at the pulsing object. This time, it didn't bounce off so much as kind of sink in, but still, the only sign of impact was a slight flare in the blue glow of the veins where my attack had connected.

I studied the veins and noticed that the glow had shifted slightly. A small amount of green was mixed into the blue. I could also see minute cracks on the surface, with the telltale green glow of poison fire, but they were so small, it wasn't readily apparent damage had been done. Still, that was a good sign, so I hauled back and started wailing on it. I tried to focus hard enough to make the blows sink in, since that seemed to be what had done the most damage.

Instead of using DS Mastery, I decided to get in some Balam training. I had the others step back and started trying to work up my rotation, slamming my tonfas into the surface of the heart from different angles and positions, trying to make my blows land with as much force and momentum as possible. The forms of Balam were pretty adaptable, so I was able to slowly get a grasp on which movements and attacks fit best with my weapons.

Blunt weapons worked similar to the strikes I'd been using, with the main difference being the reach. I had to change up my rhythm and adjust my grip a few times before I got the hang of it, but before I knew it, I could see that telltale green glow beginning to spread, interrupting the blue. I was having a blast, the bounciness made this thing feel like a punching bag, and I couldn't get enough of wailing on the dark surface.

Sadly, nothing could last forever, because after a minute or two of blurringly fast blows, the thing started to shudder. The cracks began to grow on their own without any help from impacts, and Callie and Benny grabbed my shoulders to drag me back. My girlfriend seemed sad to cut me off, but she did it anyway. "Whoa there, babe. That's enough. We need to get out of here. That thing is shaking, and while I don't *know* it's going to explode, it seems likely." I flushed and scooped her back up.

We bolted for the edge of the platform, hurling ourselves off and into the cavity inside the Wyvern. The space was shifting even more, and gaps started to form in the darkness coating the bones as we drifted down. Benny followed with his density manipulation skill. We touched down on a rib then waited for a gap. Slipping through, we fell a much shorter distance to the ground than we had to get to the gap we left through.

As soon as we hit the grass, we started running, bolting at top speed to get out of range, and it was a good thing. We'd just barely made it out when the entire Wyvern went up in a huge wave of blue green poison flame, throwing the three of us from our feet.

Chapter Twenty-One

MARTIN AND CELINE met us as we got to our feet after the explosion. The whole place was covered in flames. Given how spread out the attack was, Martin had been able to block it for the two of them. Sarah and Jessie had Cark to hold back the fire. The same could not be said of the ghost cavalry that had been arriving as the Bone Wyvern went up. The wave of poison fire had mostly been funneled up into the air, and it ate through a massive chunk of the spectral forces, pushing the others to bank away hard.

Our friends looked worried. Martin checked us over for damage. "Are you all right? That was crazy. What the hell happened in there?" He looked up at the column of flame with wide, disturbed eyes. That was fair—I was rather disturbed too. The structure I was in had just exploded. That was a first for me, and I honestly wasn't sure I would have survived it from inside the belly of the beast, so to speak.

I turned to look behind us, not sure exactly how that worked. "Also, not to look a gift Wyvern in the mouth, but why the hell aren't we dead? Because the explosion really should have gone the same distance in every direction, shouldn't it?"

Hell, I wasn't sure why it had been so volatile. I guessed all the stats had been in that heart, and a mixture of poison fire and dark magic had caused some kind of destabilizing effect and made it go critical or something.

Callie narrowed her eyes at the cloud of flame for a second before they widened. "The pocket space. That heart was at the top of the Wyvern skeleton, right up against the spine. When it blew, up was the only direction that wasn't impeded by a whole bunch of unstable expanded space. It must have swallowed most of the blast. The top was right against the outside, though, so it just blasted right through. All the excess flame vented up."

I blinked. Why hadn't I thought of that? Still, it was easily the best outcome here. The venting flames had wiped out a big chunk of the ghosts, and the drifting wisps of poison ghost fire that floated around after the blast were keeping the sky clear for now. If we could kill this damn Lich, we could get the hell out of here before any stronger ghosts could reinforce and avoid that whole ghost army issue entirely.

Benny shrugged. "Oh well. I mean, bullet dodged. Let's go help stop our friends from dying, and then we can get the hell out of here."

That seemed to wake everyone else up, and we took off at a dead sprint in the direction where the others were fighting. Cark was raining down blue Armageddon on the Lich, and it was pretty damn visible. With our Might, making it over to them was pretty much a non-issue, and we didn't even have to hold back because the H-rankers wouldn't be much good here.

As we'd seen from farther away, Cark was the one mainly engaging the Lich. Waves of fire came off him like an aura, and he was intercepting most of the magic the undead hurled. It was actually kind of hard to see, since the Lich was using that same ghostly blue flame burning in his eyes. Cark's fire was also blue, though that was where the similarities ended. Based on the ground nearby, the Lich was using some kind of cold flame that sapped energy and froze everything it touched.

In small quantities, that wasn't really viable against Cark, but the Lich's staff seemed to massively boost the power of his flames, allowing him to output about three times the amount Cark was using, which was barely keeping our pyrokinetic at bay. The Lich probably would have engaged physically before this, but Jessie had wrapped his legs in a dense tangle of glowing green vines that actively repelled the cold fire, and Cark had him too distracted to focus on them.

Sarah was in the background, getting in slaps with her Holy Hand from a distance. She was only H-rank, so sadly, the attack didn't have as much effect as she would like, but it broke the Lich's concentration. It was kind of hilarious to see it get slapped in the face whenever it wasn't paying attention. The entire mess seemed to mostly be a stalemate.

I felt myself start to flag and cursed. My Afterburner had worn off, which meant I was now in a weakened state. The timing on that wasn't great. Despite that, I still had all my active skills going. Leaf on the Wind and my poison fire would both be active for a few more minutes. Even slightly weakened, I should be able to help. The main issue here was that there was no fucking way I was getting close to the Lich in the middle of that weird clashing hot-and-cold firestorm, and neither were either of my friends. So we slipped over to talk to Sarah and Jessie, who were off to one side together since Jessie was able to restrain the Lich from a distance with her vines.

Jessie was pretty distracted, but her face lit up when she saw us out of the corner of her eye. "Oh, thank the Revenant you guys are okay. What the hell happened to that dragon thing? You guys went in, and it just exploded." She paused for a second, then shook her head. "Never mind, tell me later. Any ideas on how you guys can help here? Because that poison fire is going to fade soon, and we really need to kill this thing before it does so we don't get mobbed with an army of angry ghosts."

Callie frowned. "I can try some shadow constructs. I'm not sure how they'll interact with the flames... either type of flames. I suspect the cold fire won't be as much of a problem, so our best bet is probably to have me attack from behind." She turned to me questioningly. "Any chance you could manage a Mercy Kill through me? I don't think we've tried that one, and I know you're running low."

She wasn't wrong. My charges for the day were dangerously depleted, but I still had some in me.

I reached out for her hand, taking a deep breath. In my weakened state, it would be much harder than usual. I'd never tried flexing my abilities like this when I was compromised. Still, she was right that this would be a powerful combination. Since her constructs stuck around, the power boost should theoretically count the actual construct as the attack and boost the power behind it. At least that made the most sense to me. If that happened, then it would completely change her combat capabilities when we were working together.

I squeezed down on her fingers and triggered Mercy Kill. This was my nineteenth charge of the day, leaving me with six. Even with the cushion, in my weakened state post-Afterburner, trying to alter the shape of the skill was agonizing. I gritted my teeth and pushed past the pain, but my head was throbbing. I made a mental note not to do this when I was weakened again. It was hands-down one of the most painful things I'd ever experienced, like digging around in my own brain with a rusty spoon covered in lemon juice.

Still, despite the pain, I managed to shove the skill over onto Callie. I got a feel for exactly why this was so difficult. Mercy Kill was meant to be a single-use finisher. It was a compact and dense skill that wasn't intended to cover two people or even to be altered. It had one purpose—to crush the enemy with overwhelming force. That made it much harder to mold or shape it, and when I finally did get it over to Callie, it was by literally brute forcing the whole damn skill out of myself in a highly unpleasant way.

I hadn't noticed any real variations in skill manipulation, aside from difficulty, but it seemed like not all skills could be altered as I saw fit. Some skills were more malleable and more fluid. It made me eager to study the ways the skills shifted and moved and how they related to their natures. If I could understand the makeup of the way the energy formed a skill from DS Mastery, not only would I be able to rank up DS Mastery, but I might even be able to learn one of the skills well enough to turn it into an independent Skill I could use without charges.

Of course that was a problem for well in the future. Much like my own ability, I needed to study the way this worked and learn to use it to its fullest when I had the time. For now, I just stepped back, more than happy with Callie getting full access to Mercy Kill. Once it was gone, she pulled my hand to stop me from falling over as my legs wobbled from exhaustion. I was happy to let her handle this surprise attack or whatever, because I was barely able to stand. I needed a minute before I was ready to take off with the others.

I could see Callie almost vibrating with the energy inside her, and I wondered how it felt to have another person's skill inside you. That made me kind of consider how it felt to have my *own* skills inside me. I hadn't really considered it before, and it was one more aspect of my skills to add to the pile. I shook off the thoughts and focused on the battle and on my girlfriend's contribution to it. She shifted into stealth, and her skill was high enough that I had trouble following her. I gritted my teeth and activated Seek Hidden despite the drain so I could watch.

She circled around behind the back of the battle unnoticed, though that may have been less about the stealth and more about the fact that the Lich was wrapped up in life vines and trying to stop Cark from lighting him on fire while getting holy slapped in the face every time he left an opening. Still, Callie was like a living shadow as she got into position. Once she was there, she reached out to the darkness around her. I expected a big wave of shadow energy to smash him from behind, but Callie had clearly been considering the best way to do this.

Instead of just hurling the huge amount of shadowy power she was gathering, she started to condense it. She pulled more and more of the shadows together, twisting them as she did. Despite condensing, the shadow construct didn't get smaller as she layered on more and more energy. The final product was a long spiral spike of tightly wound darkness. With the utmost care, Callie held the shaking construct, so densely packed that she was barely able to hold it together, and began to inch forward slowly, moving in complete silence as she took advantage of the light show to maximize her stealth. As soon as she got within range she stopped, took a deep breath, and drove the lance of darkness forward.

As it sped toward the Lich's back, the shadows started to unwind, causing it to spin rapidly like a drill at the moment of impact. The Lich threw its head back and roared. As it did, Sarah grabbed its face with her Holy Hand, keeping its mouth open. As its attention wavered and the waves of cascading blue cold fire flickered, Cark whirled his whole offensive into a tight vortex as wide around as a fist then shoved it right down the undead bastard's screaming throat, immolating him from the inside.

Chapter Twenty-Two

I HAD TO ADMIT, on a scale of one to crazy, a whirling funnel of blue flames jamming itself down the throat of a screaming corpse was one of the crazier things I'd seen so far in my life. As the flames were crammed into his mouth, his body seemed to bulge as if it would explode. I half expected to have to dive for cover, but apparently, Cark's flame didn't react with the cold fire the same way mine did. After a bit of bulging, the Lich just sort of… popped, like a soap bubble, with all the pieces dissolving into fiery ash.

We all just stood there, staring. No one had been expecting that. This was some huge endgame fight, and we'd been expecting to have to throw down with everything we had, but despite the stats and everything, this was real life and not a game. Sometimes things just… died. Lucky for us, but I doubted that luck would hold, so we needed to get out of here now.

Callie scooped up the staff and tossed it to Cark. "See if that works for you. If it does, put up a wall behind us to block our way. I want each of the H-rankers carried by a G-ranker. We don't have time to take it slow. We need to get the hell out of here."

Benny grabbed Celine, I grabbed Martin, and Jessie grabbed Sarah. Cark wheeled to try to put up a wall to block our exit, checking to see if the staff could do for him what it did for the Lich. Since he had the most Might of all of us, we all took off at a dead sprint back the way we'd come. As we ran, I pulled even with Jessie, yelling to Sarah. "Hey, weird question, did that seem… too easy? Because I know you guys were fighting him for a while, but that Lich died really fast. I kind of expected more based on all the hype."

Sarah actually giggled at that. "Oh, he isn't dead."

I stumbled slightly, yelping but managing to adjust my foot as Callie caught me. We both looked at Sarah for an explanation.

"Liches aren't just undead wizards. They're a special class of being. A Lich removes his soul from his corporeal body and stores it in a special container called a phylactery. Even if you destroy the body, the Lich is fine as long as the phylactery is safe. No Lich will bring their phylactery into battle with them. But we don't need to worry about that."

That seemed pretty damn optimistic, and I couldn't help but glare at her. "Why the hell not? Because I feel like a powerful undead who can't be killed is exactly the type of thing we should be worried about, especially one that has a vested interest in destroying us." I paused for a second. "Wait. Do we have its phylactery? We stole a bunch of shit from that treasury. Maybe it was in there."

She just shook her head. "I doubt it. He would have been much more upset. That was just typical undead arrogance. They get uppity because they think of themselves as immortal. If not, though, like I said—no need to worry. Liches are incredibly powerful and dangerous, but they're also limited. They're bound to within a certain radius of their phylactery. Once we get out of this cavern, there's almost no chance it'll be able to follow us to the surface, and even less it could trail us into the forest." She paused. "The ghosts probably could, but they don't do great with sunlight, so it wouldn't be a smart call."

We were interrupted by an explosion of heat rolling over us, and I looked back to see a massive wall of fire filling the cavern. Apparently, the staff *did* work for Cark. Callie was already next to us, and we all slowed down to wait as Cark came barreling across the field, doing his damnedest to escape the horde of ghosts being held off by the firewall.

The original explosion of the Wyvern had chased off a bunch of specters, but apparently, that had been a scouting party or something. Now they were out in force, and some G-ranked spirits among them seemed to be commanding. A few rode ghostly chargers and wore armor, while some were clad in fine silks and fancy noble clothes woven from silvery light. I assumed these were nobles and members of the Grave Lord's court. Luckily, they were shying away from the flames too. We kept looking back for about five or ten minutes, sure not to slow down as they finally broke through the wall.

My view was cut off as we hit the edge of the cavern and entered the tunnel back to the surface. Without having to sneak or look for enemies and without holding back for our H-rankers, we were moving about twelve times faster than we had going in. The odd scout would phase through the wall ahead or next to us and try to attack or slow us down.

I dispersed more than a few with poison fire, and Cark blasted others away, while Sarah slapped them out of existence from Jessie's back. The ghosts that managed to find us were only a threat because the otherworldly wail seemed to signal others, forcing us to change directions a few times. I had to trigger Seek Hidden again to make sure we didn't get lost on the way, and I stumbled as a wave of exhaustion hit me. I was running pretty close to the end of my rope as I approached my charge limit while still weakened.

I was able to find the same ethereal trail in the air as before, and I took the lead, showing the group which direction would take us to the surface without running into any dead ends. A single blockade would have pretty much doomed us, because while we were more than able to handle a few stray ghosts as they came through the walls at us, if they pinned us down, we would have been absolutely screwed. Even with the advantage of fire and holy energy, we couldn't take out a whole army of the things.

In my current condition, flexing the skill was agonizing. Without a doubt, I was going to refrain from using Afterburner so liberally in the future. I honestly couldn't imagine going through this again, and the next time I decided to invoke that skill I would make damn sure it was at the very *end* of an operation, not right in the fucking middle of it. Granted I hadn't known about the Lich attack when I'd used it, so maybe this was just a case of bad luck rather than bad timing, but either way, I needed to be more careful.

I was able to keep my feet, though, and being at the front of the group meant it would be obvious to the others when I was having trouble and they would be able to help me. As we went, we ran into a few groups of H-rank undead of the more physical variety, and Cark used his new staff to steamroll them.

Even the two Dullahans in our path were no match for his new staff, and despite the blockages, we made good time toward the surface. Unfortunately, the tunnels were at a fairly steep incline, which meant Cark couldn't plug them up with firewalls without flooding the tunnels we were in with bursts of heat and smoke that rose from the lower positions. Luckily, our Impact was more than enough to protect us from the sweltering heat.

Finally, we made it up to the ledge we'd viewed the original cavern from. Despite our speed, all the turns and obstacles had made this trip much longer than the return across the cavern floor, but once we got up there, we officially needed that firewall. The open ledge was a killing field for the specters to hit us from, and Cark nearly passed out from the exertion of using his fire to block it off.

Callie sealed the entrance to the labyrinth of hallways with shadows to prevent the heat from making them impassible, and she carried Cark since the rest of the G-rankers were otherwise encumbered. Getting back through the halls was much easier. I was able to drop Seek Hidden because we'd been this way. Plus, there was a trail of undead corpses to follow (though I wasn't sure if 'undead corpses' was an oxymoron or a tautology). Still, we made excellent time despite the turns since we knew the way, and as we broke through the doors of the crypt and into the fresh air of the admittedly still pretty dark field we all breathed a sigh of relief.

It took everything we had to slam the doors shut, and as soon as we did, I heaved with all my might and *shoved* Consecration of Flame into the doors when the others were clear. The metal groaned as fiery energy flooded the two doors, transforming them into mediums to channel my skill. My head swam so much that Martin, who was still on my back, had to hop down and catch me. I could barely move. Not just because of the nearly twenty-three charges I'd used, but because I'd overworked my brain. It was officially done.

Cark, luckily, had rested up during the run and was able to stand again, leaving my girlfriend free to carry me. She scooped me up in a princess carry, giving me a gloating smile. "This is just to pay you back for earlier. Thank you ever so much for carrying me to safety." She batted her eyelashes, and I would have chuckled if I could fucking move.

Then we all took off for the forest. It was daylight outside... somehow, but we needed to get outside of the Omen Star's reach before that would be of value.

As we ran, I looked back over Callie's shoulder to see the doors to the crypt warping and shaking. Even imbued with flame, the ghosts were throwing everything they had at them, but they didn't need to hold long. Cark was carrying Martin, and at top G-rank speed, even our lowest Might score was enough to get us out of the range of the army before it broke through the huge barricade.

There was an unearthly howl as the doors were torn apart and the ghosts poured out, barreling toward us as we slumped down on the ground, exhausted. We didn't even pay attention to the things as they bullrushed the edge of the field then... stopped. They howled and shrieked, but they wouldn't pass into the sunlight of the empty clearing we were sitting in. We blocked them all out, and Callie set me down to rest, lying on my back in pain and exhaustion. We were free, and we had time to take a breath, which was good, because I wasn't going anywhere for a while on my own.

Chapter Twenty-Three

WE DIDN'T ACTUALLY NAP RIGHT THERE in front of the barely restrained army of ghosts. We weren't idiots. We rested for a minute to get some strength back and let Jessie top us all off with life energy. Then we made the trek back to the hatchery, where were we could finally collapse into a nice restful sleep. I couldn't wait for my head to stop throbbing.

Despite it being light out, we'd all been underground so long we had no legitimate clue what time it was. Nothing screwed up your internal clock like delving into an underground city of darkness, and when we all woke up, the sun was just starting to set. Luckily, we were pretty far from the crypt, not to mention specters were apparently wary of auras much like goblins (which was understandable since they were literally spiritual beings), and Zeke's presence acted as a passive deterrent to them trying to come after us.

Even after a rest and a charge-up from Jessie, my head still pounded. I was pretty sure I'd overdone it with my skill manipulation. I couldn't imagine how bad it would be if I'd kept going and actually blacked out from using all my charges. Still, we were back and fully stocked up on new mats, so I just took the time to lie back and decompress. Even with Jessie pumping us full of life energy, there was a mental component to relaxation that just didn't recover without actual rest.

After some time chilling, though, I got bored and decided to go eat… breakfast? Dinner? A meal. Since my cooking skill was the highest, I decided to do the cooking myself, which had the added benefit of meaning I could make whatever I wanted. I checked the storage room (or at least the room of the hatchery where we were keeping our stuff) and was pleased to see Zeke had brought a bunch of food with him… somehow. I assumed he had a spatial artifact somewhere on his person.

Since Zeke had never bothered to learn to cook, he let me take supplies in exchange for labor whenever I made food. It didn't count as helping me because he was directly compensated. I grabbed a big crate of eggs, some ham, a few bell peppers, a block of cheese, as well as a spatula, a skillet, and a knife. Then I headed outside to cook in the twilight. The clearing was big enough that I wasn't worried about animals smelling the food, so I started a fire and got right to prepping.

I found a relatively flat rock and used Boiling Cloud to steam clean it. I was recharged for the day, and I didn't flex it, so it wasn't a strain. Getting the fire going was simple enough. Thanks to my Might, the old stick-rubbing trick was easy with super strength, and I let the flames crackle away as I started chopping.

I diced the peppers, cut the cheese into cubes, and sliced the ham into thin strips before cracking the eggs into the skillet and whisking them with the knife. Once the eggs were all diced up, I dumped the sliced veggies and cheese in and held it over the fire. Instead of rushing it, I held the skillet higher over the flames and just… enjoyed myself. I loved cooking. It always made me feel so at peace. It was nice to enjoy some time to myself and just breathe for a bit.

As much as I loved hanging with my friends and cultivating, it was easy to ignore the slow build of tension and anxiety during the course of my adventures. I got so used to being on edge that it felt like I wasn't on edge at all, at least until I had a minute to slow down and really process what it felt like to relax. That was most of the reason I got overwhelmed—I got so excited fighting, training, and looking for new loot, I didn't even realize I was burning out until I was beyond my limits.

I scraped the eggs off the bottom of the skillet with the spatula and smiled. Times like this were good for me. No one to impress. Nothing to fight. Just me and my ingredients. Scrambled eggs were harder than most people thought. You had to cook them slowly, or half the egg ended up sticking to the bottom of the skillet, especially if you didn't use butter. It was an exercise in patience, but I didn't mind at all. I slowly pushed the cooked egg out of the way, letting the raw take its place as it cooked all the way through, melting cheese and searing ham and pepper alike.

The smell was amazing, and I closed my eyes for a second to soak it in. Perception could be a hell of a gift sometimes. I stayed like that for a few minutes, slowly cooking the eggs by keeping the skillet just far enough off the fire to make the heat weaker. Finally, I finished it, and I carried it inside to the storage room to scoop it all onto a huge platter and then headed up to the raven room. I called everyone on the way, figuring if I was up, everyone else would be too.

I'd made about a dozen eggs. The skillet was pretty large, and there was enough for everyone to have some, albeit not a huge amount. It was mostly just a nice breakfast to help everyone greet the day and give us some time to unwind before planning our next move. The smell of the eggs permeated the whole building, and I laughed as I saw Callie stumble through the door, sleepy and slightly confused.

I'd called for plates and forks when I told everyone about the food, and I couldn't help but smile to see her grasping the plates blearily as she looked around in confusion. She swallowed slightly before croaking, "Food?"

I couldn't take it and dissolved into laughter. I set the skillet on a table and went over to get the plates, prying them from her fingers and leading her to the table so I could make a plate for her. I put the fork on top and pushed it over, wary of her as she began to voraciously devour the eggs.

I made my own plate and started eating while she did, though I ate slower. I wasn't sure if Callie usually woke up too groggy to function or if this was a factor of her exhaustion, but honestly it was kind of adorable. I just enjoyed seeing her come to life as she ate, her eyes clearing and sharpening as she woke up more. Meanwhile, I enjoyed my own eggs immensely. The cheese was perfectly melted and the eggs were incredibly fluffy, a testament to my Cooking Skill rather than any practice or anything.

Once she finished, she sighed and pushed the plate away, leaning over to kiss my cheek. "Thanks, babe. That was delicious, as always." She slumped back in her chair, enjoying the quiet before everyone else showed up.

Callie was always more relaxed when it was just the two of us. The pressure of being in charge was a subtle thing, but as I'd noticed when I woke up, sometimes pressure could mount even when you weren't aware of it. I was glad she felt safe enough with me to relax for at least a little while. It was one of the few ways I could easily help her deal with her role.

As I finished the last bite of delicious eggs, the mouth slit in my mask closed back up, and I pushed my own plate away. "Of course. Glad you liked them. So, what are we doing today? We still have to get those items appraised. Hopefully, Zeke can tell us what they are. No clue how we're going to pay for that, but hey, maybe he'll agree to take one of the objects as payment once he's finished." I figured more than anything, we all needed a day off, and this was a good way for us to take that.

While we were in a time crunch, Callie needed a break even more than the rest of us. Given her love of treasure, I was sure the idea of spending a day identifying and cataloguing the artifacts from the Necropolis would be both fun for her and something that wouldn't weigh too heavily on her desire to push forward. It was a nice middle ground for all of us, given the others probably wouldn't even care enough to be involved.

As I'd expected, she seemed thrilled at the chance to find out what we'd ended up with after raiding the crypt. I knew she was planning to trade at least some of the objects in question to other teams if possible, to try to fill out our own list. Some of them might be too valuable for that to be cost effective, but I was certain there were some passingly useful artifacts in the bunch that could reduce the amount of work we had to do. Especially for the things from the treasury, the chances of some being list items for teams besides ours were pretty high, given the specters' dedication to collecting powerful items.

If they found other objects in their territory like the corpse-eating grass, the treasury was where it would have ended up, and I refused to believe there were so many treasures like that out in the wilderness that they'd found a dozen powerful artifacts and literally none of them were on the lists for the hundreds of other teams out here with us. Callie had made the smart call when she decided to collect the extra stuff with the intention of trading it, because I didn't think I had five or six more raids like the Necropolis in me, and sure as hell not within a single week.

Zeke, who had just come in when he smelled the eggs, dropped into a chair next to the table, scooping some of the eggs onto a plate. "What's this about me and artifacts?"

Callie excitedly filled him in on our idea. He made a pensive noise as he ate, taking a moment to savor the eggs as he chewed and stewed. "Hmmm. That's not… impossible. I'd be willing to identify a few things in exchange for my pick of the resulting artifacts. I get first right of refusal, though. My Identification Skill is substantially higher than anyone else you would find, and as such more valuable."

I rolled my eyes, pointing my fork at him as I countered his point. "I call bullshit. We only need the Skill to be strong enough to identify G-ranked artifacts. Anything beyond that is just pointless excess, and there are plenty of people in Rajak who could do that. It's not like we're paying for prestige either since we aren't going to be telling anyone you were the one who did it. We're getting the same information regardless of who does the job."

He smiled proudly at that and gave me a conciliatory nod. "Fair enough. Fine, first right of refusal with a single veto. That's the best I can do."

I grudgingly agreed.

He smiled. "Now, I'm going to finish the rest of my eggs—great job, by the way—and then we can get started."

With that decided, he lost himself in his food again, and I turned to focus on the bag in the corner that contained our spatial box. Time to finally see what we had on our hands.

Chapter Twenty-Four

DESPITE THE RUSH of excitement Callie and I were feeling, Zeke didn't seem in too big a hurry to start. He took his time clearing the table and putting it away so he could have free space on the floor then had us put the box down on the ground for him to open and sort through.

Despite his power, I couldn't help but issue the same warning we'd been repeating ad nauseum. "Some of that stuff is probably cursed, man. Not that it could probably hurt you much, but still, it's something you might want to take into account."

Zeke, however, just seemed bored by the idea. "Curses are a type of ability, and like all other skills and abilities, they become markedly less viable against an enemy when they're used against someone more than one or two ranks above you. The Impact alone just makes it nearly impossible for them to take effect. They can theoretically lock onto me, but it's the difference between an ant biting a baby or a block of carbon steel. The latter just isn't going to have an effect. Even if there were a thousand G-rank curses in here, they couldn't put a scratch on me."

That made sense, though I wondered if there was a theoretical number of curses you could stack to reach enough power to hurt someone that much higher ranked than you. This wasn't the time for that, though. Zeke's first move was to flip open the backpack and pull out the box, looking it over slowly. His eyes glowed slightly as he stared at the storage device. "Huh, low-grade spatial artifact. G-rank. The low rank is why it's so bulky. You can only fold space so much at the lower ranks. It's why you see lots of spatial expansions on buildings and cars but no rings and pouches on planets like this."

I hadn't considered that, but it did make sense in a weird way. Fantasy worked by altering the world to fit an idea; being able to fit a big pocket of space into a big real space was easier to envision than fitting a building-sized area into a ring. As a layman, I wasn't exactly sure how the process worked, but the idea at least made sense. Having a much higher Fantasy stat would undoubtedly make packing more space into a smaller area easier... if that was how it worked. Hell, maybe that assumption was the entire reason it *was* easier—it wouldn't be the first time weird impressions screwed with reality where cultivation was concerned.

He flipped it open and turned it upside down without any preamble, and I wished we'd had some warning because that shit was *loud*. A cascade of gold coins poured out of the upended box like a tsunami crashing into the seawall of an island fortress. The absolute torrent of shining yellow metal sounded like nothing I'd ever experienced before, and even my Focus couldn't prevent the sound from overwhelming me because of my Perception (probably because the former was so much lower). Callie and I both covered our ears to block out the noise until we saw it finally come to an end.

We glared at Zeke, who just shot us disapproving frowns. "Gold? What are you? Gremlins? Mortal gold is absolutely useless. Why would you fill up fully half of this damn thing with pathetic sparkly soft metal?" He shook his head in disappointment. "You two were mortals *way* too recently. You have to shake your attachment to things that used to be valuable now that you've begun your Ascent. Hoarding is a bad habit to develop when you're low rank."

I rolled my eyes. "Please, you have like hundreds of low-ranked masks lying around. You're telling me you don't keep souvenirs?" I hadn't seen Zeke stocking up on random stuff, but he'd never been the type to get rid of anything that seemed useful. I knew him well enough to be pretty sure he was a packrat, even if I couldn't think of a specific example of the behavior off the top of my head.

That got a genuine bark of laughter. "First off, kid, I *make* those masks. They're part of my powers, and they're intrinsically tied to me. Second of all, I said hoarding is a bad idea at *lower* ranks. Not that you shouldn't get good stuff, but keeping a huge stockpile of valuable goods on you without the strength to back it up is just asking to get robbed, and useless junk just takes up space for no reason. Once you're stronger and have the spatial artifacts to hold it all, you can of course carry as much bullshit as you want. I have more useless cultivation bullshit on my person right now than there are items on this planet."

That made sense. Damn it. "So what? We should only carry a few things on us at once? Do we stash the shit around the planet and come back for it? Put it in a bank? Or are we just supposed to live like monks until we hit D-rank? Because we're going to be collecting a ton of shit during this hunt, and I don't know what the hell you're suggesting we do with it." Even though I knew he was right about the gold, I wasn't planning to leave a bunch of useful artifacts behind.

He just shook his head, sighing in exasperation. "Sell them. No matter how much money you have on you, there's always going to be people richer to rob. Expensive cultivation materials can draw greedy eyes and dastardly plans, but despite being useful, money is by far more ubiquitous in the universe. It's easier to rob some fat store owner than to track down a rare Ascendant material. Any stuff you aren't using to enchant or cultivate, you should sell, at least for the foreseeable future. You never know what crazy asshole might need that exact artifact or material."

Callie, obviously, looked murderous at the idea of having to offload almost all of our loot whenever we got some. I, on the other hand, understood Zeke's point, but I also suspected he might have lost some perspective on exactly what being lower ranked was actually like. Being strong for such a long time would definitely have given him a higher viewpoint than most, but it was easy to look down on a G-ranker. I wasn't entirely sure we were as likely to get robbed as he thought, but I couldn't discount the advice either.

Zeke wasn't perfect, and because of all the crafting I did, giving up materials wasn't ideal unless I knew for sure I could replace them. Seeing we weren't convinced, my uncle just shrugged and moved on. "Anyway, quite a few items in here are worth at least a bit, though obviously nothing I would consider valuable personally. I'll probably just pick whatever is worth the most money as my compensation, though again, you do have a veto if it's something you need."

He started sifting through the gold, smiling fondly at some of the things he was finding. "Been a while since I've seen most of this junk." He picked up the glass box with the hand in it. "Hand of Glory, G-rank, decently useful thieving artifact. Not cursed but generally unpleasant to make." He set it down and picked up the red crystal butterfly. "Heartbeat Monarch. You sync it to someone's heart rhythm, and it lets you keep track of them from a distance. It works pretty much anywhere and is a good way to make sure loved ones are still alive and healthy."

He picked up the black rock rose. "Rotprick Blossom. Naturally releases a decaying poison." The dagger was next. "Spectral Severer. Cuts things that aren't physically there." He paused. "This one is actually interesting. Physical weapons that affect the immaterial without needing skills or elemental affinities are kind of rare." Setting the dagger to the side, he gave me a contemplative look. "I'll put a pin in that one, actually. None of this is useful to me, but that's a neat gimmick at least."

Shaking off his interest, he got back to identifying things. He picked up the pair of earrings. "Okay, now *this* is cursed. Makes you unable to read social context and perceive threats to your safety outside of direct attacks. That *is* nasty." Rather than worried, he sounded interested, and eventually, he slipped them in his pocket. "Haven't seen a foe-blinding curse this low rank before that still functions. The design is pretty economical. Most curses are stat hogs that limp in with *way* too much Fantasy to offset bad design fundamentals. I'm keeping these, unless you want to veto it?"

Neither of us did.

He smiled and got back to work. He picked up the hourglass, frowning at it for a minute. "This one is *very* interesting. Peak G-rank. When you flip over the hourglass, it starts a minor time loop that resets as soon as all the sand hits the bottom. So, probably five or ten minutes. Only usable once. May not seem useful since you have to actually activate it first, but it's pretty amazing for delicate operations that require you to guess something. Won't be much use to anyone more than a rank or two over G since it'll burn out faster under higher Impact, but I'd hang onto this one. Never know when a do-over will come in handy. Just don't tell anyone else what it can do, and you should be fine."

We both gaped at the object, shocked by the sheer power it held, but when he pointed out exactly how limited it was, we calmed down. Luckily, intent was required to trigger it, so just flipping it over did nothing. I was able to check the exact time on it that way, and it only turned out to be ten minutes or so, which also somewhat lowered the value. The last two artifacts were the small wooden hammer and the cane, and Zeke picked up the hammer first. "Judgement Gavel. Reinflicts every healed wound from the last hour. Also single use, but nasty in the right context."

He finally picked up the cane. "This one is a beauty. Kinetic cane. No death affinity despite the morbid theme. Basically, the whole thing is designed to charge off kinetic strikes and energy. Once it's full, the rubies in the eyes glow, and you can discharge it in one swing on the next attack. It's pretty much peak G-rank in terms of composition, so it can hold a *lot* of force, but it'll take a monstrous amount of time to charge based on the amount of force leached with each hit."

That *was* cool. It reminded me of my tonfas, but better in some ways. It wasn't enchanted to increase force, but I had skills for that, and it was a flat upgrade in terms of durability. Plus, it would give me a legitimate ace in the hole if I ran into something really scary in the future. I held out my hand, taking the thing from him and twirling it between my fingers, liking the balance. I might have been due for an upgrade at this point. I would be F-rank soon enough, and my own Enchanting Skill wasn't good enough to keep up.

With all the treasures identified, Zeke flipped the box lid closed. "Anyway, we're done here. I'm taking the earrings if you don't want them. You can decide what to do with everything else. Also not cleaning this gold up. Sorry not sorry."

He turned and dashed from the room, leaving us both scowling at his retreating form. I knew he was fast enough to vanish entirely if he wanted, so he was clearly messing with us. I snorted and shook my head, turning to Callie and holding up the cane with a smile. I wondered if I could get sole ownership of it for a wish.

Chapter Twenty-Five

IT TOOK ABOUT forty minutes to pack all the gold and artifacts back into the box and return it to the bag. I debated keeping the cane out for myself, but since it was communal, I could probably use it as payment for a wish, so I decided to wait. Once we had everything set up, Callie and I walked over to sit on the edge of the open top floor of the hatchery, staring out into the forest. It was still dark out, we'd come back midafternoon and slept for hours, putting us firmly in the middle of the night at the moment, and it was absolutely breathtaking looking up at the stars out here.

This view wasn't the same as the one from our first night here, because not only could we see the night sky, but the forest out into the distance below it. The whole thing, heaven and earth, had a sort of serene balance to it that just eased my heart. I put an arm around my girlfriend, and she laid her head on my shoulder as we watched the night. We even saw a shooting star, and I took the opportunity to make a silent wish to get more nights like this with her. The silliness of wishing on a star when I could literally grant magical wishes wasn't lost on me, but my power didn't work for me so honestly it was probably the best I would ever be able to do.

We sat together like that for a while, just relaxing, but eventually, I decided to be the one to break the ice and mention the hunt. I knew Callie well enough to know it was on her mind anyway. She was just avoiding being the one to broach the topic because she knew I wanted to rest. That said, talking didn't mean we needed to go out and hunt down materials, and forcing her to avoid the topic while she was dwelling on it would have the opposite effect of helping her relax. Better to talk out our next steps so we could move on with our day off. "So, what do you want to do next?"

I felt her shoulders slump and had to stifle a chuckle. Sure enough, she'd been focused on our next move and had just been holding back so as not to ruin the evening. Her slight sigh of relief made me even more sure of my choice to mention it.

"I say our next move should be to scour the internet for local searches for Ascendant materials," she said. "If we can track down some other teams who have been looking for any of the things we just found, we can fill out our own list without having to go on a bunch more raids. I doubt we can completely avoid moving out again, but if we play this smart, we can put a serious dent in our list without having to do any more fighting too soon."

I'd assumed that was the direction she was leaning, and honestly, I appreciated it. I wasn't the only person who felt burned out after the mess in the Necropolis. The others needed some downtime, too, and this was a good way to make progress. "Sounds like a plan. Do you have any leads so far? I have zero idea how to hack anything so I don't know what the timeframe or effort needed for that is. Speaking of, when did you learn hacking, anyway? It seems like something you would have needed to spend a lot of time on."

Callie sat up, chuckling to herself. "Oh, I'm not a hacker. I just use a bunch of premade programs and tools to accomplish certain tasks. The types of message boards that freshmen at the Academy have access to aren't particularly well defended, so I can get away with it, especially with Batty's ring. It doesn't take long, but I don't have any leads so far. We just found out what everything is, and I didn't recognize any of the names from the brief look-over I gave my information. Nothing from our own list, obviously, but we'll need to feel things out to see if anyone else needs any of it."

She seemed unsure, and I gave her a confident smile. Our masks sat off to one side as we cuddled. "Hey, don't worry so much. There can't be an infinite number of Ascendant materials out here. The chances that one of those items is on someone's list is crazy high." I decided dwelling on this wasn't conducive to relaxing after all, so I decided to change the subject. "What about our training? We can do some Balam lessons later tonight. The geas shouldn't be pressuring you since I have the forms down and just need to practice them, but it's still something we can do together."

She raised an eyebrow at me. "Only one or two dates in, and you're already going for 'let's wrestle,' huh? I'll have you know I'm not that kind of martial artist." She gave me a teasing grin, but it faded into a solemn expression. "But seriously. If you want direct training, you need to master the forms first. Half the benefit of Balam is its adaptability. If you try to spar with me without establishing your own style first, you're going to adopt my habits. The forms are a guide to help maximize the individuality of your combat technique."

I could tell from her serious expression that she meant every word of it. She was worried about training me incorrectly and giving me bad habits. I gave her a reassuring smile. "Okay, no problem. I'll put in the work. We can train later." I leaned in to give her a slow kiss. "I prefer spending time with you relaxing anyway. We don't always have to be fighting or training, and yes, I realize how absurd that is coming from me. Despite how much fun it is, I think we both spend a little too much time focused on cultivation."

She just chuckled, snuggling back against me. "You're not wrong." She frowned, her face taking on a pensive cast. "I know I tend to hyperfocus. I spent such a long time wanting to prove myself, to show everyone I could be strong on my own despite who my father was. I know, intellectually, that it doesn't matter, that I should be comfortable just enjoying my life, but some part of me still feels like when people look at me and see how strong I am, they give him the credit, and I absolutely hate it. I feel like I'll never get out of his shadow."

If my dad ever did anything I approved of, it was not telling me about his cultivation. Seeing Callie so distressed after years of both she and everyone else comparing her to her father, I could only be glad I didn't have that same drive. Not that I didn't want to get strong, but despite wanting to ask my dad some very pointed questions, I wasn't driven by the need to surpass him. I was fully confident it would happen eventually, but it wasn't a priority for me. Not like it was for Callie.

I gave her a reassuring squeeze. "I get it. But you're on a whole different track than he is now. We're going to keep getting stronger and leave this planet behind, and in another few years, you're going to have completely eclipsed him. This isn't me doing the boyfriend thing and saying, 'Oh, you're going to be better than he could ever be.' At this point, given the team we have and the effort you're putting in, this is basically objective fact. Your father is a nonentity to you at this point. The rest of the planet just hasn't figured that out yet."

She grinned viciously. "In some ways, that's even better. I kind of want to leave before it becomes obvious. I want to be long gone and let stories about me spread back here, so he can only sit around and seethe about being known as Nightstrike's father and nothing else. He spent decades crafting his reputation, and being forced to acknowledge that I'd done more for it just by existing is going to drive him crazy. Especially given I've made my disdain for him well-known, so it's not like he's going to get the credit for it."

That got a laugh out of me. "See. So despite how it feels, it's okay to take breaks. To let yourself recharge. You're not just a hero. You're a person, and it's okay to enjoy that. I've been getting as caught up in all this as you, but I feel like if we just live for getting stronger, then what are we getting stronger for? Protecting people we love and helping them accomplish goals is good, but we need to have lives, too, or what the hell is the point of living for such a long time? If we never ranked up again, we would both still live for almost a thousand years."

While Impact slowed aging, Vitality kept you at perfect health for that age. In nine hundred sixty years, I would be the physical equivalent of a hundred year old, but I would be the healthiest damn hundred-year-old imaginable. It didn't expand the lifespan as much as make living to the absolute maximum possible, but still, even independent of the Impact mechanic, most Ascendants could live to the anatomical age of a hundred to a hundred twenty before dying of old age, and quality of life before that happened was pretty damn good too.

But all that lifespan meant nothing if I just used it to grind away. I'd been too focused on the part of my future plans where I got stronger and had access to more places, and I'd overlooked that in order to actually enjoy being a powerful explorer who went out and saw things, I had to enjoy actually *seeing* them. Living for some hypothetical future adventure that would be better than all the others was a stupid way to do things. I needed to enjoy the ones I was already having just as much, and that meant savoring moments like this.

Callie wasn't exactly working on the same life plan as me, but I could tell she wanted to slow down a bit too. Now that she didn't need to worry about surpassing her dad, she was trying to live in the present more. I wanted to help her with that as much as I could. Hell, all of our friends could probably use more of that. We were all either looking forward or looking back, and I was pretty sure it wasn't good for anyone not to be able to live in the now.

In some ways, I'd overcorrected for my past aimlessness. I needed to find a middle ground between living with zero idea of what I wanted to do and focusing constantly on my future goals. The past and the future were important, but not as important as the present. I made a decision, standing up and stretching.

I pulled Callie to her feet. "Let's go swimming."

She raised a questioning eyebrow at me.

I laughed. "There's a creek over there we've been completely ignoring. Just staring at it for no reason. Let's get everyone together and go for a swim in the moonlight."

She giggled at my ridiculousness. "I'm pretty sure deciding to just have a life isn't something you can rush. But I'm game, I guess. I haven't been for a swim in ages. I'll go get the others."

She leaned up to give me a quick kiss and headed down to talk to the rest of the team. She didn't wear her mask, but honestly, I approved of that. I wasn't going to wear mine either. Living in the now meant appreciating our friends. Everyone here had earned my trust after all we'd been through. Solomon had been through a lot with these people. Now I felt like I could introduce them to Shane.

Chapter Twenty-Six

THE SWIM WAS RELAXING and fun, of course. I'd always loved swimming, and despite not having been in the water like that for years, I took to it quickly. Still, it didn't last forever, and after we all finished our swim, we spent the rest of the evening just chilling out and talking, learning more about each other and introducing ourselves to everyone else sans masks for the first time since we'd met them.

In the end, we realized we still needed to actually work, so Callie got back into looking around for someone who needed what we had. She was poring over her screen with interest, scanning through documents, when she finally froze then let out a whoop of joy.

"Yes! We got something. Someone has been running searches on that stupid red crystal butterfly, and they even searched it by name. Unless they have an appraiser and found another one, the only reason I could think of for that to happen would be if it was on their list."

That was actually kind of disappointing. I thought the butterfly was kind of cool, and being able to link it to a loved one and always know they were all right was kind of sweet. Still it was admittedly rather limited. Though the fact that it worked from anywhere was a dimension of power that explained why it was G-rank. Being able to maintain its effect across the whole universe was pretty crazy, even if that effect was mainly sentimental in nature.

I leaned over her shoulder to try to read the details, but she smacked me away with a glare. "I keep telling you not to do that. It drives me nuts when people read over my shoulder."

I stuck my tongue out at her childishly, which turned her glare into a smirk she had to actively suppress, but she shook off her amusement and annoyance and focused on the details again. "Anyway, the information here implies someone nearby is looking for what we have, and hopefully, they have something we need to trade for it."

I took a step back, trying to stand up on my toes to read over her shoulder from farther away, which got me a sharp glance but no actual comment from my girlfriend. "Okay, but does it say where they actually are? We won't be able to trade with them if we can't find them. Also we need to do some recon on the group in question before we make contact. If they're too much stronger they're more likely to fight it out and try to rob us. While peaceful cooperation isn't prohibited here, it *is* way less attractive than being a greedy bastard and just taking everything."

Callie shrugged. "It's a false dichotomy. That option is always available no matter where you are. Anyone you meet could decide to rob you blind, as Zeke so generously reminded us. The question here is whether people will get backed into a mental corner by the hunt. The Academy specifically framed the interaction here to be combative, but the fact is that we don't *have* to fight each other. Alliances and cooperation are a viable option, unless someone makes them *un*viable by refusing to acknowledge them."

I could see her point. The Academy wanted us to compete to sharpen us, but I was sure we would be just as heavily rewarded for finding other solutions. Cultivators had a very "ends justify the means" sort of mindset, but that sort of made it easy to hyperfocus on violence. We spent so much time gaining power that *using* that power in a way that made us gain more became as natural as breathing. Some of that was recursion for sure, but some of it was just the human tendency to take the path of least resistance.

Not that I thought we could revolutionize cultivator society or some nonsense. But knowing the problem made it easy to look out for it in ourselves and others. Falling into the trap of always resorting to brute force might seem like the best way to approach every problem given all the attention it got us, but achieving results was its own form of advertising. Making ourselves more well-rounded and policing our cultivator instincts to just blow shit up when it made us angry was likely to yield positive results long-term.

Not to mention gaining a reputation for that kind of deliberation and foresight would have recursive benefits for the way we thought in the first place, forming a virtuous cycle. "You have me convinced. I'm sure you'll talk the people we need to work with into avoiding violence, too, but the fact remains—we have no idea whether they have what we need, and you still haven't said if you know where they are."

She grinned at me, gesturing out the opening in the side of the building where the ravens would exit. "We have the best possible recon specialist, and as for where they are, I do have a heading. Granted, it's hard to know exactly how far they are with only two points of data to rely on, but I can at least estimate distance. Jessie will be able to reach them with her ravens, and we can feel out their response to a peaceful trade."

I hoped Callie's plan worked out. Granted I would kick some ass if it was necessary, and I did like battle. But I was burnt out on the normal combat grind—which actually gave me an idea. "You think we could tip the balance on either of those things in our favor? I've been wanting to experiment with my Wish ability more, and we saw from the siege that we can do more than just directly affect things. Can you think of any ways we might be able to use that?"

I could, a few of them, but I knew that if I gave her the ideas for the wishes, they wouldn't be viable. She needed to come up with them on her own, though I could steer her in the right direction if she couldn't think of anything after a bit of time. I wasn't sure that just telling her the answer would make the wish invalid, but since I wanted this to work for my own sake, too, it seemed safer to let her come to her own conclusions. Honestly there was a decent chance she would come up with a better idea than I could anyway.

Callie was, of course, more than up to the challenge and immediately got to work considering the issue. Rather than jump the gun, she decided to talk out her decision aloud, which was fine as long as I didn't try to tweak the wish to benefit me more. "There are a few ways to do that. Wishing for them to be more open to negotiation seems... wrong. Aside from mind control like that being a slippery slope, I doubt a wish like that would be cheap anyway. I was okay wishing for the sleepers to be pushed a specific direction, but they were already being controlled."

I felt the same way. "Agreed. I don't like the mind-control thing. It reminds me too much of the Black Sorrow Cult. People's brains belong to them, and I don't like monkeying with that." Just because I could do something didn't mean I should. The versatile nature of my Wish ability was a responsibility as well as a benefit. That was presumably why my power always gave me the choice to grant a wish or not. If someone tried to wish for something awful, I was free to decline the request.

Callie didn't look finished, though. "That said, there are other options. We know that Wishes can play with probability, but what about things like Quantum Uncertainty. If we assume that the group closest to us will find something new soon, we can leverage the fact that no one knows what that is. Considering the Wish ability and how it interacts with secrets, I bet shifting undiscovered materials out for other more useful ones would be way less expensive than any changes to something that had already been found."

I blinked. I could follow the logic on that. It was like looking in a box. Once you checked the box you knew what was in it, but until you opened it, hypothetically, anything could be in the box. Callie was guessing that it would be cheaper to wish for something specific to be in the box than to change the object you already knew was there. It was actually brilliant, considering how attention and belief interacted with stats. Like she'd said, the whole secrets thing proved that my wishes were heavily impacted by perception, whether public or personal.

It also explained the luck thing. Good luck was notoriously fickle. No one had any reason to believe they would specifically have good luck at any given time; we'd mostly been conditioned to think of it as completely random. That impression most likely helped leverage my power more efficiently without the need to fight back against an entrenched mindset that something couldn't happen. Once again, I found myself in awe of the original Wishmaster.

As far as I knew, the Unity didn't exist yet when the original Wishmaster created the ability. And that made it all the more impressive. Since ability-based cultivation was a relatively new thing, the Wishmaster was most likely using the job system or something similar when he created the skillset I was using. Then he'd brought it up to a high enough level to become a bloodline. It was a crazy thought that made me wonder exactly how many skills had gone into the Wish ability and exactly how long it had taken to get them all, synergize them, and continue to improve them all together until he reached S-rank with the result.

Callie worried at her lip for a minute as she collected her thoughts. She had the idea, but she wanted to make sure she optimized her wish based on what we knew about my powers—things like conceptual resistance (the name I'd just made up for the fact that widespread belief made some actions inefficient) and the potential benefits versus costs of making vague wishes that my power had to compensate for. The Balam wish had turned out well, but it had also cost a *lot*. We were pretty sure that was because of all the heavy lifting my power had to do.

Finally, she seemed to settle on her exact wording, speaking carefully and slowly as if deliberating even as she voiced the wish on how to structure it best. "I wish that nearby group that needs the Heartbeat Monarch will stumble on something from our list as their next find." She seemed to be considering making it more specific or adding conditions, but eventually, she just nodded. She smirked and reached into the box. "In payment, I offer you sole ownership of this cane as the leader of the team that found it."

I grinned. I felt the rising static across the surface of my body as the words rolled across my vision in purple flaming letters.

Wish detected. Grant wish?

I confirmed.

Stat points sufficient. Requirements: 36 Impact, 63 Fantasy, 150 Might, 96 Creation.

Since it didn't say "compensation required," I assumed that the cane was enough to pay it off, and I immediately confirmed again. The static charge built through me before finally exploding out, dissolving into the ether. I slumped down into a chair. Now we just had to wait and let Jessie's ravens do the work.

Chapter Twenty-Seven

BETWEEN THE RAVENS and Callie's ability to track their scan ring, we were able to get eyes on the new group we wanted to trade with pretty quickly. As before, Jessie was able to describe them to us when she found them. Celine knew exactly who they are. Her noble Job clearly gave her an advantage in statecraft and cultivating sources that the rest of us just couldn't measure up to. Jessie, eyes glowing with life energy, was happy to pass on the information on this new team to our main information specialist, and I had to note yet again how useful this building was in conjunction with her ability.

Jessie was facing out into the night air, a habit she had developed when she sent out her ravens, despite being able to see through their eyes regardless of what direction she faced. Her brow furrowed, she focused on a target none of us could see. "The group Callie asked me to target is six people. Four men and two women. They're all dressed in dark serviceable combat gear, and they're fighting much more in sync than most of the teams I've seen in action. They're fighting a horde of goblins right now, and the group seems to be mowing through them with superior tactics more than brute force."

That meant they were probably H-rankers for the most part, which meant we had a much better chance of interacting with them peacefully. Back-stabbing was pretty unlikely from anyone with one sixth of our impact, regardless of what kind of training they were employing. Even if they were hyperfocused on one stat and had a series of stacking skills that made them strong enough to punch up ranks, Callie and Cark were both pretty damn powerful. My Might was no joke either. Not that I expected it to come to that.

We all turned to Celine. She looked as impassive as always.

"That's probably Raleigh's Raiders. They're a school club offshoot of a much larger mercenary company with postings all over the planet. They tend to be on the weaker side due to renown dilution from sharing the spotlight, but it is a consistent way to gain stats over time through accumulation. It has more in common with the way people cultivate in the Empire as a social class than individual training, but it works."

Jessie nodded slowly. "I could see that. They move like an army. The goblins have them massively outnumbered, but they're just dismantling them in the most efficient way possible. Two of them seem to be staying out of it, though. I think they're G-rankers. I guess they're letting the others get some training in on weaker enemies. Still, it's impressive how in tune they are. They must have trained really hard to get this good. Do you want me to make a map to where they are right now?"

Callie shook her head. "No. We're waiting for them to find their next material. I want to check something." She gave me an excited smile, which I returned. Callie enjoyed researching my power as much as I did, and we were both eager to see the result of this wish. If it worked the way we thought, we would be able to completely change the way we went about the rest of the hunt. She returned her gaze to Jessie. "Just stick to them for now and keep us updated on what they do. We can move in once we know they've found something we can use."

Surprisingly, Cark interjected, despite usually staying out of plans. "I've seen Raleigh's Raiders work, by the way. You're going to want to keep your distance, bird or not. They train their people to notice every detail, so don't get too close. Their Perception may not be very high, but they'll definitely be cranking it to the max."

Jessie nodded and got back to focusing on her recon.

Cark turned to Callie. "I can go with you guys to make contact if you want. I have a bit of a rep in bounty hunter circles in my area, and the Raiders have worked in my neighborhood before."

It sometimes slipped my mind that Cark was this badass bounty hunter who'd managed to hit G-rank with zero support from any larger organization. It hadn't come up out here, but I could see how it would probably come in handy now.

Callie gave a grateful nod. "Of course, we'd appreciate that. Anything to stack the deck in our favor. Every object on the list we don't have to fight for is time we save for the harder things we can't find to trade."

Cark didn't seem to take it to heart, he felt he owed us more than he could pay back, and this was apparently the least he felt he could do. Still, I would remember this and try to help him out in the future too. Even when we'd saved his sister, he'd gone out of his way to stay and help us instead of just taking off—he was good people.

Speaking of his sister, I looked around quizzically. "Where is Cass, by the way? I haven't seen her at all today." Granted, it was nighttime, but I hadn't actually seen her in a while.

He just snickered. "Asleep. She went out exploring in the forest today. Apparently, Zeke's protection extends past the building, and she wanted to go look around. Since she's safer with him than she would be in a literal bomb shelter made of the most durable metal on this whole planet, I didn't see a reason to stop her, despite your uncle's pleading gaze. Poor bastard. Better him than me, though. I love my sister, but she can be a menace when you let her run amok."

The thought of a small child forcing Zeke to follow her around the woods and protect her from literally everything was admittedly hilarious. Still, I couldn't imagine Zeke agreeing if he didn't want to go. He'd promised to protect Cass, but that didn't mean he had to obey her every whim. He could have locked her in a room or something. It would have been a dick move, given her recent imprisonment, but it was on the table. Clearly, he thought she needed to get out and do stuff and wasn't willing to prevent something that might make her feel better.

Cark seemed to get this too, and despite the teasing mockery in his tone, I could easily see the gratitude in his eyes. Zeke was actively doing his best to help Cassidy get over her imprisonment.

I hesitated a bit before asking. "How is she doing? Really, I mean. I know she's been acting like she doesn't care, but she can't possibly be as unaffected as she's been trying to let on. Does she need anything?" I felt responsible for Cass, given my part in rescuing her, but more than that, I *liked* the little girl. She was fun and had an attitude, and she gave everyone in the group something to focus on.

He just sighed. "She's been… inconsistent. Sometimes, she seems fine. Sometimes, she forgets and gets a bit quiet. The worst is at night. The dreams have been pretty bad. She won't talk about them, but she cries in her sleep all the time. It's getting better, though. I think being out here is helping. It's markedly different from home, where she was taken from, or the place they held her. The new environment is giving her something to focus on other than what happened."

That was good. She would probably need therapy in the long run, but if avoiding the places that made her feel unsafe was helping, I was glad. If it had been necessary, we could have sent her back. Having Cark around was damn useful, but his sister's mental health was more important. "Is there anything I can do for her that might help? Some kind of food or something she likes? I can try to track down ingredients." I'd been spending too much time with my girlfriend, because the only thing I could think of to try to cheer Cass up was to feed her.

The question got a genuine laugh of surprise out of my teammate. "She never turns down free food. If you want to make her something, she would like pancakes. That would be the easiest. She eats them every time she gets sick. She puts strawberry jelly on them instead of syrup. I can promise as long as you don't burn them, she'd love whatever kind of pancakes you make."

I smiled at that and decided to check the pantry for relevant ingredients. I was pretty sure Zeke had brought more than what was lying around in there, and I could probably convince him to hand the stuff over if I cooked for him, too.

Seeing that I was putting thought into this, Cark smiled, clapping me on the shoulder. "Thanks, Shane, really. It means a lot that you've all been here helping with this." He laughed ruefully. "I stayed to help you out and pay back some of the debt I owe you, but I ended up owing even more. Not just you—Jessie has been spending tons of time with Cass when she can. That girl is a ray of sunshine, and even my sarcastic brat of a sister can't stay upset around her. She's been helping keep Cass's mind off everything. Benny has been spending time with her whenever possible too. Plus Callie is basically her hero. Your girlfriend has made quite the impression."

I grinned widely. "You're a friend. You don't owe us anything. But yeah, Callie tends to do that. Back in Velan, Nightstrike was a household name. Callie is the real deal—no doubt about it. Even I was a fan before we met. I'm glad everyone is helping out. Benny spent lots of time with his little sister growing up, so he's pretty good with kids, and like you said, Jessie is just the sweetest person ever. Cass is going to be okay. We made sure there were no side effects, and other than that, this is something she needs to work through, even if that takes a while."

While it would be theoretically possible to just wipe her memory of it ever happening, I thought that would be a mistake. Losing weeks of your life as a child would be massively unnerving. It would have a profound effect on her, and I still felt uncomfortable messing with the brains of people who didn't knowingly consent. Cass was nine years old—she absolutely wasn't capable of making long-term decisions about wiping her own memories.

If she came to me when she was older and wished to get rid of the memories, I would be fine helping her out, but for now, helping her work through things naturally seemed like the right thing to do. I was pretty sure Cark was of the same opinion, because he hadn't even brought up a memory wipe. My team would be there for both of them as best we could be, and hopefully, she would get through this okay.

Our conversation was cut off as Jessie made an excited sound. "Guys!"

Everyone turned to look at our healer, who was grinning ear to ear.

"They just found something. Some kind of glowing gold mushroom." She raced over to snatch the list from Callie. "I don't know much about this identification stuff, but I'm almost positive that this thing is a Midas Toadstool! We hit the jackpot!"

I gave Callie a wide grin of triumph as that sunk in. I'd known the Wish would work (they always did) but it was still amazing to see it come through. We had a way forward, and it was a good one.

Chapter Twenty-Eight

THE TRIP TO meet Raleigh's Raiders was *not* a fast one, for several reasons. Firstly, we were now a few days into the hunt, which meant people would have finished their base prep and started making their way out to start scavenging. We'd done some scouting of our own already, but assuming that Jessie's ravens were foolproof was a good way to get knocked out of this thing early. We were taking our time with the trip, keeping our eyes peeled for enemies we hadn't spotted or that the ravens couldn't detect.

We were also moving slowly because there were still *lots* of useful materials and artifacts scattered around here.

"So, we've been seeing lots of interesting items that aren't simple materials," I said to Celine as we walked, "things that seem like they were made by Enchanters. Like this." I held up my cane, indicating the obvious rune carvings spiraling across the dark wood surface.

Unsurprisingly, Celine knew her business. "Artifacts are seeded in the area when needed, though in the case of the Necropolis, that wasn't necessary. The corpses harvested by the Lich in his attempt to build his army allowed for a great variety of useful items to accumulate in this area, I'd imagine. In less impressive or occupied biomes, you might see some artifacts donated by alumni of the Academy or flawed products produced by Enchanters that didn't manage to reach the grade they were aiming for. Nothing broken or useless, just subpar products that should be better."

That seemed like a decent way to do things, but her explanation was so thorough, I'd finally decided to just come out and ask something I'd been wondering for ages. "Okay, how do you know so much? Like, I get you're a noble and you have Skills for making spy networks or finding sources or whatever, but you seem to have the answer to every question. I can understand knowing who everyone is—keeping track of the promising freshman makes sense—but how do you know so much about the hunt itself?"

She just gave me a flat look. "While I do indeed possess a gift for acquiring intelligence, I'm afraid you're going to be disappointed in this particular answer." She reached into her backpack and pulled out a slim book. "I went to the library on campus and asked them for a rulebook. Didn't you bother to check if there was official literature pertaining to the rules and content of the event?" Despite her normal flat expression and calm tone, I could swear I saw a glint of smug mockery in her eyes.

I froze then turned to look at Callie, who looked just as poleaxed as I did. We had not, in fact, checked to see if there was an accessible source of information about the hunt, which, in retrospect, was... really dumb. This was a school-sanctioned event, and it was common sense there would be a rulebook somewhere. "If there are official rules, then why did that guy at the beginning bother to give us his whole 'you might die here, nerds' speech? Why not just send us off into the forest and assume we knew what was up."

Celine just shrugged. "They don't announce the rulebooks. Most people don't bother to check, so they treat it as a sort of pretest. There are all sorts of helpful tips and bits of information in these, and they give anyone intelligent enough to bother looking for them a strong advantage."

Once again, despite her tone and expression being entirely even, I got the distinct impression she was mocking me. I briefly wondered if that was one of her noble Skills. The ability to make someone feel like an idiot could be pretty powerful in the right circumstances... though I also might just be projecting.

The rest of the trip to where the Raiders were was pretty relaxed. We didn't run into any monsters, though Jessie did send her raven out a few more times to double-check. Apparently, the goblins were close, but so many G-rankers together was too rich for their blood. Since the goblins had attacked the Raiders, either they were comfortable with one or two higher ranked foes if the odds were stacked enough, or the Raiders had some way of hiding themselves from them even more effective than Zeke's ability. I doubted it was the latter personally, so we had Jessie keep an eye out for a huge goblin army just in case.

Unfortunately, we didn't run into any materials on the way there, but that had been a pipe dream. Still, by the time we made it to where the Raiders were camped for the night (the necropolis had really messed up our sleep schedules), we had managed to get some concrete details on how their base was set up so we could plan our approach ahead of time.

The Raiders were using a mobile base system, which made a lot of sense for a group of H-rankers with only two G-rank members. We'd had the room for supplies to make the hatchery and could have easily brought along a campsite ourselves, though it would have been less stable. Despite not being ideal for us though, not staying in one place for too long was a good way for a weaker group to avoid raids.

Once we got close enough, we sent Cark out to talk to them. We'd decided his immense Might stat, combined with being known to the organization, made him the most sensible decision. He had the same twelve Impact protecting him, but if things went south, he was better able to mount a quick and brutal defense that would probably scare the Raiders out of continuing their attack.

Not to mention Cark carried the staff we'd found in the necropolis. The weapon's blue glow was oddly different after a few uses from the pyrokinetic. The previously ghostly blue of the staff had begun to slowly leach to something more energetic, closer to the vital blue of Cark's own powerful flames. While the improved connection didn't seem to have increased the yield of his flames, it certainly looked like it helped him to better control what he was able to conjure, the focus acting as powerful helper in micromanaging the fire.

In fact, he'd been training with it extensively, even using it to put on a fire manipulation show in the clearing when we were all swimming, much to the delight of his sister. The bounty hunter seemed to delight in creating realistic and intricate shapes and movements in the flames to entertain everyone, and it had been a really nice moment of relaxation that truly encapsulated my desire to try to live my life and enjoy the power I was accruing even as I accrued it in the first place.

The staff would allow Cark to not only react immediately to an attack, but also control that reaction delicately enough not to accidentally turn the rival H-rankers to charred meat. We were trying to avoid harming any of the other contestants unless they tried to hurt us first and were strong enough to force the issue. None of us had any stomach for killing, and we all still deeply regretted the loss of the two sleepers who had been killed in the siege. The last thing we wanted was more bodies on our consciences.

Some of the people in this test might not give us that option, but I really hoped we didn't meet anyone who pushed the issue.

Cass wasn't the only person having nightmares. My dreams hadn't been peaceful lately either. The sight of those eight G-rankers having their heads blown up still stuck with me. I'd been through lots of crazy shit since getting my ability, but most of it was... surreal. The trauma was easier to handle because it was almost like a fever dream. That had been shockingly real and horrible, and I'd had to bury it immediately to even keep functioning.

Giving us all a cheerful nod, Cark headed out of the tree cover and towards the camp, hands raised and ready to stop immediately if they called for it. He was doing everything he could to make sure he didn't seem threatening, and though he had the staff out, it mostly just looked like a stick, so hopefully they wouldn't be too focused on it. It was still glowing, which kind of drew the eye, but Cark was a big guy, so maybe that would be enough to keep them from caring too much.

I had to say, his relaxed demeanor as he approached probably helped quite a bit. Cark was able to stroll into the clearing with confidence without coming off as aggressive at all. It was a kind of niche vibe that said, "I could kill all of you if I wanted to, but luckily, I don't, so let's be pals." I tried to memorize how he was doing it for later, because I didn't think I had that kind of swagger in me, and damned if it probably wouldn't be useful at some point. The whole fake-it-till-you-make-it thing was a big part of my strategy for interacting with other people as an Ascendant.

Raleigh's Raiders, as it turned out, were every bit as careful and attentive as Cark had mentioned. They were already waiting when he walked out of the woods, and despite noting the staff, they seemed to sense Cark wasn't someone they wanted to engage with. Though they were clearly concerned about him, they didn't try to make the first move, watching him like a hawk but not drawing or leveling a weapon as he came closer, despite how reasonable that might have been.

It occurred to me that if they sensed him, they could easily have some means of detecting *us* too. We hadn't used stealth on our way in, specifically because we wanted them to know someone was coming, though also because plenty of our number didn't actually have the Skill. If they knew we were here, it would make even more sense that they hadn't tried to turn this into a throwdown. Not only did we outnumber them outright, we had their number of G-rankers beat more than twice over. Still, it showed they were smart enough to listen, which was a good sign for Callie's planned trade.

Cark was smiling amicably as he came within range of the fire in their camp, his features illuminated by the dancing flames. "Hello the camp!" He paused and then snickered. "Sorry, I've always wanted to say that. Hey there, my name is Cark. I'm a bounty hunter from one of the megaplexes that was brought on by one of the Academy teams as a contractor. I actually know your organization. I worked with Flegmann's team a time or two. I come in peace—we all do. We were just hoping to talk to you about a mutually beneficial trade."

Despite the tension, they seemed to calm down at his words. I didn't know if it was because they knew of him or because they assumed a force that was as superior to theirs as ours wouldn't need to bother with tricks or subterfuge (which was both fair and accurate), but they relaxed marginally.

The leader, a tall somber man with a red mohawk, gave a slow nod. "Well, if you're just here to talk, then I don't see a reason not to welcome you. Please invite your friends out of the trees to sit by our fire. It sounds like we have quite a bit to discuss."

Chapter Twenty-Nine

RALEIGH'S RAIDERS WERE LESS... military than I'd expected. Given the theme and vibe that the others had described, I was expecting uber-serious soldier-of-fortune types, but everyone was actually really laid back. Red mohawk guy, whose name was Chester, was the leader and one of their G-rankers. He sat us all down and got us drinks, and within a minute or two, he was talking to Cark like an old friend. The others were mostly friendly too.

The other G-ranker, Olivia, was a tiny blonde girl with a tight ponytail and a severe expression. She seemed less trusting than Chester, but not overtly hostile, and the others were mostly friendly too. They made a point to introduce everyone one at a time so we would feel comfortable with our hosts. First, since there were less of them (only one) they introduced the women. The only other female member of the team, Constance, was a tall, thin woman with short black hair and an easy grin.

They didn't mention her ability, but she gave me a cheerful hello before moving on to introduce the others.

The other three men were Thomas, Edward, and Caleb respectively. Thomas was a tall dark-skinned man with a serious expression, Edward was a tanned man with an easy grin, and Caleb mostly avoided any contact, keeping his pale-blue eyes on the fire and his blonde hair mostly blocking our view of him.

Cark asked questions, making polite chitchat for a while, but finally had enough of the pleasantries and decided to get down to brass tacks. "So, Chester, we actually did come to talk, like I said. Specifically to talk about something you might be looking for. We heard on the grapevine that you might be in the market for a Heartbeat Monarch. We happen to have one in our possession, if you would be interested in getting your hands on it."

I realized I'd underestimated Cark. I would probably have asked about the mushroom first, and that would have started the conversation off on the wrong tone. In retrospect, it was a simple but sensible idea to bring up what they would get out of things beforehand, given our superior forces and numbers. While my impulsive and excitable response would have screwed up this negotiation, the bounty hunter clearly knew how to handle people, despite being a mainly combat-oriented Ascendant.

Obviously, once they heard their target mentioned, they seemed interested, but Olivia also immediately became suspicious and started to look agitated. That was a totally understandable reaction, given that the "grapevine" had given us information no one but they were supposed to have. Us knowing the contents of their list meant we either had some kind of source for the list from the Academy, which shouldn't have been possible, or we'd figured it out since they got here, whether with an inside man or some kind of spying or prediction ability.

We, of course, knew it was the latter, but we couldn't tell them the truth without giving away secrets we absolutely did not plan to mention to anyone else.

Olivia, the suspicious one, seemed to naturally transition into the leader role as she questioned us. "Really? What exactly would you want for something like that? Because it seems stupid to just give it away." Obviously, she rightly suspected we had knowledge of not just her list but what they had on them at the moment. The main issue was that we didn't have full understanding of either.

Callie took over at this point—being the leader, she was the most qualified to negotiate. "That depends. What do you have to offer? We have a decent idea of what you might be able to trade, but we don't know how you feel about any of the materials we're looking for. Able and willing aren't the same thing. Why don't you give us a rundown on whatever you don't need for your list, and we can go from there." She kept her smile bland and cheerful, a perfect poker face.

Olivia narrowed her eyes. She obviously knew Callie was looking for more information, but since she *also* knew we had something they needed, she kind of had to play along. They needed the Heartbeat Monarch and had zero chance of taking it by force. While it was a solid reputation boost for us to negotiate, *they* had no choice but to do so. Who knew if there was even a second Heartbeat Monarch in the whole testing area? Honestly, I was leaning toward not. She frowned for a bit before sighing and starting to list off a few things she would be willing to trade.

I personally didn't have any skills at negotiation, though Benny did step in to help with his haggling Skill. While the leadership talked, though, I noticed something out of the corner of my eye. Nothing solid enough to really tip me off that something was going on, but some instinct of mine told me I should check it out. I stood up, nodding to the others to stay seated as I moved to the edge of the clearing their fire was in. To my surprise, Chester stood and followed me, stepping up behind me quietly and making sure I knew he was there.

Once we got a bit of distance, he leaned in, lowering his voice. "What happened? You were sitting there like nothing was wrong, and then you got all antsy." His voice was serious, and I was actually really impressed. He not only noticed my discomfort but went out of his way to check what was going on. The guy was a pretty solid leader, from what I could see. Even my own people hadn't bothered to check what I was doing. They also knew that I had the skills to escape from almost anything and the power to push back whatever attacked me long enough to call for backup.

I couldn't actually tell him, because I didn't know myself. But I'd seen... something. I just shrugged in frustration. "I don't know, honestly. I caught some movement out of the corner of my eye. I don't see anything over here, but I could swear something moved, so I figured I'd check it out. Probably just a rabbit or something. No need to follow me. I'll be back after I do a quick sweep out in the trees."

I was a bit restless anyway; negotiating wasn't my strong point. I was better at punching problems than talking through them.

I wondered exactly when that had become the case. Before getting my abilities, I wasn't a particularly violent person. Sure, having super strength now made it easy to just kick ass, but it was almost always my first choice now. I was Ascending, becoming more than I was, but in some ways, I was also becoming less. The more I threw myself into this, the farther I got from the person I'd been before.

The issue was that I didn't know how much of the old me I even *wanted* to keep. I hadn't exactly been anything special before. Changing and growing was a good thing, as long as I didn't lose myself. I felt like taking the time to focus more on the present and enjoying what I could do was a good step toward a happy medium. I had my friends to help too. If I ever forgot who I was, I could always ask Benny. He'd known me longer than anyone and would be happy to expound at length about my flaws before I'd become an Ascendant.

I shook off those thoughts and focused on Chester, who seemed to be giving me time to have my introspection before saying anything, which I appreciated. I cleared my throat in embarrassment, and he just chuckled.

"It's fine. I'll come with you just in case. Never a good idea to travel alone at night. The forest can be a pretty terrible place." His tone said he wasn't sure I'd seen a rabbit either. This wasn't entirely for my benefit—he was worried there might be something out there too.

More than anything, that convinced me to let him come along. "Sounds good. But let's try to move quietly. Don't want to tip off any animals that might be out there. If we don't need to start a fight, we should avoid it."

He gave me a solemn nod, and the two of us headed out towards where I'd heard the noise. I was focused on stealth, so my footsteps didn't make much sound, but to my surprise, Chester was pretty damn quiet too. I wasn't sure if he had the stealth Skill or if he was just well-trained, but it was nice to know he wouldn't be dragging me down if we got into trouble.

When we got out into the woods, I slowed and started searching around. I could use Seek Hidden, but I didn't even know what I was looking for. Just "any traces of any entity or object that might be moving" wouldn't work. I needed *something* to cut down the possibilities. Like down in the tunnels, when I was looking for traces of the people responsible for the rat king, I'd focused on the idea of an organization and, honestly, partially my guess that it was the Heartrippers.

I searched the general area where I'd seen the movement for any signs of what had been there. Person, animal, inanimate object. Something had moved, and while it might not have been anything important, it should have left a trace, even if it was just a bunny or something. I leaned down, studying the ground thoroughly. I really wished I had the Tracking Skill like Callie, but I had to work with what was available, so I just leveraged my Perception and paid attention to what was in the spot I was focused on.

I saw... forest—leaves, dirt, grass... I didn't really know what the hell I was supposed to be looking for. In the movies, the main character would spot a broken stick and deduce that the enemy had stepped on it exactly five minutes ago. Judging by the severity of the break, they were exactly six feet and one hundred eighty pounds, and one of their legs was longer than the other. Despite my heightened Perception, I didn't have any sort of actual basis in reading signs like this.

I didn't want to admit that and look like an idiot, but it was looking like I was going to have to, when I spotted another movement out of the corner of my eye off to one side. I stood up, making sure to stay in stealth, and headed in the direction I'd seen the flash, pretending I'd found something that showed me where to go. We made our way over slowly, taking our time and trying to be as silent as possible. When we got to where I'd seen the movement, I leaned down to move some bushes.

The bright-gold eyes on the other side did not seem friendly as they glared at me. Huge razor-sharp teeth dripped saliva from a mouth that smelled like rotting meat and blood as I stared up into the face of the biggest fucking wolf I had ever seen. I'd grown up in a city, so the list wasn't long, but still, this was a big fucking wolf. I did *not* stumble wildly back scrambling to get away from the massive animal, because I am a hero, and wolves don't scare me. My perfectly calm-and-collected retreat put me out of the tree line and exposed enough of it that I could see the shapes of several other wolves emerging. Wolves with thin green humanoids on their backs.

Goblins. G-ranked goblins. A bunch of them. Fuck.

Chapter Thirty

TEN. Ten G-ranked goblins riding giant wolves and backed by a much larger force of goblins on foot, all glaring at me like they wanted to tear me apart. Normally, ten G-ranked cannon-fodder monsters wouldn't scare me, especially not with my team around, but those wolves had *big* teeth. Something about the fur, the smell, and the glaring hate in their eyes made them much scarier than the Bone Wyvern, which while huge had really just been a big fuck off skeleton.

Making sure to keep my voice even and casual and my eyes locked on the wolves, I addressed Chester. "So... any chance you got followed back to camp last time you were out? Because these guys seem like they might have been planning this for a little while." I'd gotten back to my feet and was slowly backing away, hoping Chester got the hint and did the same. He did, and the two of us retreated calmly and rationally as fast as we fucking could back towards the firepit and our respective teams.

Unfortunately, we got about three steps before the wolves decided they weren't open to the idea of a retreat. Given stealth was now out the window, I just bellowed, "Chester, hold tight, I'll be back! Guys! Monsters!"

I didn't have a chance to say anything else because the wolves went from a charge to a full-on lunge, and I had to compensate. Hoping Chester was going to be okay, I used Leaf on the Wind and shoved off, heading for the nearest tree that looked too tall to climb. With the power in my legs and the decreased gravity, I touched down gently on the branch to overlook what was about to be a battle.

My warning had given Cark enough time to spring into action, and the pyrokinetic had conjured a huge wall of blue flame that was holding back the tide of goblins and preventing them from getting to our people and the Raiders both. It looked like keeping the wall stable and up was straining him, though. Down in the necropolis, he didn't keep his constructs together for such a long time, mostly just using them to maneuver attacks to hit multiple enemies.

I wasn't sure if he could hold it long term. The walls he'd left behind in the Necropolis had only lasted a minute or two after we got past them. They hadn't needed to last longer than that because we'd been moving fast enough that our pursuers got left far behind with that much of a lead.

Not to mention this was a huge open area. The heat from the flames was rising like heat always did, which meant the power was dissipating. He would need to pump more energy into the blaze to keep it going, plus cover much more space to protect everyone.

I looked back to check on Chester. I'd bolted to safety without him because I wanted to get the lay of the land, but I wasn't going to leave him down there. I couldn't stretch Leaf on the Wind to him because he didn't know me well enough to trust the skill when it spread to him, so my options were strictly of the attack variety. When I looked down at him though, I was surprised to see he didn't need any help after all. I'd been preparing to use my Mistwalking to cover the battlefield and slip him out into the woods with Seek Hidden, but the big man was standing his ground.

The G-ranker with the red mohawk was standing in a boxing stance, and behind him, a huge behemoth of solid rock jutted out of the ground. The construct of stone was only visible from the waist up, but aside from being featureless, it heavily resembled Chester in form and shape. The construct had its huge stone fists up and was flicking out blurringly fast jabs in a staccato rhythm, knocking approaching wolves away from the shadowboxing form of Chester, whose movements the construct was mimicking exactly.

I called down to the big man, "Hey, you all right? I was setting up to extract you with stealthier methods, but it looks like you're holding up okay!"

The goblins noticed my yelling, but since I was behind the line made by the construct, it was basically irrelevant to the situation. Chester was laying down a blanket of blindingly fast punches into the air in front of him, seemingly unconcerned with anything happening and barely even breathing hard despite the insane speed he was working with.

He chuckled, calling back. "No worries. I saw you getting ready to jump back in, and I heard what you said. I'm not quite in as good a position as I look, though!"

I wasn't sure what he meant by that until I took a closer look. Despite the literal rain of powerful blows, the goblins weren't dying when the construct hit them. As it made contact, I was able to tell that the thing was made of hard packed dirt, *not* stone. The Skill or ability he was using might be G-ranked, but the earth here wasn't. Even propelled by his power, it wasn't enough to get the job done when spread over such a large area.

That was less than ideal. I wondered about his ability, (could he make it smaller to make it stronger, but went big to cover more distance?) the arms of the construct were big enough that their range created a protective bubble around the man as he danced through his boxing forms. It was absurdly potent as a defense even if it apparently lacked the kick to finish off the goblins in its current form. The damage seemed to be so diffuse, it wasn't even killing the H-rankers, but the G-ranked goblins weren't actually any heavier, so the huge earth fists were still sending them and their mounts flying.

Luckily, I had something that would help. I stepped off the branch, letting gravity take hold and haul me downward, but landing softly on the densely packed forest earth as Leaf in the Wind resisted the pull, making the first step a quick and easy one despite the long drop. When I got down there, I bolted over to Chester.

"Stall for a minute longer, man. I can help turn this around."

With just the two of us on this side of the firewall, we needed to fight smarter, not harder. While each individual goblin might be less than a threat, there were ten G-rank goblins *and* ten wolves of the same level.

I hurried over to the construct and put both hands on it. I closed my eyes and reached for DS Mastery, knowing this would seriously fuck me up but also knowing it was the perfect solution. First, I strained at Stone Limb, using it to cover the whole golem. Since the thing was dirt and rock and part of the earth, that was less of a stretch than I'd been expecting. The next two were tougher. Consecration of Flames and Touch of Tears both washed out of me, and my knees buckled at the strain.

When I opened my eyes though, the huge dirt construct had become a hulking black behemoth of cracked stone with glowing green poison magma surging through it. I fell back on my ass, letting Chester work as I yelled, "Got it, go!"

The big man unleashed his flurry of punches again. The poison magma goliath was unleashing a rain of hellish basalt destruction on the goblins, and unlike before, it was working. The wolf riders were taking the punches as best they could to shelter the army, but every blow was getting them more and more poisoned.

I was kind of in awe. The combo of my earth and fire skills created magma, and the combination of my poison and fire created acidic poison flame, but the three of them together was something else. Seeing it all merge in this giant form was something I couldn't have imagined, and it was earth shatteringly terrifying to behold. The flying fists were slowly whittling away at the bastards, and everyone nearby was staring at the combination of my DS Mastery Skill and Chester's ability.

The magma-infused fists were raining down on the goblin army, basically vaporizing the H-rank goblins when they hit. The longer it went on, the more the goblin riders got worn away. My earth skill was reinforcing and enhancing the already-mighty construct, bringing it to a level where it could inflict real casualties on the goblin forces. The number of wolf riders started to drop as one of them succumbed to the poison flame, leaving a hole for another few punches to demolish a dozen more goblins.

The behemoth was holding them back so effectively, Cark even dropped the fire shield, and the G-rankers on my team headed in to help with the fight. Given the wolves and their mobility, sending the H-rankers in seemed like a mistake. Olivia stayed behind with both sets of lower-ranking members while the others joined the battle, whooping with joy. Jessie, the lone exception (having hung back to heal), stopped to charge me back up with her life force, and despite a small headache, after a few seconds, I was good to get back into the thick of things.

With the others here to deal with the little ones, Chester seemed to have reigned in his symphony of destruction to a more manageable series of slaps and grabs, focusing on pinning down the other nine wolf riders and their mounts, with Cark and Callie pulling off one of each pair to try to relieve some of the pressure. Since I needed to get some training in against stronger enemies and these wolf riders were all poisoned, I drew out my cane and slammed the head down on two of the wolves before leaping clear, drawing them off and leaving Chester with five riders, Benny and Jessie offering support.

I touched down a bit away from the group with the pair of wolf riders on my tail. This was my first time using my cane in battle, which wasn't ideal, but to be fair, I'd been training to hit people with sticks for a few months now, so it wasn't really that different. The main change was the way the new grip changed my options in terms of striking. While a close-fisted grip on the cane worked and was useful most of the time, the shaft was thin enough to spin between my fingers, which opened up a lot of options given my new fighting style.

I slipped into my Balam form, getting ready to deal with the two wolves and the goblins riding them. I had a feeling this was going to be infinitely more difficult than taking out a bunch of skeletons, but I didn't regret getting into this at all. As much of a crutch as I knew it was, combat helped me center myself and clear my mind. All the complicated things I thought about when I was free of distraction and in my own head melted away.

Ever since I became an Ascendant, this had just come naturally to me. I wasn't great at making plans, I wasn't good at self-control, and I didn't have Celine's head for politics or Callie's drive to learn more about our world.

But I could fight. I could win. Much like wishes, combat was something I could contribute to the group, something I could do to show I was valuable. I knew that was stupid, but I needed it. Needed to feel like something other than a walking stat dispenser. Needed to be good for more than just my ability.

But hey, bonus, I was pretty sure getting lost in a battle frenzy was a great example of living in the now.

Chapter Thirty-One

THE FIGHT against the wolf riders taught me multiple important things. First, most of my combat training had been against humanoid opponents, and animals were distinctly different in terms of goals and execution during fights. The wolves also worked together *much* more fluidly than any other enemies I had encountered. I really needed to address that flaw if I was going to keep fighting monsters.

Secondly, the new rotation with my cane made it a fantastic weapon for Balam, but it also meant I had to learn the mechanics of the forms over again, which was inconvenient at best, but it still helped me learn to make the style my own a bit better. Finally, wolf riders were wolves *and* riders, and those little bastards attacked separately. I was dealing with four attacks from two directions. The goblins weren't exactly revolutionary combat geniuses, but trying to deal with them while I avoided the wolves was tough.

The one benefit of Balam in this situation was that the circular-spinning fighting style was mobile, which let me stay in motion so I could track the wolves. The vicious beasts were circling me like sharks in bloody water. As I tried to compensate for the attacks, I realized how thoroughly their instinctive grasp on timing had been developed. Though I spun fast enough to keep them in my sight, albeit alternately, one of them dipped in and bit down on my leg. I winced and managed to pull away before the thing could set the bite properly, but I still had a bloody hole in my calf.

The damage wasn't severe enough to immobilize me, but the distraction let the other one jump me from behind as I smashed my cane down on the first with a snarl. I had to drop to let it fly over my head and avoid getting my spine ripped out, which barely let me get out of the way of the second strike from the wolf that originally bit me. During this, the goblins were trying to pin me with spears, and I felt a pair of hot lines along my side as they sliced me open pretty damn deeply with the surprisingly sharp weapons.

I stopped when I could, taking a second to calm down. The wolves timed their attacks flawlessly, each tearing into me while the other held my attention, switching between attackers with almost no warning at all. The goblins made the issue even worse, but they were easily handled if I could get them off their mounts. Even at G-rank, they couldn't compare to me in terms of power, but as harassers who exploited gaps in my defense, they were a nightmare.

That said, half the problem was my reactions. I was getting caught up in their tempo, reacting instead of acting, and they didn't need to predict my moves if they were pushing me to make them in the first place. I was dancing to their tune, and that was the exact wrong way to play this. Despite that, taking the initiative wasn't an option either. If I focused on one, the other would maul me from behind while I wasn't paying attention, and I wouldn't be able to do a thing about it.

That was why I stopped to take a breath despite maybe opening myself up to attack. As they circled me, slowly getting in position, I had an epiphany. While they were making me dance to their tune, they were also dancing to each other's. There was a rhythm to this fight, and I just had to learn it. I watched carefully, eyes on the goblin in front of me and its wolf, the ones I knew weren't going to attack me. My leg was throbbing, and the cuts from those spear wounds were highly unpleasant, but I focused through the pain.

The wolf I was watching had moved, but since I was watching, it wouldn't be attacking. It was distracting me to line up the shot for the other beast. I whirled my cane around to strike out behind me, actively avoiding looking where I was hitting because if I took my eyes off the first wolf, it would just pick up the attack. I felt a meaty thump and heard a whimper as the wolf was knocked clear. The first wolf started to come in to distract me but realized I was waiting and backed off along with the other, opening up some breathing room from the massive beasts and their riders.

The goblins were not pleased by my little turnaround, and the creepy little green bastards narrowed red eyes at me and bared their needle-like teeth. It was obvious the greenies were carnivores from their chompers, rows of small triangular teeth, razor sharp and clearly made for tearing flesh. Their bat-like ears flapped in agitation as they hissed, seeming to be a secondary method of communication adding nuance to their sibilant hissing tongue. They brandished their spears threateningly at me, obviously trying to throw me off my game again.

But I wasn't having any of it. I was getting it now. Not only were the wolves less of a threat once I learned their tempo, this was an opportunity. Their circular attack pattern was something I could learn from given some time to focus on it. I couldn't mimic it exactly because there was only one of me, but with my weapon and my own limbs, it was possible to vary my attack methods. Besides, I'd figured out some of the tempo, but it wasn't like I'd solved some code. I'd just gotten a better grasp of their timing, and they were more than capable of varying that again at any time.

In the spirit of learning more about their style, I let myself fall back into a predictable rhythm. That was dangerous because I could easily get hurt doing this, but I was pretty confident in my ability to at least avoid fatal injury. Jessie's power also made it easy to overlook possible harm if it was to my benefit. Even though my aching leg reminded me not to take it too far, I knew there was something here for me to learn. I could feel the inspiration on the edge of my mind.

I was still trying to create my own style of Balam. It was, as I'd noted before, highly customizable, more of a series of forms and guidelines than a hard style with specific techniques. Something about the effectiveness of the wolves and their riders made me think that their tactics could be applied to my skill to create my personal version of Balam. As I tried in vain to figure out my next move, the two wolves moved again. The one in front of me attacked, lunging at my throat. I heard the snarl as the one behind me attacked, and expecting the feint I'd seen before, I lashed out behind me, only to hit... nothing.

My eyes widened in panic as I jerked my cane back in front of me to try to intercept the lunging wolf I'd thought was faking me out. Apparently, they had learned from the last attack. When the first wolf had lunged, it had been setting up a feint from the *second* wolf to distract from its *own* intent to follow through. It explained the obvious snarl of the one behind me, clearly trying to draw attention to its false charge. It was a complete reversal of tactics I hadn't even considered.

It also showed me one of the major benefits of the wolves' combat style. Adaptability. When the wolves attacked, they didn't need to set up a sure kill strike and a feint to distract. Either of them could make any false attack real with nearly no notice, and their seamless cooperation made it nearly impossible to properly counter. Defending wasn't about telling what was real and what was false because both attacks were neither and both at the same time.

While it might seem like that wasn't applicable to my situation, in reality I could use that realization in my own style. The idea of feints that became real attacks that became feints was an intriguing one when combined with the spinning, dance-like qualities of Balam. It was a performance. I could make them think or expect whatever I needed to and then do the opposite. Excited to try out my idea, I hauled on the cane and pitched the wolf over my shoulder at the other one to try to buy some time and create some space.

Surprisingly, the goblin on its back managed to stay mounted as it flew through the air, but sadly, it didn't hit the other wolf, which dodged out of the way as the soaring wolf twisted midair and landed on its feet.

I rushed forward, not wanting to let them get their tempo back now that I had a better idea of what I wanted to test on them. I flicked my cane out at one of them and lashed out with a kick at the other. I spun the cane away before it made contact even as the first one feinted and the second one dodged, only to take the head of the cane to its skull as I whirled it around behind my back, extending it well past the foot the wolf had just dodged.

I grinned and switched up my targets again. Then I started on the Balam forms, applying the lessons I'd picked up in the fight about adaptability and subterfuge. The style was surprisingly organic and blended well with basically any combat style, so I was able to work in the new elements seamlessly, and as I spun and whirled, my blows started to land much more often.

Of course it wasn't perfect. This was training, and I was learning a new Skill from the ground up. I had a bit of experience, but it was still very much a Minor Skill. I was honestly just grateful that I hadn't run into more combat capable monsters. The wolves were clever and adaptable, but they weren't trained, and the goblins appeared to be mostly just trying to stab me really hard when I got close. Any monster with actual martial ability would have torn me apart.

I spent a few minutes landing hits, getting more used to my new style and their changing patterns until I was pretty sure they didn't have anything else to show me. Then, when my next shot landed on a wolf's leg, I unleashed my force charge. It was nowhere near full, but I'd been tapping the cane against every surface I came across since I got it, just quick casual tapping as I walked. That, plus all the blows from this fight, had added up. It landed on the wolf's fragile foreleg, and the unleashed force plus the power I put into the swing snapped the leg, bringing one of the wolves crashing down.

I caved in the head of the goblin riding it then dipped out of range of the downed animal and dealt with the other goblin and broke a leg on the other wolf, which was much less difficult when dealing with just one of the damn things.

I didn't kill the wolves. I couldn't. I was a dog person, and I suspected Jessie might be able to take charge of them after healing them up, since they didn't seem to be sapient. The others had the same thought, apparently, because when we finished, there were nine living wolves.

As I checked on the others and made sure they were okay, I couldn't help but wonder: could *we* ride the wolves now? I resolved to broach the subject with our healer because that sounded awesome.

Chapter Thirty-Two

WE DID GET THE MUSHROOM, bringing us up to four items on our list. With proof of concept, we spent the rest of the week using a combination of wishes and determination to track down a full twenty-three of twenty-five items. Unfortunately, that was when we ran into a little snag. The fewer items remaining on the list, the more expensive the wishes got because of the smaller number of variables in play. By the time we got to the last two items on the list, they were too expensive to wish for with our current method.

Still, despite missing out on the one-week mark like we'd been aiming for, we were doing amazingly well. The recordings had started, and I was fairly sure they showed us doing pretty damn well, but with the last two items being up in the air, we decided to hold a team meeting. It was internal only (just the four of us) because we would be discussing my ability, and the others didn't need to know about that. I was willing to trust and open up to my new friends, but there was sharing, and there was being reckless. It would be stupid to tell people willy-nilly about my real origins.

Callie was leaning back against Rallia, the black wolf she'd claimed for herself, using the big beast as a pillow as she considered our options. With nine wolves left (one had been killed by that poison fire construct), we had exactly enough of the big animals for our group to each get one. After Jessie healed them up, her life energy allowed her to take control of them. She spent the next three days with Cark watching her back as she trained them all, using her ability to enforce commands and positive reinforcement to show they would be rewarded for certain actions.

I'd kind of expected it to be harder, but given they had originally been ridden by goblins, they took to the positive treatment much faster than expected. Jessie still kept them topped up with life energy when we rode them, in case she needed to take control of them if one snapped, but all in all, they were pretty smart creatures for non-sapient animals. As long as we fed them well and gave them attention, they seemed to actually love being around us. Even us riding on their backs didn't bother them, and their speed as G-rankers meant increased mobility when we moved as a whole group.

My wolf, Jin, was black with a white spot on his forehead, and he was the biggest of the lot. He was one of the two I'd fought. We'd connected after our battle, him clearly seeing me as strong enough to follow. The rabbits I kept catching and cooking for him probably helped too. Regardless, I had a kickass war mount now, and I couldn't wait to bring him back to the city. I'd been worried about whether we could, but Callie said tamers were a known thing. There were provisions for docile monsters and animals, and the wolves were apparently the latter.

Callie blew out a long breath. We were on the top floor of the hatchery, and the others were out training with Cark. We were pretty sure they knew we wanted them out of the way for a bit, but they didn't seem to mind. Cass and Zeke were downstairs. Cass was mortal, so we didn't need to worry about her hearing, and Zeke knew my secret. I decided to break the ice.

"Okay," I said. "We didn't make it to the end of the list before the week was up, which isn't great. But we're pretty close, and we might still be able to get first place if we find the last two items. Callie, what's last on the list?"

She grimaced. "Akkadian Fire Beads and the Heart of a Greater Mountain. I might be wrong, but based on the activity from the searchers nearby I'm pretty sure they set up the last two to overlap on almost everyone's lists. Both of them will be in the same place, though. A volcano. Jessie has been scouting and managed to find one relatively close by, but if we found it, so will others. And there's a good chance this competition is going to get pretty intense." She didn't sound too pleased with the Academy, and I could see why.

We'd been doing this whole thing as quickly and painlessly as possible. Not everyone would agree to trade, and we'd had to pick some fights, but we'd mostly been able to avoid all-out brawls. This was going to be the definition of a brawl—literally everyone left, or at least bunches of them, all going for the same item. On the one hand, that would be a huge pain in the ass, but on the other, it did have a benefit.

"We can use that too though, can't we?" I pointed out. "We can demonstrate our skills against the other fighters for everyone to see."

That got a grudging nod from my girlfriend. "That's true. We want to get at least some impressive time on the cameras. We're going to be part of the stream for this when it gets released, and the better we do, the more they include us. We've done okay so far, but we've also been leaning into the wishes to get things easier, which definitely makes us look efficient, but it also makes us look absurdly lucky and like we aren't relying on our own abilities. One last big fight will definitely give us a chance to show off, but I'm not entirely sure it's worth it."

It was a tough call. We had weaker members we would need to protect. We could leave them behind sure, but then we would be robbing them of that prime-time footage we were all looking forward to and the sweet, sweet gains we would all get from it. I didn't have an easy answer. "We could leave the others behind? We'd have to check and see what they think about it. We are a team, but if this is going to be the free-for-all you say it is, bringing the H-rankers might be too dangerous."

Benny looked dubious, which, considering his relationship with Celine, wasn't surprising. I wasn't sure if they were actually dating yet, but the two of them spent almost all their time together. The idea of asking her to give up her chance to make a name for herself would obviously bother him, but I could tell he wasn't any more enthused about bringing her into a G-ranked war zone.

"We can still bring the wolves, right?" Benny asked. "The H-rankers would essentially have not only a means of escape but an actual weapon that they can use against higher-ranked enemies."

I turned to Jessie. "You're the one who got them to the point they're at. I'm a big fan of Jin, but can the wolves be trusted to have our back in combat already? This is a new setup. In fact, depending on the circumstances, it might be *more* dangerous to send the H-rankers into battle on the wolves. If they consider the H-rankers to be an impediment to survival, their instincts might tell them to eliminate the threat. But again, not really my area of expertise. What do you think?"

She bit her lip, looking uncertain for a minute, before finally shaking her head. "No. They wouldn't do that. You need to understand I haven't just been using life force to make them do things and then giving them treats. My connections don't just allow me to control them, but to share thoughts and impressions. The same way I can see through the eyes of a raven, I can feel what the wolves are feeling and can communicate my feelings. They don't really do complex thought, mostly acting on instinct, but I've been able to show each of them that we're part of their pack and that we care for them as they care for us."

Even without going into the psychology stuff, that was really impressive. Jessie's power had *much* more potential than I had realized. I looked at Jin, who had his head cocked at me. He didn't understand human speech, and I doubted he would anytime soon, though theoretically if his Focus got high enough, he might be able to learn. I doubted he had pretty much any points in that stat, though. Animals weren't known for that, and from what I could tell, they ended up Might and Vitality heavy most of the time, with a few exceptions. Still, he clearly felt comfortable around me, and I was glad we had decided to keep the wolves. They were powerful supports. Plus, I'd always wanted a dog as a kid, but Zeke didn't feel like cleaning up after one.

We all gave Callie space to make the final decision. After some thought, she finally sighed. "In the end, this isn't really up to us. I could claim authority and tell them to stay behind, but it's not my place. If the wolves can help keep them safe, there's no reason to forbid it. We'll give them the choice to go or stay behind and see what they decide, but it's their future on the line, not ours. It's not right to try to decide how they do it. Sure, going with us is dangerous, but cultivation is inherently dangerous. Trying to coddle them now just means they'll be weaker when we aren't around anymore."

Clearly, she didn't like making that argument. I imagined it struck her as far too much like something her dad would say for her liking, but she wasn't wrong. Our lives *were* pretty dangerous. Ascendants *did* die in the city when fighting monsters and criminals. If there was no danger involved, we wouldn't get nearly as much renown for victories. It wasn't our place to deprive them of training or exposure that could help them survive, even if it was to protect them. They were our friends, but in the end, they weren't actually part of our team. They had their own priorities, and we had to respect that.

I reached down to scratch Jin behind the ears. "Fair enough. I suggest we wait until tomorrow before we go, though. We can get those five wishes in for the day. Might put us behind the others if they found the place already, but I think the wait will be worth the boost in power. Ten points isn't going to be a crazy amount, but it's enough to make a difference in a pinch, and I'd rather have it and not need it than need it and not have it. Although maybe, eight would be better—leave a wish in case of emergencies."

We'd been using up all of our wishes one at a time getting the proper items for our list. It had been four days, and we were already almost done, which showed just how useful the technique could be. Still, not having any spare wishes on hand in case of an emergency had been bothering me, and that didn't seem like a smart way to go into such a precarious situation, considering we would be up against some of the best teams in the Academy. Anyone who'd gotten this far this early was going to be tough to beat.

Putting the last two items on everyone's list meant that only one team could actually finish the hunt, which kind of explained why they had that whole "first place gets all the exposure" rule. I'd been wondering how they would pick first place—if it would be based on time, effectiveness, or the like—but having it so only one team could finish was certainly a simple way to decide.

I was pretty sure they were trying to show us that cultivation meant being the best, and that while useful, alliances weren't viable in the long term if we really wanted to reach the top.

Regardless of the reasoning, I was determined to win. Now we just had to plan out how this was going to go. Hopefully, Jessie could at least draw us a map.

Chapter Thirty-Three

To the surprise of literally no one, Grimmengap *did* want to come with us on our last raid. It hadn't even been a question. Danger was a fact of life for cultivators, but this kind of opportunity for self-promotion didn't come along every day.

If our team got the last item, everyone who was on their last two items would be done, and everyone else would be finished when they reached that point. I suspected the lists would update themselves then. It seemed more dramatic, which was pretty much their style. I wondered what would happen if two different teams each got one. Would the judges default to time? Would the teams share first place?

In any case, once we clarified that they would be coming with us, we let them know we planned to go the next day and that they should get some rest. Then we all turned in. We got up the next morning before the others, and Jessie used four wishes to pump her Vitality by another eight points. We'd debated for a while about who would get those wishes, but in the end, we'd decided pumping up our healer would have the broadest utility. She paid for it by giving me some of her memories of the first aid Skill. Not enough to get me to Lesser or anything, but enough to grant me the Skill in a general sense.

Once that was done, we ate breakfast together then met outside to mount up and talk through our strategy based on the information Jessie had accrued from her scouting last night before bed. Seeing everyone riding on giant-ass wolves was admittedly pretty inspiring.

Despite the amazing visual effect, Callie commanded everyone's attention as per usual. "All right, people. This is going to be rough. We'll try to avoid confronting anyone for as long as possible. Luckily, it seems like most of the teams haven't gotten to the point where they're looking for the volcanic materials yet. Agria, what are we dealing with here?"

Jessie was becoming much more confident with her briefings and didn't even hesitate before she picked up the thread. "Like Nightstrike said, not many teams have advanced far enough to look for these specific materials. I'm guessing the ones who haven't are staying away from the Volcano for obvious reasons, which is good for us. Bad for us is that the really scary teams will be on the way. Right now, though, our biggest problem isn't a team. It's a person. Fisher is already onsite and heading into the Volcano, and that means we're probably going to have to fight him to get to the materials, or worse, to get them back if he finds them first."

That was less than ideal. I remembered Fisher from Jessie's briefing at the start. The motorcycle rider who could phase through objects. He was supposed to be one of the ringers in the hunt, and his decision to go solo only made his absolute confidence more obvious. Of everyone we could have run into, I honestly wanted to fight him the absolute least. His ability sounded like a pain in the ass. Luckily, we weren't entirely helpless in that particular department. We had a counter to his power, even if it was a small one.

I set my bag on the ground, dug out the dagger that could hurt incorporeal entities, and held it up. "What are the chances this thing will hurt him? I know it's mainly meant for use on ghosts, but he's going to be incorporeal, and that's kind of the whole point of the dagger." Zeke wouldn't have been nearly as interested if it was just a ghost-stabbing dagger. There were plenty of ways to hurt ghosts. I knew it wasn't a perfect solution, but I figured it would at least give us an edge, no pun intended.

I tossed it to Callie lightly, and my girlfriend snatched it out of the air by the hilt. She had dagger training from her Balam Skill, which was higher than mine, so she was the optimal person to use it. She looked it over, chewing her lip. "It's better than nothing, but we should try our best to avoid running into him." She turned to the others. "If we do, I want Grimmengap to run. The wolves are powerful allies and protectors, but their defense only works if they can stop the thing that's trying to hurt you. A phaser will just ignore them. Better to take off and let us deal with it."

Celine looked displeased, but she didn't object. "Very well. We can continue on and try to find the materials while you hold back the threat if we run across him. Still, with advanced knowledge of exactly what we're going to be facing, we could easily avoid him. Our best bet is to rely on Agria's map to help us navigate." She looked to our healer-slash-recon-specialist. "Exactly how comprehensive can we expect this map to be? Will it be able to lead us to the actual materials themselves?"

Jessie looked abashed. "No. Sadly not. Most of the Volcano biome is underground. There's a sort of magma labyrinth up top that leads into the depths of the mountain, but there are about a dozen entrances at different points, and there's no way at all to know which is the closest to our target." She looked at me subtly, and I nodded.

"No way at all" wasn't exactly accurate. We'd saved a wish for an emergency, but more importantly, Seek Hidden could be of help depending on the size of the objects and how I chose to use it.

I got her point, though. That was why she had only warned about Fisher. She didn't know who else was already down there or who could end up down there since there were so many ways in. The underground portion of the Volcano biome eliminated her raven as a scouting option, though I supposed going after something called the "Heart of the Greater Mountain," we were bound to be working underground at least a little bit.

Once that was done, it was time to go, and we mounted the wolves and headed for our new destination to try to finish this hunt once and for all.

One huge upside to the wolves' presence, aside from combat capabilities, was that a long-distance trip could be accomplished at G-rank speeds even while our H-rankers were with us. Of course we couldn't go *too* fast, because if they fell off while going at top speeds, they might die, but even so, we managed closer to my own foot speed than say, Sarah's. Which was good because the Volcano was *far*. Jessie had been able to spot it in the distance because it was a Volcano, but it had taken her hours as the crow (or raven) flies to reach it for recon.

Luckily, with G-ranked transport that came out to like, twenty minutes on paw, which was faster than we ever could have managed with the others following on foot. Not to mention with the wolves being on four feet instead of two, the ride was pretty smooth.

As we drew closer, we slowed down, dismounted, and led the wolves and H-rankers to the top of an outcropping Jessie pointed out to us so we could do our own scouting. We took up position on the ridge, staring up at the rim of the Volcano and searching for any incoming threats.

Callie looked uncomfortable with our possible approach. "Okay, guys, not a fan of this. That Volcano is completely exposed because of the height. We'll be spotted if anyone looks up there, and we can only climb it so fast. Unfortunately, I don't see another choice. No stealth or lightening skills will extend to all of us, especially not with the wolves, and we can't leave them behind, because it would leave the H-rankers vulnerable. That means we take the slow way up and try to avoid being visible by sticking to the cracks we find in the stone."

I saw her point. The Volcano was a towering spire of black rock cut off at the top like some immense being had taken an axe to a normal mountain. The gaping opening at the top spewed out black smoke, though luckily no actual lava, despite the warped and uneven dark stone of the spire making it clear there had been eruptions there in the past. Anyone who took even a short glance up at the thing would spot us if we went straight up, but the same hardened lava rock deposits created small trails and recesses in the mountain that we could use to cover part of our approach.

She turned to Jessie. "Agria, can you send the bird out to do a circuit around the Volcano and try to spot any incoming threats? If we know what side any nearby enemies will be on, we can try to stick to the opposite slope at least. It might give us a cushion when we don't have cover."

Jessie had brought her raven with her of course, though once we got to the peak and started into the maze of lava rock where the entrances were, she was going to send it back. It wouldn't do us much good underground, after all.

Jessie didn't even ask for details, just lifted her wrist falconer style and dispatched the bird to do a wide, slow circle around the entire mountain. As she did, Callie started trying to map a way up the slope from the side we could see, just in case. I could see her eyes scouring the uneven surface, trying to find a place with at least some incline to make sure the wolves could make the trip too. Luckily, the slope wasn't actually sheer, so it shouldn't be too difficult for the canines to find purchase for their paws.

Honestly, it might have ended up being easier for them than it would be for us.

Finally, after ten minutes or so, the bird came back. Jessie had been watching the landscape through its eyes, so its return wasn't really necessary for a report—she just considered it the end of the scouting mission. She took a second to take stock before laying out her findings. "Okay, I saw four teams coming in. Three of them are on the other side, and one is coming up from behind us, though not directly. We have a while before they get here in either case. Still, I don't recognize any of them. Once we're out of the way, maybe Celine can fill us in, but my suggestion is we move before the team behind sees us.

Callie, who had finished coming up with a relatively safe path to the top, nodded. "Agreed. I think I know how we're going to make it, so stick with me. I'll put up a dome of shadow over us. Given the dark color of the stone, that should give us some extra protection from sight, not to mention catching someone if they happen to slip." She looked over her shoulder. "All right, guys, let's go. We need to get in there as fast as possible, but don't move so fast you have an accident. Keep pace with me, and we should get in there safe and sound."

With that, she climbed to her feet and set off down the outcropping toward the base of the Volcano.

Chapter Thirty-Four

WE DIDN'T GET SPOTTED by anyone on our way up the Volcano, thankfully. It was also lucky Callie kept that shield around us, because more than one of us fell on the way up. Though we had incredibly powerful physical bodies, most of us couldn't actually fly, and the mountain was much less durable than we were. The rock crumbled out from under us a number of times, but because we were going slowly, and being careful, the few times someone slipped, we were able to intervene before they fell. Even the wolves made it to the top of the Volcano safely.

Once we made it to the top, we all stopped to catch our breaths after the nerve-wracking trip, constantly worrying the fucking ground might collapse out from under our shoes.

The rim of the Volcano was much more stable. We stood, looking down on the sprawling maze of dark rock walls that made up the bottom of the Volcanic bowl, which to my immense relief, was *not* coated with actual lava. While we couldn't assume it was entirely dormant, it was pretty clearly safe to interact with the rock up here.

We all crouched down inside the rim so no one could see us from farther away. High Perception stats made things like that possible, and it was better not to risk it. Staring down into the labyrinth, I saw shambling forms that were barely visible from up here, even with enhanced Perception. Callie was able to see them best, given her talents, and she relayed their appearance to the rest of us, but no one knew what they were. Despite how prepared we were for the undead biome, no one here had any special knowledge of these kinds of monsters.

Luckily, there were other options. We still had our scan rings, and while outside, we had signal, so we could do a bit of research. We spent twenty minutes or so tracking down monsters that fit Callie's descriptions.

Returning from a scouting foray, Callie crawled over to us, wincing as the sharpened bits of volcanic gravel scraped at her legs, though her higher Impact prevented any actual damage. I suspected there were higher ranked stone shards in there, or it probably wouldn't have even hurt her. When she got close enough, she turned her screen so we could all see the picture. The creature was a large upright monster made of the same lava rock as the labyrinth, which explained why we couldn't make them out very well.

Callie looked less than enthused. "They're called Tinderlings. A type of G-ranked lava construct. They form naturally when low-grade fire elementals possess lava rocks. In their base form, they're basically small rolling pebbles, but over time, they accrue more stone and build themselves stronger bodies. When they rank up, they merge into their rock form entirely and become a completely new creature. Tinderlings are durable, being made of stone and all, but they're mainly Might attributed, which makes them both stronger and makes the heat they give off more intense. These are not an easy enemy to fight, and avoiding them is going to be our best bet."

The gravel shifted slightly as the wolves adjusted themselves, clearly not enjoying being stuck on their bellies in sharp gravel, whether it could actually hurt them or not. They even whimpered slightly, though Jessie was able to shush them into silence again. Despite the wolves bonding with each of us, Jessie was still their main point of contact, and they seemed closer to her than the rest of us. I didn't mind. She would probably be working with them more than we would. Her life energy could even help them evolve over time if I understood her power correctly. They were mounts for us, but for Jessie, they were a huge force multiplier.

"Will we be able to avoid them?" I asked Callie. "The labyrinth is kind of sprawling. We might be able to work around them if we use the ravens, but what happens if we run into one of these things after we enter the tunnels? We have no way to tell what the setup is like down there, and we might be completely penned in with them." For that matter, I didn't know which entrance we should even pick. I might be able to use Seek Hidden to find the closest to our target, but I would feel better if we got closer.

Luckily, she seemed less concerned. "Like I said, they're absurdly Might heavy. Their Perception is pretty much rock bottom, probably because no one expects rock monsters to have particularly sharp senses, especially given the lack of eyes and ears. We should be able to sneak by them easily enough, though if we get penned in like you're worried about, we might have to fight in a few cases. Fighting a few of them, though, is better than fighting dozens, and we don't exactly have a way of avoiding them completely."

I grinned. "That might not be accurate. Remember we're standing on a big-ass mountain. This entire thing is made of rock. I had an idea when I saw this place, but now that we made it up here, it's beginning to become an actual plan. What if we avoid the labyrinth and the monsters entirely? My Sucking Mud skill can turn the earth liquid in a ten-meter radius. What if I narrow the effect and use it to reach farther down? We might be able to literally sink through the ground and into the tunnels while bypassing all the dangers."

Callie looked less than enthused by my idea. "Solomon, that... That is *incredibly* dangerous. What if we don't pick a spot over the tunnels? What if someone sinks down into the earth and then gets stuck down there? They could drown in the mud. That sounds horrifying to even imagine. I'd love a way to avoid all this danger, but I can't in good conscience let anyone take that risk." Her voice quavered, and I wondered if she had some sort of phobia about being buried alive.

Luckily, I hadn't just spouted the idea without considering it. "Not at all. I thought of that. I can use Seek Hidden to find the tunnel system. It's huge, so it won't be hard to locate. As for getting stuck, our bodies are way more powerful than they used to be. Tearing ourselves free of some dirt wouldn't be hard for any of us, and we could put a rope around the person's waist just in case so they can follow it back up. Plus with our Might, we can hold our breaths *way* longer than we used to. I noticed it when we were swimming the other day."

I'd actually been pretty confused about how that worked. My best guess was the increased suction from inhalation condensed a lot more air into our lungs, but I hadn't had a chance to ask anyone. It was one of those weird side effects of Might that no one really mentioned because it didn't usually come up in the day-to-day.

I could see Callie still looked uncertain, and I stepped forward, putting my hands on her shoulders.

I gave them a squeeze. "Hey, no one was suggesting you do it first. I'm the one with the Sucking Mud skill, so I'll try it out. If something goes wrong, I can use the skill again, and you guys can pull me up by the rope. No muss, no fuss. Okay?"

Her eyes looked clouded for a second, as if she weren't looking at me, and I wondered what the hell had happened to her that could cause this kind of reaction to the idea of being buried. It wasn't an underground thing, because we'd done that plenty since we got here. It was specifically the idea of being buried alive.

Still, it wasn't the time or place, and was possibly not my business. I made my intention to ignore it obvious, and I saw her come back to her senses as she noticed me letting go of her shoulders.

She shook it off, giving me a brittle smile. "Yeah. Of course, that sounds like a smart safety measure. Let's do that."

We started to make our way down the crater slowly, towards the edges of the labyrinth. In order for this to work, I needed to be close enough for Seek Hidden to find both the right entrance and the tunnels themselves.

Luckily, the Tinderlings had shit for Perception, so even a basic application of stealth let me range ahead of the group without fear of being noticed. I let the others fall behind as I slowly made my way forward to the edge of the labyrinth. When I got close enough, I closed my eyes, took a deep breath, and activated Seek Hidden, targeting the entrance closest to the Akkadian Fire Beads. I'd considered doing the Heart of the Greater Mountain, but based on the name, I suspected it was big enough for me to use the tracking skill on it directly when we got to that point.

I felt the skill activate, and given the size of the entrances, I didn't need to strain it or change its application to make it work. I opened my eyes, staring out into the labyrinth, and after a minute or so of searching, I managed to catch sight of a dim red glow. I gestured up to the others to follow at a distance and began the process of sneaking around the edge of the labyrinth, drawing closer and closer to the slowly brightening red glow of the entrance we needed to make use of to get to the Akkadian Fire

Beads first. I was pretty sure getting the Heart was going to involve fighting for it, but if we could secure the beads, we could ensure we at least had a chance to win or tie regardless of the outcome.

As we drew in close to the proper entrance, I waved the others in closer and nodded to Benny, who passed me a rope he was able to conjure from his torso. Since Benny himself was G-rank, and the rope was at least H, it would be more durable than average. I tied it around my waist and cancelled Seek Hidden, waiting a second before activating it again, searching for the tunnel system beneath us. Unlike the entrance, the tunnels were massive, so I didn't even need to look to see them lit up like a lantern.

I made my way over to a tunnel that I saw connected to the entrance we wanted and extended past the edge of the labyrinth before turning to the others. I kept my voice low as I spoke, still somewhat worried about the Tinderlings hearing us. "All right, I'm going to head down to test out the process. It isn't too far, so it shouldn't be a problem. Plus, my mask will keep my face clear, and I can hold my breath on the way. If you feel a tug, though, pull me up, and if the ground hardens, wait a minute. I'll use the skill again." I cracked my neck, readying myself for the next task. "Wish me luck."

I just hoped I wouldn't need it.

Chapter Thirty-Five

DESPITE MY EARLIER WORDS TO Callie, once I found the right spot and got ready to use Sucking Mud in the way I'd envisioned, I found myself hesitating. Callie's fear at the idea of being buried alive might have been more extreme than I expected, but as I was preparing to actually submerge myself in temporarily liquid earth, it was hard to ignore the horrible images in my head. Despite being stronger, faster, and more durable than we had been before, we *were* still mortals deep down. We still hadn't completely let go of who we used to be, and honestly... being buried alive sounded fucking horrifying.

Clearing my head of the theoretical but incredibly unlikely potential consequences of my actions, I focused on the ground under me. I triggered Sucking Mud, but instead of extending it out to ten yards, I confined the effect to a small three-foot circle around my body, directing the excess energy into increasing the depth instead of the width. Since the skill was designed to be variable, it wasn't actually much of a strain to change the shape of the mud pit. I had to flex a little, but it was barely a change. It was more like holding something lightweight. I was sure it would get annoying after enough time, but for now, it was easy.

Once I triggered it, I began to sink. Slowly. Really, really slowly. Like an inch or so every few seconds. I groaned internally. This was taking longer than expected. Was a smaller radius making it slower? I didn't know enough about science to make that call. Maybe it was just because the ground here was harder.

Regardless, after about two full minutes, I was finally fully submerged. On the upside, the extremely long wait banished any possible terror or suspense from the situation. Even illogical fear could only last so long, and after two minutes of waiting, going under just didn't scare me the same way.

After inhaling strongly before I submerged, I spent the next two minutes or so holding my breath. Finally, the mud underneath me gave way, and I was left slowly dropping out of the mud an inch at a time. Dangling with my legs completely exposed was annoying, and I tried my best to remain still and let the weight of my lower body drag me free before dropping into the tunnel below. Despite having plenty of air left and my face never having been covered, I still felt the need to exhale and take a deep breath, so I did.

Once I was free, I untied the rope around my waist. After tying the end around a small rock as a signal, I tugged it, and the rope was quickly pulled back up. I used Sucking Mud again, just to make sure it was active for long enough, and I waited. After a few minutes, I saw a familiar pair of black boots emerge from the ceiling of the tunnel. With a flash of insight, I jumped up to grab them and used my weight to drag Callie down through the mud faster so she didn't have to stay submerged for too long. It worked, but as she came free, she collapsed on top of me, hacking and coughing up mud.

After she cleared her airway, she lay on top of me, glaring down in a way that made me pretty sure I shouldn't say anything.

"Why?" she asked with deceptive calmness. "Why would you think that grabbing me by the feet and dragging me into the depths of the churning earth would be a gesture I would appreciate? Holding your breath only works when you actually hold it. Screaming while your head is submerged in mud negates any benefits someone might get from having incredibly strong lungs." Her voice was shaky, and her breath was coming in short, shallow pants.

I could tell that had really messed with her.

I wiped away some of the mud and leaned up to kiss her on the forehead, pulling her down against my chest. "I'm sorry. I wanted to get you out of there as soon as possible, and when I saw your feet sticking out, I thought I could help end it faster by pulling. I didn't think about how you would react."

She leaned against me for a minute, breathing slowly and calming down. Her body relaxed as she pulled herself together.

After she finished getting her head on straight, she pushed herself up off me, climbed to her feet, and helped me up. "I understand. I appreciate the thought, but in the future, maybe we can come up with additions to the plan like that before they actually happen so I know what to expect."

I nodded but didn't say anything, staring at her and waiting.

"You want to know why I'm so afraid of being buried alive?"

Without even nodding this time, I just waited patiently.

She sighed, pulling off her mask and wiping her face to make sure all the mud was gone. Then she untied the rope around her waist. That shit got everywhere when we went under, and I was going to be cleaning it out of every crevice of my armor for weeks.

I tried to brush some of it off, which didn't work, and then shrugged. "If it's a really traumatic story now might not be the time. We have a few minutes until whoever is coming next gets down here. Besides, it sounds like something you don't want to talk about. Honestly, I can't see this coming up again anytime soon. It's not like we go mud diving for fun."

She giggled, snorting a bit then covering her face as mud came out her nose, which made me start laughing. "I guess that's fair. Maybe we can talk about it after things calm down. For now, let's just get everyone else through the mud." She bit her lip. "Maybe avoid the feet grabbing. Even if there's a decent reason, the surprise is… unpleasant."

I pulled her into a hug. After a minute, I gave her a quick kiss, and we turned to watch the others come down. It was admittedly kind of hilarious watching Benny kick and squirm his way through the ceiling. Even Callie was giggling as he finally slurped through the final layer and fell, sprawling onto the floor of the tunnel. The black mud covered his face completely, leaving him unable to see, and he flailed wildly. Although he'd dropped straight onto his back, the distance hadn't knocked the wind out of him.

Sadly, none of the others were quite as clumsy coming down. Cark landed flat on his feet and didn't even stumble. Celine landed in a crouch. Martin came down on all fours, and he caught Sarah when she dropped through.

Jessie came last after taking control of the wolves to make sure there were no incidents as they came down. She was able to assuage their annoyance by giving them treats she'd been lugging around in the backpack, but regardless of the bribery, they were not at all pleased to be covered in soot-colored muck.

Once everyone was down, I let the skill drop. I wasn't tired so much as slightly sore, and in a way, that made suspect it would fade pretty quickly. Once Sucking Mud vanished, though, we realized there was a slight unintentional side effect of using the skill that way—the mud all over us had all become solid again. While helpful for getting it *off* us, that was not particularly pleasant to experience. When mud turned back into sharp rock, sand, and stone in a lot of really unfortunate places, it was bound to cause some discomfort.

Once we all shook out our armor (and those of us with cloaks or long coats beat the damn things out like an old dust mop), we were finally ready to proceed. We all turned to check in with Callie.

She noticed us looking and rolled her eyes. "Yes I *know* it's my call where we go next. Can you give me five minutes, people? We just got down here. Let me formulate a plan."

We all just stared at her, waiting expectantly.

"Fine. Vultures, we go that way." She pointed down the tunnel in the direction of the entrance I'd originally spotted with Seek Hidden.

Of course I'd used my skill to find the right path while we were waiting for the others, so we knew which way to go, but I suspected she just wanted to lighten the mood. It worked, and the others snickered as we headed down the tunnel towards the Akkadian Fire Beads. Speaking of which…

"Did anyone do any research on what the hell an Akkadian Fire Bead is? Because I didn't, and if we're supposed to find this thing, we should probably know at least what it looks like." I hadn't bothered to look that stuff up before we left, which in retrospect, wasn't great planning.

I was getting too used to charging in without bothering to pay any attention. I had teammates who did that kind of thing, but I should have at least checked. While my ability and my combat skills contributed a lot to our group, I wasn't in this alone. I couldn't just decide my own role in things— that was something all of us needed to decide on together. Luckily, the others picked up the slack, and as usual, Callie had dug into the origin of our target.

My girlfriend was clearly feeling much better. Her walk and attitude were more upbeat after getting through the ordeal, and she didn't seem to mind being our walking textbook this time. "Akkadian Fire Beads are a specific type of elemental crystal that are often found in Volcanoes. They're the result of hyperdense fire energy flooding into a specific type of gemstone with a reputation for energy storage. Akkadian crystal is tough to find, even without elemental affinity, and it's a pain in the ass to fill up, so they aren't common."

That sounded useful for crafting, though not particularly useful to any of the crafters in our group. Still, we would be able to sell them after the hunt, and I was betting we could get a decent price for them. "So, I imagine they appear in hot environments. Where should we start looking in terms of setting? Is there someplace the things are native to?" While Seek Hidden could always find the beads if I could get close, or a trail if I wanted to mess with the skill, it would save me a lot of pain and effort if we knew where to start.

Callie, who was looking ahead, straining her eyes for something, turned and grinned at me. She pulled me ahead to the tunnel exit, nodding toward the new cavern we'd entered. "The easiest spots to find them are places with an absurd amount of fire-attributed energy. You know, forest fires, forges... magma pools." She gestured off to the side of the chamber, to a huge pool of glowing molten rock.

I winced. "Oh. That might be a problem."

Chapter Thirty-Six

THERE WERE good and bad aspects of finding the location of the Akkadian Fire Beads (I used Seek Hidden to confirm we had the right pool just in case). The upside was we knew where to look, not to mention the Tinder-lings weren't lurking around here guarding this place, so we had time to figure out how to retrieve the crystals. Unfortunately, we couldn't actually get into the damn magma pool to retrieve the beads in the first place.

I stared down into the magma then picked up a chunk of H-rank stone and tossed it into the pool. With a flash of fire, the magma literally consumed the rock. I turned to the others. "Okay, I don't know exactly what that stuff is other than molten rock, but I'm pretty sure it's hot enough to really mess us up."

Callie nodded. "It is. The fire energy in the beads is concentrated into the crystal, but the spillover is most likely responsible for this pool. It'll be hot enough to melt our flesh down to the bone, which does somewhat impede our ability to… you know… get them. We need some sort of plan to retrieve the crystals. Anyone have any ideas? Because I have literally nothing."

Benny leaned down to hold a hand out over the lava, intent on the pool. We all stared at him. I wondered if he had a device he hadn't mentioned that could get around this, or maybe some new Skill he'd been training? I was fascinated to see what he could do to fix this problem. He knelt close, moving his hand above the lava as if searching for something. He made a noise of understanding before standing back up and turning to the rest of us with a serious expression. "This stuff is super-hot. I'm not touching it."

We all glared at him, no one saying a word.

He crossed his arms over his chest and looked away.

I very deliberately turned away and ignored his nonsense. "Okay, Cark, what about you? Fire is sort of your jam, right? Do you think you could coat yourself in flames to hold back the lava long enough to reach in and grab the crystals?" I'd seen him use his flame armor to stop attacks before, so that might be viable.

It was my turn to get the looks. Cark just shook his head. "Sorry, man, but that's... not how any of that works. I can't clothe myself in fire to prevent me from being melted in lava. What about your magma-skin thing? Would that work long enough to reach into the pool and grab the beads? Not sure how it stacks up against actual lava. Or magma or whatever. Regardless, that seems like our best bet to me. Assuming it's dense enough to make sure it doesn't, like... melt and burn you to a crisp."

That was a decent idea, but I wasn't anxious to test it. Sure, it might work, but if it didn't I wasn't sure even Jessie's power could fix what this shit might do to me. I didn't think a thin layer of stone or magma would protect me.

We were all kind of... stuck. No one had any idea what to do, and we all spent the next fifteen minutes talking over Skills and abilities that might let us get around the problem, but nobody had any plans that could help. The lava pool was hands-down the most dangerous thing we'd come across.

Jessie, who'd been staring hard at the pool along with the rest of us, suddenly let out a gasp, and her eyes lit up. "I have an idea! What if we create another pit? A deeper pit. Then we can make a channel between them and let the lava drain out until the beads are exposed." She turned to me. "Solomon, can your Sucking Mud skill make the ground soft enough that Nightstrike could use a shadow scoop to shovel the mud out of it and create a hole in the ground?"

I blinked. "I... don't know. I've never considered using the skill to actually move earth, but it *should* work... theoretically. Hell, if we get the hole deep enough and at an angle, I could use the skill to soften up the channel itself and then let the earth between the pits slop into the deeper one. That would prevent us from having to dig around or mess with the magma. Hell, we could make the channel at the very bottom of the magma pit so it drains out completely. Agria, that's brilliant!"

It was also going to be fucking exhausting. Sure, making a big pit wouldn't be that tiring, but for it to be deep enough, I'd need to repeat the process a bunch of times. Still, this was by far the safest, most reasonable plan anyone had come up with, and it was definitely doable. I looked at Callie to make sure, and she nodded, confirming that this was something her shadow constructs could handle, not that I'd had many doubts.

I had everyone step back (the last thing we needed was someone slipping into the muck or accidentally tripping and falling into a pool of G-ranked magma) before starting my work.

I considered how best to do this. I was at about twenty charges, so I had some room to play with it a bit. I considered doing the same thing I'd done earlier (concentrating the skill into a smaller area and forcing it down) but I realized I was making this more complex than it needed to be. I could do this much simpler by just using the skill as intended multiple times.

So that was what I did. I activated Sucking Mud in a ten-yard radius, as usual, though it only went down a few feet. When I nodded to Callie, she created a huge shovel from her shadow abilities and started scooping out the muck, dumping it in a random crack a few feet away from us. Once she got most of it, I let the skill fade and did it again—rinse and repeat until we'd managed to hollow out a massive depression in the rock.

The hole was huge, ten feet around and about twenty down, and it took about four uses of Sucking Mud to reach the point where it was deep enough to drain the magma in the way we needed. At least we hoped it was deep enough. We couldn't actually see how far down it went, but the hole was deep enough that we could drain out some of the magma and use that to estimate exactly how deep the pool was to start with.

With the pool finished, I had everyone stand back and readied myself to cast Sucking Mud again, this time with a bit of a twist. I activated the skill but altered the shape and size. There was a one or two foot gap between the two pools, just so the magma didn't melt through the side before we were ready. With a flex of my mind, I created a cylindrical shaft between the two of them with Sucking Mud at an angle, making damn sure there was plenty of room for the magma to come through.

Because of the angle I'd made the cylinder at, the mud inside it slowly flowed out and dropped into the pit, leaving a big open cylindrical hole in the wall of the pit, directly connecting to the pool. Slowly, much slower than I'd expected, the magma began to flow through the channel and spill into the pit. Watching the glowing stone roll through the passage and drizzle into the pit was... an interesting experience. It was a beautiful sight, and that made taking it seriously a bit harder, though I was smart enough to know that was a stupid reaction.

The weird dichotomy of how easy this had been relative to the difficulty of the task made it tempting to do... something. Since we were just sitting here and waiting for the thing to drain surely there was some way to speed it up, right? But we were all smart enough to know that despite how peaceful and boring this little light show was, it was also absurdly deadly and potentially fatal, and we couldn't make it go by any faster without taking far too many risks.

Despite how annoying the hurry-up-and-wait aspect of the process was however, it *was* working. The level of the magma was slowly dropping. It was easy to see the marks on the sides of the rim as the level of the pool dropped a bit at a time, and we all watched with bated breath as more and more of the pool was exposed by the dropping magma level. I looked around as we waited, anxious that someone might sneak up on us, but I didn't see any sign of enemies.

I returned my gaze to the magma pool and watched in awe as the level of the molten stone finally dropped low enough to expose what we had come here for. The glowing liquid receded, a bubble of translucent red energy was exposed. Within the bubble floated three crystals, rotating around a single point of light. The crystals were linked by a series of energy tethers, seemingly part of a harmonious system, and each time they rotated, the crystals themselves pulsed. The fiery nova of energy was barely visible in the depths of the stones, flaring as the central point of light dimmed.

Akkadian Fire Beads. They were absolutely mesmerizing to behold, and all of us stared, our breaths caught in our throats as we finally saw what we'd come for. Carefully, Callie conjured a net of shadows, lowering it down to scoop up the floating crystals. As the shadow touched it, the translucent sphere of red popped like a soap bubble, and the light in the center winked out. The three crystals dropped into the net, and Callie retracted the thing slowly, careful not to touch the still-hot beads.

I grinned at her. "Got them. I have to say—that was easier than I expected."

She levered them up, and I opened the bag and flipped up the lid of the box so she could drop them in. We all heaved a sigh of relief, which was cut short as an amused voice split the air behind us.

"That's funny, I was just thinking the same thing."

We all turned slowly to find a trio of yellow-and-blue-clad Ascendants. I recognized their features from the report a few days ago. The Wavestriders. Now it was my turn to sigh. Nothing could ever be easy. Oh well, hopefully the fight would at least be fun.

Chapter Thirty-Seven

As DESCRIBED, the Wavestriders (which made zero sense as a name because none of them had water powers) were a pretty intimidating group, visually speaking. The leader, Boreas, *was* short, but the green-haired bearded man made up for it with some seriously wide shoulders. The really huge dark-skinned guy, Raleigh (presumably no relation to the raiders) was holding a huge hammer in his heavy braceleted hands, as we'd be warned he might, and the small and delicate looking Astara was resting her hands on a pair of very thin and pointy-looking daggers.

They were all standing in a way that made me kind of assume they had practiced this in the mirror, because there was no way that pose was natural. Despite the somewhat-silly nature of their stances, they did actually look like a threat. Boreas had a cocky grin on his admittedly handsome face as his green eyes bored into the bag we'd just finished pulling closed. "I admit, I didn't expect the team to beat us here would be some randos we've never heard of. I thought for sure Fisher or MacDonald's crew would be the first ones to the beads. It's impressive you made it so far, but I'm afraid this is going to be the end of the line for you folks. Why don't you pass us the beads, and we can let you leave in peace."

I raised an eyebrow, not that he could see it behind my mask, and looked around at our group. "You... You know there's three of you, right? Because we have five G-rankers here. Plus wolves. Like, so many wolves.

More wolves than most people. I don't mean to come across as arrogant, but this doesn't seem like it's going to go the way you think it wi—"

I noticed a slight shimmer near Astara and spun on my heel, acting on instinct, dropping my cane and catching it two handed near the tip as I spun, swinging it like a bat at the spot where the redhead was just now appearing to try to grab the bag.

She gave a squeak as she saw the silver head incoming and tried to dodge. I clipped her narrowly before she vanished again, reappearing back at their side without the bag. She was also holding her shoulder, where I'd apparently made contact, and glaring at me.

I tsk'ed loudly. "See, that was just rude. I was talking, and you just pop over here to try to steal our shit? Not cool. This is why everyone says you can't trust a teleporter." I paused. "Okay, they don't say that. But I do. Or I'm going to start."

I heard a loud sigh from my side. Callie cut me off. "Sweetie, you're babbling. You were nailing it there for a second, but you kind of spiraled at the end. You landed a hit. Just take the win."

I shut my mouth. She wasn't wrong, I wasn't really sure where I'd been going with that. Astara popping up had shaken me a bit, and I tended to run my mouth when I was nervous. I'd gotten way too used to fighting monsters. Callie reached over to give my arm a squeeze (I assumed to apologize for cutting me off) but I just put a hand on hers and squeezed back, not bothered at all.

Boreas, who apparently was not a fan of being ignored while I was monologuing, cleared his throat. "To answer your question," he said forcefully, obviously trying to drag our focus back to his much more strained-looking smile. "We are the Wavestriders. We're some of the strongest freshman in the whole Academy, and we aren't worried about a bunch of nobodies or their stupid dogs."

Aforementioned "stupid dogs" might not have been people-level intelligent, but they were still smart enough to pick up on his disdainful gaze. The growls rumbling from their barrel chests was intimidating enough that it somewhat derailed Boreas's sneering tangent.

I snickered when I saw his face pale slightly.

Callie was smirking as she responded. "Sorry if that disturbed your rant. Regardless, we aren't handing over anything to you. Like Solomon said, there are more of us. Plus, no offense, but you seem like kind of a dick, and I don't want to give you anything you ask for just on general principle."

Raleigh's lip twitched, and I got the impression Boreas was a big enough asshole that even his own teammates enjoyed seeing him taken down a peg. Astara didn't seem amused, but mostly that was because she was trying to glare a hole in my skull while forcefully (and from the sounds of it, painfully) popping her dislocated shoulder into place. Her blue eyes were boring into me so intensely, it was actually making me a little uncomfortable. Like, I knew that had hurt, but damn, someone had to have hit her before at some point.

Boreas, whose grin had now officially faded to a look of steely anger, spat to one side, presumably to be intimidating, though it didn't really work. "Fine. You must be new transfers. Anyone who had been around a bit longer would know their place. I guess it's up to us to teach you how things work." He took a menacing step forward, but before he could close the gap any more than that, a wall of shadows slammed down over the whole room courtesy of Callie, blinding everyone in the place.

I wasn't sure how long she could keep it up, but I was guessing teleportation was a no-go in the dark, when there were fucking lava pools around, and I was determined to make use of the distraction. I activated Seek Hidden, happy they were close enough for me to be able to spot them, and then Leaf on the Wind as I dove forward to try to take out the redhead before the shadows came down. She was their most mobile fighter and would be the hardest to pin down once the blinding effect ended.

I used Mercy Kill as I came in, aiming for the shoulder I'd hit earlier. Assholes or not, I wasn't willing to kill these people. They were students at the Academy, not monsters who were brainwashing innocent people. If I messed her up badly enough, her concentration would be shot, though, and I didn't imagine it was safe to teleport around a magma chamber when you were hurting too bad to focus.

I triggered Consecration of Flame and Touch of Tears right before the cane made contact.

I'd used the combination on my tonfas plenty, but it seemed like it was more effective on the higher-ranked material of my cane. I could feel more power in the blunt weapon than I ever had before, though it still wasn't enough to have any chance of killing a G-ranker in one hit. Her vitality would resist the effect like any of my friends would, so as long as I only hit her once, it was pretty safe to use on her. I slammed the cane down on her injured shoulder, and she bellowed in agony as I released what little force I had along with it.

The poison and flames invaded the injury, permeating the damaged flesh and causing what I assumed was unbearable agony as I leapt back out of the way. Raleigh had heard the impact and lashed out at the spot where I'd been standing with unnerving accuracy, As I dodged the impact, his hammer crashed down into the stone of the cavern floor with enough force to crater it. I continued my backpedal, rejoining Callie and the others, and grabbed my girlfriend's hand to make sure she knew I'd accomplished my goal.

She dropped the shadow construct, revealing the entire room again—that was a smart call, given our friends and the wolves completely lacked the ability to move around in it. When the darkness cleared, Raleigh was holding Astara, who was clutching the top of her arm tightly, teeth clenched in extreme pain as the green glow of poison fire spread from beneath her fingers. Her eyes were closed, and her face was screwed up with agony and turning bright red. I was pretty sure she wouldn't be tele-porting anywhere for a bit.

To his credit, Boreas actually did look really pissed about the damage to his teammate. I wasn't sure if it was an affront to his pride as a leader or if he actually gave a shit that she was hurt, but I decided to give him the benefit of the doubt and assume he cared about his friends and wasn't just stupid green hair and a too white smile in a way too colorful costume. He stepped forward, gritting his teeth as he hissed. "That was a mistake rookies. We could have done this the easy way. Now we're going to have to hurt you."

Callie just sighed. "Do you? Do you really? Is this really worth it? Can't you just walk away and sell whatever you got here for a nice profit? I get that you want to win, but even if you get the beads from us, you have no guarantee that you'll be able to take down Fisher and whoever else shows up to get the Heart of the Greater Mountain. And they will show up. Lots of them. It's going to be much easier to find than this was, and I would be shocked if that whole thing isn't a free-for-all by the time any of us get there."

The gritted teeth turned into a sneer, albeit a much angrier one than earlier. "You think we're just going to give up? Figures you nobodies wouldn't get how important this is. We need to win this. It's our best chance to stand out. We may be impressive to the freshman class, but we're nothing compared to the next few years. Those people are all older and stronger and have their own publicity bases. If we're going to beat any of them, we need to be the ones who win and get featured in the wrap-up stream and publicized. You might as well ask us to quit being cultivators."

Once again, I was thankful for my ability. If I didn't have the power I did, we would be completely at the mercy of others, just like all the other Ascendants. Sure we needed to pay attention to that stuff, but it wasn't something that controlled us. We could redistribute points to the stats we most needed and make our powers more impressive, which made it that much easier for us to get attention—especially me since I had the option of trading stats from other people and not just among the team.

Still, now wasn't the time for that observation. Despite having most likely taken their teleporter out early, we still had a team to deal with, and they weren't going to be pushovers. The only major upside was that looking around I didn't see any of the H-rankers. I assumed Callie had moved them with a construct and pushed them out of the room to make sure they didn't get caught in the middle of this. Their wolves had gone with them, leaving us with just our five strongest people and five wolves. Hopefully, that was more than enough to take down these posers.

They obviously noticed the missing team members, but since Callie had chosen to keep the bag with us (presumably to prevent them from going after our weaker teammates), they focused on us instead. With everyone visible, it was easier to coordinate all of our teammates, so we weren't at a disadvantage, especially not with Cark here. As a high G-ranker, he had enough muscle to counter one of their brutes. Here was hoping that would be enough.

Chapter Thirty-Eight

BOREAS AND RALEIGH came at us hard, leaving Astara once it become clear that her wound wasn't going to get worse. There was no bleeding because the tear in the flesh had been cauterized shut with poison fire, which while excruciatingly painful, was actually helpful in terms of keeping her alive. Can't bleed out if your wound is seared shut, and her body was more than capable of fighting off the poison, though the process of purging it would take a few minutes.

Boreas, despite being shorter and less imposing, was the bigger threat. His elemental abilities had some range, and Raleigh's weight trick only worked by touch. Cark, knowing we needed to settle him down or he would shred us all like tissue paper, stepped up to engage the shorter man, hands alight with blue flame. He took up a boxing guard with his staff tucked behind him in a tube he'd brought for just such an occasion.

The smaller green-haired man didn't seem to take my friend seriously and came at him with a fist wreathed in a swirl of green wind, which Cark tanked with an upraised arm and a flare of his power that burned off most of the air around the punch, bleeding off the effect in a burst of fire. It was amusing to see the wind user's green eyes widen as Cark flicked out a jab that he had to catch with both hands, coating them in wind to try to disperse flames in the same way as Cark had managed to blow away his attack.

Sadly for him, Cark had clearly learned from that experience and condensed his flame more around his fist. The resulting explosion of flaming air blew the smaller man back from our team's pyrokinetic. He caught himself easily enough unfortunately, shaking off the heat, which while dangerous, had been dampened enough not to do much more than give him a light-red burn across his face.

Cark didn't give him a chance to recover, using his much larger range to dash in and pin the green-haired man with a blistering storm of jabs coated in blue flame. Boreas spun up his wind strikes again and did his best to weather the storm of attacks, using the spin and the explosive force of the collisions to deflect most of the force as the air cracked with explosions of heat and force at their continuing exchange of punches.

I wanted to keep watching because it was fucking awesome, but Raleigh was coming around the battle to engage with the rest of us. I knew we couldn't possibly take him head-to-head. He was G-rank, but he was Might focused and farther along than us. I didn't know how much of his progression had gone into Might, but I wasn't willing to make the same mistake I had with the Dullahan.

I dashed in to attack, but I went in at an angle, trying to strike as I went by and triggering Flurry of Blows so I could land a series of fast hits. My poison fire would do most of the work if I could hit him enough times. Raleigh deflected about half the strikes off those huge bracelets as he tried to bring the hammer around to hit me, but was interrupted by a massive black sphere on a chain came around from the other side to slam into his head right in the blind spot, staggering him.

I grinned at my girlfriend from behind my mask as she pulled his focus. When he turned his head to pay attention to her, I smashed my cane into the back of Raleigh's knee. It buckled, and he aborted his turn to deal with me before freezing with indecision, not sure which of us to go after. This left him open for Jin and Rellia to dip in from behind and try to bite down on his calves, only to evade as he kicked out at them.

Because Callie had taught me how to use Balam and my own Balam style had been influenced heavily by the wolves, the four of us synergized pretty well. We circled around him, baiting him out to create openings for the others. While fighting two wolves (even with goblin riders) had been a pain in the ass, it was nothing compared to fighting four different combatants his own rank with a massive, slow weapon like a hammer. Even with his ability, we were giving this guy a huge problem.

Callie and I moved like a single unit as she matched her speed and style to mine with her superior affinity for Balam, and the two wolves fell into our pace quickly enough. I slammed my cane down on Raleigh whenever I could get a clean shot. While the first and second blows didn't do much, the more I landed, the slower the big man got and the more openings he left.

From the corner of my eye, I spotted Jessie and Benny as they headed for the teleporter, who had managed to get to her feet. Benny attacked with a devastating drop kick, and I was shocked to see her teleport out of the way. She appeared behind him, only to be buried in an avalanche of fangs and claws as a trio of wolves perfectly coordinated by our healer fell on her. She only barely managed to teleport out after they hit her hard enough to tear a scream from the redhead.

She appeared just in time for Benny to attack from behind, but I didn't get a chance to see any more as my vision was taken up by a massive fuck-off hammer moving way too fast for something its size. I got my arms up in the way, making sure my cane was laid across my forearms so it took more of the impact. Even with my armor soaking some of the impact, my arms were on fire as I was sent flying, barely managing to tuck myself up and over into a tight backflip to get my feet under me again and land without flying tail over teakettle.

Raleigh had noticed my distraction and tried to make me pay for it. Luckily, my cane absorbed force, because I was pretty sure if it hadn't leached off some of that strike I would have broken both arms with that block, costume or not. Luckily, he wasn't able to follow up because the wolves and Callie had laid into him from behind when he committed to an attack, and he was currently howling with pain as Jin tore a chunk out of his thigh on the way out of a vicious attack. Callie landed that huge shadow ball in the back of his skull as he tried to wheel around to attack my wolf then backed off.

My arms hurt. A lot. Not enough that I thought they were broken, but enough to confirm that even with Raleigh heavily poisoned and with all the mitigating factors, that asshole hit hard. I was guessing he'd lightened the hammer a ton then snapped it back to being heavy as fuck once it built up momentum. I kind of got why he used the thing now. I needed to do some damage here, and I knew one surefire way to manage it. I stacked Mercy Kill and Flurry of Blows before charging in at Raleigh, using Leaf on the Wind to come in from above.

I swung my cane down straight at the bastard's collarbone. I wanted to seriously fuck him up but not kill him, and a broken collarbone would hurt like a bitch, but was pretty much never fatal. As I swung, I used Afterburner, massively boosting the damage of the whole skill. Afterburner was my finisher, and while it was exhausting and left me weakened, it also had a uniquely powerful effect. Afterburner boosted the power of an attack in totality, which meant each and every part of it.

It increased the speed and power I got from my active skills even further, as well as the heat and acidity and power of my poison fire. It even increased the force damage I had stored up in the cane, as little as it was. The amount of that last hammer blow it had soaked up wasn't much, but multiplied with Mercy Kill then increased again with Afterburner, the entire strike was a fucking whopper. The silver skull head smashed down on his collarbone, releasing a massive burst of power into his torso and fucking shattering the bone with the impact.

Raleigh threw back his head and howled, the incredibly powerful burst of poison fire connecting to the stacks already on him and driving him to his knees in a surge of venomous flame so deadly, I was forced to cancel the damned skills because I was pretty sure they would have killed him. He fell forward, literally smoking, but alive and on the mend. I hit the ground staggering in exhaustion from literally all of my energy bottoming out after Afterburner faded.

Afterburner was an extremely potent skill for me especially because I relied on DS Mastery so much. The skill caused an explosive increase in overall power, but it did it by increasing the power of every aspect of the next action. Of course it didn't need to be an attack. I'd used it to increase my speed during our escape from the undead fortress, though it had been a strain to fit "escape" into the definition of the skill. Still, the more skills I could pack into a single attack, the more effective Afterburner would be.

I stopped staggering as Callie appeared next to me, steadying my footing and slipping under my arm. "Easy there. I've got you. That was a hell of an attack just now. I'm impressed—I didn't know you could hit that hard." She helped me over to a nearby rock to let me lean against it. "Agria should be able to juice you back up when she's done. She and Clockwork are in the middle of finishing off Astara." She gestured over to their fight, and sure enough, Astara looked like she was about to drop.

Benny's damn tranq punches didn't do much to G-rankers as a one-off (the original device had been H-ranked, after all), but stacked ten or twenty deep and with the enemy already injured and fighting off a dangerous poison, plus obviously not high in Vitality, it was enough to whittle her down. I looked over in time to see the wolves pin her down for Benny to punch her in the face with his tranq hand, finally putting her out before slumping to the ground in exhaustion. Jessie came over and pushed a surge of life force into him, healing any injuries and getting him back on his feet.

She headed over to us, the wolves dragging Astara by her feet, not having to be too careful because of her costume. She had them drop the girl off next to Raleigh then headed over to me. "Wow, that guy looks like shit. Congrats on the win. Come here."

I stumbled to my feet, and she slapped both hands down on my chest, flooding me with a pulse of warm green energy that revitalized my flagging body. I sighed with relief as the aftereffects of Afterburner were mitigated, though from Jessie's expression, that was harder than it should have been.

We all turned to look at Cark, who was still beating the shit out of Boreas, but the green-haired man was flagging already. Their Might may be similar, but Cark was a pyrokinetic. He was resistant to his own heat, and those blasts of fire that kept going off when flame and wind met weren't doing nearly as much damage to him as to his opponent. Finally, Cark landed a brutal right cross that put Boreas on his ass, and we all headed over to where he was tying the green-haired man up.

Once we had all three subdued, we triggered their emergency beacons as we started sorting through the materials and artifacts they had on them while Jessie healed them up. Callie was right. Loot *was* fun.

Chapter Thirty-Nine

DESPITE THEM BEING ASSHOLES, we had Jessie patch them up first thing. The last thing we wanted was their deaths on our conscience, and since we'd triggered their beacons we didn't need to worry about them attacking us. They were out, and they'd lost all their materials to us. Obviously, they didn't have the last thing on our list, but they *did* have a bunch of really expensive shit we could sell, which was just a nice bonus and an excellent note to go out on after we got the last item.

To my surprise, though, none of them seemed particularly angry once we healed them up. I expected more sneers and insults, but they actually seemed to have gained a measure of respect for us. We had them restrained at first, but Boreas brought that up once his teammates were all healed. "Well... that was impressive. Teach me to underestimate the new bloods, I suppose. You can release us, by the way. We're out of the hunt, and attacking you now won't just look bad; it'll count as outside interference and bring the whole Academy down on our heads."

Knowing the Academy punished interference was interesting, because it made me even more certain Aiden had people on the inside helping him avoid detection. Still, I didn't sense any dishonesty.

I glanced over to Callie. "What do you think? I don't see a reason to keep them tied up. Hell, they could probably break loose if they really wanted to. That rope is only H-rank, and lack of leverage or not, I doubt it would hold up to a serious attempt to get loose." They were sure to have noticed the rank of their restraints already, so telling them cost us nothing.

She stared at them for a second, then sighed, gesturing for Benny to cut them loose, since the rope was his and he had the easiest time handling it. "Oh, what the hell. It's not like we lose anything by being polite. But if we're springing you early, we could use a bit of information on the remaining players. You mentioned another group besides Fisher. Info about them and any of the others you can mention seems fair." She phrased it like a demand, but let Benny keep freeing them even before she got an answer.

Boreas, who was the first untied, rubbed his wrists. "That's... borderline interference. But since you had us captive, we can consider this payment for our release. That should be valid, at least according to the rulebook." I tried to hide my wince at the reminder that I'd been a total idiot and forgotten to even see if there was a rulebook, but once we freed the others, they all sat back against the wall to wait for their pickups while they told us about the other players we might run into in the final leg of the hunt.

Astara, who was rotating her shoulder to loosen it up and glaring at me, was the first to speak. "Okay, well first of all—ow. Also, fuck you. Second of all, who do you want to hear about first? We don't know everyone who's involved. Hell, half the people we expected to make it to the end might not have stuck it out. Our own loss kind of makes that clear. The participants this year are crazy—this is probably the earliest things have ever come to a head." She gestured unhappily to her group. "We were some of the favorites to win, and we got taken out by nobodies. No offense, but we literally didn't know you existed."

Callie probably could have taken that badly, but instead she just shrugged. "Fair enough. We're pretty new to the party. But yeah, that does kind of leave the option of a shakeup on the table."

It was less probable than they seemed to think. We weren't exactly average joes in terms of freshman ability.

"So tell us about the group you mentioned before," Callie said, "and Fisher. We're pretty sure he at least is still in the hunt. We saw him recently from a distance. Chances are good we'll run into him when we go for the Heart."

Astara nodded. "Fisher is… Shit, Fisher scares me. There are some vicious bastards at the Academy. Some of the upper ranks grew up with power, and it shows. It isn't really common. Recursion tends to take the rough edges off the real psychos, but Fisher isn't vicious in that way. He isn't hateful or condescending or cruel. He just… does not give a fuck about literally anyone. He *will* hurt you. Not because he wants to or because he doesn't like you, but because he wants you out of his way and that's the fastest way to remove you."

That wasn't… great news. But it also wasn't what we needed to know. Hearing how this guy would torture us all without feeling bad about it gave us no actual tactical info.

"Yeah, we get it," Callie said. "He's a cold bastard, and we should be very afraid. What can you tell us about how he fights, anything about his weaknesses? We know he phases through stuff and rides a motorcycle. We know he has chains that he wears around his body. Anything to add to that? Anything at all?"

Astara looked sheepish. "Sorry, not really. Fisher doesn't really have long drawn-out fights. I can tell you he's efficient. He doesn't believe in dragging things out. Every time we've seen him fight someone, he ends it fast and brutal. The least effort for the most result. Economical. If that makes sense. His bike is *fast*, and it synergizes well with his powers. He can go up walls and shit, not just through them, and he uses those chains to catch people as he goes by. They aren't just chains either. There are hooks on the end. Getting caught up in them doesn't end well, so avoid them if you can."

None of this sounded particularly reassuring. But still, the more we knew, the more prepared we could be. I kind of wished she wasn't stuffing that information full of so much fatalism and doomsaying, but hey, beggars and choosers, right?

"Okay, tell us about MacDonald. Your boss mentioned him earlier." Callie looked to Celine. "Is he another one of the freshmen most people have heard of?"

Celine just shrugged. That was fair—we couldn't expect her to know everything.

Astara, who was apparently the spokesperson of the group, sighed. "Mac-Donald is one of the freshman favorites, yes. His father is an E-ranker, so he grew up on the fast track. He's kind of like that shitbag Cold Snap, only he isn't useless and annoying. MacDonald is one of those people that manages to keep just high enough of a profile to be consistently talked about without being the center of attention, and he likes it that way. He tends to move around quietly, but that's what makes him so dangerous."

Boreas groaned. "For the love of the revenant, Star, you are the worst at this. You're just repeating useless hype that doesn't tell them anything of worth in a fight." He rolled his eyes at the now-glaring redhead. "What my extremely dramatic teammate is trying to say is that he downplays his power by making it hard to notice in battle, but everyone is pretty sure he's telekinetic. He's Might focused. We tend to have the advantage in the early ranks because Might-based powers are more impressive at low levels. Point is he's subtle with how he uses it. Coats his body in a force field that lets him exert his strength more effectively through physical combat."

I had noticed the plethora of Might-based Ascendants who dominated the public eye. The fact that Might-based powers had an advantage early on made a lot of sense. Might tended to be the driving force behind big flashy powers. Stats like Fantasy and Perception were much more subtle until they scaled to a high enough level. Still, that physical enhancement trick sounded nasty. He was essentially getting twice the bang for his buck Might-wise. Not to mention the flexibility of telekinesis outside the way he was using it.

Sadly, our question-and-answer segment seemed to be at an end, because the beacons flashed a warning, letting us know to prepare them for extraction. Without much fanfare, the space next to us cracked, and a door made of blue light ripped its way into existence in midair. A bored-looking man in a yellow-checkered suit stepped out. Spotting the Wavestriders, he said, "I'm here for a pickup? I was halfway into my nap when you called, so if you could hurry up and get your things together that would be great."

I stared at the blue doorway in the air in shock. The last time we'd triggered the beacons, the pickup had been with shuttles. Granted, we had been outside, but I hadn't realized the Academy had a long-range teleporter with a portal power on hand. I couldn't imagine what kind of power was needed to tear a hole in reality across a planet, though I supposed he could have just been nearby. Either way, that was impressive. I was guessing he was firmly in the E-ranks. Though I supposed he could have been F-rank. I didn't really have any context for the scale of powers like that.

Hell, even at my current scale, I could kind of see something like that being possible. I could run fifteen hundred miles per hour, so having enough power to tear a hole in space could easily be within the realm of G-rank possibility. Longer distances could be F-rank. Who knew how shit like that even worked? Hell, I could probably grant a wish for long-distance travel with the stats I had now.

Boreas, Astara, and Raleigh all stood up. The bigger man turned to give me a onceover, shooting me a grin. "You've got a mean swing on you, man. Not to mention you're annoying as hell to fight. Don't think that'll work on me if we ever go up against each other again, though." Raleigh held out his hand. "Thanks for showing me where I need to improve."

I smiled and shook his hand.

He nodded then headed through the portal first, and Boreas went next. When it was Astara's turn, she lingered behind.

She turned to look at Callie. "Hey, try to win this, okay? If we have to get beaten by a bunch of rookies, I want all the other favorite teams to lose too. It's only fair. You guys aren't too bad. Just be careful, and you might actually pull this off. Remember what I told you about Fisher and MacDonald. Whatever Boreas says, that was solid advice. Fighting is about more than moves. Knowing how your enemy thinks and acts is important." She gave one last nod then walked through the tear in the world, vanishing into the blue light.

The guy in the yellow-checkered suit didn't even bother to acknowledge us. He just followed them into the light before letting it wink out, leaving us alone in the huge lava cavern.

Callie looked around but didn't get up. "Last leg of the journey, guys. Let's take a break before we go looking for the Heart. I have a feeling this next part is going to be tough. Might as well make sure we're in top shape."

None of us could argue with that. We all just leaned back to get a quick rest. If The Wavestriders had been telling the truth, we were going to need it.

Chapter Forty

WE WERE ALL PRETTY exhausted after the fight. The Wavestriders had been tough, and this had been one of our first run-ins with an elite Ascendant force from the Academy. If anything, we'd gotten lucky because they weren't taking us seriously, but it had really shown us the difference between our group and some of the tougher teams out here. With all our advantages, it was easy to consider ourselves the best of the freshman class, but this fight had shown us how wrong we were about that.

I'd known the higher years would be more powerful, but it was pretty absurd how much stronger than us even the other first years could get at the higher end of things. If this fight hadn't gone exactly the right way for us, we would have been screwed. Raleigh was *much* stronger than I was (stronger than any of us besides Cark, really) and if he'd been more prepared to deal with our coordination, we never would have won the fight.

I sidled up next to Callie, putting my arm around her shoulder. "Credit for your thoughts?"

She hadn't said much since announcing our break. She didn't seem upset or anything, just… distracted. I was pretty sure she was going over the fight in her head and coming to the same conclusion I had: we needed to get stronger. That meant we needed to win this hunt and get the promotion we were entitled to, as well as the points to move us up the rankings.

She shook off the trance she was in pretty quickly. "Sorry, I was just thinking about how much further we still have to go. It's easy to get caught up in how fast we've been advancing and lose track of how weak we still are in the grand scheme of things."

I understood what she meant. While I could get more points from others by granting wishes, my teammates had to trade their own points or valuable memories to get them. While we could move points around for them to optimize their abilities, they still needed to advance the old-fashioned way.

Being able to change around points to maximize their strength would help a lot with that, but it was by no means a done deal. We had a lot of hard work ahead of us to get stronger. Not to mention once we finally got strong enough to get off this planet, we still had to deal with larger forces, which included the other Wishmaster Candidates who would be just as broken at the very least. We had to make the best possible use of our time here and get as strong as possible, because at that point, our advantage would be gone.

Hell, it was worse than that. The other Candidates may have come from larger and more developed planets, giving them a head start on resources and a larger value pool to draw from for wish payments. My only real advantage was the fact that my parents had been strong enough to ensure I started with every single stat unlocked, which had given me an incredibly solid foundation to build my strength on. I'd been doing my best to lean into that and keep my stats fairly even, but I needed to pick up the pace.

Callie reached up, pulled my mask away, and leaned in to kiss me soundly. When I blinked and looked down at her dumbly, she smiled. "No getting lost in your own head. I'm already freaking out about the future. Somebody in this relationship has to stay grounded and not let what's coming get them down. Whatever is on the way, we'll face it together. All of us. In the meantime, you just need to keep your head on straight. We aren't out of this hunt yet, even if we're getting close. We need to keep our heads in the game."

I let out a loud breath. "Yeah. You're right. I'm really bad at this living-in-the-now thing, but there's still a ton to do to finish up this event." I gave her a boyish grin. "Plus, I can't get too distracted. I have to finish this and make sure we all get out okay. I don't want anything spoiling our big date or our visit back to meet your mom."

That got a blush from my girlfriend, and it was my turn to lay a kiss on her. Once I pulled away, I got to my feet and offered her my hand, pulling her up to a standing position.

I slid my mask back into place after shooting her a wink.

She turned to look at the others. "Okay, guys. This is it. The big one. The last thing on the list. If we get through this, we're the winners of this year's freshman scavenger hunt. We'll get a ton of points to bump us up the rankings, not to mention we'll be promoted throughout the city by the Academy and we'll get priority in the stream of this competition when it's released, all of which will result in a huge windfall of points for everyone here."

I hadn't actually considered how huge the windfall would be, but it absolutely would be enough to kick Grimmengap all the way up to G-rank. Hell, I had no clue where my own strength would end up, but I was pretty sure it would be a very nice cushion for all of us, and plenty more points to redistribute for the others to keep them in peak shape. Direct points trading was the fairest and most even method of wish making I knew. Hell, I could even suggest those because the inherent nature of the one-for-one trade made it a fair exchange, even if it was my idea, so I didn't need to worry about invalidating the wish with my interference.

Jessie was the one who brought up the obvious. "I'm a little worried about fighting this Fisher guy. The chains sound nasty, but those hooks are what really scare me. We don't really have anyone who specializes in durability. G-ranked hooks on chains could do some serious damage to any of us. The puppies especially will have a lot of problems avoiding that kind of attack, and I'd really hate to see them get hurt like that." She cast a worried glance at our wolves, and I couldn't help but agree with the sentiment.

Callie bit her lip, obviously just as unwilling to see her wolf injured. Our pups hadn't been with us long, but they were big warm fuzzballs we'd all bonded with. I didn't want to see Jin strung up on a meat hook—that sounded horrible. We all had armor (H-rank though it may be) that could help prevent the hooks from getting in, but the wolves just had their fur. They could avoid the hooks just as well as we could, if not better, but there was something else to take into account too.

I turned to Callie. "We should send the H-rankers back to the base. Bringing them along with the wolves was a way to mitigate the risk, but given the level the Wavestriders were at and how likely it is that everyone we run into will be at that level, I don't think it's a good idea to bring them along." I gave them a helpless shrug. "Sorry, guys. I know you wanted to stick it out with us, and you were here for that last bit and hopefully were able to get some time on the stream, but I don't think you'll be able to keep up going forward."

I expected them to be upset, but Celine nodded with a sigh. "You're right. As much as I wish we could be part of the finale, that last battle made it painfully obvious this isn't a stage where we belong yet. We can take the wolves back to the base with us if you like. Having the five extra guards with us will make it much easier to get back safely. I assume it'll be the five of you going ahead at least?"

We all looked to Callie, who nodded.

"Then I wish you all luck." Celine looked at Benny, almost shyly. "Stay safe. We'll see you all soon."

Callie looked relieved to have avoided an argument. "That sounds like a good plan. I suspect the Heart will be in an even hotter chamber in any case. The wolves aren't really designed for these temperatures. Not to mention their paws aren't optimal for this kind of ground. We saw that on the way up the mountain. You all can head back down, and we'll meet up with you back at the base once we've finished retrieving the last item on the list."

We said our goodbyes. Benny took Celine aside to have a whispered conversation while we all pretended not to hear because our Perception was way too good for it to matter. I said goodbye to Jin, nuzzling the wolf and scratching behind his ears. He seemed to like it, which was good. There was something life affirming about hugging big furry animals, though I suspected we were getting too attached. Still, we all said goodbye, then the wolves took off back to the base with Grimmengap, leaving just the four of us and Cark behind.

I shot Callie a questioning glance, and she took a deep breath and nodded, prompting me to activate Seek Hidden on the Heart of the Greater Mountain. I wasn't actually sure what it looked like, so I was wondering if this would even work or if I'd wasted a charge on something too small to be visible from a distance. Luckily, that didn't turn out to be the case, because the Heart was both not that far away and *not* small. I oriented us in the general direction, and we started walking towards it as I filled the others in on our target.

It was difficult to describe, and it took me a second to find the words. "It's a heart."

Everyone just kind of looked at me blankly.

"No, like... a literal heart. The actual organ. It looks like it's pumping, too, though I can't see exactly what. It's about the size of a door? Height-wise at least, and maybe half that wide."

It was actually pumping too, albeit slowly. We were pretty close to it, maybe a few chambers away. I wondered if they'd set these two chambers up next to each other on purpose.

I led the others in the right direction, though we had to detour a few times to find the entrance, because it wasn't a straight shot to the chamber where it was waiting. Still, we got to it eventually, and all of us were preparing to head into the room when a form came sailing by us, and an incredibly tall woman with skin like grey quarry stone crashed into the wall next to where we were standing.

Before we could react, the chain I hadn't noticed attached to her leg tightened, digging in the hook at the end as she was slowly dragged back into the room, groaning in pain. We all looked at each other.

"So..." Benny said, "I'm guessing we found Fisher."

I nodded. Seemed like we had. Though from the looks of it, we weren't the first ones to find him.

My friend grinned nervously. "But hey, if the fight is still going on, at least we still have a chance at winning."

I could always count on Benny for a silver lining at least.

Chapter Forty-One

WALKING into the chamber where the Heart was waiting, I wasn't sure what to expect, but it definitely wasn't what I found. The place was a war zone. A redheaded man, clearly Fisher, was straddling a motorcycle, chains extending from his outstretched arms. At the end of each chain was a person. One of them was the stone woman from before, and the other was a blue-skinned man with a third eye on his forehead. They were both straining against the chains, holding him in place while a shorter blonde guy wailed on him.

I wasn't sure why he didn't phase out, but I imagined it had something to do with the chains being hooked into their flesh. The stone woman was hauling on hers as hard as she could, trying to stop him from tearing off her leg or pulling her from her feet, and the blue man had the hook in one shoulder and seemed to be purposefully digging it into his own flesh.

We stuck by the entrance, trying not to get involved, and I slid up next to the wall, attempting to figure out what the hell was happening before we got involved. The others followed my lead.

I watched for a bit, noting several odd aspects of the fight. "I think... I think he's stuck. I can't swear to it, but if I had to guess, his phasing ability takes the chains with him, and anything on the hooks probably counts too. He can't go intangible because he'd have to take both of them with him, and I'm guessing a pair of huge, obviously powerful G-rankers are too much for his abilities to manage."

Or at least partly. The blonde guy was wailing on Fisher full tilt, and his punches were landing so hard, the air was literally cracking when he threw them, but Fisher was offsetting the damage or something, because he wasn't turning into meat paste under the fists of the man I could only assume was MacDonald. Whatever was going on, the situation looked... stable-ish, and that gave us time to figure out what to do.

Callie frowned nervously. "Whatever is going on, it can't continue forever. Something is going to break the status quo here, which means we need a plan. What do we do? We can try to help one of them and hope the other will be able to keep them busy after we do, we can attack them both and hope they don't try to team up against us, or we can avoid them entirely and hope they don't notice us sneaking past them to try to get our hands on the Heart. Also *how* do we take the Heart? It's huge."

Seeing the insane power the two older freshmen were wielding, it was obvious she was starting to freak out a bit, and I didn't blame her. I was freaking out, too, but hearing my girlfriend sound so panicked brought me back down to earth.

I put a hand on her shoulder and squeezed. "We use the box. It should work fine for that. As for the plan, whatever you decide, we're right there with you. You've got this. They seem impressive, but they're no different than any random villain you dealt with back in Velan."

She looked uncertain for a moment, but her face firmed with determination, and she shot me a grateful smile. "You're right. Sorry. Shook me up there for a second. Let's go with a combination plan. I'll try to sneak around with the bag to get to the Heart. Cark, you use that staff to smash them all with a huge wave of fire. Agria, keep him topped up so he can hammer them too thoroughly to pay attention to anything else. Clockwork and Solomon, guard their backs so no one interrupts her energy transfer."

As soon as she decided on a course of action, I saw the conviction in her eyes as she found her footing. I was pretty sure recursion made doing things like this easier at higher levels. My own experience with Stricture kind of proved that. I'd been a random H-ranker who had barely stepped onto the path of cultivation, behaving like I was a hardened warrior. Aside from specific recursion, that was probably something more general to cultivators as a whole, or at least heroes. Still, it was helpful here since it snapped her out of her worries.

Cark looked thrilled to oblige and grinned before pulling out the staff and stepping forward. Jessie stepped up behind him, putting a hand on his back, and started pumping in energy. With a grunt of effort, our pyrokinetic funneled his power through the staff and dropped an absolutely massive wave of blue flame onto the gathered combatants. I heard a confused roar of pain, though none of them seemed to actually be seriously injured. Still, their shadows in the light of the flames were clearly wilting under the heat as they tried to resist the damage.

Whatever Fisher was doing was protecting him. MacDonald seemed to be using his force field to hold back the heat, and the other two were obviously physical types who were more durable than most. Even with all of that, resisting the attack was not easy or comfortable. It was the perfect distraction as Callie slipped off to the side and vanished. Between her ability and the stealth skill, she was more than qualified to bypass some thugs, and that became even easier with a huge fireball smashing them in the face to draw their focus.

Unfortunately, the good times didn't last. With a howl of anger, MacDonald put both hands out and started to push. I expected that to be useless, until the bastard started opening up an actual bubble in the flames with his telekinesis, shoving away the flames to buy himself breathing room. I could actually see the strain on his face as he shoved the fire even farther back, staggering to one side so he could cover the blue guy with his shield. He snarled over at us and said something to the blue guy I couldn't hear, probably because of the shield.

I pretty immediately figured that he was going to get the guy to attack us, so I triggered Sucking Mud without any hesitation. Considering these two were stuck in a small, confined area by the bubble, it was pretty effective, and they were distracted enough by plotting our demise not to notice it for a few seconds. Sadly, the skill really shined against huge enemies, and people could pull free if they noticed it early enough. That normally would have been a difficult feat without any leverage, but MacDonald had other means.

His snarl deepened, and his face turned bright red as he heaved and... lifted the whole bubble off the ground. He hauled the telekinetic construct slowly out of the flames, and I watched in horrified fascination as they slowly but inexorably inched toward the edge of the flames. I could hear the roar of the fire as I watched them float out toward us. I paused. The roar I'd been hearing grew louder. Then, without warning, a massive motorcycle came barreling out of the fire.

My eyes snapped back to the floating shield. Where I noticed that, the chain had fallen out of the blue guy's chest as the two of them were jostled around inside. Fisher had apparently taken that opportunity to go fully incorporeal and take the rock woman with him, driving his bike full speed through the flame then through *Cark* as he roared across the chamber. He pulled into a sharp turn, cutting off the exit to the cavern as the rock woman returned to solidity and swung wide into the wall with a teeth-rattling crash.

I bellowed to Cark. "Defense!"

And our pyrokinetic condensed the massive cloud of flame covering the room into a tight spherical shield around us. It was *much* hotter than the dispersed flames and much better for keeping the bastards off us, though it was also a huge risk. Callie was still out sneaking by them. I could only hope that the sphere was distracting enough to pull focus while I came up with another plan. These guys were *way* too strong to fight head-on.

We'd outnumbered the Wavestriders like four times over counting the wolves, but these people were all as strong, and the last fight had proven in no uncertain terms there was no way we stacked up this early. We needed to fight smarter, not harder. Unfortunately, Cark was clearly exerting massive amounts of effort to keep all that fire packed down so tight. His face was bright red and dripping sweat, and if Jessie hadn't been here topping him up, I doubted he could have even managed this.

I was freaking out. We were trapped in here while a whole bunch of powerful G-rankers were getting ready to attack us. Callie was alone outside with only all the hatred we had just stirred up keeping anyone from looking for her, and I didn't know what to do. I panicked for a moment, then realized it wasn't helping anything and forced myself to stop. I closed my eyes, breathing deeply, and tried my best to figure out our next move. We needed to distract them all, and that meant I needed to see what was going on.

I looked around at the surprisingly muted dome of blue fire and noticed a few things. First, Cark was literally pinning the heat into place. We should have been sweating our asses off, but I felt basically nothing. He was straining hard to make sure this shield didn't cook us. Secondly, he hadn't covered every inch of space, which made sense because we could still breathe, and being trapped in a dome of flames, even if you had a way not to get air fried, should be a one-way ticket to suffocation city.

Lastly, he wasn't going to last much longer, even with Jessie helping. She could top up his energy, but despite a slightly euphoric feeling during a charge, nothing would dull the edge of mental exhaustion he must be feeling at the moment.

"Cark, can you open a small hole in the top of this thing? I think I have a plan."

The straining pyrokinetic nodded slowly and tightly. Almost too subtly to be noticed, a window opened up on top of the dome. Not big enough to be spotted from the ground, but just enough for me to see.

I stared silently at the ceiling of the cavern. The whole thing I'd gone through getting in here was easily one of the most uncomfortable things to ever happen to me, but it was also a new direction for my abilities. DS Mastery especially had a lot of ways to be used other than direct confrontation. I had options for applying my skills, not just by altering their nature, but by taking advantage of it. I scanned around the top of the chamber for a minute or two before finally finding what I was looking for.

I'd needed a specific spot, somewhere near enough to the enemy to implicate them and cause chaos, but far enough that Callie wouldn't be in any danger, and I found the perfect place. Once I did, I cast Sucking Mud again, but not on the ground this time. At least not the ground we were standing on. I leveraged my skill upward and created a plane of liquid stone right through the base of a hanging stalactite a hundred or so feet up. We'd been slowly moving down since we got here, and this chamber was huge.

The H-rank rock wouldn't kill our competitors, but it wouldn't be fun. I didn't even need to flex the skill, all I had to do was create the weakness in the stone, and the incredible weight of the stalactite did the rest. The huge spear of stone came barreling down into the chamber, smashing into the ground with the speed of a charging bull elephant, and a massive boom shook the cavern as it hit. I barely kept my feet as it made contact, but I couldn't help but grin. Let's see them ignore *that*.

Chapter Forty-Two

At my word, Cark dropped the shield as soon as the stalactite hit the ground, letting the huge cloud of ash and debris cover us as everyone grabbed onto me. I used Seek Hidden to find a safe place to hole up. I had to shove at the skill to make such a vague idea work, but I was able to trigger it, and I dragged everyone over to a space where there was much less ash and no lava splashes cooling after being flung free of the large pool the Heart was suspended over.

Once we were clear, I dragged everyone behind an outcropping and took cover, hoping against hope no one had seen us in the debris. I turned to Cark and the others, and I resonated my stealth Skill with my voice as I whispered, trying my hardest to completely mask my words from any outsiders. "Okay, guys, I'm hoping they'll go back to fighting each other if they run into the others in the ash cloud, but assuming that doesn't happen, I need ideas. No wrong answers here—all we need is some way to delay them."

Jessie, who was looking pale but still in good condition, raised a hand. "I can probably do a golem if I try. It won't last long. Like at all. But if we can make it the same size as one of us, we could probably bait them into chasing after it. The only issue is I don't have a sculpting skill. Any of the rest of you know how the hell to make a reasonable facsimile of a human being out of rocks? Because if it isn't at least close, there's no way it's going to work."

Benny looked pensive. "What about Solomon's Sucking Mud skill?" He turned to me. "Could you use it to slightly weaken the stone? Not enough to turn it full liquid but enough to make it easy to mold? If so, I bet we could make something about the right shape." He gestured to a nearby rock formation that was the right size but absolutely not the right shape. Everyone else looked excited by the possibility, too, but I was personally skeptical I could manage that level of control.

The more radical the shift from the original skill, the harder it was to force the thing into that configuration. It wasn't exactly a completely different application, but making it do something so unusual was going to take a ton of effort and might even put me out of the fight, if not knock me entirely unconscious.

I just shrugged. "I... don't know. I can try, but you guys might have to drag me out of here if I do. I'm not sure we can handle me being a burden when we're trying to fight people this strong. Does anyone else have a better plan?"

Unfortunately, no one did. Everyone just sat and looked at me uncomfortably until I finally sighed and nodded. "Well, we won't know until we try. Guess I'm giving this a shot." I had to psych myself up a little. This was one of the most extreme changes I'd made to a skill up to this point. I'd done some tweaking, but it was usually more shape or scope. I knew intellectually this *was* the same thing, but it seemed a lot closer to just breaking the skill to do something else with it, and even my own perception of that was going to make it much more difficult.

The first thing I did was block out all the extraneous elements around me. The ash in the air, the sound of movement, the heat through my costume —literally all of these things were distractions I had to suppress. So I mashed them down with every bit of Focus I had and dedicated myself wholly to my task. Once I had completely detached from the situation around me (which took longer than expected because my girlfriend was still out there, putting her life in danger), I was finally able to begin the process of changing the skill.

I'd done this plenty of times now, and while I'd been in pain through every one, I'd also learned. Firstly, that skills were more likely to accept smaller changes, and secondly, that the further I changed them, the more difficult it became. Paradoxically, the best way to work on a skill was to do a lot of very small changes, but to do them all at once. As difficult as I would have once found that, it wasn't impossible. My Focus stat made almost anything mental much easier, but especially anything pertaining to the dexterity of my thoughts.

So that was what I did—I changed a bunch of little things. I changed the shape of the spell, which I'd done before. I changed the speed of the spread, which I had to do to make sure it applied to the whole rock evenly. I dialed back the severity of the change to the stone itself, making it more cohesive, as well as trying my best to spread out the time available to us, which was actually easier because of the lowered intensity. I did all of these things at once, and every one of them hurt, though not much, but the pain from all of them sort of superimposed to become more than the sum of its parts.

Despite being literally eye-wateringly painful, it wasn't as bad as I'd expected. The new method of working on the skill had saved me some of the agony I'd known was coming, which was good. I jerked a hand at the others, too overwhelmed with pain and strain to speak. Luckily, they had been watching for that and leapt into action. As I watched, barely coherent, through pain-wracked eyes, Jessie and Benny stepped up and started to slowly sculpt the rock.

I'd expected her to be impressive. She'd spent most of her time before joining the Unity doing floral arrangements to get her name out there, and she'd been popular for it. She had a definite flair for aesthetically pleasing design, so it wasn't a shock she seemed to have a solid handle on shaping the rock. Benny, though, was doing surprisingly well. He was mostly handling the major shaping, leaving the details to Jessie. I assumed they had discussed it while I was tuning everything out, but still, I was impressed by how well they were working, both together and apart.

As Jessie shaped the stone, she pushed out a steady stream of green energy. The glowing life force seemed to be almost swallowed by the dark stone, vanishing into its stygian depths like a rock into a lake, but without any of the ripples. Still, Jessie didn't seem to be worried, so I could only assume whatever she was doing was actually taking. She swayed, and I would have tried to catch her if I hadn't been in the middle of experiencing what it was like to feel my brain melt.

She stayed standing, though. After topping up Cark, this was clearly a strain on her, but she was made of tougher stuff than even we gave her credit for most of the time. I could see a stubborn determination in her eyes that I recognized from plenty of conversations we'd had before. She wouldn't be giving up on this. She kept pushing for a few minutes before finally signaling that she was done, and I let go of my tenuous hold on the skill and slumped to the ground, landing on my ass shakily as the tension drained out of me.

Jessie looked too exhausted to juice me up to help mitigate the exhaustion, which was fair. I didn't want to get too dependent on her energy jolts to get through my training anyway. She slumped down herself and then flicked her glowing eyes at the humanoid lump of rock they had made. The thing, which looked semi-human shaped but didn't really have any detail or definition, took off into the clouds of still-settling ash, and I sighed in relief as I heard the sounds of shouting.

My sigh was interrupted, sadly, by a fucking metal hook slamming into my calf. I barely had time to scream before hearing the roar of a gunning engine. The hook was yanked tight, causing excruciating agony as it jerked my leg hard and started pulling me across the floor of the cavern. Fisher, it seemed, had gotten his hooks in me, pun very much intended, and my friends didn't even have time to stop him as he hauled me full speed across the chamber. I didn't know how the hell he had the space to gun it like that even in a cavern this size, but I suspected it was something to do with phasing.

Sadly, whatever that was did not save me from the impact against the wall as he swerved and let all that momentum send me slamming into the dark rock. Apparently, he was a big fan of that move, since he'd done it to the rock woman too. Regardless, even though the rock wasn't high enough rank to break me, I was extremely sore and tired. Also, my leg was on a hook. All of which added up to me feeling pretty sensitive to pain, and the impact against the wall was teeth-rattlingly unpleasant if not outright nasty.

I heard the crunch of boots on the gravel-strewn cavern floor as Fisher climbed off his bike, yanking the chain in my leg taut and dragging me toward him. His face was cold and impassive, but I was pretty sure he was annoyed. I was kind of curious why he hadn't hooked Cark, but I was guessing it was because I was already on the ground. Still, the pain in my calf was so horrible, I wanted to throw up. I wasn't sure I'd ever been in this kind of pain. It was literally making me sick, as if my body was rejecting the agony like an infection.

I expected him to attack me or something, but he just dragged me over to a nearby outcropping and looped the chain around it. Then he stepped over me and headed back towards the bike, clearly ready to go for the Heart, which Callie was supposed to be stealing right now. I didn't think, or plan, or even give myself a chance to worry. I hauled on my injured and bloody leg, pulling the chain enough to give me some slack, and hurled myself at him, grabbing hold of one leg.

He grunted in annoyance, trying to pull free, but I wouldn't let go. Fisher was dangerous, and I wouldn't let him hurt Callie. My brain was fried. I was sore and had a hook in my leg. I was barely coherent, but I refused to let him hurt my girlfriend.

He snarled, the first real sign of emotion I'd seen from him, and I felt something… shift, like he was trying to slip away. Except he couldn't. I was holding him, and the chain was wrapped around a big-ass rock. That chain was like a circuit. It was designed to carry his ability to whatever it was attached to as long as he was in contact with it.

This situation was only barely within that definition, but it *was* within it. So he kicked me in the face. I felt my mask smash into my nose and break it at the first blow, though it didn't come off. Apparently, the ability to nullify attacks was *not* one of its many useful features. He grunted and kicked me again, driving the mask harder into the injury and almost making me black out from pain. He lifted his foot again, and I was pretty sure I wouldn't be able to take another hit, but when it came down, it stopped cold on a red barrier.

I blinked, wondering how the haze of pain I was in had stopped an attack, before realizing the barrier was coming from my emergency beacon. In fact, forcing myself to look around, I saw everyone's emergency beacon was active.

A voice split the air. "Attention, participants. The four-thousand-eight-hundred-and-seventy-sixth annual freshman scavenger hunt of the Ascendant Academy has now come to an end. Please cease all combat and return to your accommodations to await further instructions."

I started laughing, though it mostly got cut off by me choking on my own blood. Still, I was giggling as I lost consciousness. I guess we'd won.

Chapter Forty-Three

BEING UNCONSCIOUS, while not enjoyable, was a convenient way to travel. I passed out in that hot stuffy cave and woke up again on the top floor of the hatchery, mask off and costume stripped away so they could treat my wounds. I looked down at my leg, which while wrapped, mostly seemed to be healing quickly. I imagined Jessie had given me what she could and hadn't had enough energy to knit my wounds together completely.

I looked around for my clothes, feeling sort of naked without my H-ranked combat gear. Sure, they weren't as good now as they had been when I'd first received them, and I imagined they were slightly holding me back at this point. But at the same time, I'd grown so used to them, I couldn't imagine going without. My costume was my second skin—it was with me everywhere I went. Almost since I'd first become an Ascendant, I'd been wearing it constantly, and being here without it made me feel all kinds of vulnerable and exposed.

I tried to sit up and winced. My whole body hurt, but the wince made my face move, which was an agony on a whole different level than the slight soreness in my muscles. I couldn't tell if my nose was still broken, but it certainly didn't feel great.

"Hey!" Callie's voice cracked the air, and she was next to me in seconds. "Lay back down, you absolute moron. You got hurt really bad—you need to rest." I blinked and looked at her, and seeing her anxious expression, I sighed and leaned back to lie on the ground.

I groaned. "Did anyone get the number of that bus that hit me? Because ow." I closed my eyes, and it felt nice to let myself relax and shut out the light. I hadn't realized, but it wasn't helping the headache. "Also, when did we get back? And is everyone else okay? I got dragged off there at the end. I didn't see what happened to the others. I take it they aren't hurt or anything?"

Callie gave a hysterical laugh. "You got your face stomped into hamburger meat by a deranged biker, and you're asking if everyone else is hurt? No, Shane, no one else got hurt." She sounded on the verge of crying. "What the hell is wrong with you? I saw what you did as I was grabbing the Heart, but I couldn't make it back in time. Who grabs a more powerful Ascendant around the leg and hangs on like that? He could have killed you. If he'd kept kicking, I think he actually might have."

I opened my eyes again to see hers overflowing with tears. I felt like an asshole, though I wasn't entirely sure *why*. Still, I wouldn't apologize for keeping her safe. I just gave her my best reassuring smile, which admittedly probably lost some of the effect given my split and bleeding face (I definitely felt some wounds reopen when I stretched my mouth), and reached out for her hand. "Hey, I'm fine. I knew you were out there, and he was heading for the Heart. I needed to make a call about what to do, and I sort of panicked and did the first thing I could think of."

She swallowed hard and threw herself into my arms, giving me a painfully tight squeeze, but I wasn't complaining. Even with my Perception, I barely heard her as she murmured into my shoulder. "You moron. Who cares if we win this stupid hunt if you die? I love you, but you're an idiot." She held me close for a second before her body went stiff, clearly realizing what she'd just said. She jerked back, clearing her throat. "I mean, right—we won. The others are fine. We're waiting for the call to head back. How are you feeling?"

I decided to leave her slip alone—she would talk about it when she was ready. "I'm fine. Not particularly happy to be awake right now, but with my Vitality, I'm sure it won't last too long. If Jessie is okay, she can probably top me up once she's back to full charge. What did I miss? Last I saw, the hunt was ending and we were trapped in a cavern with a quartet of pissed-off G-rankers."

That got a wet chuckle as she helped me sit up. "Well, you probably saw the important parts. After we finished, they halted the hunt. But we found out the announcement wasn't across the whole event, just for the teams that had completed their lists. According to what Jessie found out with the ravens, it was us and about four others. The other teams are still actively searching for their list items. We haven't gotten any responses, but we're pretty sure this is normal. Letting the other teams finish and then cutting in some of the more interesting footage before the big drop so they can get some more airtime."

I listened to her explanation, nodding along. "Well, as long as we're out of it, I have nothing else to say. If you think about it, that makes sense. If they stopped it now, they would miss out on some decent fights. Are we still vulnerable to attack here?" I hoped not, because I just wanted to slump down and sleep off this pain. I was pretty sure Zeke wouldn't intervene against Ascendants unless they tried to hurt Cass directly since it would be violating the parameters of our deal.

She shook her head. "Nope. Apparently, the overlap items that can't be found elsewhere have faded from other lists. We were told we're protected now, though they didn't bother mentioning how. Celine is pretty sure they're using the beacons to warn people off attacking the teams who have completed the hunt. This isn't the earliest it's ever ended exactly, though it's pretty close. They're giving the other teams a few days to try to get some good footage, and then they'll run the stream and do a mass pickup. The rest of them will get picked up at the end of the month."

We sat there like that for a while, me leaning against her for stability, until I finally felt a bit better. Then she helped me to my feet to check in on the others. Everyone was out in front of the hatchery, the only exception being Jessie, who was still sleeping off the energy drain. She'd wanted to stay up and try to heal me more, but once it was clear that I was safe and out of immediate danger, Callie forced her to sleep. My Vitality could patch me up until she woke up and was feeling better.

I was glad Callie hadn't let her run herself into the ground. I would have made the same call. When we stepped out, everyone's eyes snapped to us. Celine was sitting with Benny while Martin and Sarah reclined against a tree, and Cass ran around the clearing watched by Cark and Zeke. When they saw us, everyone got to their feet.

Benny was the first to cross the distance and pull me into a hug. "Shane! Revenant, man, you were looking messed up there for a minute. That Fisher guy didn't hold back."

He sounded angry, but I just patted his back and chuckled. "Nope, but he didn't go as hard as he could have, either. I have no doubt he had the leg strength to break my neck in one kick if he was really trying to end me. I'll take living and beat up over dead and barely injured any day. I was just worried about the rest of you. I'm glad everyone is okay. Where are the wolves? I don't see them."

Benny snickered, pointing to the edge of the creek off to the side of the clearing. It was a decent distance away, but I could easily make out the massive furry shapes slumped wet and bedraggled, on the beach. "Cass decided the wolves should go swimming with her. I have no clue how she talked them all into it, but they were not happy to be soaked. They're drying off now. Everyone else is fine too. Hell, Cark is actually pretty excited."

The big man shrugged at my questioning gaze. "Honestly, I wasn't expecting any benefits from this other than finding my sister when I agreed. Now that you guys won, though, I'm going to show up in your battle footage and will get some of the same promotion as all of you. They won't be pushing the narrative for me the same way, but since I'll be there, I'm probably going to see a big bump in my stats just like all of you." He smiled ruefully. "I stayed to pay you back and ended up getting an even bigger favor. I really have no idea how I'm supposed to repay you for all this."

That got another eye roll from me. "If you keep talking about favors and debts, I'm going to think you don't like us. I told you—you're a friend, and there's no need to keep score. Any of us might have ended up dead without you here. I can't think of a way to repay you for that either. The lives of my friends are priceless. Since we both owe each other more than can be reasonably paid back, why don't we just call ourselves even and move forward as friends."

Cark had put himself in harm's way time and again for all of us, and I absolutely wouldn't hear about any of this payback bullshit. I considered him part of our group, even if only for the hunt, and I was going to treat him that way. If he benefited from working with us, then all the better. He gave me a grateful smile and clapped me on the shoulder. "Well, if you put it that way, how can I refuse? Come on. Come sit down. We were just talking to Celine about how this whole thing is going to work."

Callie helped me over to sit by a tree and we looked over to where Celine was sitting. Benny had rejoined her, and though they weren't exactly cuddling, the two of them were sitting pretty close together. I smiled at my friend, who avoided my gaze but couldn't help the satisfied smile on his face.

The elf girl waited until everyone was settled, then she nodded. "As you know, great deeds trigger stat growth. The accumulation of renown bursts out at these milestones and allows us to upgrade our strength."

We all nodded. This was something we had experienced multiple times ourselves. "As usual, the milestones tend to be fit into certain categories, triggering based on a specific event or series of events. Due to studying these sorts of milestones for quite some time, the major forces have developed methods of setting up their events to count as singular milestones over longer periods of time. This is why we haven't seen a slow trickle of points during this hunt, and are going to see large returns all at once in the end."

We'd heard this already, but I hadn't realized they intentionally did it this way. I wondered how long they had studied the way renown worked before being able to set up events like this. Either way, I was looking forward to the windfall. Celine went on to explain the payout, the timing that we could expect, and what kind of stat numbers we might be looking at (though she admitted that was mostly guesswork). By the time she was done, I couldn't help but be excited for the upcoming boost in power. Once the promotion began, we would all get hit with the points at once, and I couldn't wait to see how strong all this had made us.

Chapter Forty-Four

WE SPENT the rest of the week recovering, keeping an eye out for attackers and preparing for the points boom when the stream came out. Everyone was excited. Grimmengap was looking at a probable rank-up, and while the rest of us (aside from possibly Cark, if he got *very* lucky) weren't even close to that point. We would all be seeing a huge bump in strength from the endgame of this little adventure.

Of course, we still had to wait for the stream to air, but that would probably happen tonight. In the meantime, it was now officially the day of our return to Rajak, and despite all of us having enjoyed our time here (mostly), everyone was looking forward to getting back to civilization. Once everyone was packed up, we headed back to the field where the air shuttles had dropped us off to take them back with the other hunters. Apparently, this was part of the ritual of the hunt and would be shown as part of the stream.

When we arrived, we spotted MacDonald and his two teammates, as well as Fisher, waiting alongside another dozen teams. Apparently, in the last week, plenty more people had managed to make their way to the finish line or at least as close as the other teams could get. We eyed the other teams carefully as we arrived, not sure about our reception after the last fight, but no one seemed to be holding a grudge. Still, I wished we could have taken the shuttle back with Zeke and Cassidy, both of whom had gotten a ride back earlier to avoid any inference of cheating.

We also saw Cold Snap, which was a bit of a surprise. He'd bailed after helping us with Aiden, and we hadn't seen him since. Without the sleepers, we hadn't expected him to manage very well, but considering his personality, he'd probably bribed or bullied some random group into helping him by relying on his mom's reputation. That seemed pretty on-brand for the spoiled brat.

We all gathered up, and although there was quite a large number of people, it was a far cry from the number that had come out here with us the first time. Plenty of people were still out searching for the remaining two weeks, and some of them were probably dead. I felt a pang of grief over the lost sleepers who had died during the siege, and I made a mental note to track down their families (if they had any) and do... something.

Telling them what had happened seemed crueler than letting them think their family members had died trying to follow their dreams, but maybe I could anonymously send money or something. I should probably have done the same with the eight who'd died in G district, but they'd been wearing masks, and their heads had blown up. I wasn't sure how to go about finding out who they were. I doubted the Unity had even tried. I felt guilty over trying to gloss over what had happened, but even now, I wasn't sure I was ready to deal with it. That had been when things really got real for all of us, and I didn't think anyone in the group was really equipped to process how they felt when watching those people die.

The blink-and-you-miss-it appearance of the man who called himself Professor Tricks was less shocking now than before the hunt. He had shown the ability to come and go like that when we first saw him, but even more than that, we were just more equipped to deal with the shock now. My lack of reaction actually revealed something about this entire thing that I hadn't noticed until now.

We'd gotten better. Whether it was the pressure, the stakes, the danger, or just the constant need to keep an eye on the situation, this experience had changed us. Part of our big problem before was that we still thought like mortals, and that hadn't disappeared, but some of the rawness and the inexperience had been rubbed away. We'd gone into this a bunch of random newbies, but all the things we'd gone through together had helped us gel as a team, helped us learn and grow into more powerful versions of ourselves.

Seeing the ways the hunt had changed our perceptions of things (some of which were incidental or the result of third-party interference) gave me a new appreciation for what the Academy could do. For the way they operated. Events like this were an opportunity for more than padding our wallets. This whole thing had basically been a crash course in life experience, years of Ascendant training and adaptation all packed into a neat little fortnight, and it was obviously far from accidental.

It wasn't a perfect system, obviously. What participants got out of it depended on what they put in. We had pushed (and been pushed) and so we'd grown more than most, but that was the point. The Academy didn't care about random nobodies who hid out in a tree and waited out the month. They were trying to polish people like us, people who had the will to be more than we were and the power to make that will a reality.

It wasn't nice. It wasn't fair. And it had probably been responsible for a not inconsiderable number of deaths that we weren't aware of yet. But what it almost certainly was, was effective. Exposure to monsters, opportunities to bond as a team, and training in information gathering and tactics—there had been opportunities out here that had nothing to do with expensive magic plants, and we'd made the most of them. The only thing left to see was if it had been worth it. If our effort had led to rewards that felt justified.

Professor Tricks, still in his purple suit and wide-brimmed hat, looked mildly less apathetic when he glanced around at the crowd, as if he were looking at a particularly interesting bug, but he at least seemed to give a shit we existed this time. "Well, I see you've mostly made it back. A few deaths, more than a few wastes of space I won't even bother with, but still. This group can be considered just at the edge of competence."

I saw more than a few satisfied smiles among the crowd, and so did he, because he felt the need to shut that down pretty quick. "Don't mistake my comments for confirmation that you've reached some kind of watershed. Passing the hunt with reasonable levels of skill is the bare minimum to be taken seriously as a student, but only barely. Most of you still aren't anyone I would consider important or impressive. Maybe one or two of you will graduate in the top ten thousand rank-wise, which is what I would consider even a modicum of success in this Academy."

His eyes scanned over us, and the mild interest he'd shown earlier felt... derisive now. I was less sure it was a good thing that he gave more of a shit

221

now, because it kind of seemed like he'd gone from not caring at all to actively considering us pathetic. He opened his mouth to speak, but before he could, he paused. His head shifted slightly to one side, as if listening to someone speak, before his face screwed up in annoyance. "Fine. I'll move on to the rest of the informational portion of the evening. I suspect they get the point anyway."

He flicked a hand, and a scan ring projected a large screen above his head. I found the names of our team in the first slot, and the rest of the slots on the list were taken up by random people, though the existence of Fisher in the second slot and MacDonald in the third made it clear this was a ranking list of the event.

Professor Tricks spoke up lazily. "As you may have noticed, your exact rankings were not made clear to you when you completed the trial. I have no interest in reading them out, so find your names and make a note, because this is where you landed."

He kept it up for about thirty seconds before flicking his wrist and cutting it off. "Now, anyone who missed their name, though how anyone with even passable Focus or Perception could have with that much time, can find the list hanging in the student building. Moving on. The stream of this event is going to end shortly. In point of fact, it should be complete by the time the shuttles arrive back at the campus. I suggest once you make it back, you head for a safe place to sort through your gains from this exercise. There will be quite a bit to digest for some of you."

That sounded like a good thing to me, but I also recognized that when this ended, I would probably be getting more points at once than I ever had in my entire life. It might be reasonable to make some accommodations before it happened. I turned to raise a brow at Callie, who nodded and looked at Celine. "Think we could hole up in your rooms while we digest our gains from this? If it's going to be as dramatic as he's implying, we could use somewhere close by to weather the storm, so to speak."

Celine's smile was wry. "Of course. Given how much of our success we owe to you, it is, quite literally, the very least we can do. You're always welcome in our rooms. Even if we hadn't passed, you would be welcome any time. I feel we've been through enough together to be considered friends."

Her voice was more animated than I had heard it before, and her face, while not as expressive as some, was less blank than usual. I was pretty sure

222

this was her version of getting worked up. She was also holding hands with Benny, though she was careful not to actually look at him as she squeezed his fingers.

Professor Tricks finished up the rest of the presentation, telling us a few important bits of info, like how the winners would be the focus of extra attention from the Academy and would benefit from their marketing abilities and how the stream actually worked, as well as who would benefit from it most. He didn't look at us when saying any of this, and since we weren't exactly social with most of the other students, no one except Fisher and MacDonald recognized us, despite having seen our names on the list.

Once that was done, he released us to wait for the shuttles then vanished into thin air again. I considered going over to talk to Fisher and MacDonald but decided to leave it alone for now. We could talk it over with them back at the Academy to make sure there weren't any hard feelings, but starting a conversation here would just draw attention to us a bit too early. From her expression Callie was of the same opinion.

Finally, the shuttles showed up. We all climbed aboard and waited as they took off for the Academy grounds. The trip passed in a blur, just like the last time, and when we finally climbed out, we all headed for Grimmengap's dorm at top speed, determined to make it there before the stat points hit. The rest of the students were in just as big of a rush, scattering as soon as we reached the campus. Luckily, no one got in our way, and we made it just in time.

As the door shut behind us, I saw a familiar scrawl of purple flames across my vision.

It was time.

Chapter Forty-Five

TALES of your exploits have begun to spread. You have done a great deed, and whispers of your power are disseminating in the ether. You've received fifteen points of Vitality, twenty-five points of Focus, forty points of Perception, and thirty-nine points of Might!

My eyes just about bugged out of my head as I read that, though they were pretty quickly occupied by rolling up into the back of my head as my entire body started to basically tear itself apart from the changes.

I'd never gotten anywhere close to this amount of points in one shot before. I'd been expecting a small twinge, maybe something like when I'd taken that pill, but this was on a whole different level in terms of pain. It occurred to me belatedly that the last time I'd gotten a huge amount of renown all at once, I'd been unconscious when it hit. I hadn't gotten this much when I'd stopped Aiden, either, and what I had gotten was painless. I wondered if the slower trickle of stats had resulted in less dramatic changes or if the delay somehow increased the pain. Hell, maybe it was just the scale. I'd only gotten fifteen points tops of my highest boosted stat before.

Regardless of the reason, I was in fucking agony. My Perception had increased drastically, which stacked with the already-mind numbing torment from what I assumed was a huge shift in my recovery abilities from Vitality, and a complete cognitive upgrade from Focus was giving me massive returns on investment in terms of horrifying pain. I wanted to black out from the sensation overload, but sadly I wasn't that lucky.

Everyone else seemed to be stiff with pain, as well, so it wasn't just me. Once the misery faded, I let myself exhale in relief as I pulled up my sheet to see where I was at.

Wishmaster Candidate Status: G-rank.

Ability: Beginner Wish—Five times a day, grant a Beginner wish in return for proper compensation. Wish must be feasibly achievable by the candidate's own efforts within a three-day period with current statistics.

Might: 97
Impact: 12
Fantasy: 21
Vitality: 44
Focus: 63
Perception: 80
Creation: 32

Skills: Beginner Doom Sovereign Mastery, Lesser Enchanting Mastery, Lesser Cooking Mastery, Lesser Inventing Mastery, Minor Piano Mastery, Minor Gymnastics Mastery, Minor Swimming Mastery, Minor Guitar Mastery, Minor Singing Mastery, Minor Poker Mastery, Minor Archery Mastery, Minor Boxing Mastery, Minor Balam Mastery, Minor First Aid Mastery, Minor Herbalism Mastery

I had to choke down a whistle at the progress. I'd made some serious strides in terms of raw power. My Might nearly matched Callie's. I wondered briefly about why I hadn't managed to get any Fantasy or Creation, but looking back, I hadn't really used either of those attributes where people could see. The Might was probably from all the damage I'd managed with stacked attacks like the one I'd used on Raleigh. The Perception from the acumen I showed in tracking with Seek Hidden. The Vitality was most likely a side effect of Jessie's ability letting me keep going nonstop, and the Focus was probably just people assuming we actually knew what we were doing.

All in all, I could see the reasoning behind why people would have focused on those stats to the exclusion of others. Looking around, I grinned. As I had expected, every member of Grimmengap had advanced to G-rank alongside us. It wasn't a huge shock really, they'd been middle to high H-rankers to begin with, and I'd gotten more than a hundred points just from this one event. They had done less, and because there was less obvious impressive footage, had almost definitely gotten less, but it was pretty obvious they would make it over the line from this.

I could see the new Impact just by looking, the weight of their presence on the world pressing down on reality six times more firmly than before. I was sure they were much more powerful. Professor Tricks had been extremely clear about the fact that the stream would blatantly favor our group, making sure to cherry-pick the footage for as many premium moments for the team as possible to gain maximum yield for points.

I had no idea how it worked, but he'd stated up front that they had long since developed formulas to plot out what stats would benefit most from which areas of the city and demographics, all to make sure to get as many points for each member of the winning team as possible. It would have exponential effects too. The people who remembered us would be more likely to show their friends, not to mention more likely to spread future deeds once we established our identities outside the Academy.

It was almost scary how efficient the Academy was, but it did make sense. Cultivation was a way of life, so it was obvious the Academy would have people who studied trends and psychological conditions in an effort to make the most out of the most precious resource a cultivator had—fame. Hell, so much of our interactions with them had already made it clear that every facet of society was structured to get the most possible renown in the most efficient way. Even the existence of lower-ranked cultivators served to act as a standard by which elites could be measured, and therefore praised.

I popped to my feet easily, feeling light and nimble. The gravity around me felt exponentially weaker than it had been, and I jumped much too high and slammed into the ceiling. I actually got stuck in the plaster, even with the barely noticeable push I'd used for the motion, and it took a few seconds for the others to pull me free, with the newly ascended G-rankers doing most of the work since they had less to get acclimated to.

I fell back the ground, landing on my ass with a thud, and stayed extremely still.

Callie gave me a reassuring smile. "Careful there." She turned to the room at large. "We all should be. This is the biggest boost in stats I think any of us have ever had. In terms of percentage, I think several of us just had some stats outright double." She looked at Cark, who mostly seemed fine. "I'm guessing you probably got the smallest comparative boost, given your already-absurd Might stat. You should be mostly okay to move around, right?"

The big bounty hunter nodded. "Yeah, Might was most of my boost. It went up by about eighty. The more powerful you are, the bigger the impression, but you reach a point of diminishing returns on big jumps like this, I think. That, or there just isn't enough people to support more, but that seems unlikely. Yes, though, that eighty wasn't even a twenty-five percent increase."

I cursed. This kind of issue wouldn't be as big of a problem later then. We would just have to acclimate to the boost slowly over time. I looked over at Celine awkwardly. "Sorry about your ceiling by the way. I can pay for it, I'm sure." They'd let us come use their room, and we hadn't even been smart enough to keep it from being wrecked. Well, ok I hadn't been smart enough. Still though, it would be shitty to ignore it. The plaster was seriously mauled. I was just lucky this place had such a high ceiling or I might have gone right through the whole floor.

The elf girl just chuckled, waving it off. "It's a dorm, and as someone technically on a diplomatic mission, they'll hardly make me pay for it myself. You can count this as them paying for their own failure to warn any of us. We probably would have done it by accident if you hadn't. Besides, ranking up is easily worth the fees even if they had made us pay. The lifespan increase alone is staggering. Not to mention all the publicity will make ranking up again that much easier. You've done us a tremendous favor."

Now it was my turn to wave off a comment. "No way. You guys stuck by us through the siege and even helped us make it out. I know you were a huge help to Jessie with her tree defenses, and Sarah was invaluable in the Necropolis. Regardless, if you aren't against sharing your secrets, what did you all get the most stats in? I know it's a bit personal to ask for the actual numbers, but I figure sharing our biggest gains shouldn't be a problem. Mine was forty in Perception. Though again, no pressure."

Mostly, I didn't want Cark to be stuck as the only one sharing. He'd told us his before I mentioned the possibility of keeping it quiet, and given all he'd done for us, some solidarity was the least I could do. I suspected the others had gotten theirs more spread out, because hearing my number made them all flinch in genuine shock. Or maybe it was just that no one had gotten nearly as much in the way of Perception points.

Benny, always happy to have my back, raised a hand to get everyone's attention. "Well my highest was Focus at thirty."

That was pretty damn impressive. I could only assume they had included some production clips from him or something. I knew he did some crafting just to stay sharp, and as an inventing-based-ability user, it made sense to lean into that stat. It just went to show that they had done some serious research into us before cutting things together. Focus was one of Benny's main stats and an integral one to Inventing.

Jessie was up next, and I could tell she wasn't even hesitant about sharing. "Fifty Vitality. Not as much as Cark, but I did pretty well. I think being in multiple roles all dependent on the same stat helped give me a boost. I got a pretty big chunk in a few others too, and even though I didn't unlock any stats I didn't have before, I'm pretty happy with how all of this turned out."

Callie seemed the least excited. She just shrugged. "Thirty points in Creation. Not my preference exactly, but it does make sense based on what they saw me doing, and it does play a role in my ability even if it isn't my current main focus. Seems like they tried to push us each into a specific role to maximize our gains. Using footage that highlights a distinct strong point seems like a good way to ensure we all made the biggest possible impression on the audience." She finished, very careful not to look at Celine, obviously trying not to pressure her to go next just because we'd already mentioned ours.

Celine and the others weren't strangers, though, and they were happy to share. Celine got twenty-five Vitality as her highest, while Sarah had twenty Creation and Martin had twenty Might. All much lower than ours, but then they had spent quite a bit of time in the background, so it made sense they wouldn't have made an impression as big as ours. It seemed like the Academy knew what it was doing though because they'd all gotten enough to rank up, and that was plenty for them.

With all of us having shared and gone through our upgrades, we were all itching to get home. We agreed to wait until the next day to check our ranking boosts and set up a time to meet and sell off some of our materials from the hunt. Then my team and I headed for our skyride, offering to give Cark a lift back to our place where Zeke would still be watching Cass. He accepted, and we all piled into the car, glad this was finally over. Of course, we still had to discuss the rest of our stat acquisitions, but that could wait. For now, we could just relax.

Chapter Forty-Six

We got home in short enough order, Jessie driving of course, and headed inside to check in on Cass. When we arrived we found her sitting in front of a huge screen, watching a replay of the stream from the scavenger hunt. Since she hadn't been able to come with us, she hadn't seen everything that happened, but watching all of our adventures during the stream, not to mention the adventures of the other teams, was obviously thrilling to her.

I had to admit the people at the Academy knew their stuff. Not only had they strung together all that footage in a way that firmly made us look like the stars, they'd managed to create a cohesive narrative with the clips they picked. They arranged it so that the other teams looked good and got a bit of screen time too, but we certainly seemed even more powerful in comparison. Punching out a bear was way more impressive if you just watched that bear kill a mountain lion, so to speak.

Cass was sitting on the couch in the middle of the orange living room, hiding her face behind her hand and watching it from between her fingers whenever she found a point where her brother was in a fight too big for him to handle. She gasped and cheered and was clearly completely enraptured in the action. I wondered if someone at the Academy had some kind of storytelling skill, because this was actually really good.

We didn't have the heart to interrupt her, so we went over to check with Zeke, who was sitting on a different couch, arm thrown over his eyes and clearly trying to sleep. Despite not being able to see us, when we came inside and walked over behind the couch it was simple for someone with his Perception to notice us. "You're back. Good, you can watch the kid now. I'm going to sleep. I'm counting this job as over. You can make crepes for breakfast to make the wait up to me." He hopped to his feet, landing nimbly and reminding me of my own humiliating mistake earlier.

Despite his apathetic words, he shot another look over at Cass to make sure she was okay, and I had to smile internally. My uncle liked to pretend to be a lazy good-for-nothing, but he was a big softie deep down. He'd acted the same way about me when I was a kid. I could tell he liked the kid, and I decided I would check to see if Cark wanted to take one of the spare rooms here. The place was huge anyway, and having them around would be convenient as well as fun. Besides, Cass livened things up around here. Having someone who wasn't a cultivator nearby would make sure we did things other than train.

Of course I'd check with Callie and with Cark himself before I offered in front of the kid, but I didn't see anyone having a problem with it. Now wasn't the time for that conversation though, so while Cark stayed downstairs with Cass, the four of us went up to talk over our new stats in their entirety. We picked one of the training rooms, but rather than start the training, we just sat down to go over what everyone got. Since we'd already sort of chosen an order, I decided to tell them everything I got first, and everyone seemed pretty impressed.

Benny seemed the most annoyed. "Man, other than Focus, I didn't get any huge lump sums like that. I'm guessing all that Might came from some of those huge blows you landed. I saw that one that put Raleigh down, and that was fucking monstrous. Other than the thirty Focus, I got ten Creation, which was a new stat for me. Fifteen Vitality, five Might, fifteen Perception, and ten Fantasy. No clue why I got any Fantasy at all, to tell the truth, probably one of my item effects, but still, that was another new one and marks a full unlock for all my stats, so I'm not complaining." He wrote out all his totals just to be clear.

Benicio Cortez: G-rank.

Ability: Lesser Mechanical Embodiment—Allows the integration of existing inventions into the user's body for the purposes of strengthening and enhancing them.

Might: 40
Impact: 12
Fantasy: 10
Vitality: 31
Focus: 75
Perception: 17
Creation: 10

Current integrated tech: 8/10.
Torso: extending rope.
Right fist: triple punch.
Left forearm: long range attack attraction.
Left fist: minor slow acting tranquilizer effect.
Right foot: density shifting to create heavier kicks and more powerful jumps.
Left foot: momentum neutralization to allow stopping instantly.
Head: slight cognitive boost to allow more thinking time.
Back: ability to grow a shell to tank damage.

Skills: Minor Cooking Mastery, Beginner Inventing Mastery, Minor Haggling Mastery, Minor Stealth Mastery

I had expected him to get more Might, but I supposed he'd been kind of playing a background role and relying more on his support abilities. Maybe the Fantasy was from his tranq punches. It also explained why he hadn't seemed nearly as fucked up from the stat dump, since his were more spread out. I noted he'd also gotten less overall than me, but that made sense since Callie and I were the stronger of the four of us, and the recent G-rank members of our team probably stood out less in comparison.

Jessie was up next, and she seemed just as excited to share as before. "As I mentioned, I got a full fifty points in Vitality, which as you might expect, was my largest gain. I did get a decent bump in both Creation and Fantasy, though, at twenty each. That was basically it. I didn't get any new stat unlocks like Benny did. I guess my ability is one of the ones that people tend to typecast as using certain stats. I'm super pissed I didn't get any Might especially, but I figure I can move some of those Fantasy stats around." She wrote hers out just like Benny had.

Jessica Evans: G-rank.

Ability: Beginner Lifeweaving—Infuse living things with life itself and direct their actions while the user's power flows through them. Control has limited effect on sapient entities. Prolonged exposure to life energy may cause lasting effects in controlled non-sapient subjects.

Might: 32
Impact: 12
Fantasy: 28
Vitality: 108
Creation: 28

Skills: Beginner Horticulture, Beginner First Aid, Minor Herbalism, Minor Flower Arrangement

She wasn't wrong—people had definitely focused more on her healing-related stats, but still, she got some use out of most of those. Not Fantasy so much, but those were good points fodder to buff up her other main stats. Her Vitality had already passed a hundred, which was nuts. It had taken me ages to get a stat even close to a hundred, but to be fair, I had sort of gone out of my way to keep my points more evenly spread.

Finally, it was Callie's turn. I knew she'd gotten a huge bump in Creation, which was still good even if she would have preferred Might. Creation helped her make *more* shadows, while Might gave them physical presence and Vitality gave them enhanced mobility as she could breathe more life into them. Still, I was sure she'd gotten at least some Might points. She'd been kicking plenty of ass in the hunt.

She didn't seem upset by her gains, though, and she talked as she wrote out her totals. "As mentioned, I got a big bump in Creation. I also managed to get another twenty Might, twenty-five Perception, eighteen Vitality, twenty-five Fantasy, and twenty-eight Focus. Focus was the biggest change for me, and where most of the pain that hit me during the upgrade came from, I think. Still, all in all, I'm happy with the outcome. I think the big Focus boost shows that people had a good impression of me as a leader and a tactician, which I'm happy about. The other stuff is mostly shine on the apple—those stats were already high."

Calliope Reynolds: G-rank.

Ability: Beginner Shadow embodiment—Ability to control and shape shadows, either molding them into constructs or imbuing them into specially prepared objects to enable enhancement and control.

Might: 127
Impact: 12
Vitality: 164
Fantasy: 75
Focus: 68
Perception: 175
Creation: 142

Skills: Minor Tracking, Beginner Stealth, Beginner Disguise, Lesser Balam Mastery

It was interesting how clean Callie's sheet looked compared to the rest of ours. She had fewer skills, but they were all much higher than most of ours, and while she was obviously focused on specific stats, her points were pretty spread out. It was intimidating to see what proper understanding and a good build could do. Callie had created a strong foundation that made continued progress much simpler. I was just hoping that we'd manage the same for Jessie and Benny. My build was basically a lost cause.

Callie looked absolutely thrilled with everyone's growth. "This is amazing, guys. I can't begin to tell you how quickly we're improving compared to most teams."

I was pretty sure we had a decent idea, but it was nice to know she was happy with the results. We also had tons of spare points now to funnel into more important stats from ones we used less.

We had all this gear to sell too, and all that money was bound to give us new opportunities to grow. Even if we couldn't turn it directly into strength (which we could in some ways since none of us had even scratched our ten percent elixir limit in G-rank), we could still benefit from the cash. We could buy expensive, powerful gear, hire people to run us through missions, or hell, post our own missions to take care of problems.

After we discussed our future plans and talked each other out of peeking at our Academy coins before the agreed-upon meeting time, we officially decided it was time for bed. Benny and Jessie headed back to their rooms, leaving Callie and me alone. I pulled her against me, and we both slumped back onto the floor to stare up to the ceiling.

I spoke casually. "So, we got through it. When were you thinking we would go back to visit your mom?"

She snuggled into my side, sighing happily. "Not sure. Don't want to think. I'm just so damn relaxed. I've been stressed as hell during this whole thing. I know I'm not the only one who has to be responsible for the rest of the group, but being the leader makes it feel like that. Don't get me wrong. I appreciate you guys putting your faith in me, but it's still a lot. I'm going to enjoy some downtime."

I felt the same way and told her so, and she smiled, leaning over to kiss me soundly before getting up. "All right, well, I'm heading to sleep. Get some rest. I need you in top form tomorrow—we have to sell all that stuff. I know Benny has the haggling skill, but I trust your judgement." She turned and strolled off down the hallway, a bounce in her step.

I hopped to my feet and stretched widely. I was tired, plus I had to get up in the morning to make breakfast. There was no point in forcing myself to cook while sleepy. With that I headed off to bed, thinking about what Callie had said. Hopefully, things would stay this peaceful.

Chapter Forty-Seven

AFTER BREAKFAST the next morning (I made quiche), we headed for the Academy to meet up with the others. We took the skyride back over, though we left Cark at home with Cass since he wasn't a student. We'd promised to hand him a cut of the sales from the hunt, despite his attempts to turn it down. Cark had definitely done his part, and it would be wrong not to cut him in for a portion.

Since it was my idea to begin with, he was more than willing to trust us to sell everything and give him his cut when we got back. So we met up at the crafting hall with the others to sell our wares. As expected, Grimmengap was waiting for us when we got there, along with the wolves. I'd brought Jin with me back to the house, and Rellia had been with Callie. Jessie and Benny had left their wolves with Grimmengap, though, because they wouldn't fit in the car comfortably, even with the space expansion.

Seeing Jessie, her wolf, Lily, leapt onto the small blonde and licked her excessively. With her Might, Jessie was able to stay up pretty easily since the wolf wasn't trying to hurt her, and she giggled nonstop as the wolf licked her face. Rolf, Benny's wolf, was much more circumspect and walked over to bump my friend's leg with his nose then enjoyed the petting Benny gave him as he scratched behind the big canine's ears.

I nodded to the others. "Hey, guys, you all ready to find out what our new rankings are?"

Celine was uncharacteristically jittery and nodded quickly. "Of course. All at the same time, I take it?"

We all agreed and, as one, reached down to pull out our coins. Celine stopped, staring hard at the object in her hands. She took a deep breath, clearly putting lots of pressure on this new rank. I could understand that. This was more than just the result of the new points—this was the foundation they could use to get a foothold in the Academy.

I had my own coin out, and I flipped it over. Two hundred fifty thousand six hundred ten. I had to fight down a whistle. That was a pretty big jump. Over a hundred thousand places higher than my previous ranking, especially counting the inevitable drop when I didn't do anything for a few days. This put me around the top twenty-five percent of the entire Academy. I knew there were still tons of powerful G-rankers much stronger than I was. Just because I was high up the list didn't mean I actually had combat power in the top twenty-five percent, but it was a start.

Everyone showed off their new rank, and we confirmed that the whole team had made it up over three hundred thousand. I was higher than the others because of my Might ranking, and Callie was even higher than that, but we'd all made it to a respectable placing in the ranking boards. I could see Celine was pleased with the rank-up, though my team mostly didn't care. We had our own methods of cultivation. While a higher rank was helpful, it wasn't absolutely necessary for us to get stronger.

This was only part of what we were doing here. Callie remembered too, and since my girlfriend could never get enough of loot and treasure, she was quick to steer us back to the matter at hand. "All right, guys, we still have to sell off our gains from the hunt. I've been doing some research on pricing, and we can get a pretty good chunk of change for everything, but there's still the matter of what everyone wants to keep. I think that everyone should get to pick one item, if that works for all of you. Solomon already got his, of course." She nodded at my cane. "What about the rest of you?"

Benny raised a hand. "I want that hourglass. I know it basically just gives you a controllable vision of the future, but I can definitely use that to try out different combinations for inventing. It'll let me save on rare and expensive ingredients and get the best bang for my buck. I'm looking at designing a few new devices for my embodiment ability, and that will help me get the best possible outcome."

Despite being incredibly interesting, the usefulness of the hourglass was somewhat in doubt. Sure it could be used to find hidden dangers in your path, but since it was a one-time-use item, relying on it for that was kind of a waste. Benny using it would give him a possible powerful artifact to use as part of his actual combat strength, so it made sense to let him have it. The others didn't seem to mind at all, so Benny took the hourglass, happily stowing it away as he got ready to use his cut of the cash to buy new materials.

Callie kept the spectral severer, because it was interesting and there wasn't much else she needed. Jessie, Martin, Sarah, and Celine all took materials from the list that lined up with their combat styles so they could commission some weapons. I was pretty damn good, but there were plenty of Enchanters here better than me, so they were planning to pay for them. Wishes might have been able to make something more impressive, but most of them didn't know that, and honestly, with the kind of money we had to throw around, that wasn't even a guarantee.

Benny got in on the haggling, and after an hour or two of negotiations (helped along by my using Seek Hidden to find the people most in need of our materials) we walked away with ten thousand G-ranked chits. More money than any of us had ever seen in our lives. Each of us got a thousand, and we decided to give Cark two thousand because he hadn't picked a material and would need the money to take care of Cass in the future. We'd have other chances to do events like this, but he might not, and we wanted to make sure our friend was taken care of no matter what happened in the future.

I'd been considering what to invest my share in, but I figured I would ask Callie what she thought. I had a few ideas, but I was pretty much equally leaning towards two different options. I pulled her aside.

"Hey, I was wondering if I could get your opinion on something."

She hung back as the others kept walking, tilting her head quizzically at me.

"I was thinking on what to do with my share, but I'm torn between getting a new car, possibly even a shuttle if we can afford one, or a new costume. This one is kind of wearing out at my current rank."

Callie didn't even hesitate. "Costume. The car we have now isn't perfect, but isn't bad, either. That H-rank armor has been holding you back, though, and it's gotten you hurt more than once. I get that it doesn't feel like it's been quite as big a problem as it should—having a dedicated healer helps with that—but I'm guessing you have more than a few rips and tears in that thing. It was great when you were in H-rank, but you need a better set of gear for combat purposes at least."

I sighed, knowing she was right. "Yeah, fair enough. The question becomes should I order a new set in the exact same style or try to update my look?" I glanced down at the familiar light armor, now covered with scratches and damage, despite my best efforts to keep it in good shape. It would be simple enough to get some Skills that would let me patch it up properly, but I knew deep down that it would just be treating the symptoms rather than the disease. I'd outgrown my old clothes, and part of me wanted to use the opportunity for a change.

Callie seemed to get that, but she shook her head. "Massive image over-hauls like that are counterproductive to a rising Ascendant. My personal suggestion is maybe make some small changes. Keep the armor style and exchange the cloak for a coat or something. As long as you keep the hood, you'll still be easily recognizable. You can change your image, but you want to do it slowly over time. One element here, one there. That way, people slowly acclimate to the alterations without losing their impression of you. Image management is incredibly important to cultivators."

That was an interesting take on things. I'd mostly been focused on the fact that changing my vibe this early would let me avoid losing out down the road, but a slow shift in image would probably work better. "Speaking of, what rank is your gear? You've been G-rank since I met you, so I assume it's that level too, but is it as good as what you can get here? The materials you can find in a place like this would be a lot better than anything you can pick up back in Velan. Or did you get that on your visit?"

Callie's famous Nightstrike outfit had been in solid condition since we got here, despite not covering as much as mine, and it was clearly much more durable. I'd never actually given any thought to where she got it.

She just shrugged. "I special ordered it. There are delivery services that run between here and Velan. I was a guild executive of the Velan branch, so I was able to worm my way onto the approved list. Of course it was still expensive as hell, but I have a few sponsorship deals back home, so I was able to save up for it."

With my question answered, I figured it was time to track down someone to make me a new costume. I liked her jacket idea and was planning to include it, but before we could move very far, I heard the chime of my scan ring getting an incoming call. I spun it up to open the call, only to find Zeke on the screen. He rarely called me first, so I expected this to be important news, but rather than looking serious, he seemed like he was about to break down laughing.

I raised an eyebrow before remembering I had my mask on and cocking my head. "This can't bode well. What had you laughing so hard?"

Zeke grinned widely at me. "I wanted to be the one to tell you because I wanted to see your face. I just got a call from Stella."

I waited, glaring into the screen as he took a deep breath, dragging this out.

"She told me we're getting a visitor from Velan. Another local moving up to the big leagues. Specifically one nobody saw coming, and he brought his people with him." His grin was so wide, I wondered if his face hurt, and it took him a few seconds to finally get it out. "Mr. Jack-tastic broke through to E-rank. He brought his whole crew to Rajak. The Jerks have officially moved up to a planetary-scale organization."

I froze, my blood running cold. I'd seen plenty of terrible things since becoming an Ascendant, but nothing matched the sheer lunacy of the territory the Jerks had ruled over. That had been when Mr. Jack-tastic was running a section of a much smaller town. There were still plenty of other E-rankers, but probably not that many, and he had a way of grabbing attention.

Rajak had just become a much weirder place. May the Revenant have mercy on us all.

Chapter Forty-Eight

WE DIDN'T commission new costumes. We went home. Immediately. If Zeke felt the need to tell me Mr. Jack-tastic was in town now, there had to be a reason for it. I didn't believe for a second he'd just been informing me because it was amusing. This had some relation to me, and I wanted to know what it was before those absolute lunatics filled my car with spray cheese or something. I still had nightmares about the day I'd spent in the Jerks' territory.

Callie was at least sympathetic, because she agreed to head home with me. Benny decided to stay back at the Academy with Grimmengap and most of the wolves, though Jin, Rellia, and Lily came with us. Without Cark and Benny, we had the room to barely squeeze everyone in. When we got home, Jessie went to go deliver the two thousand chits to Cark while Callie and I cornered my Uncle.

He smirked when he saw us. "Ah, hurried home I see. I'm not surprised. I figured you would be curious."

I dropped onto the couch across from him. "Okay, let's get the obvious out of the way. Why or how are you allowed to tell me they're in town in the first place? Doesn't this fall under the whole 'do it yourself' category?" That was going to bug me all day if I didn't get it settled. I was still figuring out the rules for how all of this worked. The more I found out about Zeke's geas, the more I could work around it if necessary.

That got me a disappointed head shake and a tsk of disapproval. "That was a waste of a first question, honestly. I told you—Stella called. She would have passed the info to you all eventually anyway. I was just acting as an intermediary. I didn't tap into any resources or information lines you couldn't normally access." He grinned at me tauntingly. "Now that you asked the dumb question, how about the smart one?" He didn't even try to hide the condescending glee he felt at making me dance to his tune.

Sighing, I rolled my eyes. "Fine. Why does it matter to me that Mr. Jack-tastic has come to Rajak? You wouldn't call and tell me that just because that stupid gang haunts the darkest parts of my nightmares." At least, I hoped he wouldn't. Though saying it out loud like that made me wonder how accurate it was. Zeke's sense of humor could be obnoxious sometimes.

He gave a satisfied nod, and I felt more and more that I'd just stepped into some kind of trap. "Because they came here partly for you." He paused. "Well, no, they came here because breaking through to E-rank means Mr. Jack-tastic is a top-tier existence on this planet now, and as such, being at the center of the action means he gets a bigger slice of the pie, but you being here definitely helped them make the decision to come over more quickly. After all, you're very important to them."

Okay, I liked the way that sounded even less than I liked how gleeful he was being about this whole thing. Despite the sinking feeling in the pit of my stomach, I didn't take the bait. I stayed calm and said in a very level voice, with absolutely no teeth grinding, "And why, exactly, would I be important to the Jerks, when I met a total of, like, six of them in the entire time I was in Velan?"

His smile got wider, if that were even possible. "Oh, you don't know?"

I had to literally force myself not to lunge across the room and try to choke him.

"I just assumed that you were aware. Apparently, you were responsible for foiling the grand entrance of Mr. Jack-tastic's only son into the criminal underworld of Velan. He decided that you were his nemesis and has decided to accompany his father to Rajak in order to do glorious battle with you."

I believed he must have been tapping into his seven-digit Focus score to get that all out before he dissolved into gales of laughter.

The blood drained from my face. "Oh, you have got to be fucking kidding me. Please tell me his kid wasn't Carl." It could have been Stephen the Shoe, but Carl had at least had *some* brains, not to mention he had seemed like the one in charge.

Zeke just grinned at me, clearly savoring my pain.

I pointed at him accusingly. "You are *way* too bored if you're this amused by my misfortune. Forgetting for a moment your complete lack of any sort of life, how exactly did Mr. Jack-tastic of all people hit fucking E-rank?"

His smile dimmed but didn't vanish as he rolled his own eyes at my critique of his entertainment. Still, his voice became more serious and slightly impressed. "In a similar way to how Unity did it, actually. In retrospect, it's actually kind of brilliant. By making his name both ridiculous and included in the name of his gang, combined with picking the weirdest and most eccentric people possible, he farmed renown for years, building up his profile in a way that the other gang lords just couldn't."

I blinked. "I mean, I figured he was pushing the crazy angle for renown—I think we all did—but I guess I never really noticed how any interaction with the Jerks was filtered through the lens of them being his subordinates. Even more so than the Queen of Hearts and The Nobody Man. I got the impression they were all sort of equal. If he kept from tipping people off, he must have been playing things pretty close to the chest. I guess the whole 'genius or idiot' question kind of answered itself, huh?"

Callie looked absolutely thunderstruck. She'd been an executive in the Velan branch, not to mention a frequent visitor to the WCP. A case could be made that she was the member of the Unity with the most connection to the underworld in all of Velan, and this had obviously completely blind-sided her. I knew how she felt.

I turned to Zeke, trying to convey with my tone that I wasn't kidding around anymore. "So, this Carl thing. How much trouble can the son of an E-ranker make for me? I mean I know you can stop Mr. Jack-tastic himself from messing with me, but what about the other Jerks? Also, why didn't we know about Carl to begin with? I figured Cap would be aware of some-thing like this."

Zeke looked a little annoyed. "Apparently, it was something of a secret. Carl is an idiot, but he's a prideful idiot. The only reason we found out about the connection was that Mr. Jack-tastic—gods that's such a stupid name—because Jack exerted personal influence to spring him from jail. As much as we might pretend otherwise, after a certain level, powerful cultivators can basically do whatever they want. Just him showing up in person was enough to pressure them to let Carl go."

It was hard to throw stones there. I'd benefited from Zeke's powers when he came to help with the sleepers. Still, Mr. Jack-tastic wasn't the only F-ranker in town at the time. Even if he had been approaching E, not many people knew that. "Wouldn't that be a huge risk, though? Putting pressure on the authorities like that? I mean, rank isn't a magic medicine that makes you invincible. Even without being as high in stats, the other F-rankers would still be a threat if push came to shove. Unless his ability is really that overpowered? I don't think I've ever heard what he can do."

Zeke didn't seem to care, but given his insanely high rank, that wasn't a shock. "He's a beast caller. It's similar to what Benny does, but with animals. He binds the spirits of monsters and beasts into his skin like tattoos and can tap into their abilities at will. It's less versatile than an embodiment skill because it's permanent, but it's also more powerful because the beasts can actually grow as he does. But you aren't wrong— Jack isn't invincible at F-rank by any means, but he doesn't have to be. He just has to be strong enough to be inconvenient."

Realization dawned on me. "The F-rankers in Velan are balanced. Taking on Mr. Jack-tastic means potentially getting hurt or even killed, leaving your territory open for the others. Stella might not have that same problem, but she also can't afford the blow to her image. If she wants to keep growing, she needs to be the unassailable guild master. It's the only way she has a chance of making an impression after someone like Midknight passed the torch to her. Stopping him from springing some random weakling, son or not, isn't worth burning those bridges, so they just ignored it."

It was interesting to hear more about the way people interacted at higher ranks, and more than that, it made some of the unspoken rules clear. It was obvious that the E-rankers in the capital could have converged and destroyed all the criminals on the planet if they wanted, but what would be the point of that? Heroic cultivation required spectacle, and spectacle required enemies.

Of course, there were certain things like Stricture's killings that crossed the line, but even then, there seemed to be rules in place. They had sent a single F-ranker to deal with the issue, keeping the power structure in the city mostly intact. Even that had been compromised for Callie to get the credit (which she ultimately hadn't. I could only assume she'd gone out of her way to make sure my role was disclosed. I'd never asked her about that), showing that the E-rankers had even more complicated motivations past the preservation of the current order.

So the question became, what was Carl going to actually do? I doubted he was going to ignore me, but I wasn't exactly running around town, and the city was way too big for that to matter anyway. The only thing I could think of would be coming to the Academy, but it was a Unity-exclusive institution. Then I paused. Was it? The Unity pretty clearly didn't care about outsiders attending—Celine had made that obvious. "Is it possible that Carl might end up at the Academy? Like could Mr. Jack-tastic pull some strings to make that happen?"

Zeke didn't seem surprised by the question. "Sure. Building good relations with an E-ranker would be worth admitting someone to the school. They do that kind of stuff as a political gesture all the time. In fact, that would be a decent reason for coming here. The Academy isn't just a concentration of force; it's a recruitment tool. The events they hold weed out the most promising candidates from the student body and give them a chance to see what they're capable of. It's one of the fastest ways to get to a higher-ranked planet."

That was good to know. I was guessing such recruitment was aimed at F-rankers. Given their status in the Academy, it would make the most sense. In fact, I'd always wondered why the F-rankers stayed on as student instructors and helpers after graduation, but if it involved some kind of opportunity for promotion, that made perfect sense. I shot Callie an excited look, and I was sure she was having similar, if not identical, thoughts.

We thanked Zeke for the news and ignored his snickering about the fact that I had an insane stalker. This had given us a lot to think about, and we both headed to the training room for a spar. We had Balam lessons to continue, and after the big power boost, we both needed to get used to our new capabilities. I was happy to take some time off from thinking for a while. Not that it would necessarily end soon—I was pretty sure with the Jerks in town, none of us were going to be making much use of logic.

Chapter Forty-Nine

We ended up back at the Academy the next day, specifically in the dorms. We'd decided to ask Celine about whatever F-rank events were going on around here. Chances were good she would know, given her sources at the school and her position as a diplomat. Of course, some questions were still unanswered, like how Carl would even get to F-rank in time if he was planning to enroll, but I was pretty sure there would be ways to help pump someone's stats if you were strong enough. If there wasn't, Zeke's geas wouldn't be so damn restrictive about how much he could help me.

As expected, Celine was well aware of what we meant. "Yes, of course there's a scouting event for higher-ranked planetary forces. Or rather, a scouting event for a scouting event. It's something of an open secret. This year, in particular, the tournament is incredibly important. The winner of the F-ranked combat tournament for Callus is guaranteed a spot in the black-abyss dungeon. It's an Ascendant territory. The top participants from all the E-ranked planets are allowed entry."

I remembered Callie mentioning dungeons at one point. I knew materials were incredibly abundant there, but that wasn't too important at the moment. If we were right about Carl's reasons for coming, then that combat tournament was a much more pertinent issue. "So if Carl is aiming for that, aside from getting to F-rank—which is kind of a crazy hurdle on its own—how would he get a spot in that tournament?" If this was a year out, maybe he had some way of rushing it, but mostly, I just wanted to know exactly what the Jerks were going to be doing. I didn't believe for a second those crazy bastards wouldn't come up with some stupid weird plan to help their boss's kid.

She shrugged. "Same as anyone else. Missions, rankings, events. There isn't really a way to cheat the system with resources or manpower. It has to be done that way since so many of the Ascendants here come from powerful families. More than that, though, producing talented Ascendants reinforces the Academy's reputation. The better the students do, the more convinced people are by the school's press. Allowing nepotism to compromise their process would only decrease their overall effectiveness."

I sighed. I'd been afraid of that. The Jerks weren't the grand-diabolical-scheme type. They just did literally whatever popped into their heads. It was part of what made them so unpredictable. I sighed and shook off the weird sense of urgency. I'd gotten so used to there being some emergency to deal with that I'd jumped into problem-solving mode without thinking. I would just have to deal with Carl and whatever stupid bullshit he and his lackeys came up with.

To that end, I focused on the immediate future, turning to my girlfriend. "So, ignoring this nonsense for the moment, what's our next move?" Part of the reason we'd come here was to ask Grimmengap what they had planned and possibly invite them to work with us a bit more. We all made a hell of a team, and especially since they'd hit G-rank, it wouldn't be a bad idea to have them on our side.

Sure enough, Callie turned to Celine. "Actually, I was wondering if you all would be interested in continuing our partnership. We worked well together back in the hunt, and we know that up to ten-person teams are viable. We can still take on missions as a group, and our experience working together should make that much easier."

As expected, Celine didn't seem against the idea, and neither did the other two.

It made sense to keep working with Grimmengap—we liked them, we had a good rapport, we understood their abilities, and most importantly, we'd already invested in them. Whether it was giving them the wolves or elevating them to G-rank through the hunt, we'd put in plenty of work getting them to the same level we were at, and it made sense for us to keep that relationship going. Everyone was happy with our collaboration so far.

Celine also allowed the unspoken caveat that Callie would remain in charge. While we weren't in the hunt anymore, Callie was still the strongest member of either of our groups, as well as the most experienced. Letting her continue to run things was the smartest play, and Celine clearly had no issue ceding control as long as she and her teammates kept benefiting like they had been. Not to mention I knew she still wanted Benny around and needed Jessie to make sure things went well with the wolves.

Callie, graceful as ever, accepted her trust without comment and switched gears immediately. "Okay, then, our next move is obviously to keep building up our strength and reputation, making the most of the fame from our stream." She glanced at me. "There might be a way to keep an eye on the situation developing with the Jerks, too. Celine, is there a place where we can get info gathering missions? You seem to have a ton of sources here. That kind of information can't just come out of nowhere. Even if you built your networks, they would need some kind of foundation, right?"

Celine gave an embarrassed smile. "About that... I may have exaggerated my reach. While I have been making inroads with the student body and expanding my circle of friends, a large portion of my information came from the information hall. So yes, it's not really publicly stated, but it's an open secret that the Perception faculty operates something like an information broker within the Academy and the city at large. The kind of mission you're talking about is exactly what they do there."

I snickered. I didn't blame Celine for the misdirect. If anything, it was a brilliant use of resources. We were Ascendants, and convincing people you're secretly a spymaster when you buy all your information from the local broker was classic PR. The fact that we fell for it just went to show that sometimes cultivation made us a bit too willing to believe the amazing and fantastical. Just because people were capable of doing the impossible with their abilities didn't mean that every action anyone took was inherently rooted in them. It was a good lesson that logic didn't completely go out the window where cultivation was concerned... just mostly.

I think more than anything, Callie was embarrassed that she didn't know that. Perception was one of her specialties. She'd even done the test over there at one point. The fact that she didn't know about such a big part of what should have been her own faculty clearly didn't sit well with my girlfriend. I didn't blame her, though. We'd been so wrapped up with the Heartrippers that we had completely ignored the Academy as a whole. The hunt itself had shown us that there were some impressive people here, and our ignorance of this place was firmly to our detriment.

We needed to get a better lay of the land since we were going to be here for the foreseeable future. Step one was looking around, but we also needed to engage more with the whole Academy system. Taking missions at the information hall would serve multiple purposes in that sense. I could see Callie thinking through all of this even as I did, and I didn't even need to meet her eyes to know it. Despite that, when I cocked my masked head at her, she smiled brilliantly, somehow able to pick up what I was thinking in my body language. Maybe because of all that Perception.

Callie and I hadn't been together that long, or even known each other for as long as we could've, but one of the reasons we did so well in combat was that we understood each other. The way our brains worked just tended to click. Callie understood me better than most people in my life (even better than Benny in some ways) and aside from my crush, that was one of the major reasons I wasn't worried about how fast things were moving with her. We just... fit. It wasn't scary or intimidating. In fact, I barely even noticed it mostly. Things with her were just comfortable, and I found myself falling into an easy pattern with her without trying.

That wasn't to say I always agreed with her decisions, but even when we butted heads, we found a way to work it out because of that mutual understanding. Callie was my first serious girlfriend, but I was pretty sure the rapport we had was a rare thing. I was definitely grateful for it, because it was one of the things that kept me balanced with all the building pressure on me emotionally, and I liked to think I was a stabilizing influence for her too.

I understood more than ever what Zeke had meant when he told me not to put off having a romantic life until I got stronger. I wasn't sure I would have gotten to where I was without her, or if I had, I wasn't sure I would be the same person. Just the rapport we had was worth its weight in... some material more valuable than gold. Being an Ascendant really screwed up some of my favorite idioms. I wondered what she was thinking about as I considered all this. I doubted it was the same thing. We were pretty compatible, but we didn't read each other's minds.

Luckily, she was better at communication than I was, not that it was hard to be, given my tendency to get lost in my own head. "We'll take an info-gathering job, something related to discovering new forces if they're looking, if not something that will take us to whatever neighborhood they're in if we can find out where."

I felt my shoulders relax. I had this vague feeling whatever nonsense the Jerks were going to get up to would suck me in. Carl's little vendetta was only part of the reason. The rest might be paranoia, but it was better to be proactive.

Despite what I'd said about the tournament and the school being true, I very much doubted an E-ranker had only one reason for coming here. Rajak was a big city, and Mr. Jack-tastic had been around on Callus for a long time. You don't get to be an E-ranker by thoughtlessly or stupidly doing anything, no matter what impression you gave people. I imagined recursion made him more prone to erratic behavior, but anyone who stuck around that long was bound to have strong willpower.

E-rankers were the real powers of this planet, and Rajak was where most, if not all, of them were gathered. There was no way to add another one, especially one as weird as Mr. Jack-tastic, that wouldn't upset the apple cart. Maybe it wouldn't involve me, maybe I could just skate through whatever they had planned without being noticed, but my luck since becoming an Ascendant didn't give me much confidence of that.

Whatever was happening, I wanted to at least find out the details. If we could avoid whatever was about to go down (and I just couldn't shake the feeling something was), at the very least, we wouldn't be blindsided again. I was getting sick and tired of reacting to the crazy things that happened around us last second. Knowledge was power, and I wanted as much power as I could get.

Chapter Fifty

I was interested in the Perception faculty. I'd never actually been. Callie had gone at least once to do the test, but since she hadn't known about the missions or the information gathering thing, I assumed that part of the faculty was kept separate from the testing grounds. Like the golem battle dome was out of the way of the Creation faculty but still nearby. Since Callie didn't bring it up, I asked Celine myself. "How come we haven't heard of this place, since we've been to the Perception faculty building?"

I said *we* despite never having gone, because if Callie hadn't noticed it, there was no way I would have seen anything. Her Perception was leagues ahead of mine, and she paid more attention than I did. I caught a fond smile out of the corner of my eye when I asked that. She knew I'd only brought it up because she was embarrassed to say anything, though I was also legitimately curious.

Celine shrugged. "Like I said, it's something of an open secret. No one really talks about it. The thought is that if you have enough of an interest in Perception to be there, you'll find it. It's not a rule or anything, more of a silent agreement, so I don't care too much about letting you know." Left unsaid was the fact that this was something she used as an advantage. Sharing the information with us like this was a peace offering. She was sharing one of her secrets with us because she considered us part of her team.

It was taken in the spirit it was offered. As nice as the gesture was, it wasn't enough to convince me to tell them about my ability. Mine was a secret in a completely different league. Still, it was appreciated, and I would try to pay back the trust as best as I could.

When we arrived at the Perception building, I almost missed it as we walked by. The building was set back into the trees, and something about the lines of the construction, the shadows, and the way the trees drew the eye made it so that place was really easy to overlook. When we stopped, it took me a second to lay eyes on it, and once I did, I wondered how I had missed it.

The building was, contrary to what the blending effect would imply, not exactly subtle or unremarkable. It wasn't loud or flashy, but the construction was obviously high quality, and there was a kind of dignity to it that made the building pull focus, at least once you were looking at it. The front doors were wide and thick, with a heavy frame of light wood carved with pictures of animals like foxes and hawks—animals known for keen sight or the ability to vanish. It was a beautifully made door, and I was betting the carpentry Skill of the person who'd carved it was at least Beginner level.

Callie pulled the doors open, flinging them wide so we could all enter, and I noted as we passed the threshold that the wooden doors made no noise as they opened, not even on striking the building. That was an interesting effect. When we stepped inside, we looked around to see a series of comfortable-looking couches set on plush carpet, with a nice water feature on each wall. The place looked like a lobby. Since Callie had brought us, I was pretty sure this was the testing area.

I cocked my head. "Hey, I figured we would do the missions first. This isn't the information hall. What are we doing here?" I'd been interested in doing the test for a while, and with my Perception at eighty, I could probably manage at least the early aspects of whatever it was. I'd expected to have to wait and come back myself, though. I could see the others hadn't been expecting to show up here either.

The smile on Callie's face was slightly wicked. "I figured we could all come take the test together. I know Agria hasn't unlocked Perception yet, but Clockwork has, and yours just got a big bump. Plus my own Perception is almost at two hundred, so it'll be interesting to see what I can manage here." Despite the slightly teasing tone, it was nice she wanted to give us the chance to try it out. Even if we would probably end up getting subpar scores, it wouldn't do much, and we had the potential to get ranking points daily if we scored well.

I figured based on her excitement that the test was probably much different than the Might stone, and I was looking forward to seeing what they had come up with. We headed up to the counter to sign up for the Perception test, and once we got registered, I was ushered forward on my own as the others were led away to different entrances. Callie gave me a kiss for luck and told me to have fun, so I knew it wasn't dangerous, whatever it was. The faculty member led me over to a door in the back, opened it up, and ushered me into a dark hallway.

The door shut behind me, but before it did, I saw a few gleams of metal. Once it shut, I stood completely still in the darkness before activating my Seek Hidden skill to see what exactly I was dealing with. I focused on finding the metal glints I'd seen when the door opened, and suddenly, the whole place was full of a series of red lines as Seek Hidden lit up a network of wires strung across the hallway end to end, covered with bells.

It was odd using Seek Hidden in the dark like this, because despite the light in my vision, the glow didn't actually cut the darkness at all. There was no illumination outside the dim red gleam of the wires and bells. Skills were fine in the tests, so I just considered this a good matchup, since Seek Hidden helped a lot with a test like this. I took a step forward, figuring I was supposed to Perceive the wires and avoid the bells.

The second my foot touched the beginning of the flooring beneath the wires, though, the wires began to roll in gentle waves, tossing the bells about up into the air, though somehow not actually ringing them. When all of them were in motion, I realized why this was a Perception test. I was supposed to find the way between the whipping wires. I stepped up and stood in place for a minute. Then, with all my concentration, I rolled forward through a gap in the wires.

I came to my feet staggering, stomping down hard to stop the momentum of my roll, and the second my foot met the ground, I felt an impact on the sole of my boot. That impact made me stumble forward, and I reacted with every bit of grace I had, doing my best to avoid the wires. Every time I rang a bell or my feet made a noise, I felt an impact. I was able to dodge some of them once I realized the impact targeted whichever limb had made the noise, but I still didn't manage to get more than ten feet. As soon as an impact struck the same place I'd already been hit, there was a loud noise, and the test ended.

The lights came on, and I saw that I'd been moving down the hallway toward a door on the other end. Closer to the door, the wires got thicker, and there were more bells hanging on each one. I heard a snicker and turned to see my girlfriend waiting at the door.

She gave me a wide smile. "That's a good color on you."

I looked down, and rolled my eyes as I saw the paint that was covering me. It was mostly white, though I had a small splattering of pink on one shoulder. Apparently, they used the same color system the Might stone did.

I raised an eyebrow behind my mask, then I grinned widely and bolted forward at her. She squeaked, eyes wide as she realized that I was close enough to grab her while still covered in paint. She shrieked in protest as I wrapped her up in my arms, making sure to get as much paint on her as possible, but the shrieking turned into giggles as she pushed me off. "All right, all right, I deserved that. Fine, I should have warned you. I just wanted to see how you would do going in cold."

She was wiping the white paint off her with a big smile, and the faculty advisor who had let her in was leaning back against the wall, rolling his eyes, clearly not even remotely interested in our flirting. That was fair enough, so I followed them out of the hallway, and the advisor passed us both towels. I shrugged as I cleaned myself off. "I knew it wouldn't be anything dangerous, or you would have told us, so I didn't mind going in blind. I was pretty interested to see what they would come up with. I think I know how it works, but can I have a rundown?"

She chuckled as she wiped the last of the paint off. "Sure. It's not complicated. When you make any noise, the tunnel launches a paintball at the point of contact, if a paintball hits the same place a second time your run ends. The further down you go the faster the wires and the more bells. You got hit with a bit of pink, which means you made it into the hundred-Perception section of the tunnel, probably with a skill, since I know you're shy of that milestone. Pretty impressive for your first go. I figured it might be fun for everyone to try it. The paint wipes right off, so it's not too inconvenient, and it's kind of fun."

I snickered. "I'm not entirely sure that Clockwork is going to agree with you, but fair enough. It was definitely… interesting."

It wasn't what I'd expected for the Perception test. I could see how it was a good measuring stick, though. With the right amount of perception, you could plot the course of the wires based on the sounds, which I probably should have at least tried. Even if your Might wasn't too high, you would be able to react to the paintballs enough to avoid getting hit in the same spot twice. Between that and controlling your footsteps, an obvious feat of stealth, I could see plenty of layers to the test.

Callie eventually left to do her own test, managing to make it to the three-hundreds range based on her stealth abilities. I was thoroughly impressed. The others came back covered in white paint. Jessie had decided to give it a try for fun, and without a single point of Perception, she had completely fallen flat at the beginning. Benny had used his projectile-attracting arm, but since two hits in one spot ended the exercise, that had actually back-fired, much to his chagrin.

All in all, Callie had been right—it was a fun thing to do as a group and a good idea for team building. We all wiped off the easily removable paint and made our way toward the information hall with Celine leading the way, and everyone was in a good mood. As we walked toward the building, I sidled up next to Callie and put my arm over her shoulder. I'd really needed to relax.

Chapter Fifty-One

WE WERE all in a fantastic mood when we arrived at the information building. Like the testing hall, this particular structure was tough to spot unless you knew where it was. I still had no clue how they'd achieved that, but I imagined it had something to do with the stealth Skill. It was interesting to consider how it was done, like maybe they'd built it using Perception-oriented materials and while resonating the Skill. Would that make it a building with a Skill? Or maybe you needed an architecture Skill to do things like that so they had used both Skills in its construction.

Whatever the case, once we were aware of it, we could see it just fine, and we made our way in through the doors, which, while similar to the white ones from the testing hall in design, were pitch-black. That was pretty much the only similarity, because once we made it into the building, it became clear that the inside was far from the lobby-like appearance of our previous destination.

The inside of the info hall had hardwood floors as opposed to carpet, and wall-to-wall boards were covered with tacked-up pieces of paper. Much like the mission system back home, it seemed like people here favored written postings as a method to avoid leaving any traces. The whole place was filled with people, though most of them were covered in cloaks or hoods, even on top of existing costumes, and more than half wore odd temporary masks that all looked the same. Anonymity seemed to be the order of the day.

Callie gave a low whistle as we stepped inside. "Wow. This place is… interesting. My Perception is only just high enough to even notice some of these people. A couple of them seem to be in a perpetual state of stealth, and I'm betting there are a few even I can't see." She turned to Celine. "Is there some kind of sorting system for who can take what jobs? I imagine you can't just accept any assignment."

With the kind of people here, there was no way they were taking the same kind of jobs as we were. Their stats would put them on a whole different level.

Celine smiled. "Well spotted. Yes, there are small colored dots on each mission if you look. The color corresponds to the range of your abilities in the test. The ones over here"—she pointed to a series of nearby missions— "are blank missions. Ones that anyone can take. They correspond to white on the mission boards. The missions need to pay more the further up the spectrum you go. Obviously, people use points to pay for them, much like the crafting hall missions. All of my postings have been blank missions."

I blinked. "Well, that's… convenient? Or not? I honestly don't know. Do all of us have to reach the required standard to take it as a team? Because if so, we're stuck at blank missions, but if not we can take orange missions because of Nightstrike." I wasn't sure if I had a preference there. We might not really be ready for any higher-level missions, though I assumed the higher pay would be useful.

Celine nodded. "Teams are only allowed to take missions based on the placement of their lowest-scoring member, so yes, we can only do blank missions. Still, that shouldn't be too big an issue. There are bound to be multiple levels of missions for recon, and since a decent chunk of this new force will be lower G and even H-rankers, there should be at least one mission for investigating those elements of the organization." That was a decent point. Mr. Jack-tastic might have reached E-rank, but the Jerks as a whole were still mainly the same gang.

Having an E-rank boss was bound to affect their ability to grow—we'd seen that from the Flame Riot Militia. The boss being one of the elites of the planet definitely had a qualitative effect on the members' reputation, but it was hardly going to take effect so quickly. We were dealing with a gang from a lower-tier city, and even those lunatics would have to hold back somewhat while they built up their rep, though I wasn't sure how capable of that they really were.

Callie headed over to the nearest board, having scanned the other notices to double-check from a distance and closed in on one that would be useful. She strolled up and snagged one of the notices. After reading over it and rolling her eyes, she passed it to me. I scanned the posting and had to groan at the contents. "How? How did they manage to find a situation like this so quickly after getting here? It's been like a few days or something, right? I figured they would be taking things slow."

My girlfriend snickered. "Like they even know how." She held up the page to the others. "From what this says, an unknown group with a character-istic colored mohawk has apparently laid siege to an area in the south of the WCP's G district. The territory of..." She checked the page again. "Cicero Castleton's Captivating Circus Cavalcade? Oh, I can already tell I'm not going to enjoy dealing with these people. Anyway, someone is offering a hundred points per person to look into it and find out what's going on."

That was odd. "I know it's pretty big, but I feel like I would have noticed a circus in G district when we were last down there. We were all over that place. Where exactly is this... cavalcade?" I was honestly kind of curious what an Ascendant circus would even look like. It sounded like it would be kind of crazy, exactly the kind of place where the Jerks would feel at home.

Callie just shrugged. "I doubt we covered more than half of that place, not that it was easy to tell. But we avoided the major population areas. The marks were all in out-of-the-way spots where no one spent time by neces-sity. It'll be interesting to see some of the more lively parts of the WCP. My major issue with this is that it's posted here at all. Isn't the WCP supposed to be a completely separate force? Why do people at the Academy even care what's going on down in the WCP?"

This one, Celine did know the answer to. "The Wish Curse Palace is an important part of Rajak. It's heavily involved in local politics and the distri-bution of local forces and resources. The information hall isn't just built around information from the Academy. It covers the whole city, and the WCP is a necessary part of that networking. I won't say all or even most of the jobs here are based down there. It isn't that big of a space compared to the whole city, but there are certainly a decent number of missions aimed at that area."

It also made sense that they would go straight down there when arriving. The WCP was a neutral area, even if only nominally. They would have a much lower chance of running into political complications while moving around down there. I was curious if the Jerks even had enough G-rankers to operate in the G-ranked district. They only had a few that I remembered. Then again who knew what "laying siege" actually meant in relation to them.

I turned to Callie. "You're the one with the most experience with their G-rankers. Can we handle them?"

She snorted. "Easily. But only if they actually fight us. This is recon, not an elimination mission. Plus, if they're running up against a noted G-rank force, they must have gotten some upgrades. The only way I can imagine that happening in any reasonable time frame would be if they did some recruiting. With Mr. Jack-tastic at E-rank, it should be simple enough to find people who would be interested. Even if they would have to make allowances for... stylistic differences."

That was the nicest way of saying they needed to find crazy people that I could imagine, but I somehow doubted in a city this size it would be too hard to find people willing to act like idiots for a chance to get more powerful. The Jerks were... colorful, but they drew attention, which was its own kind of draw. With their boss at E-rank, people were bound to see working with them as an opportunity, even if they had to dress like a dumbass and act ridiculous.

Our decision made, we headed to the desk tucked into the back corner, where we informed the person working behind the counter (whoever they might have been, since they were in a thick-hooded cloak, and I literally couldn't penetrate the darkness with my eyes) that we wanted to take the mission. Since it was a blank mission, we didn't need to present any proof of capability or anything, though Celine mentioned we would if we'd tried to take something higher rank, and then we headed back to the dorm.

We'd left the wolves back at the rooms, since they drew a lot of attention when they were around. Since Jessie was technically a tamer, we could bring them around with us, but since we'd been indoors and in a more sedate area like the information hall, we had decided to leave them at the dorm. Celine and the others had splurged on some treats and didn't mind sharing them, so they mostly just chewed on some dried meat and waited for us, but they were still really excited to see us when we got back to the dorms.

Once we arrived, Callie sat everyone down. "All right, I figure we can drop in tomorrow to take a look at this circus. This particular mission will probably take a while, but we shouldn't go in costume. G district isn't exclusively costumed individuals, and a circus is the kind of place where civilians would blend in. Since we don't want to draw attention and Jerks will *definitely* recognize me in costume, it makes more sense to dress normally. We can even bring Cark with us, since he knows the area well from his time looking for Cass."

We could even bring the wolves with us. No one in Velan would associate them with our personas, and we hadn't had them long enough to be known for them here yet. Plus, they would be good protection when we didn't have our gear on. That said, since it was a recent addition, I could at least carry my cane with me. We went over the details before deciding to head home. If we were going down to the WCP tomorrow, we needed to be well rested. Plus, we needed to ask Cark if he felt like coming along.

Benny stayed behind with Celine, and Jessie drove, so Callie and I spent some time together talking in the back of the car on the way back. We decided since we were going as civilians, it would be a good time for us to have that date we'd been planning. Benny would probably be fine to head off with Celine, and Jessie volunteered (she was eavesdropping) to take Cark out to look around while Martin and Sarah did their own thing. With a firm plan in mind, we sat back and enjoyed the ride, petting the wolves as we headed home. Tomorrow was going to be a big day.

Chapter Fifty-Two

IT FELT weird wearing my civilian clothes down to G district. I got the logic —none of the jerks would recognize me without my mask (even the original ones I'd met had seen me in a generic WCP goon costume), but I felt exposed. Still, having the others and the wolves with me helped allay my concerns about being vulnerable to attack. Giant terrifying wolves are a real confidence booster in basically any situation, and Jin's teeth were about the size of my hand. Plus, he was fuzzy, which made him an excellent pillow.

I consider spamming my wishes before we went down there to give us an edge, but in the end, having them on hand as a trump card seemed like a better use of my ability. The previous day's wishes had given me twenty points of Creation from Jessie in exchange for twenty points of Might. She'd been unhappy with having the lowest Might in the group, and she didn't really use her Creation stat since she depended mainly on her Vitality for healing and control. I, on the other hand, was falling far behind on that stat, so I was happy to have a boost.

We headed for the station again, this time at a more relaxed pace. It was nice to take our time and just take in the sounds and sights of the place. We climbed into the metal canister. The wolves got a few looks from the families in the crowds, but we didn't draw much attention in the actual G-rank conveyance, and we all sat down to prepare for departure. We took up a sizable space because of the wolves, but there was plenty to go around, so we weren't crowded or anything.

The most amusing part of the day had to be how flustered Celine was. When we were all interacting in costume, it was easy to keep things official, but since we were out of our masks, this was more like a first date for her and Benny. The elf girl had a semipermanent blush on her face as they sat together, hands folded in her lap, and it couldn't have been more clear that her diplomatic training had skipped over any sort of romantic entanglements. Benny, for his part, looked pretty nervous too, and the sheer awkwardness of the two of them sitting together was so comical, I had to fight the urge to crack up.

It was probably mean to take so much amusement out of their awkwardness, but to be fair, Benny had never missed a chance to make fun of me when Callie and I had still been dancing around each other. Still, Celine was a nice girl, and I didn't want to pile on, so I would keep my mockery to the ride home, when she wasn't around. For now, I just sat with Callie, an arm around her shoulder, and enjoyed my own date. Despite having to keep an eye out, this *was* a date, so I had to do my best to make sure she had a good time.

Cark had been co-opted into escorting Jessie around, which I don't think he minded. He'd considered bringing Cass, but despite us being dressed as civilians, this *was* a G-ranked area in the WCP. Not exactly the place for mortal children. He had promised to bring her back some circus food, though, and Jessie was planning to win her a bunch of stuffed animals and prizes. She and Cass had bonded even more since they'd started staying with us, and I thought their relationship was really sweet. After losing her brother, it seemed like it was good for her to be the older sibling in a sense.

As we arrived in the old-fashioned square, I headed for Spruce Bunny's place to get a sausage. While he wouldn't recognize us, he had a decent idea of goings-on down here and could probably point us to the circus. Plus, the use of the word *cavalcade* seemed like it implied some connection to whomever these circus people were. Sure enough, when he saw us, the masked man lit up. "Well now! Welcome, new friends! Such a variety of guests, and even some hungry-looking canine companions! What can Spruce Bunny get you fine folk?"

I'd forgotten how intense this guy was, but it seemed more fun than campy. I passed him a few chits. "We'll take one for everyone. We also heard from some friends that you know your way around down here, and we couldn't help but notice your shop's name. We were wondering if you could give us direction to Cicero Castleton's Captivating Circus Cavalcade? Or is the word *cavalcade* in your name a coincidence? We didn't want to assume." I honestly didn't care either way. I was just starving. I loved the sausages here.

The rabbit-masked man laughed. "A common question, my friend! Have no fear—I can indeed point you to my cavalcading confederates! For such wonderfully generous customers, a mere directional discourse is simply the least I might do! Simply follow the main thoroughfare to the east along the boulevard! Might I interest you fine friends in a coupon for a free cotton candy?" Left unsaid was the fact that we'd just spent literally sixteen times what most people would already, but still, it was nice of him to offer.

We decided to take him up on it then headed down the street toward the circus, enjoying the sausages.

Sarah seemed particularly thrilled with the food. "This is amazing! I've never been down here. H-rankers can technically come down, but we always avoided it. It can be kind of dangerous. I'm definitely getting another one of these the next time I come down here, though." She took a huge bite of sausage and I had to chuckle at the enthusiasm.

Callie also took a bite, savoring the flavor. "Agreed. Not the best thing I've ever eaten, but it's up there in terms of quality for mortal food. I don't know if rabbit guy made this, but if so, he's a culinary genius. Best cooking I've ever had without high rank ingredients."

I made an affronted sound, and her eyes widened.

"Oh, I mean… in terms of street food. Obviously, I love your cooking, sweetie. I'd rather you make dinner for me than anyone else."

I gave her a suspicious look but decided to ignore that, taking a sulky bite of the admittedly fantastic sausage. "Anyway, I kind of understand how we missed the circus now. We were avoiding the big flashy main streets. Like you said, the marks were out of the way. Even the bar where we met Cark was down an alley and out of the way. Still, I'm excited to see what the main parts of the G district are like. I've never been to a circus before. I've read stories about them, though, and they're supposed to be lots of fun."

Callie gave me an exasperated look and leaned up to give me a kiss before leaning down and snagging a bite of my food. I gasped, but she just chewed it up rapidly and swallowed it before I could really react.

She gave me a vindictive grin. "What? Your cooking is better, right? This is just some random street food. You wouldn't begrudge your girlfriend a bite of that?" Before I could take a revenge bite, she shoveled her own remaining bites of sausage into her mouth and gulped it down.

I held the rest of mine up in the air away from her. The extra foot of reach didn't affect people with our physical abilities, but it at least kept her at bay. Despite the absurdity, I couldn't really hold it against her since I was laughing almost as much as the others. She pouted as I held it away and buried herself in my side, and I took the opportunity to scarf down the delicious food before she had a chance to go for it again. I put my arm around her shoulder and continued down the road.

I looked at the others. "How about you guys? Ever been to the circus? I'm pretty sure Benny hasn't. If there was one near our place growing up, I'd have heard about it." I paused. "Though you did have all sorts of weird rich people hobbies, so maybe not. Still, you probably would have told me, right?"

Jessie and Callie had both grown up in other parts of Velan, and who knew what the hell Elves did for fun? Not to mention the members of our group who'd grown up in Rajak itself.

Jessie nodded. "Yes, actually. There was a circus that went through town when I was younger. It was a mortal thing, but still lots of fun." Her face was wistful. "Alan took me. I ran off and got lost in the house of mirrors, and he spent the entire night running all over, looking for me. By the time he found me, I'd cried myself to sleep. He woke me up and saw how scared I was, so instead of yelling at me for running off, he got me an ice cream cone, and we rode the Ferris wheel. That was a really special night."

We all smiled at the happy expression on our friend's face. Ever since she'd gotten back the hope of reuniting with her brother, she'd become a lot more willing to talk about him. The memories of her life growing up with him had become much less painful in retrospect when she learned they might not be the last she would make. We all encouraged her to talk things through because sharing those memories helped her open up to us, and we were more than happy to learn more about her.

She shook off her wistfulness. "Anyway, I've never been to an Ascendant circus. I can't wait to see what kind of things they have here. I bet the food is pretty great, and the games are probably crazy. Where are you guys headed first? I know we're mostly splitting up to do our own thing. Tony and I are going to check out the midway and play some of the games. I want to see if I can win something fun for Cassidy."

Benny and Celine were apparently just going to head over to take in the acrobats, and Sarah and Martin (who none of us were actually sure were dating or just close friends) were going to see the animals. They weren't kept in cages or anything since the circus had a tamer, so people could actually interact with them. Callie and I were planning to take in the Big Top, where all the main acts were going to be. They had a separate tent from the acrobats, and it would be the place where we could get a good idea of what was going on the easiest.

We weren't sure where the Jerks were, and we'd arranged for any of our group who ran afoul of them to post in a scan ring chat room we'd set up. The description we gave the others was distinct enough that no one was worried we wouldn't be able to recognize the Jerks. We'd heard they were "laying siege" to this place, but who knew what that even meant. The Jerk version of a siege could just be winning all the good prizes so no one else was enjoying the games much.

Finally, we rounded the corner and saw Cicero Castleton's Captivating Circus Cavalcade. The massive rides, tents, and animals were lit by colorful and constantly shifting incandescent bulbs as hundreds of people milled about, enjoying all the amenities the circus had to offer.

Callie turned to the others. "All right everyone. Make sure to keep an eye on the wolves. This is a G-ranked circus so we can bring them in, but don't let them get into any trouble. Other than that, have fun. We'll see you all later."

And with that she grabbed my hand and dragged me off into the crowd.

Chapter Fifty-Three

THE CIRCUS WAS BEAUTIFUL. I had expected it to be interesting, but not beautiful. There was a sort of dark ambiance to the place that made it impossible not to scan the crowd and the attractions constantly. Aside from the morbid aesthetic, the most impressive thing about this place was that every attraction seemed to add a bit to the whole, despite being wildly different and unique.

There were food stands, art displays, games, rides, and every single one of them was totally unlike the others, but in such a way that it added to the whole. Like a mosaic, where each tile is a slightly different image or material that are all just close enough to complement each other, while also making the whole picture into the image that it's supposed to present at the same time. It was absolutely breathtaking.

The most beautiful part, though, was the expression on Callie's face. She was rapt as she stared at everything nearby, and despite it being my first circus, I was infinitely more interested in viewing it from her point of view. It was a rare thing to stare at my girlfriend without her mask, and I found myself bowled over by how lovely she was, smiling and excited like this. If nothing else, coming here would be worth it just to see this look on her face.

She pulled me back and forth, stopping to get some cotton candy, then to do a ring toss, then a ridiculous game where we had to shoot a thin stream of water into a small hole for long enough to fill a meter. Even with Callie's Perception we didn't manage to successfully complete the challenge, which had something to do with the hole being on a spinning pinwheel that whirled around on an arm, sometimes dipping behind other cutouts to prevent us from getting a solid hit on the game target.

I was pretty sure the game master had cheated, but I also didn't care, because it was only a single I-ranked chit to play. I hadn't even seen an I-ranked chit before, and they made change for us, so I didn't mind wasting a bit to make Callie happy. She got so excited playing, and I was worried she'd be upset at the loss, but she just laughed it off and grabbed my hand, dragging me to buy a funnel cake.

We stopped at one booth where an artist was drawing caricatures of people with overly large heads, and Callie paid for the picture, pushing me down into the seat and dropping in my lap. She stared ahead raptly as the artist began to draw, trying her best not to move, but perfectly happy to speak as we waited. "So. I figured after we finished this we could do some of the rides. I want to try the tilt-a-whirl, and maybe the tunnel of love, oooh and the haunted house!" She spoke rapidly, her excitement clear in her voice.

I laughed and wrapped my arms around her middle, burying my face in her shoulder from behind. "Whoa there. What's got you so excited? I know we haven't been to the circus before but you don't need to rush. We can take it one thing at a time. There's no hurry." I didn't add that I thought her excitement was adorable, because I thought there was even odds she would be embarrassed about it.

She chuckled wryly, letting her body slowly relax back against me. "Sorry, sorry. I know I'm getting ahead of myself. It's just…" She blushed. "This is kind of our first date. Especially as civilians, being out together like this. I've never really done anything like this before. Just… spent time with someone out of costume. Like obviously I've spent time with people, but not *with* someone."

I nodded against her neck. "I get it. I'm the same way. I'm excited to be here with you too. But we'll have plenty more nights like this if you want. Hell, we can come back here specifically if you want, and try out every-thing there is to do. It's not like we're short on money or time. It would be easy to fit in visits between training. Just focus on having fun—as long as you have a good time I will too, and we can get to everything in its own time."

She leaned over and kissed my forehead. "Good. And you're right." The artist finished up the caricature, though I got a small glare for wriggling around so much. Still, Callie folded the picture carefully and slipped it in a pocket before dragging me off again, this time much more slowly, to the next stop on our tour—a big scale type thing with a mallet where people could test their strength.

I decided to try this one. Callie had higher Might than I did, but I had skills to boost it. I was surprised to find that this was an Ascendant meter, though one within the G-rank spectrum, maxing out at a thousand Might. It was such a random use for Ascendant materials that I figured the device was created via Inventing.

There were prize levels for every hundred points, and the one hundred mark had this cute little stuffed hummingbird Callie was staring at. When I volunteered, she grinned and put her hands up, surrendering her dreams of getting the stuffed bird to my capable hands. With ninety-seven Might I was a shoe in, especially with skills, but I suspected like the other games here this one might be slightly weighted in their favor.

Knowing I couldn't break it, I hefted the surprisingly heavy hammer, hauled back, engaging all my muscles, and triggered Mercy Kill and Flurry of Blows, adding the enhanced speed to the flat damage increase to boost the impact of the hammer. I'd been right to assume they would rig the thing—even with the extra boost I barely hit the one hundred mark. Still, it was enough, and when I handed her the hummingbird Callie squealed and threw her arms around me happily.

Definitely worth it.

After, we walked around for a bit. I saw Callie scanning the circus grounds, looking for any sign of our targets. When she saw me looking at her she smirked. "As much as I'm enjoying spending time together, we do have to at least try to accomplish the mission. Not just because of the reward, but because I know how worried you are about this too. Luckily the Jerks are less than subtle at the best of times. Based on their usual MO we're looking for behavior so obvious they would grab less attention with an actual billboard."

I snickered. "True enough. But we can look more easily from higher up. How about we take a ride on the Ferris wheel, and we can expand our perspective?" I figured since she wanted to do the whole romantic first-date thing, we could hit two birds with one stone by using the Ferris wheel to look out over the whole circus. The view was probably gorgeous from up there.

Callie tugged my hand and almost ran over to the Ferris wheel. It was easy enough to spot since it was basically the biggest thing in the park, and as we drew closer, I had to whistle in appreciation at the intricate carriages on the wheel. They were each wooden and carefully crafted, looking like the wooden housing on a horse and carriage. We paid the man at the base, and he let us in. We settled into a plush, padded interior made with dark wood and maroon cushions. There was even a dim bulb providing light to the car so we could see.

We waited as the wheel began to turn, slowly carrying us up above the circus proper, and Callie leaned against me as we stared out the window, entranced by the beauty of this amazing place. Of course, we were still on the lookout for the Jerks and their ridiculous multi-colored mohawks.

I pulled her against me and, given the atmosphere, finally said something I'd been thinking for a while. "Hey, Cal?"

She turned to look at me curiously.

"That thing you said? I love you too."

She blinked at me, clearly not expecting the confession, and I immediately started trying to think of a way to take it back when she didn't respond right away, because I thought she hadn't meant it and I'd made an idiot of myself. That thought quickly melted as she hurled herself against me, kissing me fiercely.

We ended up riding the Ferris wheel all the way through without seeing any of the Jerks. But to be honest, I wasn't really looking very hard.

When we got to the bottom, I was a little dazed, and Callie looked to be a mix of smug and thrilled as she pulled me back into the crowd by my hand. I was about to suggest another ride when I noticed something out of the corner of my eye. I poked Callie in the ribs and pointed to the retreating figure of a huge man with no shirt, leather pants, and an absolutely nauseating bright fuchsia mohawk. I raised an eyebrow at her, wondering if she knew who it was.

She rolled her eyes, looking annoyed at the interruption. "Great. The absolute most absurd person in the whole gang. Ronnie the Beef."

She'd mentioned Ronnie the Beef before, though she hadn't told me anything specific about him. All I knew was that he was one of the only G-rankers the Jerks had, though who knew if that was still the case? Still, we'd come to do recon, so we followed him quietly from a distance. Not that it was hard. Despite being a G-ranker, Ronnie the Beef wasn't particularly observant. Go figure.

Unfortunately, not being subtle made following him harder in some ways too, since he didn't seem to mind bulling past all the circus goers as he made his way through the fairgrounds. Even among G-rankers, this guy was attention grabbing enough to move people out of the way, given that the Jerk G-ranker was a full seven feet tall, towering over even someone like me. He also happened to be much wider at the shoulders, and I wondered how much of that physical presence translated to Might stats. I bet a guy this big had a rep as quite a bruiser.

I slowed down to pull Callie slightly back. "So, why do they call him Ronnie the Beef exactly? With the Jerks, it's even odds whether he has some infamous tendencies to hold grudges or likes to eat steak." I kept my voice low so Ronnie wouldn't hear. His Perception must have been low, because he didn't seem to notice a word I said. Though, to be fair, we were pretty far back, and there were plenty of chattering attendees between us.

Callie just snorted. "He once beat someone to death with a cow carcass. You were pretty close on both counts, I guess." She stopped talking, eyes widening. "He just ducked into that tent. Let's slip into stealth and follow him in. I'm betting whatever is in there is going to tell us everything we need to know about what the Jerks are doing here."

She took a deep breath, and the two of us entered stealth, suppressing all traces of our presence as we followed the huge man into the tent. I had to admit, I was pretty curious myself. I just hoped we could get back to our date after we finished our recon.

Chapter Fifty-Four

THE TENT RONNIE THE BEEF slipped into was not an empty one. The place was one of the show tents, and the man in the middle was breathing prismatic fire while riding a unicycle across what looked like a literal hair. I didn't know what power would do that, or if he was even using one instead of some magic gear, but it was impressive to watch. Ronnie the Beef made his way over to a crowd of other Jerks, who were all sitting crowded around a black-cloaked figure.

We sat within listening distance, though only barely with all the noise, and tried to hear what they were saying. It didn't work out too well. I could tell even from a distance that the other Jerks were mostly H-rankers, though I didn't see Punchin' Carl or his shoeless friend. Thankfully.

The hooded figure at the center wasn't visible under their cloak. I assumed that was some kind of magic effect, because the cloak itself wasn't very big, and my Perception should have seen through a bit of shadow.

I leaned over to whisper to Callie, not worried about being overheard by the Jerks from so far with all the people talking in here. Callie was listening in on them, but even she didn't seem to be getting all of it, just the odd word here or there. My voice seemed to jerk her attention to me. "Hey, can you see the face of whoever is in the cloak? I can't, which is weird, but their face is in shadow, so I figured you would have an easier time."

She scowled. "No. I was trying, but there's just… nothing. Probably some kind of identity protection item. Those aren't too rare, but having one that can block me even in the shadows means whoever the person under there is, they aren't a nobody. That's probably an F-ranked artifact. What the hell someone like that is doing meeting with the Jerks, I have no idea, much less why they would be meeting them *here*."

That was a good question. "Why are they even allowed here? When I heard *siege* in the mission, I imagined a running battle through the tents or something. They're just walking around here like their normal idiotic selves. How is this a siege of anything? Except possibly the good taste of everyone who has to watch them walk around with those awful haircuts and ridiculous outfits… if you can even call them that."

That got a snicker from my girlfriend. "Agreed, but no. I think sieges down here are different. Given how stable things are, picking an actual fight in a place this central to their power would be stupid. Even for the Jerks. If I had to guess, I'd say it's something like trying to make them look bad by ruining games and stuff. That seems more like the Jerk style of doing things anyway. You know what they're like."

I did know that, and she was right, but I still didn't know who the cloaked figure was. It wasn't their style to make shady deals with weird people… well, with *subtle* weird people. I felt the need to point that out. "Isn't this out of character for them? Shadowy meetings with hooded figures in dark tents? Well, as shadowy as people like them can manage. There's a huge crowd of multicolored idiots over there, but this may be the one place where they don't draw undue attention for their very existence. Clowns are colorful too."

I could see on her face that she was worried about that, too, and I could see just as easily that she was trying to play it off as nothing.

She gave me a strained smile. "I'm sure it's nothing. This isn't exactly their own territory. It makes sense for them to change things up a bit. Whoever that is probably reached out to Mr. Jack-tastic when he got to town to curry favor with the new power player, and then arranged for them to meet in hiding because they were embarrassed to be seen in public with lunatics like that."

Despite her comforting tone, I could tell she didn't believe that. It wasn't that it was crazy—hell, it made as much sense as anything, but it didn't *feel* true. When you'd been an Ascendant for a while, you started to get a feel for trouble. It might have been some kind of learned subconscious tell we picked up, or it might have been something more ephemeral like some effect of Fantasy letting us read some ethereal changes in fame within an area. I'd heard lots of theories.

Whatever it was, it was a notable fact that lots of the most powerful Ascendants had something of a sixth sense for trouble, even if they often used that sense to run *at* the trouble instead of away from it like a sane person. I hadn't really noticed myself having it before, but to be fair, I'd been gaining lots of renown. It was possibly a consequence of me actually becoming someone of note, or starting to at least. In any case, Callie had it too clearly, and she and I both felt like this was a big deal, even if we didn't know why.

Of course, articulating that wasn't really an option, it would sound crazy, but I trusted her instincts, and she trusted mine, even if we didn't bring them up out loud. So when the Jerks and their hooded guest stood up to leave, the two of us dipped back into stealth to follow behind them, determined to make sure that we knew exactly where they were going and what they decided to do. I wasn't sure this was something I wanted to be dragged into, but considering Carl's vendetta, it wasn't exactly impossible, so it was more than worth the effort. Plus, we still had recon to do, though this bit of info might have fulfilled the mission on its own.

Still, we stood up and slipped out after them, moving through the crowds silently, leaning into our stealth Skills to avoid being spotted. Callie held back as we went, keeping her stealth closer to my level so she didn't leave me behind. She knew this was tough for me and that she had to give me time to make sure I was able to keep pace. Her stealth Skill was much higher than mine at Beginner, after all.

The biggest issue was that while in some ways, getting lost in a crowd was easier, it was also much harder because of how stealth worked. With the stealth Skill, you used Perception to find and erase traces of your passing, detecting and isolating sound and visual cues through the filter of the Skill. It was incredibly complex even at the best of times because it required constantly keeping track of and eliminating multiple variables to make sure you couldn't be detected.

In a crowd like this, there were hundreds more people to see and hear me, to sense me; more angles to cover and revise and keep track of. At these levels, stealth actually relied heavily on Focus, as well, though only the aftereffects like how much processing power we had. Of course, we weren't eliminating all traces, just the ones we picked up, so people with higher levels of Perception would be able to see right through us, but given the number of people here and the fact that our Perception was pretty high, we would most likely be fine as long as we weren't too obvious about tailing them.

Still, stealth in a crowd this big was taxing the hell out of me, and Callie had her hand in mine, resonating her stealth Skill to help take some of the burden off me by channeling it through my body.

The Jerks weren't exactly watching for us, though, and were busy shoving each other and shouting insults back and forth. If I made any slips, they didn't catch them. I was worried about the hooded figure, but it was hard to tell if the person in the cloak had noticed anything, given their obscured face.

The Jerks bulled their way down the thoroughfare in the middle of the circus, bumping into people who avoided making a scene when they noticed Ronnie's hulking fuchsia-haired form looming behind them. As we followed them, the crowds became thinner and thinner until we finally took a turn down a side path and had to slow down because we didn't have as much cover anymore. Callie called the shadows to us, cloaking us even more deeply as she supplemented her stealth and mine with her ability. We stuck to the sides of the tents, where shadows were more plentiful as we trailed them.

They came to a stop in a dark and secluded area behind a towering roller coaster. When they came to a halt, the Jerks surrounded the cloaked figure, forming a wide circle that showed they wanted to put pressure on the person without risking themselves. Ronnie seemed much less worried and stalked up to the hooded form, making the slight figure look positively miniscule in comparison to the massive hulk of a man. I could see the figure was probably only about five feet tall, but they seemed unconcerned by the difference, if body language was anything to go on.

Ronnie glared down into the blank-faced figure. "We've been here for days! Why are you just now showing up again? The deal was one a day, not one whenever you felt like gracing us with your presence. We've held up our end, putting pressure on the cavalcade. Are you going back on your part of the bargain? Mr. Jack-tastic isn't some punk kid you can push around, no matter where you come from! An E-ranker isn't someone for you to disrespect!" His voice was deep and rumbling, but surprisingly articulate for a Jerk. I supposed at G-rank, you had to pick up some Focus, even if only by accident.

Even without a face, the hooded figure somehow managed to show how bored it was without a face, a kind of knack for body language that most Ascendants picked up after wearing a mask for a while. Even if I hadn't already known this person was G-ranked, I would have guessed they were Ascendant from that.

The voice that come out of the hood was surprisingly lyrical and feminine. "I said one a day, not one daily. I can do more than a single payment at one time, so shut your pie hole. You get three today, and my respect or lack thereof for your boss is none of your damn business."

Ronnie growled at the smaller girl, clearly angry, but just as clearly much less willing to start trouble than he was to talk shit. I didn't blame him. The hooded figure sounded way too calm regarding his anger. People that confident usually had a few nasty tricks up their sleeves.

He glared down at her for a minute. "Fine. Let's get this over with. I'll be collecting payment for the day. Hands out." His tone was nasty, but he refrained from any actual insults, showing his fear of the figure.

The hooded form reached out a hand from under the cloak, revealing a slim and relatively well-muscled form in efficient-looking black armor and two thin, delicate hands. Ronnie took hold of them tightly, glaring down into the hood. "I wish for three more points of Might. Payment is services rendered for the ongoing task we've been hired for."

The bottom dropped out of my stomach as I saw a series of purple sparks play over the hands clasping Ronnie's. I stared in horror as the figure granted Ronnie's wish. That was the Beginner Wish ability.

The cloaked figure was a candidate like me. This was… not good.

There was another possible Wishmaster on Callus.

About the Author

Malcolm Tent is, in fact, smarter than a fifth grader. He enjoys reading, writing, and spending time with his dogs. He's lycanthrophobic and addicted to Cajun food.

Author website:

About Timeless Wind Publishing

Founded in late 2020 by Lorne Ryburn and Silas Sontag, Timeless Wind Publishing is an up-and-coming indie publishing house. We love sci-fi and fantasy—progression fantasy, power fantasy, LitRPG, time loops, cultivation, system apocalypse—genre fiction of all kinds! We're prolific readers within these genres and endeavor to bring awesome books into the limelight.

We look forward to helping authors (aspiring and published alike) develop and expand an audience of readers who believe in their vision.

Our logo is an exotic cat from a Palmyrene ruin. The word along its back roughly translates to, "Alas!" or "What a shame!" This word is present on all gravestones in Palmyra. It's a recognition that all things come to an end… even the best people and stories. Alas!

We hope our readers will have "alas" moments when they finish our books.

Connect with Timeless Wind Publishing
TimelessWind.com
Facebook.com/timelesswind
Twitter.com/timeless_wind
Instagram.com/timelesswindpub